I0556804

# Lucky 13

T. James Reese

**Veritas et Virtute**
**Media Production**

Copyright © 2012 by Timothy James Reese

All rights reserved.

Cover design by Timothy James Reese

No portion of this book may be reproduced, stored in a retrieval system or transmitted in any form by any means, electronic, mechanical, photocopy, recording, or otherwise, except for brief quotations in printed reviews, without the prior permission of the publisher.

This is a work of fiction. All characters and incidents in this novel are the products of the author's imagination. Any similarities to people living or dead is purely coincidental.

Manufactured in the United States of America

ISBN  978-0615733531

First Edition

For you, Mom, my inspiration...love you, miss you.

*"You may not change the world, but you may change the person who changes the world."*

# CONTENTS

# PROLOGUE

September. Something stirs. The leaves aren't all that's changing; darkness grows, a deep despair, as the warmth of summer subsides and the gloom of impending winter looms in the storm clouds overhead.

Thunder cracks as lightning flashes. Rain falls in New York City. The dark streets glisten in the glow of passing headlights, reflecting the once celebrated beauty of this fading empire, a symbol of freedom, of man's triumph over disparity, the American dream. But memories are the only dreams now: nightmares lay ahead.

Still, it rains; a never-ending downpour of sorrow and decay. Day after day, like the heavens crying down on this forsaken place, it rains. The light is gone. Darkness shrouds the wicked and the righteous hide in shadows.

On the outside, the city is elegant, its massive architecture stretching high above the sprawling streets as millions of people march like ants across its beaten pavement. Whispers of the future echo from the rooftops. But there's a darkness lurking just beneath its surface.

In one hand, goodness resides. But evil hides in the other's clenched fist, a fist raised high in its own accomplishment, praising itself for its insecurities.

Even so, the goodness is still there, somewhere. Perhaps it's wandering the streets, hunting down evil and cleansing the city on a quest for redemption, or maybe the city itself is searching for goodness? But redemption will come: it always does...always.

# I

## THURSDAY NIGHT

The door creaked open, its hinges fighting against the age-worn frame. A placard on the wall read *7A*, the paint faded and peeling. Dim light from the hall outside filtered into the dark entryway where a couple stood, their bodies close, her hands holding his, as the shadow of their goodnight kiss shown on the wall.

"See you at work tomorrow," she blushed, her slender figure disappearing behind the door.

She leaned against it as it closed, the bottom grating over the old, cracked weather stripping on the floor. A smile stretched across her pretty face. The deadbolt clicked into place, followed quickly by the clattering of the sliding chain-lock. Hanging her purse and jacket on the coat rack that stood in the hall, she turned and headed for her bedroom.

She ran her fingers through her rain-soaked hair, pulling tangled strands from her dark green eyes, as she kicked her shoes off onto the old hardwood floor with a thud. A hairbrush rested on the top of her dresser. Happily, she picked it up, then stepped into the bathroom, brushing her long blond hair. Young, beautiful Kayla Rose stood flushed, feeling a bit foolish, maybe in love, as she thought back on that evening's events: dinner followed by a quiet stroll through Central Park.

*More foolish than in love,* she told herself, setting the brush on the counter, then making her way back to the living room, picturing how funny they must have seemed running hand-in-hand through the park, in the middle of a downpour and no umbrella in sight.

Passing her fireplace, she glanced at the pictures displayed on the mantel. One was of her parents when they were young, nearly her age, just married and so happy. Another showed her brother and his wife, as well as their three children, playing in the backyard of their home just outside of Chicago. Two more pictures sat beside that one: the first was of her grandparents; the second, her oldest brother, wearing full police dress, the words "In Loving Memory" engraved in the silver frame.

The last picture was of a girl, just as beautiful as Kayla, but younger, her little sister Ashley. She'd started college that fall at Penn State, a stone's throw from their family's hometown. But when Kayla moved to New York, Ashley followed, transferring to Colombia. They were best friends, inseparable.

Kayla walked into the kitchen, thinking how lucky she was to have such a great family. She reached into the fridge for a bottle of water as her thoughts returned again to her date, recalling the long kiss under the shelter of a tall tree, its fall colored leaves rustling in the wind, moonlight shining through its crooked branches.

*Definitely foolish.*

She twisted off the cap of the bottle and took a long drink. Nothing could stop her from thinking about that night.

*It was just a date, nothing special,* she told herself, but it couldn't wipe the happiness from her face.

Yawning, she grabbed a handful of pretzels from a bowl on the counter and headed back to her bedroom, walking again past the fireplace. An oddly cool draft filled her apartment, like she'd stepped into a freezer; goose bumps ran up and down her arms.

Kayla's attention was drawn to the apartment door, now standing wide open. Her pretzels dropped to the ground, breaking apart as they hit the wooden floor, her water landed just beside the pieces and spilled, spinning onto its side. Kayla froze; a faint tapping coming from over her shoulder. She looked back at the mantle; the frame with Ashley's picture in it was lying face down.

She blinked her eyes, trying to clear her head, as she looked back to the front door, now closed, the deadbolt locked, just as she remembered doing when she closed it earlier. Her smile had finally faded.

Kayla righted the fallen frame, but quickly stepped back, her hands shaking. The frame was empty. Where had the picture gone?

\*\*\*\*\*\*\*\*\*\*\*\*

The shrill cries of a woman filled the crisp night air, the darkness shrouding an indescribable pain. Squad cars lined the street, *N.Y.P.D.* emblazoned on the doors, their red and blue lights dancing across the buildings' façades. A black-clad strike squad assembled at the foot of the crumbling cement steps that led into a rundown apartment complex.

"Keller."

"Yes, Sir?" the Sergeant answered.

"You take Team One. I'll follow you through with the second unit," First Lieutenant James Sykes grunted as they double checked their guns and walkie-talkies. "Make it a sweep and clear. My boys will mop up any leftovers, understood?"

"Yes, Sir," Keller grinned. "Okay team, ready on my command. Let's move!"

Loud cracks of gun fire echoed out as the team smashed through the decaying front door and into the musty, dark building, floor tiles crunching beneath their boots, splintered wood flying through the air. Bursts of suppression fire rattled back from the enemy inside, their guns blazing, hardly taking time to aim.

"Clear!" a voice called from around the first corner, a man standing in his tactical gear, a bullet proof vest strapped across his chest, fallen bodies strewn at his feet.

"This room is secure!" echoed another man from behind the hazy visor on his helmet as he tramped down the dark hall, the beam from his rail-mounted flashlight illuminating segments of dust and wall.

Room by room, they searched for survivors, but found nothing. Again, they divided into two groups: Keller and his men trudged up the stairs toward the sound of the screaming woman, now silent, assumed dead; Syke's team headed for the basement.

"This could take all night," Keller muttered, the butt of his MP5 raised to his shoulder.

\*\*\*\*\*\*\*\*\*\*\*\*

An old man sat alone in a dark room, flickers of candle light and flashes of lightning illuminating his face. He quickly scribbled in a small wrinkled notepad, the text filling page after page. Sweat rolled down his forehead as he transcribed the thoughts flowing through his mind, his memories spilling onto the pad. He was writing so fast, unintelligibly fast.

The pencil point snapped. The scratching of the lead on the paper was almost deafening. Then, silence.

\*\*\*\*\*\*\*\*\*\*\*\*

The squads covered ground quickly, thoroughly, the way they were trained. As Keller led point, the rest of his men swept the dust-filled rooms that lined the darkened halls. The flashes of muzzle fire had subsided, but the smoke still lingered, limiting visibility, creating a gray haze that clouded the old building. There was no one left to counter. The aggressors were dead. The job had become search and rescue.

The upper floors were filled with trash, makeshift beds, and the memories of broken lives. Empty closets, littered with fallen plaster, tainted with the smell of mildew, hid no secrets.

Finally, they came to the last apartment, darker than the others, mysterious, evil. Sergeant Keller entered the room, his SMG slung across his back, panning the walls with the light on his Glock as his men took cover positions around the door frame. Jagged shadows jumped across the dirty, torn wallpaper: a decrepit chair, a cardboard box, and finally, the raggedly clothed figure of a woman standing, slightly hunched, in the corner, deathly still, her back to the door.

"Ma'am!?" he called out, his light focused on her.

No reply.

"Clasp your fingers together and place your hands on your head."

A chill swept through the room. Pipes rattled from within the walls and the roof creaked above.

"I'm not here to hurt you, Ma'am," he assured. I'm going to step towards you!"

Silence.

"Ma'am!?"

Silence.

"Get on your knees and put your hands on your head," he urged, now standing just behind her.

Keller reached out, placing his hand on her shoulder. She didn't move. Tugging gently, he attempted to turn her, his squad aimed and waiting.

Suddenly, she whipped around, snarling like a dog as she bit deep into his arm, her skin ghostly pale, her eyes black as night. He cursed, looking into her face. The booming of gunfire shook the tiny room as her bullet-riddled corpse fell to the floor. Blood ran from the hole in his sleeve. Angrily, he fired one last round into her already dead body.

"Let's hope Sykes is having better luck!" he said wincing, nursing his arm as he headed for the hallway, his heavy boots clomping across the dusty wood floor.

************

A broken man sat slumped in a chair, his bloodied head in his hands. His elbows rested weakly on an old splintered table. Makeshift bandages hung from his brow, soaked, almost useless, his disheveled hair matted and sticky. He wore a dirt-smeared black suit with scuffed shoes, his tie pulled loose, the top buttons of his shirt torn away, lost.

Another man sat across from him, the darkness shrouding his face; a perfect antithesis, his suit freshly pressed and wrinkle free, his arms crossed arrogantly. He was like a shadow, pitch black, except for his eyes, glowing brightly, as if filled with pure light.

"What do you want from me? There's nothing I can tell you!" the beaten man cried out. "Do you hear me?!"

The man stared on silently, his head cocked as if disgusted by his prisoner. The room reeked of sweat.

"Why won't you answer me?!"

He uncrossed his arms, then set his hands palm down on the table, his gloved fingers fanned out, "What you don't understand is that you know something that you don't know you know. You believe a truth that isn't truth at all. And although you know that truth to be the truth, you do not embrace it, do not *live* by it, even though it is the *truth*. I despise the truth."

The spite in his voice resonated within the thickly walled room. Dim light cast weak shadows on the peeling paint that covered the space.

"Truth? What truth? I don't have any idea what you're talking about!" he shouted, his frustration beginning to boil over as his patience wore thin.

"You will," the dark figure replied, leaning into the light, his face hidden beneath a sadistic black mask, the mouth roughly stitched into a hideous grin stretching from ear to ear.

\*\*\*\*\*\*\*\*\*\*\*\*

Syke's men tromped down the metal stairs to the basement, the sound of their quick footfalls bouncing off the narrowly walled stairwell. The Lieutenant's radio buzzed to life.

"Sir," Keller grunted, "the upstairs is clear, we had an encounter, but no personal casualties."

"Copy that, head towards the lobby we're checking the bottom level now," Sykes replied in his gravelly voice. "Make a final perimeter sweep and call for cleanup."

"Ye..."

The reception on his two-way crackled out and disappeared. Sykes froze. These radios had never given him trouble before. He slammed the bottom of it against his palm.

*Static.*

A shadow moved across the far end of the hall. He squinted into the darkness, but couldn't see a thing. Still, it felt like he was being watched. Purposefully, he forced himself back to the task at hand.

*Get your head straight, Jim.*

His team stopped at a steel door, rusted from age, but still solid, its hinges frozen. A battering ram was brought up from the rear. With a deafening blast, the door was breached, the broken lock clanking against the worn cement floor. Slowly, they stepped into the darkness, a definite chill in the air as a cold draft flowed from within the splintered frame. The thick smell of blood and rot hit them like a wall. The men entered cautiously, scanning the room with their lights, their fingers uneasily resting on their triggers. It was sickening, incredible, beyond words. None of the team had ever seen anything this disturbing, nothing like...*this.*

Faint smoke from candles lingered at the ceiling; spiders crept across the exposed wooden beams as a rat scurried through a hole in the aged once-white brick walls. Thirteen bodies lay in a circle at the center of the room. The victims heads were still intact, but just barely, their throats cleanly slit, their blood drained into a pattern that had been gouged into the floor, a pentagram.

As the men stood in disbelief, a ghostly laugh, long and deep, echoed through the building. Sykes stepped back through the door and away from the carnage, his radio crackling again.

"Gary," he stuttered in nauseous disbelief, "you read me?"

*Static.*

"Gary!"

"Yes, Sir?" the answer finally returned.

"We need more than cleanup down here, Sergeant."

Keller was right. This would be a long night, a night they wouldn't soon forget.

\*\*\*\*\*\*\*\*\*\*\*\*

Ashley woke suddenly, her heart racing. Peering into the darkness, she could see glances of her nightmare cast all around her. Cries for mercy still rang in her ears.

"So much blood," she whispered, "what an awful dream."

Climbing out of her warm bed, she stumbled into the bathroom and felt across the wall for the light switch. The fluorescent bulb mounted above her medicine cabinet hummed to life. Her bare feet slapped against the cold tile floor as she shivered, startled by her own reflection staring back in the mirror. She pulled her short brown hair into a ponytail, still unable to shake the horrific thoughts from her head, like they'd been burned into her, a part of her.

"I'll never get back to sleep now," she complained, flipping on the shower and getting undressed.

\*\*\*\*\*\*\*\*\*\*\*\*

"Jamie!"

Kayla woke with a start. She'd fallen asleep on her couch, the television screen flickering in the darkness. She glanced at the clock that hung on the wall above her TV.

*3:00 am.*

Her ankles were cold. She looked down at the cuffs of her pants, still wet, soaked from the rain. Rubbing the stiffness from her neck, she made her way to the mantle and looked once again at the empty picture frame. It made no sense, and now this dream.

She stepped into her bedroom and pulled her sweater off over her head, neatly folding it and placing it in her top dresser drawer. Then, she slid off her khakis and hung them up to dry over the back of the chair that sat at her vanity.

Kayla slipped into an old sweatshirt and checked the time set on her alarm clock, then climbed into bed. The covers felt warm, reassuring. She closed her eyes and tried to sleep, tried not to think about her dream. But as she lay there, images flashed through her mind: the missing picture, her perfect date, his warm smile, *her nightmare*; a shadow looming in the haunted, dark places of her mind.

Outside, lightning flashed and thunder boomed across the city, echoing off of buildings and down dark alleyways. Rain spattered down upon the rooftops. As the city slept peacefully, the world grew dark and cold, and in that instant, evil woke.

# II

## FRIDAY MORNING

Morning came quickly. Blinding sunrays painted the city in brilliant hues of gold as the rising sun chased away the darkness. New York's nighttime skyline crept into the shadows. The daily bustle began, a million worker ants scurrying about their endless routine. It was a new day, maybe a better day than yesterday. *Perhaps...*

In Manhattan, the homicide office was silent, even as the daily grind set in throughout the rest of the precinct. Captain Patrick O'Donnell stood in front of his detectives. In one hand, he gripped a manila folder; a report on the previous night's bizarre events. The other hand clenched a tightly rolled newspaper with a thick rubber band wrapped around it. The headline read, *Mysterious Murders: 13 Victims Found, Killer at Large!* A dozen unblinking eyes stared at him, all reading the tension on his face. Anxiously, they braced for the rant to come.

"Here's the deal," O'Donnell grunted, his face red, his blood pressure on the rise, "we've got thirteen John Does in the basement of an abandoned apartment in Harlem, a lady dead for biting Sergeant Keller, and last but not least, a morgue full of shooters dressed like they came from a frickin' Halloween party. Plus, the media is having a field day with this thing: *killer at large...*

Last night, these nut jobs opened fire on an officer, and as of yet, there doesn't seem to have been any motive whatsoever, a completely random shooting. I think that just about sums it up. Oh, and before anyone asks why we're on this case instead of the northwest precinct, the Mayor considers this priority one. We got the call, enough said!"

O'Donnell slammed the folder and the newspaper onto one of the detective's desks, then paused, taking a moment to wipe his profusely sweating brow and attempt to tug his sagging pants back up to what semblance of a waistline he could muster. Then, thoughtfully, he picked up his cup as he twisted his head to one side as if to give his neck a good crack, obviously trying to steady his nerves.

"So, does anybody have any clue what was going on in there?" he asked, his teeth gritting into a blatantly forced smile, his attempt to calm himself failing miserably.

His shirt, as always, was stained with sweat, dark patches growing under his arms. Now, he was about to add coffee to his tie if he wasn't careful with the cup he was waiving around.

"*Nobody!?*"

The silence was deafening. No one could find the words when the Captain was in one of his moods, and for good reason. He had a self-proclaimed short fuse, an anger management problem he cared for with a bottle of Jack Daniels, his best friend.

"Good job!" he shouted, his office door slamming behind him, the coffee cup sloshing into a trash can as he disappeared behind the frosted glass window.

Everyone cast knowing glances back and forth. He was definitely in one of his moods. This was going to be one of those days.

Creaking, the Captain's door popped back open. His red forehead crept out, followed by his angrily squinted eyes.

"Frickin' unbelievable. Find something out, *NOW!*" he barked, the door slamming shut once again, the glass rattling.

"Why did I come in early today?" Detective James Branson asked as he yawned sleepily, looking across his desk to where his partner sat, then giving the digital clock on his perfectly organized desk a subtle glance: 7:20am. "I don't think I've ever set foot in this office before 8am."

She looked up from her paperwork, her beautiful, green eyes piercing into him, her soft lips curling into a smirk.

"Because you *live* for this kind of thing, remember? Or at least, that's what you told me when we were assigned together...or was that just an excuse to talk to me?" she teased, her smirk opening into a full smile, her face glowing.

"Whatever you say," he chuckled, a slight blush in his dimpled, street-hardened cheeks.

Jamie slumped back into his chair opposite hers, his shaggy brown hair flopping about, and pulled a pencil from a mug-turned-organizer on his desk, attempting to distract from his embarrassment. He seemed much younger than he really was. Everyone even called him Jamie, though it made him feel like a kid. Still, he never let it bother him. In fact, though he would never admit it, he was even beginning to tolerate the name Jamie, maybe even like it, especially when *she* called him that. He played with the pencil, rolling it between his thumb and forefinger, searching for a scrap of paper or a notepad, anything to look busy.

He grew up in this city. The street life he once knew had made him tough, distant, but not cocky. His thirty-two year old frame held a boyish charm, a child-like curiosity, making him a great partner for a twenty.-something young woman hungry for action and adventure, especially an ambitious one like Kayla.

Though she had what many at the station considered little experience when the Captain promoted her, Kayla's confidence and go-get 'em attitude had earned her a standout spot on O'Donnell's team of detectives, a distinction she was always quick to add, especially at her age. And, despite what some of the other detectives believed, she deserved it, especially when considering her degree in criminal science and excellent marks at the academy. Still, at times, her eagerness to prove herself showed how green she really was. Her badge made her feel invincible, bulletproof, even though she'd rarely had the need to draw her sidearm in action.

Kayla was from a cop family, a born and raised public servant. It was in her blood. Her father had retired earlier that year, commended for his honorable service. Her two brothers served on the force as well, one dying tragically during a routine traffic stop, shot in the chest by a man who wanted to avoid a speeding ticket; the other worked forensics out of a Chicago precinct.

Initially, Kayla's desire for a career in law enforcement was fueled by her brother's murder. She said she wanted to clean up the streets, a novel idea no doubt. Even so, her bitterness was evident, though well hidden behind a coy demeanor. But after a couple of short years on the force, she had seen more than her overzealous twenty-five year old eyes were ready for. She soon realized it would take more than just her to clean up this city.

************

"Taxi!" a young man, late twenties, yelled over the rumble of traffic as he tried to hail a cab, his arms flailing above him, a leather briefcase at his feet.

Cabbies flew past, one after another: yellow blurs. One came close to the curb, splashing a puddle from the previous night's rain all over his freshly pressed black suit. His arms dropped to his sides, fists clenched, his knuckles whitening. Rage burned in his eyes.

With a sudden burst of blinding light, a shockwave of force exploded from his body, the surge of energy throwing everyone on the street to the ground. Passing cars lifted off the pavement and hurtled into other lanes, slamming the traffic into surrounding buildings. Chaos ensued as cars ripped through store fronts, fireballs and explosions tore apart the asphalt, plumes of smoke clouding the street.

As people regained vision and climbed to their feet, they looked for an explanation, but there wasn't one, just panic. The man was gone; two burn marks where his feet had stood on the sidewalk.

************

"The mayor is holding on line 4," the receptionist's voice squawked over the intercom on Capt. O'Donnell's desk.

Settling into his chair, he reached for a half empty pack of cigarettes that lay next to the phone.

"Thanks, Nancy," he mumbled, placing one between his lips and nervously flicking his lighter.

Hopelessly, he stared at the blinking red light on his phone. Talking to the Mayor was one of his least favorite things to do, especially now, with a case like this on his hands. Slowly, he raised the receiver to his ear and forced a greeting.

"Busy day, Patrick?" Mayor Bradford bellowed through the phone.

"You could say that."

"I'm just calling to find out where you're at on the Harlem murders."

"Well," O'Donnell paused, taking a long drag on his cigarette, "I've got my best team on it as we speak."

"You mean Luke?"

"Um...yes, Sir."

"You'd better," the Mayor replied with a less than convinced tone, "Election time is coming up. The last thing I need is blood on my streets, and this is a lot of blood!"

"As soon as I find anything out, I'll let you know."

"Don't think you're just going to keep me in the loop," Bradford barked, "I am the loop. Sometimes I think you forget that!"

"No, Sir."

"Good. I want to see some results."

"Yes, Sir."

O'Donnell frowned as the sound of dial tone echoed in his ear. Hanging up the phone, he rubbed his cigarette in his ash tray, thin wisps of smoke filling the air. He had to get this case moving: he had to show some results.

\*\*\*\*\*\*\*\*\*\*\*\*

Ashley sat in her art class, tapping her pencil slowly on her desk. The teacher rambled on about Georgia O' Keefe and a painting of a flower. Although she appreciated the picture, she personally didn't like it.

The bored tapping of her pencil slowed as her professor continued to lecture about brush strokes and blending. Ashley's head drooped forward, her chin nearly touching her chest as she slipped into a quiet sleep. She hadn't slept well the night before: her horrible nightmares woke her long before her alarm would have.

Suddenly, her head jolted back up, her eyes fluttering open as a flash of light woke her. The teacher was still going on monotonously, her dry-erase marker squealing across the white board as she wrote.

Ashley was overcome with the same fear she'd felt last night, the hair on her neck tingling again. She had had another dream, a man standing on a sidewalk, an explosion of light. The horrific screams still echoed in her head.

\*\*\*\*\*\*\*\*\*\*\*\*

"You two," Capt. O'Donnell ordered, his index finger pointing at Jamie and Kayla, "in my office, *now!*"

Reluctantly, they stood and headed towards the door with O'Donnell's name etched ominously into the glass. As they entered, he motioned for them to sit. They could tell he had something on his mind.

"Before you say anything," the Captain grunted, "I want to get something clear. I don't know what's going on between you two, but keep it professional. Understood? I can't have my two best detectives off gallivanting with thoughts of romantic fancy while a psycho killer is loose on my streets."

Kayla glanced at Jamie from the corner of her eye. His jaw was flinching: he wasn't happy.

"That said," O'Donnell continued, "I'm pulling Luke off this case. All he got out of that apartment last night was a bunch of lousy photos, not a single finger print, hair, or DNA sample. It's like he wasn't even trying."

"What about all the blood on the floor?" Jamie challenged sarcastically.

"Unless the killer sprang a leak, I'm assuming the blood all belonged to the victims," O'Donnell said in a disgusted tone. "Besides, it all ran together, so I'd hate to be the one at the lab trying to sort that mess out and sift through blood types right now."

"So what do you want us to do, Captain?" Kayla asked, trying to ease the tension between her boss and partner.

"I'm putting you two on the case," he shrugged as he crossed his thick, hairy arms. "I've got the Mayor so far up my backside, when I get heartburn, he feels it too. So, do what you do best. Find the guy who did this."

"And Luke," Jamie asked, "didn't the Mayor request him on this case?"

"Let me handle the Mayor, now get out of here!"

The door slammed behind them as they walked back to their desk. Jamie stopped for a cup of coffee.

"Where do we start?" Kayla wondered.

"We'll get Luke's notes and go from there," Jamie answered as he loosened his tie and sat down in his chair.

"Hey Rose!" a detective hollered from a desk on the far side of the room, "line one."

Kayla picked up her phone. The blinking red light flashed to green.

"Yeah…okay…uh huh…we're on our way."

She placed the phone back on the receiver, a perplexed look on her face.

"What's up?" Jamie asked as he watched Kayla reach for her jacket, and instinctively did the same.

"Not sure," she frowned, shaking her head as she flipped her blonde hair over her shoulder, "but we need to get downtown."

\*\*\*\*\*\*\*\*\*\*\*\*

Kayla stepped from the passenger door of Jamie's BMW and straightened her skirt as Jamie walked around the front of the car, notebook in hand, leading her onto the sidewalk. Police cruisers barricaded the street. Several officers were already there taking witness statements and attempting to calm passer-byes, while firefighters and EMS searched for survivors and attended to injuries. The two walked a quick perimeter, listening to all the various descriptions of what had happened.

"The truth is going to be tough to decipher out of all this crap," Jamie smirked.

"Yeah," Kayla agreed, "this is the weirdest thing I've ever seen. These people are talking about 200 mile per hour wind in the middle of New York City on a calm fall day. It just doesn't make any sense."

"This place looks like Beirut," Jamie said frowning, taking in all the destruction, remembering what Times Square looked like on any other day.

Looking at the ground, they stopped, the two burn marks in the concrete staring back. This definitely defied explanation.

\*\*\*\*\*\*\*\*\*\*\*\*

"Do you think there's any connection between the killings last night and what happened today?" Kayla asked, thinking more or less out loud.

Jamie paid the cashier then stepped around to the end of the counter as another girl poured their coffees and handed them to Jamie, a cute smile on her freckled face.

"Thanks," he grinned.

Kayla gave him a little jealous nudge, followed by a smirk as they walked away. Jamie passed her a coffee.

"I don't have a clue," he finally answered, returning to their conversation, as he popped the lid off of his cup and stirred in some sugar.

Kayla did the same and replaced her lid, sipping carefully on the hot coffee as she thought.

"Wonder why we got the call?" she questioned as they sat down at a tall table facing the windows. "Sure, everyone thought Luke was on the murders till O'Donnell flipped them to us, but still..."

"This is an odd one." Jamie smiled, finishing her sentence.

They shared a flirtatious grin and then went back to their steaming cups.

"Even after what we just saw, I still can't get those file images of the murders out of my head. We need to get into that apartment building," she finally said after several moments of silence. "We need to take a look at that crime scene."

"That's what I'm thinking," he replied. "We'll go there next."

Her cell phone rang, startling both of them as they stared out at the passing traffic.

"Hello?" she answered, flipping the phone open and raising it to her ear.

"Kayla..." the voice trailed off, weak, scared.

"Ashley?"

Silence.

"Is that you Ash?"

"Yeah, I'm here." she answered with a sniff. "Can we get together for lunch? I really need to talk to you about something."

"Uh..." Kayla thought aloud, looking at Jamie for an answer, though he didn't have a clue what the conversation was about, "Things are a little crazy today."

"Please?"

"Sure," Kayla said reluctantly. "Is that little café uptown okay?"

"Um, yeah. Anywhere is fine," she slowly responded.

"Are you alright, Ash?"

Her tone had Kayla worried. She was usually so upbeat.

"Yeah, I guess. Look, let's just get together and I'll tell you everything, okay?"

"Alright, well I'll see you around 1:00 then?"

"Yeah, see you then."

Kayla closed her phone and set it on the shiny wooden table top, a very concerned look on her face.

"Who was that?" Jamie asked.

"My little sister."

\*\*\*\*\*\*\*\*\*\*\*\*

Ashley Rose sat on her bed, her legs crossed, a drawing pad on her lap. She stared at the blank page, pencil in hand, trying to think of what to draw, but her mind was clouded by her dreams.

She was Kayla's younger sister, just eighteen and headstrong. She was enrolled at Penn State, but, against her parent's wishes, she transferred to Colombia University.

She loved to draw. She'd been drawing her whole life. Her imagination seemed to flow from her pencil into beautiful works of art. She had sketch book after sketch book filled with portraits of people she'd never met, people that existed only in her mind. Other pages danced with imaginary creatures, fairies and warriors, knights and princesses, telling elaborate stories through her pictures. It was her passion.

Over summer break, Ashley had moved into a small apartment in Morningside Heights and found part-time work at an art studio and exhibit on the Upper West Side. But this was her first semester, in a new school, and a new city. Kayla always helped her out whenever she could. After all, New York could be a lonely place if you didn't know anyone.

She gripped her pencil tightly as her thoughts drifted from a scattered vision of an elfin princess and dashing knight to her dream, her blood-hued memories bringing tears to her eyes. Ashley closed her sketchbook and laid it on the bed beside her, placing her pencil on top of it as she cleared the images from her mind.

Looking out the window, she wondered if Kayla was going to believe what she was about to hear. The sun's warm rays highlighted a potted flower on the sill. It gave her hope.

*************

Jamie lifted the yellow police line that cordoned off the entrance to the apartment where the murders took place as Kayla stepped through the splintered doorway. Shaking her head in disbelief, she looked around at the bullet-riddled walls and broken pieces of tile scattered beneath their feet.

*Maybe this wasn't such a good idea?*, she mumbled, second thoughts urging her to turn around.

"Luke's notes say the bodies were found downstairs, in the basement." Jamie said, flipping on his flashlight and aiming the bright beam down the dark, musty hallway.

"Well, Luke should be down here doing this," Kayla complained, following Jamie down the hall, their steps echoing in the silence. "I don't even know how he made detective."

"He is the Mayor's nephew," Jamie said, looking at her over his shoulder and motioning towards the stairwell. "It's not like anyone is going to tell him he's doing a bad job. I mean come on, even O'Donnell is intimidated by his uncle. Mayor Bradford is one guy I wouldn't want to cross, that's for sure."

As they reached the top of the stairs, Kayla glanced back at the front door, the sunlight fading away as rain clouds hung ominously overhead. The faint rumble of thunder threatened somewhere in the distance.

Slowly, they made their way towards the basement. It was so dark: they could hardly see the steps as they descended. The beam of Jamie's flashlight bounced around, illuminating the grimy, mildewed walls in the stairwell. Decades of old green paint cracked and flaked to the floor.

They stepped onto the gray basement hallway and gagged. A rotten egg-like smell filled the air.

Kayla peered into the darkness. As they approached the doorway where the bodies were found, she was sure she saw a shadow flit past the frame. Shaking off her fear, she pulled her flashlight from her jacket and pointed it at the room ahead.

Passing through the battered door, she stepped into the room. Every hair on her arms stood up, as if electricity was coursing through her. It hadn't been noticeably cold in the building, but this room was freezing.

Jamie took a pair of latex gloves from a small leather pouch on his belt and pulled them onto his hands with a snap.

They stopped and scanned the room with their flashlights. Old tables covered in melted candle wax lined the walls. A dusty, broken chair leaned in the corner.

Kayla stared at the floor in the center of the room. A large circle of dried blood showed where the bodies had been. Kneeling, she took a closer look at the stain on the floor, but found nothing useful.

"So what do you think *really* happened down here?" Jamie wondered aloud as he examined one of the dust covered tables.

"I don't know," Kayla frowned illuminating the pentagram on the floor with her flashlight, "but this had to be some kind of ritual or occult thing. Halloween is just a month away you know."

Jamie grinned at her as he headed towards the chair in the corner. He examined it, but, like the blood, there was nothing to draw any conclusions from.

"Find anything yet?" Kayla asked, shining her light at him.

Raising his hand to cover his eyes, he shook his head in disappointment.

"I was so sure we would find something down here," Jamie said sadly, "something Luke missed."

Slowly, he panned the wall with the white beam of his flashlight. Something caught his eye.

"Hey..." he called out, "take a look at this!"

Kayla stepped around the pool of dried blood and looked where Jamie's flashlight was pointed.

Roman numerals were etched into the faded cream paint on the wall. Kayla turned, shining her light on the surrounding walls.

"The numbers go all around the room," she observed.

"How high do they go?" Jamie asked, looking at all the numerals.

"Up to one hundred, at least," she replied thoughtfully.

Jamie stopped and stepped closer to the wall.

"Check this out," he grinned. "I think we found what Luke missed."

"What?!"

The two stared at the wall in front of them. An X and three I's seemed burned into the cracking plaster, right over top of the etching. A ring of blood encircled the letters. It was the only number like it.

"Thirteen?" Kayla wondered.

"I don't know what it means," Jamie smiled, "but it's a start."

She pulled a digital camera from the inner pocket of her tweed jacket and snapped a couple pictures of the wall, puzzling over the number. Jamie traced the numeral with his finger.

They had all but forgotten the rotten egg smell till the sound of something hitting the floor startled them. Quickly, they turned towards the far wall, their flashlight beams darting back and forth. A yellow sulfurous haze hung in the room. A candle rolled across the pentagram and stopped at their feet.

Cautiously, Jamie picked it up and headed towards the table it fell from. In the very middle was a round empty place where the candle had obviously sat, the wood of the table top showing through. The rest of the surface was covered in wax.

He placed the candle down in the opening. It fit perfectly.

"There's no way this fell," Jamie grunted.

"Let's get out of here. This place gives me the creeps."

"Yeah..."Jamie said slowly, turning and staring once again at the Roman numeral thirteen on the wall, "I think we've seen enough."

Heading up the stairs, they became aware of the sound of rain pattering off the building's roof. Floor boards creaked above them as they headed towards the door.

Jamie glanced at Kayla and stopped, his flashlight aimed at the ceiling. Dust fell from a hole above them where a beam showed through. Kayla kept walking. She had no intention of investigating further. Jamie's flashlight flickered and then went out.

"I just put new batteries in this thing!" he said, shaking it angrily.

"Forget about it," Kayla urged as she headed for the door.

Stepping out onto the front steps of the building, they were greeted by a sudden flash, followed by a loud clap of thunder. Then, as if on command, the rain stopped.

"This is a really weird day," Kayla laughed as she fastened her seat belt and looked back at the abandoned apartment, the yellow "crime scene:

do not cross" tape that hung at the building's front entrance fluttering in the light breeze.

"Tell me about it," Jamie mumbled as he put his BMW in gear and pulled away from the curb.

************

"So do you know what you want then, or are you waiting on one more?"

"Oh, no," Ashley replied, fidgeting as she sat at a small, round glass-topped table outside of her favorite, street-side eatery. "I'm not ready yet. My sister is meeting me."

"Okay, hun. I'll check back with you in a few minutes," the waitress smiled curtly, hurrying off to another table.

Ashley glanced at her watch: 1:30pm. Kayla was late.

*So much for one o'clock.*

Several minutes passed. She looked for ways to distract her self, finally settling for people watching, her artistic nature analyzing the passer-bys.

"Alright," the waitress prompted, refilling Ashley's water glass with one hand as she flipped open her receipt pad with the other, "ready to order?"

Ashley had been observing a peculiar looking woman walking her peculiar looking dog and was lost in the curious thought that many people's appearances tended to reflect that of their pet, in this case, a poodle's svelte pompadour, the woman's hair a perfect match, both in color and volume. Now she felt the impatient stare of the waitress and looked up with a smile.

"Um, one corned beef sandwich on rye with Swiss cheese and light mayo and a turkey melt on the poppy seed Kaiser roll with no lettuce or onions, just cheese and tomato" she decided, reading off the menu, "oh and sweet potato fries with both of those, please."

The waitress nodded, jotting down the order with her dulling pencil, then picked up the menus and headed off to the kitchen, her water pitcher in tow. Ashley checked her cell phone: the minutes were ticking by absurdly slow and she hadn't missed any calls.

*Kayla is never late...this isn't like her; I hope she's okay.*

Ashley dialed Kayla's cell number, the buttons beeping with each press, and then raised the phone to her ear. It began ringing. A hand squeezed her shoulder, giving her a start. She quickly looked up, nearly dropping her phone.

"Kayla!"

"Jumpy today huh, sis," she laughed as she pulled a chair out from the table and sat down, giving Jamie a small wave as he sped off into traffic.

Ashley smiled up at her with a sad, almost fake expression.

"Sorry I'm late. I've got a couple of crazy cases you wouldn't believe, *so crazy*, Jamie says he's never seen anything like this. We just left a crime scene. It was definitely," she thought a moment, "*odd.*"

"I might believe anything right now," Ashley admitted.

"Sorry to interrupt, ladies, but what can I get you to drink?" the waitress asked Kayla shortly.

"Oh," Kayla hesitated, her thoughts still fixed on what her sister had been saying, "water with lemon, please."

"Sure. I'll be back with your drink and food in just a moment."

"Is it just me, or does the she seem irritated with us?" Kayla wondered, watching their waitress lean flirtatiously over a table of well dressed professionals, her tightly fitting, low-cut shirt displaying her assets, the men obviously noticing, laughing and ogling as she played her perfected innocent, young, unaware-of-her-own-attractiveness role without missing a step.

"I think she knows she'll get a better tip from them than us," Ashley mused." So sad..."

Kayla huffed, shaking her head, then returned her attention to their previous conversation, "So you said you would believe just about anything right now, what do you mean?"

"Well," Ashley shrugged, "I've been having these dreams. They don't make any sense, only bits and pieces, but they scare me, *a lot.*"

"Like nightmares?"

"Sort of, but not exactly; for example, I saw the news report about last night's killings at that apartment in Harlem, and well, it's strange. The reporter said the police had yet to disclose any details, but I *knew* what had happened."

The waitress brought their food to the table, placing two wax paper-lined red-plastic bistro dishes in front of them. Their food looked wonderful.

"Thank you," Kayla smiled as Ashley checked to make sure her sandwich was right.

"What do you mean you *knew* what happened?" Kayla wondered, picking up her corned beef sandwich.

"Well," Ashley hesitated, "my dreams were about the murders, about everything that happened. I had the dream last night, around midnight, just before the news said it took place, but it wasn't like I saw what happened from my own perspective, it was like I lived it, you know? It was my hands I saw covered in blood, my hands that I watched slit the throats of those poor people!"

"How do you know that, about their throats?" Kayla questioned in a whisper, hoping the other tables hadn't heard what Ashley had said. "That was in our files only, the media doesn't have that information."

"I told you I had dreamt it," Ashley answered, nibbling at her fries.

"So you dreamt that you killed those people?"

"That's not all, this morning I dozed off in class and I had another dream about a guy blowing up a bunch of cars downtown, not with a bomb or anything like that, but just because he thought about it, like he used his mind."

Kayla stopped mid bite, her teeth just sinking into her mouth-watering sandwich, "What?!"

"Yeah, it really shook me up. I tried to convince my self that last night was just a nightmare, a freakish coincidence and that I took what I heard on the news and fit it into the confines of my dream, but then this second one was so outlandish, last night's dream just has to be a coincidence."

"So you don't know?" Kayla sighed, dropping her sandwich into her basket.

"Know what?"

"That actually happened, an explosion, today: a block of Times Square was devastated."

"Shut up!" Ashley exclaimed, the table of business men turning to look at her inquisitively.

"Yeah, Jamie and I were there already, we got the call. It's our case. But you had no idea it happened?"

"No! I walked home from class and waited there till it was time to meet you."

"Well, your dreams have to be a coincidence," Kayla reasoned, trying to convince herself as much as she was her sister." I mean, stuff like that doesn't really happen. Dreams are just a collection of jumbled thoughts and memories, something you saw on TV or in a movie that your brain superimposes into another event or discussion that you remember as you lie sleeping, oblivious to the tricks your mind is playing on you."

"So you know what happened in that apartment?"

"Funny you bring that up, because Jamie and I are investigating that as well. The Captain decided we were the right ones to head up the case."

Ashley sat back in her chair, not sure whether she was relieved or more afraid now that she'd gotten her feelings off her chest, "Well, I didn't know how to tell you, or that you'd even believe me, that you'd think I'm crazy. But it is the truth."

"You're sure?"

"Definitely, I can feel it, you know? It doesn't make any sense to me either and I'm scared, Kayla. I'm afraid to sleep, I'm afraid of what I'm going to see," she said, tearing up.

Kayla wanted to tell her it would be okay, but she didn't believe that herself. She'd thought her dream about Jamie was nothing more than that: a nightmare; but now, if Ashley was right, then maybe her dream too was more than just a dream. Fear began to well up inside of her. Ashley wiped the tears from her eyes and steadied her voice, changing the conversation by asking Kayla how things were going with Jamie.

"Really well," Kayla smiled, glad for the chance to think on happier things. "We've been seeing each other a little over a year now. I can't believe we've been able to keep it a secret at work this long. But..."

"*But?*"

"It's funny we're talking about dreams, because," Kayla said, her thoughts quickly wandering right back to the subject she was trying to avoid, "because, last night, I had one too. I dreamt that Jamie was being held captive, interrogated like a hostage or something. Some man was asking him questions. Jamie was beaten up pretty badly."

"What did the guy look like?" Ashley wondered.

"I don't know. I never saw his face," Kayla lied, turning away to watch traffic for a moment, the eerie mask grinning in her mind.

Ashley finished her sandwich. Kayla's appetite was gone. Uneasiness churned in the pit of her stomach.

"So you believe me?" Ashley asked after a few minutes of silent staring.

"Yeah," Kayla smiled, still picturing the mask, "I just don't understand how it's possible."

"I don't get it either, but I'm not going to pretend it didn't happen. I just want to get the images out of my head. Do you know what that's like?"

Kayla didn't answer. She simply nodded her head. She knew exactly how her sister felt.

************

"Come on, Branson," Detective Luke Bradford mocked in a whiney tone, "aren't you tired of playing cop? Why don't you leave this case to the big boys?"

"We can handle it."

"Who, you and the little princess?"

Jamie edged right up into Luke's face, nose-to-nose. Bradford didn't back down.

"I want your notes and the rest of the reports on last night's homicide." Jamie growled, trying to hold his temper.

He wasn't succeeding.

"What do you mean, *rest of the reports*? This is my case!"

"Not anymore. I've got the coroner's report on the old lady, but I need the rest, your photos, evidence you collected, everything."

"On whose orders?" Bradford huffed.

"O'Donnell's. If you've got a problem with that, you can take it up with him. I'm just trying to do my job."

"You...little...piece of..."

"Easy now," Jamie interjected, "I'd hate to have to shut you up, again. Like I said, I'm only doing my job."

Bradford stepped back, his eyes on fire. He glared at Jamie as he walked over to his desk and unlocked the file cabinet attached to it. Angrily, he pulled all the folders out of the drawer and slammed it shut.

Jamie watched him, amused. This wasn't the first time they'd butted heads. He was sure it wouldn't be the last.

Luke pushed his way past him, bumping shoulders, as he stomped over to Jamie's desk and dropped the folders onto it. Bradford wasn't going to forget this.

"Thanks a lot, Luke!" he hollered, watching him disappear around the corner sulking.

Jamie sat down at his desk and sorted through the files, putting them into a proper order. He smiled gloatingly, picturing how angry Bradford was, and now, he had the paperwork he needed. Jamie couldn't wait to dig in.

\*\*\*\*\*\*\*\*\*\*\*\*

Just north of the residential town of Sleepy Hollow, a quiet manor sat amongst the trees, hidden from the world that progressed around it. It was original to the area, there before any of its neighbors had laid stake to the surrounding properties. In a way, the community was built up around it, preserving, yet forsaking it all the same. Long ago, the landscaping had become overgrown as the forgotten memories of the property's former glory faded away. Now, only rumors of the centuries old house being haunted remained. Witnesses claimed to see faces in the windows and lights dancing in the dark of night.

No one recalled what happened to its previous owners, but a few decades back, it was purchased by an unknown party. Apparently no one ever moved in by the looks of it. Still, it had potential. But its better days were in the past.

At the end of the long gravel drive, a large steel gate slowly creaked open, weighed down by years of vine growth and rust. Six black Mercedes Benz sedans pulled through, dust kicking up from their tires, the windows tinted, hiding its passengers. They traveled to the rotting front stairs of the old house, each parking as part of a perfect diagonal line. The cars' passenger doors swung open. Eighteen sharply dressed men, all in matching black suits, stepped from the sedans, their faces shrouded behind tight black masks; the mouth openings stitched shut, the white slits of their eyes glowing. Several of them carried briefcases, while others held large black duffel bags. The drivers waited in the cars.

A tall, distinguished looking old man opened the double doors of the manor and walked out onto the front porch.

"Gentlemen," he began as he stroked his well groomed beard, "we have much to talk about. Please, join me inside."

Silently, the men followed him into the house.

"Find a seat," he smiled congenially. "Make yourselves comfortable."

The men gathered around him and listened intently.

"I first want to thank you for your dedication to our task," he began, speaking with his hands as much as his deep, powerful voice. "The servants did well to protect you as you finished the ceremony. The mystery surrounding that night has baffled the police and has given us the time we need to regain our strength and prepare for our next endeavor. Though many of the servants fell, they will be remembered for their faith in our cause."

Several of the men nodded in approval.

"However, there is one *problem*. Thirteen, come forward."

One of the men stood from his seat and stepped to the front of the room.

"Please, stand at my side. I want you all to look at him; see his power, his pride, his...*arrogance*," the man frowned. "He is an example to all of you. He has learned to use his powers in a way that even I had not foreseen. You should strive to attain his level, each and every one of you, for he is our future."

Thirteen turned and leaned against the frame of the fireplace that stood just behind the man, cockily straightening his tie and crossing his arms. He seemed bored with the meeting.

"But, before I get ahead of myself I do want to remind you all that in his strength, his lack of self-control, showed weakness. What you did was reckless, Thirteen," the man scolded, turning to him and wagging his finger angrily as if speaking to a mutt. "You risked exposing us before we were ready to show ourselves to the mindless that walk the streets. Still, the display of your power was quite pleasing to me. I believe you are ready for the next step in your faith. Choose a replacement for yourself from among the servants. You will no longer be a member of the Tri-Six. You must become stronger, become the one who can finally lead us to glory."

Thirteen stared at his comrades, the corners of his mask wrinkling as he smiled beneath it. His white glowing eyes pulsed with excitement.

"Number Thirteen," the old man grinned, confidently placing a hand on his shoulder, "you are our future. Luck has been with you."

\*\*\*\*\*\*\*\*\*\*\*\*

"I already made my decision," Capt. O'Donnell grunted, tapping a pack of cigarettes against the top of his desk.

Detective Bradford sat across from him, his shirt sleeves rolled up, his tie hanging loose around his neck. He looked furious.

"But this is my case!" he argued.

"It *was* your case," O'Donnell replied smugly, lighting a cigarette and leaning back in his chair.

"My uncle isn't going to like this."

"Do I look like I care?" he grunted. "He asked me to put you on this, you failed to come up with any leads. So, I put someone else on this case, someone who can get a fresh perspective."

"I only had one day!" Bradford shouted as he raised his hands over his head, a look of disgust on his red face.

"And you wasted it. Your crime scene photos are crap. I wanted Branson and Rose on this in the first place. You had your chance. You're off the case."

"But..."

"I'm not saying it again. You're off the case."

32

# III

## FRIDAY NIGHT

Day turned to night as the darkness crept out from its hiding places, covering the city in its shadow. Ashley, her arms full from an afternoon of shopping followed by a stop at the corner grocery, stepped into her sister's apartment. Kayla smiled, making room for Ashley to squeeze past in the narrow entry hall, then turned and locked the door, double and triple checking the bolt.

"Paranoid much?" Ashley laughed, setting the bags down on the kitchen counter as Kayla rolled her eyes.

"Now, you know where everything is?" Kayla asked, unintentionally sounding like a big sister.

"Yeah," Ashley smiled, "I've been here a couple of times you know."

The two grinned at each other for a moment and then stood in awkward silence. So much had changed. They'd never felt this way before, never searched for words. And though they shared in the despair of each others dreams, they felt distant, like something was driving them apart.

Ashley spoke first, "I really appreciate you taking the rest of the day off to spend it with me. I needed to be with you. It helped me a lot."

Kayla just nodded her head, sorting her thoughts, thinking that Ashley was just as much of a comfort to her. Ashley dropped her bag on the floor next to the coffee table as they sat down on the couch and shared another short silence as a heaviness filled the room, a weight they could both feel. It seemed hard to breathe.

This time Kayla braved the tension, "Do you think you'll be able to get some rest?"

"Yeah, I hope," Ashley said, staring out the window.

Kayla checked her cell phone: 9:30 p.m.

"All right, well I'd better get going," Kayla said, squeezing Ashley's hand as she stood and picked up her jacket off the back of the couch. "I'm meeting Jamie at "McKellen's" in half an hour. How do I look?"

"Well I wouldn't wear that shirt with that skirt."

"Should I wear jeans you think?"

Ashley looked her up and down, then smiled, "Go with the jeans."

"Okay," Kayla grinned, then raced into the bedroom and slipped off her skirt, finding her favorite pair of jeans in her dresser and pulling them on. "Belt or no belt?"

"Are you tucking your shirt in?"

"No..." Kayla decided as she buttoned them and tugged up the zipper.

"No belt."

Kayla hurried back into the living room. Ashley turned to see how she looked.

"Well?"

"Great," she replied.

"Good!" Kayla glowed. "Don't worry and try to get some rest."

"Do you think he'll believe what you're going to tell him, do you think he'll believe...me?" Ashley wondered, her voice full of doubt.

"I don't know, but I'll tell you one thing I know for sure; whatever is going on, my gut says it's just the beginning."

\*\*\*\*\*\*\*\*\*\*\*\*

Lightning flashed in the distance, illuminating the dark silhouettes of the surrounding skyscrapers. Kayla drove through the East Village, the glow of street lamps and headlights reflecting across her blue Honda.

*Jamie's never going to believe this.*

She ran her fingers through her hair, replaying the case in her mind, thinking about her sister's dreams, her own dream. They seemed connected, and yet maybe it all really was just a big coincidence.

*Still...*

\*\*\*\*\*\*\*\*\*\*\*\*

Ashley rested on Kayla's couch feeling very much at home, a rerun of "Friends" glowing in the background, the flicker of the television casting ghostly shadows in the dark room. Her eyes grew heavy as she slowly fell asleep.

Kayla had put her at ease in a way that only a sister could. It seemed she might finally get some rest.

\*\*\*\*\*\*\*\*\*\*\*\*

The tall, bearded man sat silently in his study; the lights dimmed, his eyes closed, his veiny hands resting on his knees. Flashes of a young woman jumped through his mind as if he had been there, watching her every move. He focused more intently and found where she was, now standing looking over her, the world a fuzzy blur around him, yet ominously there. He watched her sleep.

*So young, so beautiful.*

As he concentrated, he could see her lying on a couch in a dark apartment, all alone. She stirred, rolling onto her back. Gently, he placed his hand on her forehead and immediately found himself able to see her memories, through her eyes, her perspective. He searched through the cluttered mess of recent fear and anxiety, pleased at the part she played in his game. He saw her talking with another woman, her sister. But her thoughts grew cloudy.

He stepped back from her, now once again seeing the blurry apartment. Another vision came to him and within seconds, his mind traversed the city, narrowing in on a car, a man in a suit talking on his cell phone. The man was driving to meet whoever was on the other end of the line.

*Interesting?*

He focused his thoughts back to the apartment and placed his hand back on her forehead, finding her now tossing and turning. A faint smile stretched across his thin mouth. She was having another dream, a nightmare: *his* nightmare. He'd been filling her mind with them while she slept. He knew she would be vulnerable. From the first time he saw her in his own dark and twisted dreams, he knew they were connected, he knew she could be used.

He looked further into her memory. Pieces of her past played for him like a jumbled collage. What was he looking for? The man fast forwarded through her mind as if it were a movie, skipping over birthday parties, family vacations, and Christmas mornings. He searched by his feelings. His intuition would guide him to the memory he desired.

*There!*

His faint smile opened into a broad sinister grin. He paused, taking in the memory, studying it in his mind: the grave stone of Officer Jack Rose, her brother, killed in the line of duty. That was the connection.

*All too perfect.*

The man returned to her most recent memories. He saw the young girl with the woman she was talking to earlier that day. Intensely, he listened to their conversation; sweat beading on his brow, his smile now gone.

*Your sister is a police officer, just like dear old Jack? And what's more, she knows of the sacrifice, her and her partner.*

He pursed his lips and concentrated. Again, he saw the man in the car, but the setting had changed. The man was now sitting in a chair, blood drying on his beaten face. Across from him sat Thirteen, shrouded by the shadows, his white eyes glowing in the blackness.

*He must suffer, oh yes, he must.*

She shivered in her sleep, the room growing cold. Lightning flashed, revealing the hazy black cloud that hung above her.

"Ashley," the man whispered into the darkness, his eyes flicking open, her name rolling like a curse from his lips.

Glistening with sweat, she sat up on the couch. The dream was so real.

"Not Jamie," she wondered aloud, "just like Kayla's dream."

But that wasn't all. At the moment that she woke, she caught a brief glimpse of something, a shadow, pale, but distinguishable. She had seen the face of a man. She had to tell Kayla.

\*\*\*\*\*\*\*\*\*\*\*\*

Kayla eased to a stop as the traffic light turned red. She shifted uncomfortably in her seat, unable to shake the bad feeling that was eating her up inside, the unmistakable sensation of being watched. With a tingle, the hairs on the back of her neck stood on end.

*This light has been red for a while.*

The city that never slept was unusually quiet tonight. The normally cramped sidewalks were curiously empty. She glanced at the clock: 9:51pm. It was early for a Friday night. Kayla turned back to the light.

*Still red? Come on!*

She looked both ways, no cars to be seen, then looked up at the "no turn on red" sign.

*You've got to be kidding me.*

She sat for a moment, amused by the sudden humor of the situation. In her mind, she pictured herself sitting just like she was, but with little versions of herself standing on each shoulder, one dressed like an angel, the other like a little red devil.

"No one will know I turned," she mumbled, imagining her little devil-self giving enthusiastic thumbs up.

With a bit of reluctance and just a twinge of guilt, she pulled forward, looking first to the left, then the right. The light was still red and the coast very clear as she began to pull into the intersection.

*This is ridiculous, there's not even another car in sight!*

She stepped on the gas pedal. The car jolted forward and her angel-self disappeared in a poof of white and gold cloud.

Slam!

Something hit the passenger window hard. Kayla floored the brakes, skidding to a stop. A haggardly old man with a rusting shopping cart stood just outside the car, his middle finger exclaiming his anger, his dirty, rotting teeth sneering from behind his grizzly beard.

"You made me drop my booze!" he yelled, his middle finger still in the air, his eyes glowing red with hate.

Kayla's heart was pounding. She gave a little apologetic waive and turned right. As she passed under the light, it changed green. Her hands were still shaking as she glanced in the mirror for a last look at the old man, but he was gone, as if he'd vanished into thin air.

*That's what I get for even thinking about running a red light.*

The corners of her lips formed a slight smile. She felt so foolish. A horn honked behind her. Her smile quickly faded as she became suddenly aware of all the people that packed the sidewalks and the now very busy, traffic filled street.

"Go, lady!" a man shouted from the window of his SUV, his arm motioning for her to move.

Kayla shook her head in confusion and hurried on around the corner. The image of that man and his angry, red eyes still loomed dauntingly in the back of her mind.

************

Ashley sat in silence, trembling, as she pulled a sketch book from her messenger bag and leafed through the pages. She had seen a man's face in her dream, a face she didn't recognize.

Stopping at a blank page, Ashley took out her pencil and sharpened it to a perfect point. Anxiously, she began drawing, first his eyes, then skillfully shaping his nose and framing his face. The man had such strong cheekbones. His skull seemed to hide just beneath the surface, like the skin was stretched thin, pulled taut. His mouth was a small slit, lifeless, without expression.

Ashley went back to the eyes. They seemed so hollow.

Filling in the pupils and shading around the corners of his dark eyes, Ashley felt a chill sweep through the room. Startled, she looked up. The windows were closed; so was the door.

The drawing had taken shape. It looked just like the man in her dream: the eyes, the jaunt expression, the well-groomed beard. It was him.

As she looked at the picture, curiosity rather than fear rushed over her. Staring into his eyes, it was as if they were staring right back, reading her, piercing her soul.

*Who are you?*

Her own eyes grew heavy as her head eased softly onto the arm of Kayla's couch, sending her drifting back to sleep, her sketchpad still resting on her lap, the man's face embedded on the page. As she slipped into another dream, a presence filled the room. The picture looked so real, so alive. And then, its eyes, its hollow eyes, that Ashley had focused so intently on portraying just as she had seen in her dream, those hauntingly real eyes blinked.

************

Kayla sat across from Jamie at a small table in the rear of "McKellen's Pub." Several pool tables filled the far side of the room with a bar on the opposite end. An older man made drinks behind the counter: he was the owner, Ernie McKellen, complete with thick Irish accent and graying mutton-chop side burns. Several patrons were pulled up to the bar on stools, talking loudly, laughing at his stories, while others played eight ball or threw darts. "McKellen's" was always a pretty busy place.

Waitresses hurried about, some carrying drinks or trays of food while others flirted with customers for bigger tips, all of them dressed in short plaid skirts, white t-shirts with *McKellen's* emblazoned across the front, and tall black boots adorned with steel-gray buckles. The walls were faded, discolored from years of smoke, the ceiling low and gray. Neon beer signs lined the room and laughter was always on tap. It was about what you would expect from a little bar in a big city: full of character and memories. McKellen remembered every face that walked into his bar and the waitresses knew all the regulars.

"What are you going to have?" Jamie said, peeking at Kayla over the top of his menu.

"Oh, I don't know," she said laughing, "I always have the same thing."

"Chicken Philly it is," Jamie grinned as he motioned for the waitress. "No mushrooms, right?"

"What'll it be, Jamie?" she asked with a wink.

Kayla rolled her eyes and answered, leaving Jamie silent, his mouth hanging open, "I'll have a chicken Philly sandwich with no mushrooms."

"Green peppers and mayonnaise?" the waitress asked, looking away from Jamie.

"Yes, please."

"And what kind of cheese, American or provolone?"

"Provolone."

"Would you like fries or coleslaw?"

"Fries."

"Okay, thank you," the waitress said, her tongue licking the corner of her mouth as she wrote the order down, "and you, Jamie?"

"He'll have the meatball sub with extra mozzarella cheese," Kayla chimed in, smirking at Jamie who was now blushing as he took a sip of his beer.

The waitress nodded and headed off for the kitchen, her feet shuffling across the dirty vinyl floor. Jamie set his mug down and chuckled.

"You're in a pretty feisty mood tonight."

"It's been a long day and I'm glad to be with you. And after the coffee shop today, I want to keep you all to myself."

He smiled, picked his beer back up, but paused before taking another drink, "So what did your sister have to say?"

"Well," Kayla stalled, wondering where to begin, "it's a long story."

"We've got all night!" he grinned.

Kayla sighed. She felt a bit silly, almost superstitious, but he needed to hear about Ashley's dreams. Jamie listened skeptically as she explained everything Ashley had told her, all the details of her dreams.

Their food came. Kayla continued on between bites. At the end of her story, Jamie tipped back his drink, finishing off his beer. He placed the mug back on the table, the glass thunking against the old heavy wooden top.

He hadn't said a word while Kayla expressed her fear, rambled about her sister's dreams, the homeless man with the shopping cart, and how she believed it was all somehow connected.

His mind was spinning, full of questions. The case was already strange enough, *now this*. His partner's sister was apparently having precognitive dreams. How could he understand the truth?

"So," Kayla prodded, "what do you think?"

Jamie sat in silence, playing with his mug, sliding it back and forth between his hands on the table top.

"I think I understand," he shrugged uneasily. "Truth is, since this case began, I've been searching for something that makes sense. As of yet, I haven't come up with anything. So this just, *fits*, but you said her dreams all happened just before these incidents took place? Not like a couple days earlier or something like that? I mean, she's an artist, obviously a very creative person. Do you think there's any possibility her imagination is just getting the best of her, that maybe her timeline is messed up and she thinks the dreams happened before she'd heard of the incidents? Maybe her memory is just off? If she's as scared as you say, her fear could cause confusion, it makes a lot of sense."

"I know my sister, Jamie. She doesn't make things up, especially things like this," Kayla explained. "She is genuinely scared and I want to get to the bottom of it."

"Well," he yawned, scratching his elbow as he thought for a second, "if your sister really is seeing things in her dreams before they happen, maybe she can help us. Maybe she'll see something that could lead us to the perpetrators in action. Maybe she can find them. In the mean time, let's stay focused on what we know for sure."

"I know," Kayla said, a bit disappointed that Jamie wasn't more excited about the news she had to share, "we need to stick to what we've got so far."

Jamie nodded thoughtfully.

"I'll see Ashley when I get home," Kayla continued. "I wanted to keep her close tonight. I'll ask if she can give us a hand. I don't know how or when she has the dreams, or if she'll even have another, but if she sees something else, I'm sure it won't be long before it actually happens. In the meantime, I have some thinking to do."

Looking at him, suddenly nothing else mattered. All she could picture was Jamie, beaten; resting slumped in a chair and stained with blood.

"Jamie, I need to tell you. I'm not quite sure..."

"Yeah?" he smiled, looking deep into her eyes.

They stared at each other, the world around them frozen in the moment. Her heart thumped in her ears.

"...never mind..."

Kayla wanted so badly to tell Jamie about her dream, to share it with him, but when it came right to it, she just couldn't and she didn't know why. And worse, by holding back her words, she felt like there was something between them. Maybe she thought he wouldn't believe her, that she was crazy just like her sister or maybe she didn't believe it herself. But regardless, she buried it down inside.

They continued to stare at each other in silence till Kayla forced a wide smile. Slowly, she stood and picked her jacket up from the back of her chair. Jamie stood as well. He took her jacket and held it for her as she slid her arms into the sleeves.

"See you in the morning," she said handing Jamie a ten dollar bill. "Here's my part of the tab."

"You know I never let you pay," he said, his voice softening, "besides, I thought maybe we could spend some time together tonight, maybe another walk in the park? The trees are starting to change colors."

"I'd love to Jamie..."

His face broke into a wide smile, his cheeks dimpled, cute.

"...but it'll have to wait," Kayla said, hiding her real feelings, knowing she wanted nothing more than to stay with him. "I have to get back to my sister. Thanks for listening."

She was almost out the door when she looked back and gave Jamie a smile and a little wave. He grinned and waved back. But as soon as she was out the door, his expression turned to sadness. He'd hoped they could talk, talk about their relationship, where things were going.

The waitress came to check on him. He faked a smile and ordered another beer. Deep in thought, he drank alone, drowning his frustration.

Everything had started innocently enough: a few dates, dinner, maybe a movie. Now, a year had passed, they'd become closer. They were careful to hide their interest in each other at work, afraid it would end their partnership: they were a good team, a compliment to each other. But their flirting had become more serious and their affection was obvious. And now Jamie found himself missing her, wanting to be with her, and feeling genuinely alone when she wasn't around.

Quietly, he looked around the bar, taking in the faces of the people all around him. Some looked desperate, others lost. Still, there were some who looked happy, very content, a drink in one hand, a dart or cigarette in the other.

*Am I like them?*

He finished his beer and stared at the bubbling foam in the bottom of the mug. Sadly, he felt the same way: empty. His thoughts turned once more to Kayla and he felt even worse as something deep down inside of him tugged at his heart. He wanted her to know everything he felt, get it all out in the open, but he knew now wasn't the time.

Tossing a pile of money on the table, Jamie headed towards the door and into the cool night air. There he was, alone, gazing up at the stars all by himself. He wanted to tell Kayla that he felt like he was missing something in his life and he believed with all his heart that it was her. But she was gone. And worse, she was right, even if she hadn't said it in so many words. Their relationship would have to wait.

************

Ashley woke, the sketchbook sliding off her lap. Yawning, she looked up at the clock on the wall. She couldn't believe it, she'd actually slept. Lazily, she staggered into Kayla's bedroom and undressed, then slid into bed, the comforter warm, safe. Maybe things weren't so bad after all.

************

Kayla hurried home. It was raining again, pouring. Drops splattered across her windshield as she turned into her apartment's parking garage, her headlights bouncing off of rippling puddles. Pulling into her spot, she thought she caught the shadow of a man in the corner of her eye, but when she looked again, nothing was there.

*Get a grip.*

She grabbed her purse and headed towards the elevator. Pressing the *up* button, the heavy doors clanked shut and she felt it jolt as it began its ascension up to the seventh floor. She stared into the copper-toned mirrored walls, looking at herself, her rain tangled hair.

The lights flickered. In the reflection, she saw a dark…*something*, something she couldn't describe, hovering just behind her, its glowing eyes fixed on her. But just as quickly, it was gone, and the lights were back on.

The elevator stopped on her floor. Kayla hesitated as the doors slid open. She felt like she couldn't move.

*What was that thing?*

Finally, she stepped from the elevator and walked quickly towards her apartment door, glancing over her shoulder as she fumbled with her key. Finally the lock clicked open and she turned the knob as quickly as she could.

Kayla closed the door behind her and leaned up against it, setting her purse and holster on the table in the entryway. She turned the deadbolt and dropped her jacket over the back of a chair, her wet hair dangling in front of her face.

Heading into the bedroom and changing into sweats and a tank top, she quickly brushed through her hair, wincing, tugging at knots.

Kayla looked over at the bed. Ashley was sleeping peacefully, the covers pulled up closely under her chin. She looked like she was twelve again. It made Kayla laugh as she pulled a bit of hair from her sister's face that had fallen across her cheek. She never stirred, sound asleep. Kayla set down her hair brush and closed the bedroom door.

Putting her hair into a ponytail, Kayla stepped into the living room and sat down at her computer. She clicked enter on the keyboard and it whirred to life. Logging on to the Internet, she Googled dreams, and similar unexplained phenomenon. Her query returned websites about prophecy and visions. She began reading down the list of sites, some religious, some fanatical, but stopped on one entitled "The End of Days." It was so difficult to understand. The site spoke of Nostrodamus and the Book of "Revelation" in the Bible. This wasn't what she was looking for. She typed *precognition* into the search bar and clicked *go*. The browser pulled up even more websites filled with words that looked like they were written in code. Kayla felt like she needed an interpreter.

She closed her web browser and stared for a second at the glowing screen, a picture of her with her family when she was about fourteen as her background. They were at the beach: herself, Ashley, her mom and dad, and her one brother with his fiancé, taken about a year after Jack was killed.

Kayla missed her brother. He would have been just about Jamie's age now. Maybe that's part of why she was so comfortable with him.

*I should have stayed with Jamie tonight.*

She smiled at the thought of him, biting on her lower lip.

*What am I saying?*

She forced her thoughts back to Ashley. Clicking open a folder on her desktop, Kayla scrolled through her collection of MP3's, finally finding what she wanted to listen to. Hard rock music quietly filled the room, her favorite band echoing between the walls. Walking towards the kitchen for a drink, she glanced at the wall clock, a wide yawn stretching across her face.

*One thirty! Where did the night go?*

Kayla reached into her fridge for a can of diet soda, then closed the door, popping the tab and taking a swig. A faint knock startled her as she crossed back to the living room.

*Was that the door?*

Kayla stared down the entry hall at the door, light shining through the peep hole. She took a step forward, but stopped as something passed by outside the door, blocking the light for a brief moment. She set her pop on the hall table and slid her Glock from its holster beside her purse. Loading a bullet into the chamber, she peered through the peep hole, but no one was there. She undid the chain lock, clicked open the deadbolt, and slowly leaned through the door, looking first to the right, then the left, her back up against the wall.

"Hey," a voice called out, "I hope I didn't wake you?"

It was Ashley. Kayla lowered the gun to her side as she held back another yawn.

"I could have shot you. Why did you sneak up on me like that?"

"Sorry, I couldn't sleep," Ashley explained. "I thought maybe I could stay here tonight."

Kayla paused as the words sunk in. The world froze in front of her, her mind catching up to what she was seeing.

"But you're already here?"

The Ashley standing in front of her was rain-soaked, her hair long and stringy, hanging in her face. She broke into a dark grin that reminded Kayla of every scary movie she ever sat through. The lights in the hall flickered, then the lights in her apartment did the same. An odd, almost electric buzzing sound, much like strong radio interference, crackled through the walls.

Kayla glanced over her shoulder, checking the lights. Everything seemed okay. She wondered if the bedroom door was open, but there it was, closed, just as she remembered doing. She turned back towards the hall, her ears beginning to ring from the constant hum.

Ashley was gone. The hall was empty. Kayla did a spin looking in every direction as the walls closed in on her, a panic-induced taupe blur. She was definitely alone.

The humming stopped. Kayla raced to the bedroom door. For a moment she stood there, her hand an inch away from the doorknob, wanting to enter, but afraid of what she might find. Courage prevailed. She closed her eyes, grabbed the knob, and turned.

Ashley was asleep. She had shifted in bed and the covers had moved noticeably, but she was sleeping all the same.

Kayla pulled the bedroom door closed and ran back down the hall, her hands quivering. This was out of character for her. She was always in control.

The front door was still standing wide open. Kayla slowly eased into the hall, her gun ready, and checked the elevators, but they weren't moving. Then, frustration set in. She raced to the emergency exit and slammed through the crash bar that led into the stairwell, the metal door clanking against the wall, but it was empty too.

Kayla settled back down on her couch, her gun resting on the coffee table, her arms limp at her sides. She had made sure she locked the door. But now she couldn't remember if she had.

Doubt filled her mind. Yet she knew Ashley had to be telling the truth. The same questions kept circling in her head, over and over.

*Why is all of this happening? What do these dreams mean?*

And her biggest question, the one that really had her stumped: *Why Ashley?*

\*\*\*\*\*\*\*\*\*\*\*\*

The man from Ashley's drawing stood deathly still as he stared out the window, high above the city below, a look of uneasiness in his strong eyes. His office was pitch black except for the bright flashes of lightening that flickered, briefly chasing away the shadows that consumed him. Loud claps of thunder made the room quake.

Thirteen stood at his side, his mask shrouding his face, hiding his hate.

"I need to ask you to do something for me," he began, a faint shake in his voice. "It is something I can ask only of you."

"Anything, Sir."

"I need you to follow the girl," the man continued more forcefully, "keep an eye on her."

Thirteen grinned beneath his mask.

"Besides the obvious enjoyment of stalking a beautiful young woman," he quipped, "why do you need me to follow her? Is she a threat?"

"I don't know, *yet*," he replied solemnly, "only that her brother once came close to discovering some, *delicate*, information about me and I need to make sure she doesn't know the truth."

"I will do what you ask," Thirteen answered as he disappeared into the darkness.

"Be careful," the man warned calmly, stroking his beard, "her sister is investigating the sacrifice."

He was already gone.

\*\*\*\*\*\*\*\*\*\*\*\*

Jamie turned on his TV. He couldn't sleep. Kayla's words kept running through his head.

Grabbing a garbage bag from under the kitchen counter, he cleaned off his coffee table, filling the bag with frozen dinner boxes and a dozen empty beer bottles.

*No wonder Kayla never comes over.*

Dropping the bag off next to the trash can in the kitchen, Jamie pulled his police-issue Glock from its holster where it was hanging on a coat rack. He ejected the magazine, stripped the slide, and began cleaning the barrel, a comedy show squawking in the background.

Jamie picked up the remote and flipped through the channels: news, weather, more news, *MTV*. He stopped. Hip-hop filled the room. The screen flickered with the image of a rapper surrounded by Italian sports cars smiling wide, his teeth covered in gold and diamonds, as he threw fist-fulls of money into the air.

He finished cleaning his gun, reassembled the parts, and set it down on the coffee table. Still wide awake, he jumped up, walked to the fridge, then returned to the couch, flopping back down as he tossed a bottle cap onto the floor and tipped back a cold beer. Maybe this would help him sleep.

Half a bottle later, his iPhone beeped to life. The screen flashed "Kayla's Cell."

"Hello?" he answered, setting the bottle down.

\*\*\*\*\*\*\*\*\*\*\*\*

Thirteen stood outside the window. His feet just fit on the decorative stone ledge that protruded from the side of the building. It was cold. His black suit coat fluttered in the wind.

Silently, he peered around the frame, the glow of his eyes reflecting in the glass. Ashley slept quietly within. He liked his new task. She was beautiful. He shuffled around the ledge, gracefully sliding around the corner of the building and glancing into the living room.

*My, my, you're pretty as well...*

Kayla faced the front door, her cell phone at her ear.

"Jamie," she said frantically, "I don't know what's going on. I think I'm seeing things!"

"Hold on," Jamie replied, "I'll be there as soon as I can."

"No, you don't have to come over. There's really nothing here. I just needed to hear your voice, to talk to somebody, bring me back to reality, you know?"

"Are you sure?" he asked, pulling on his jacket and searching the pockets for his keys.

"Yeah, I'm fine," she tried to convince him. "Let me explain."

"Alright, just calm down though, okay?"

50

"Alright," she said, glancing at the bedroom door.

Kayla curled her legs up on the couch, her eyes still searching for the slightest movement.

"Just a little bit ago, I heard a knock at the door," she explained, still confused as to what she'd seen, "so I opened it."

"Uh huh?"

"And my sister was standing in the hall, completely drenched."

"So?"

"As I talked to her, I realized that Ashley, *the real Ashley*, was sleeping in my bedroom."

"Kayla, I think you need to get some rest," Jamie reasoned, holding back a slight laugh. "This case is just starting to mess with your head, that's all."

"I know what I saw, Jamie."

"Okay, okay. Maybe you should take tomorrow off, relax."

"No, Jamie."

Kayla was frustrated, Jamie could tell. Thirteen stood on the ledge smiling, his eyes closed, enjoying every word of their little spat.

"Look," he said, backing off, "I know everything's going to be okay. You just need to rest."

"Yeah, I just need some rest."

"It'll make more sense tomorrow," Jamie encouraged. "You sure you don't want me to come over?"

"I'll be fine," Kayla said, forcing a smile. "You're right. It'll be better after I sleep."

"Alright," Jamie frowned, almost certain Kayla was hiding something, "tomorrow, we'll hit this case hard, see what we can dig up."

"Okay," she yawned. "I'll see you in the morning."

Setting her cell phone down next to her gun, she looked out at the night sky. A shadow flitted past the weathered frame, startling her.

Kayla jumped up and ran to the window, searching for whatever it could have been.

*Nothing.*

She leaned against the frame, watching cars' headlights float down the dark streets below.

*Just a reflection*, she told herself sleepily.

\*\*\*\*\*\*\*\*\*\*\*\*

Quietly, Kayla slipped into bed next to Ashley. She looked at her sister for a moment, watching her sleep. Ashley seemed like she was finally resting.

Rolling onto her back and pulling the covers up around her, Kayla stared at the ceiling. For some odd reason, after all that had happened, now, as she tried to rest, she couldn't get the Roman numeral thirteen out of her head. *XIII* was all she could see when she closed her eyes.

\*\*\*\*\*\*\*\*\*\*\*\*

On the rooftop above her, Thirteen stood silhouetted against the moon. He extended his arms straight out at his sides like wings, a Japanese katana in his right hand shining, glistening in the moonlight, the fingers on his left hand fanned like talons. Rain bounced off his outstretched arms as drops spattered, soaking his sleeves. Proudly, he let out a laugh, dark and deep, listening as it echoed through the streets.

Lightning flashed, followed by a loud rumbling of thunder. In that moment, during that sudden burst of light, Thirteen slipped away into darkness.

# IV

## SATURDAY MORNING

Sun rays gleamed off New York's glass-covered skyline. Morning had come. Gray clouds drifted on the horizon, threatening to spoil what promised to be a beautiful day. Puddles lined the busy streets.

Bright light filtered through the retractable blinds hanging in Kayla's bedroom window, illuminating specks of dust hanging in the early morning sunshine. Ashley sat up and looked at her sister's alarm clock: 6:27am. The smell of hot buttermilk pancakes floated through the air. Rubbing the sleep from her eyes, she climbed out of bed and searched through her sister's dresser. It was a cool fall morning, she needed something warm.

*Perfect.*

Ashley smiled, pulling on a pair of pink fleece-lined sweatpants she found in a bottom drawer, then turned to glance at herself in the mirror, checking each angle. Satisfied, she headed into the living room. Kayla was already up, busy in the kitchen, a spatula in hand. She was standing over a hot griddle, her bath robe wrapped tightly around her.

"Good morning, Sunshine!" Kayla teased, grinning from ear to ear, the soles of her fluffy, plaid slippers shuffling across the floor as she hurried about the small kitchen.

Ashley let out a yawn and leaned against the island counter, picking up a glass of orange juice Kayla had poured for her.

"Sleep well?"

"Actually, I did," she said, a smile on her face as she took another sip of juice.

"I like your sweatpants," Kayla grinned. "Aren't those *mine?*"

Ashley looked down at the stretchy pants and grinned. They made her feel rather cute.

"*Sort of,* I hope you don't mind."

"Are you kidding? They look better on you anyway," she teased.

"Isn't six a little early?" Ashley yawned, pulling out a stool and sitting at the kitchen island, her elbows resting sleepily on the counter top.

"Not when you work at eight."

They shared a smile. Ashley missed this, the feeling of home, not being alone.

"How about you then, did you sleep well?"

"I was up most of the night," Kayla admitted, flipping the pancakes over and readying a plate. "I had a lot on my mind."

"Looks like you still do," Ashley smiled, watching Kayla's meticulous breakfast preparation. "You're worse than mom."

"No, it's just been a while since I've made breakfast for a guest and I want everything to be just right."

"So what's bothering you?"

Kayla slid the last pancake on top of her perfectly piled short-stack, then set a bottle of warm syrup down next to the butter and handed Ashley a plate.

"Dig in," Kayla grinned, pouring more orange juice as she dodged the question.

"Seriously," Ashley urged as she put a pancake on her plate and buttered it with a knife Kayla had laid out, "you want to talk about it?"

In silence, Kayla poured syrup on her pancakes and picked up a fork, delicately cutting a bite.

*I can't hold this in forever.*

"Well, last night I had the perfect opportunity to tell Jamie about my dream, even if he only took it as a warning, or something, especially after I shared with him what you've seen. I had the chance..."

"So why didn't you?"

"Because," Kayla paused, her fork raised to her mouth, a string of syrup dripping to her plate, "I think I love him."

"Have you told him?"

"No."

"You need to."

Ashley watched Kayla chew, letting it all sink in.

"So what did he think about my dreams?" she asked, trying to give Kayla something less...*sensitive* to think about.

"I'm pretty sure he believes you," Kayla answered as if waking from a deep sleep. "Jamie is a factual kind of guy, but he trusts what I think."

They finished their breakfast without another word. Kayla put on an awkward smile. Ashley felt that something was still wrong. Now definitely wasn't the time to tell her that she'd had the same dream, the dream about Jamie.

"Anything else?" she pried as Kayla began gathering the plates and setting them in the sink.

"Um, yeah," Kayla answered reluctantly, taking a final sip of her juice, then sending the rest trickling down the drain.

"Okay?"

"Well," Kayla shrugged, "last night, when I first got home, I checked in on you. You were asleep in bed. I saw you, tucked you in. Then I heard a knock at the door and..."

"*And?*"

"And when I opened it, you were standing there."

"But, I couldn't have. You said so yourself," Ashley mumbled, almost angrily. "I was asleep."

"Yeah, I know," Kayla smiled, trying to calm things down, "the you, or *whatever*, I saw in the hall disappeared before I could turn around to get another look. After it was gone, I checked on the *real* you in the bedroom and you were still there, sound asleep."

"The *real* me?"

"Yes, the *real* you," Kayla answered sheepishly, her hands raised in confusion.

"So you believe me now?" Ashley asked as she stood and handed Kayla her empty glass.

"I never doubted you," Kayla admitted, taking the glass and giving her sister a hug. "I've got to get ready for work. We'll get this all figured out."

"You're working on a Saturday?" Ashley laughed, flipping on the faucet, hot water pouring over the dirty dishes. "Sucks to be you!"

Smirking, Kayla headed into the bedroom. She'd already set out her clothes for the day.

Ashley filled the sink with water, then left the dishes to soak. She stopped at the hall mirror and looked at herself again in the borrowed sweatpants.

*Simply adorable.*

Flopping down on the couch, she turned on the television, searching for something to watch. Ashley flipped through the channels, not really seeming to pay any attention to what was actually on: a sports show, the weather, another sports show, a home shopping channel, the man on the screen yelling the praises of his cooking knives that could slice and dice right thru a chicken bone and still never dull.

*That sounds safe.*

Ashley turned to the next channel: the morning news.

*This'll do.*

The news anchor finished a light-hearted story about a heroic dog that saved a small child from a burning house. The weather man gave a friendly, rehearsed chuckle, as did the sports reporter.

"In other news," the co-anchor chattered, "another act of kindness: billionaire Dr. Maurice Triton, founder of Tri-Corp., a pioneer in the field of bio-technological development and pharmaceuticals, donated fifteen million dollars to the United American Council, a nonprofit organization promoting racial awareness and equality through the building of strong relationships between sexes, religions, and cultures by overcoming sociological stereotypes. His donation will help fund the building of the United American Academy in upper New York State. Though the facility is still in the developmental phase, the school will focus on specialized education and prepare students of all backgrounds for a successful college experience, while catapulting graduates of all ethnicities toward advanced career opportunities…"

A picture of Triton hung in the corner of the screen, a small caption with his name and company logo below it. As the reporter continued to explain Triton's contribution, Ashley sat in silence, her eyes locked on the screen, agape. Kayla walked into the room, fastening her holster to her belt and reaching for her jacket.

"You alright, Ash?" she asked. "You look like you've seen a ghost."

Ashley's eyes remained fixed on the picture of Triton. She could hardly speak.

"It's him, Kayla. It's the man from my dream," she said in shock, her voice wavering, "the man from my drawing."

"Who?" Kayla asked, quickly stepping towards the couch.

"*Triton*: the guy they're talking about on the news. He was in my dream," Ashley stammered, obviously shaken. I sketched his face."

"The millionaire?" Kayla questioned.

"No, *billionaire*," Ashley gasped back.

"Are you sure, Ash?"

"I'm positive. Look at my drawing!" she said, picking up her sketch book and holding it for Kayla to see.

"Okay, sit tight," Kayla grinned excitedly, "I'll run this by Jamie, see what he thinks. Maybe I can dig up some information on this guy at the library. I'll head there on my way to the station. My cell phone is on. Call me if you need me. I'll let you know what he says."

With that, Kayla was out the door, the lock clicking over from outside. Once again, Ashley was alone. Fear crept into her mind. She grabbed a pillow from the couch and hugged it close, pulling her knees to her chest. The news went on to another story. Ashley flipped the channel to *Cartoon Network* and set the remote next to her on the couch. She needed to distract herself, she needed to forget, if only for a moment.

*************

"I just want to make sure we're on the same page?" Triton grinned slyly as his limousine glided down Fifth Avenue, the darkly tinted windows reflecting the gray stone-work of the passing buildings that towered high above him, "because if we're *not*..."

"Oh, yeah, we are."

"Well, there are times I feel you take our relationship for *granted*," Triton urged as he leaned back into the soft leather seat of his car, letting his words sink in, his shiny metallic cell phone raised nonchalantly to his ear.

"I wouldn't say that," the voice stammered back, "it's just that sometimes, I have to be prudent. If I ran everything by you..."

"Then you would not be thinking for yourself, Mr. Bradford," Triton mused.

"Um, exactly."

"That's not a problem," Triton continued as he crossed his legs, "but, I need to know that you have *our* best interest in mind."

Nervously, the Mayor paced in his office, one hand holding his phone, the other rubbing his brow in frustration. Pausing at his desk, he leaned on the smooth wooden surface and picked up an expensive looking bottle. Anxiously, he poured brandy into a tumbler as he held his phone between his shoulder and cleanly shaven cheek.

"I don't know what brought the police out to that apartment so quickly," he said, his hand shaking as he took a sip from the glass, "but you and I both know you took a risk, doing something like, like *that*, and out in the open no less."

"*Out in the open*?" Triton laughed, "I have no idea what you're talking about, my good man."

"Well maybe your people shouldn't have shot that officer?"

Triton didn't answer, though he smiled coyly.

"Look," the Mayor continued, feeling as if he were digging his own grave, "I know you're going to tear that building down..."

"Brick by brick," Triton interjected.

"But maybe you were a little *careless*," he said, taking a deep breath, then finishing his brandy, the glass clanking against the hard wooden top of his desk as he set it down.

"My, my, aren't we feeling bold today?!" Triton chuckled. "My point is; I simply wanted to make sure the building was put to good use before it was demolished. It served its purpose. So, I don't think *careless* is the word. Just keep the police at bay as you always do, and we will continue to work together as we always have."

"Of course," the Mayor replied, filling his glass a second time. "I'll make sure their investigation runs dry. My nephew is heading it up, so we've got it covered."

"Good," Triton said emphatically, "now please, come to your window and have a look outside."

The Mayor tipped back his glass and placed it on the corner of his enormous desk, his phone still pressed to his ear. Slowly, he walked to the tall window in his office, the hand-carved peak of the deeply stained frame nearly touching the ceiling, and leaned against the pane. Dark clouds gathered as thunder rumbled ominously overhead. Scanning the street below, Oliver Bradford spotted Triton's long black limo pulled sharply against the curb, the engine running, its windshield wipers flicking away the light rain.

"I'll be down in a second," he said uncertainly into his cell phone.

*Silence.*

Triton had already hung up.

\*\*\*\*\*\*\*\*\*\*\*\*

Jamie glared at his watch. He shook his head in frustration as he held the face up close to his ear, sure the hands had stopped moving.

*Still ticking.*

Suddenly, Jamie was distracted by the unexpected sound of an empty coffee pot clanking down in the stainless steel brewer, "Who drank the last cup and didn't make more?"

Captain O'Donnell was in one of his moods again, barking angrily in the background as Jamie picked up his desk phone and dialed Kayla's cell: he hoped she hadn't left yet. Jamie hid a grin as O'Donnell passed by muttering something about old coffee grinds and doing everything himself.

"Hey," he smiled as she answered, "I wanted to let you know, O'Donnell's got us in a meeting through most of the day, so I don't think we'll get much accomplished."

"What kind of meeting?" she asked confused. "I thought O'Donnell wanted us to focus on the case."

"I don't know. There was a memo on my desk this morning saying it was mandatory," Jamie shrugged, "I guess some big-wigs are pushing their weight around or something. They told O'Donnell this had to happen today. You owe me though."

"What?" she asked curiously as she closed her car door.

"I got you out of this thing," he grinned, his voice full of mischief. "I told the Captain you were having a *family crisis*."

"Really? *Family crisis*, huh?"

"Yeah, he bought it."

"Gee, thanks."

"You bet. Anyway, I was hoping I could catch you before you made it in today so you wouldn't have to suffer through this too."

"I wouldn't mind suffering as long as you were there," she joked.

"Yeah, yeah. Can you keep yourself busy till I finish up here?"

"Sure," Kayla laughed, "This works out perfectly."

"Perfectly?"

"I've got something I can look into in the meantime. Thanks for taking the bullet on this one."

"Don't mention it," he said, getting ready to hang up his phone, O'Donnell waiving him into the conference room. "I'll talk to you this afternoon."

"Oh, wait!" Kayla cried, hoping to catch him before he hung up, three little words on the tip of her tongue.

*Too late.*

"I love you..."

************

Standing up from his chair, Jamie took one last drink from his coffee mug, placed it back on the desk, and headed toward the briefing room, following several other detectives through the door. Each man took a seat at the long conference table. Jamie tossed a notebook down, claiming his spot, and settled into the finely upholstered chair.

"This ought to be fun," he whispered, the officer next to him nodding in agreement, stifling a laugh.

O'Donnell stepped to the front of the room, a cigarette between his lips, nearly an inch of ash hanging from the tip. Two men dressed in expensive black suits flanked him on his left. Jamie had never seen them before.

"Okay ladies," the Captain began in his raspy New Jersey accent, "I'm sure by now you've all heard the rumors about Sergeant Keller's attacker, especially you Branson?"

"Yeah, Boss," he grinned, glancing across the table at Detective Bradford, "the biter."

Luke shot a dirty look his way. Jamie smiled even bigger as the group chuckled at his words.

"Well, the coroner has filed her report from the woman's autopsy," O'Donnell continued. "Listen up. She was dead five hours before our guys found her. So, it would follow that it's next to impossible she'd have been capable of biting anyone; but, apparently, she *did*."

Several detectives leaned forward; their interest peaked. Jamie had to keep his head from nodding, his eyes drifting shut.

"Now, Keller is in the hospital suffering from hysteria and severe swelling in his extremities."

"Swelling?" Detective Dennis McKenzie, Luke's partner, questioned.

"Of sorts," one of the suited men replied, straightening his tie.

"Yeah, and it gets better!" O'Donnell grunted, hardly stopping to breathe. "Not a single doctor knows what's wrong with him. They say his blood pressure is so low that his heart may as well have stopped pumping!"

The Captain was sweating heavily, more than usual. His shirt was nearly soaked. He leaned against the wall at the front of the room, mopping his face with his handkerchief, a smear of blue ink streaked across his shoulder as he grazed against a dry erase board.

"These guys will fill you in on all the rest. They're Feds, so show them some respect," he said, turning towards the men to motion them forward.

"Thank you Captain," one of them began, his eyes hidden behind darkly tinted sunglasses. "I'm special agent Dimitri; this is my partner, special agent Jones. The FBI has found this case *interesting* and your department's inability to turn any leads has led the commissioner to call for our assistance."

Jamie rolled his eyes and crossed his arms. Dimitri continued to rattle off their list of qualifications while Agent Jones set up his laptop for a slideshow.

"This is pointless," Jamie mumbled, watching the man connect the computer to a projector. "I should be working on the investigation, not listening to these two know-it-alls."

Agent Dimitri continued on, still rubbing in their accomplishments.

*I wonder if these guys ever take off their sunglasses.*

McKenzie smiled again as he listened to the Agent's rambling, whispering something not quite loud enough for Jamie to hear. He laughed anyway. Bradford huffed under his breath.

The presentation was ready.

"Let me show you what we've learned so far."

The first picture, the circle of bodies and the pentagram of dried blood, projected onto the overhead screen.

"Here you see the bodies of thirteen victims," Dimitri explained, "the blood drained, apparently involved in some sort of ritualistic killing, possibly voluntary, like a mass cult suicide."

"So they slit their own throats?" Jamie laughed, thinking these men couldn't be serious.

The agents looked at each other as Dimitri continued, ignoring Jamie's question. Jones clicked on to the next picture.

"There's no evidence of restraints," he said, aiming at the screen with a laser pointer, the red dot dancing across the grizzly black and white photos. "If you look here, there's no bruising or hemorrhaging of the wrists or ankles, so we can assume these people walked into the room on their own accord."

"Where'd you get these pictures?" Jamie asked, his head cocked to one side, puzzling over the images. "I've never seen them in any of the reports."

Jones almost answered. Luke cleared his throat unnecessarily loud, giving the agent an opportunity to move on. Jamie leaned back in his chair, sighing in disapproval as O'Donnell gave him a scolding stare.

"But the coroner's report states that she found acute subdural hematoma in all thirteen victims, most likely caused by sudden trauma from a blunt impact," Jamie challenged coolly, referencing a page in his notebook, "similar to instances involving an attack with something like a baseball bat."

Dimitri paused. Jones took over.

"However, as you all know, they never walked out."

Jamie nearly fell out of his chair as the men disregarded him once again.

"Now, other than the blood used to create the symbol," he said, motioning at the pentagram, 'there's no trace of it anywhere else in the room. The bodies also show no sign of lacerations, besides, of course, the throats. However, two small rows of arched holes were found in the lower back of each victim, at the base of the spine. But as you can see in the picture, the wounds are small and couldn't generate the flow necessary to drain a body of its blood. And as the report explains, the marks are quite deep, and strangely cauterized, which as of yet has no explanation."

"Some kind of bites?" Luke's partner asked, noting the pattern resembled teeth, or more to the point, fangs.

"Possibly," Dimitri shrugged.

"And their throats," Jamie grunted, "were they cut before or after the blood was drained?"

"I don't know, Detective," Dimitri gave in, finally acknowledging him. "But maybe that's something you could find out; actually solve this one, if it's not too much for you?"

Bradford's face lit up like a kid on Christmas. Someone finally put Branson in his place. Dimitri straightened his suit coat as Jones shut down the computer.

"This is where we leave you. We'll look deeper into the puncture wounds and their origin. I assume you've already identified the victims and begun detailed background checks," Dimitri said smugly, turning to Capt. O'Donnell.

"Absolutely," he reassured the agents, his face growing even redder, a bead of sweat running down his brow. "We should have histories on each victim by the end of the day."

"Good. We'll be in contact."

With that, the FBI agents were out the door, black briefcases in hand.

"Jamie!" O'Donnell yelled, "get started checking the victims' histories, pronto. Find out anything you can, what they did, where they ate, the name of their dog, everything. Bradford, you and Dennis get back to work on the mob shooting. This was wasted time people, let's make it up."

Jamie stood up, his feet hitting the floor, "Yes Sir."

\*\*\*\*\*\*\*\*\*\*\*\*

Ashley stared at her sketchbook, Triton's face so lifelike. She tossed it onto the coffee table and turned her attention back to the TV. A cartoon cat chased a big eared mouse with a frying pan.

*There's no way such a good man is involved in anything so evil.*

\*\*\*\*\*\*\*\*\*\*\*\*

Jamie sat down at his desk, his worn chair squeaking on its old casters, and dialed the records room.

"Hey," he said smartly as the secretary at the coroner's office picked up, "It's Jamie in homicide, I need updated autopsies, notes, anything Dr. Hedgewick hasn't sent me yet."

"Actually, I have them right here," she said in a tone too bubbly for a woman whose job dealt with corpses. "Gloria dropped them off this morning."

"That's Gloria," he mused, "always a step ahead, and on her day off too."

"I'll go ahead and have them sent up, Detective Branson."

"Thanks," he grinned, hanging up the phone and rubbing his hands together anxiously.

\*\*\*\*\*\*\*\*\*\*\*\*

Mayor Bradford sat stiffly across from Triton as the limousine cruised smoothly down the boulevard. In silence, Triton pulled a cigar from his inner breast pocket and lit it. Thick puffs of dry grey smoke filled the cabin of the car.

"Where are we going?" Bradford finally asked, coughing lightly through the haze.

"There's something I want to show you." Triton grinned, the car pulling away quickly into traffic.

"Like what?" the Mayor asked as he shifted nervously, the thick leather seat squealing beneath him.

"When was the last time you visited the Statue of Liberty?"

************

Kayla pulled to a stop in front of the New York City Public Library, large arched doorways reaching high above its marble steps, Romanesque columns flanking the entrance. It looked as if it had been painstakingly moved to the city from some ancient European villa stone by stone, an edifice designed to invoke awe, pulling inspiration from the centuries of books it housed, but it had yet to celebrate its hundredth birthday. Kayla looked out her car window, taking it in, knowing she'd driven past it a thousand times, but never gave it her attention, never appreciated the stark contrast between its classic architecture and the modern stretch of towering Fifth Avenue Manhattan that surrounded it. Now, having never been there before made her feel quite foolish.

"It's so beautiful," she wondered aloud.

Pulling a shiny, black id tag from her glove box, an N.Y.P.D. shield with the word "Detective" printed across it, she hung it from her rearview mirror and stepped from the car. Still staring up at the imposing entrance and heavy bronze doors, she glanced at one of the two imposing lion statues that guarded the library, then headed up the steps, her shoes clicking on the smooth stone surface.

*Here goes nothing.*

Inside, the building was even bigger than she'd imagined, making the university's library she used in college look small in comparison. It was almost overwhelming. She had no idea where to go. Determined, she made her way for the elevator.

Reaching the first floor, she stopped at an information stand and read over her options.

*Periodicals could be good, room 108* she thought. *Microforms? Room 100: maybe I could dig something up there? Okay. Here we go. Third Floor: General Research Division, Room 315.*

Taking the elevator to the third floor, Kayla stepped out into the hall and made her way toward room 315. Entering the main reading room, bright eyed wonder stopped her dead in her tracks. The ceiling rose high above, large chandeliers ran from one end of the cavernous room to the other illuminating dozens of neatly lined tables, all in perfect rows. A lower level of books lined the walls as a balcony holding even more stacks wrapped around the upper level of the library.

*So much knowledge.*

Kayla followed the signs through the labyrinth. The directions seemed to take her all around the floor of the library. She felt like she'd been searching forever and she didn't even know where to begin. Kayla looked at her watch: 11:42am.

*I've already been wandering for a half of an hour!*

Kayla was starting to wonder if she would ever find what she was looking for. Turning another corner, she found the religious section. Browsing across the many shelves, she read the names of the books aloud.

"*Existentialism and You, The Universal Co-existence of Faith and Time, Do You Know Where Your Heart Is?*" she paused, her eyebrows shrugged in question.

*Who writes this stuff?*

Kayla pulled a book from the shelf, *The Fall of Man*. The cover had a picture of two naked people, a man and a woman with fig leaves appropriately placed. Behind them, a fruit tree loomed, a giant, ominous snake slithered through its branches. The man held an apple. The woman smiled.

*Weird.*

She flipped through the pages.

*Nothing interesting.*

Placing the book on the shelf, she spotted the back cover. Kayla flipped it over and stared at the picture on the dust jacket: an arrogant looking man dressed in a fine white shirt, black pants, and an overly zealous grin, sitting comfortably in a wicker chair. The print surrounding the man gave a short biography on the author, a list of his few works. Under his picture it gave his name: Dr. Maurice Triton.

Kayla's eyes were as wide as they could manage. She clenched the book, her knuckles turning white. This was an incredible coincidence, or so she thought. She'd gone to the library to research Triton and, distracted by its impressive size, inadvertently followed signs to a section of books she'd never have found interesting in a million years. And there, hidden within their cryptic names, was a book written by Triton himself. Kayla wasn't going to put it down.

"Thank you," she whispered, goose bumps streaking up and down her arms.

Holding the book as tightly as she could, she took the elevator back to the first floor and made her way to the Periodicals Room. Magazines and newspapers were filed alphabetically, organized by name and date. Discouragement got the better of her. Reluctantly, she searched through the pull-out filing drawers of newspapers and periodicals cataloged by date.

*This'll take forever.*

A group of students lingered in the corner, softly debating an article that rested on the table in front of them. They didn't notice her. Kayla looked out into the corridor and saw the entrance to the Microform room straight down the hall.

*That should be easier, maybe.*

Apprehensively, she stepped into the room. Directly in front of her were several rows of catalogued microfilm storage. To her immediate right was the librarian's station and just past that, all the microfilm readers, printers, three computers, and the open shelf newspaper indexes.

*So much for easier.*

Kayla glanced up at a *Quiet Please* sign above the entrance to the room, then over at the empty librarians' station. No one else was there.

*Do I still have to whisper in a library even if I'm alone?*

She laughed to herself as she decided to give the microfiche machines a try. Perfectly organized drawers, full of archived film, filled the shelves. Kayla began looking through the indexes. Almost every major magazine or newspaper that she could think of was represented, some dating back to the 1800's.

*Talk about a needle in a haystack! No way.*

Kayla made her way over to the research computers, hoping to narrow down the search to exact articles that she could then find and pull up on the readers.

After another hour, she'd managed to research and print out several articles on Triton or Tri-Corp., but everything she read depicted Triton as philanthropic saint and made his company seem as transparent and ethical as anyone could hope.

She'd seen enough. Disappointed, Kayla gathered up the printouts and picked up Triton's book. As she turned, her heart skipped a beat. An odd, slow, rhythmic clicking filled the empty room. Instinctively, her hand went to her hip, flipping open the safety strap on her holster as she peered around the wall of shelves.

*You're going crazy.*

Her own voice echoed in her head, blending with the key strokes of a sternly old woman sitting behind the counter. She headed for the now occupied librarian's station.

*This was a wasted trip; Triton can't be the guy.*

A woman was hunched over her keyboard, the screen's glow dancing across her thin, wire-framed glasses. She looked to be at least one hundred and ten, a fierce exaggeration in the least, but quite old none the less. Kayla smirked. She couldn't help it as she watched the old woman type. The woman's hands were deformed, arthritic, clenched like fists, except for her index fingers which she used to slowly type letter after letter, one by one as she silently mouthed the words with each click of the keys.

Finishing her sentence, she looked up from behind the small oval frames of her glasses that nearly hung from the tip of her nose.

"Can I help you dear?" she asked, her voice wavering.

"I just need to check this book out," Kayla answered, still smiling.

The old woman just sat and stared for a moment. Kayla was afraid she had died right there.

"Ma'am?"

The woman still sat in silence, her eyes fixed on Kayla, not a single blink.

"Ma'am? Can you hear me?" she asked again.

Kayla reached out and gently touched the woman's hand where it rested on the desk and read the name on the placard sitting just next to it: *Beatrice Kratz*.

"Beatrice?" Kayla called out, much louder this time. "Can you hear me?"

Finally, the old woman blinked.

"Yes child. I'm old, not deaf," she began. "It's just that you look awfully familiar. I was wondering if I knew you, that's all."

"Oh, I don't think so," Kayla answered, "I'm sure. But it's nice to meet you."

The woman looked down at the book in Kayla's hand.

"Well then, give it to me. Do you have your library card?"

"Oh, no. I'm sorry. I've never been here before," she answered, somewhat embarrassed.

"That's alright, dear," Beatrice said, sliding a piece of paper and a pen across the desk in front of Kayla. "Just fill this out and you'll be right as rain."

The old woman smiled. Her teeth seemed so white: they must have been dentures.

"You know," the old woman said with a wistful grin, "books are not allowed to be checked out of this building, dear. They are meant to be read here, in one of the library's rooms."

"Oh," Kayla frowned, her face pink with embarrassment, "I'm sorry, I didn't know."

"It's okay, child," the librarian said, her wrinkled face growing stern again, "you look like someone I can trust. I'll let you take the book. It will be our little secret."

Kayla began to fill out the form, casually glancing back at the woman. She looked like she'd fallen asleep, her eyes still wide open.

*She's so cute,* Kayla thought, signing her name on the dotted line at the bottom of the paper.

As the woman sat staring off somewhere else, lost in her own little world, Kayla realized how happy the woman seemed. She was wearing an old white crochet button down sweater with an ankle length red and blue plaid skirt. Kayla couldn't see her feet, but she imagined falling support hose and brown orthopedic shoes. The old woman's silver hair was pulled back in a tight bun and her skin seemed to just hang from her bones, but she still looked so happy, so peaceful. There was a definite *glow* about her.

Kayla finished the form and slid it back across the counter. Beatrice woke from her trance and smiled again, typing Kayla's information into the computer, one letter at a time.

"So, Ms. Rose, studying man's dark side, I see?"

"What do you mean?" Kayla hesitated, playing with the zipper on her jacket.

"Well your book here, dear, it's about sin. Are you studying religion at the university?" Beatrice asked.

"Oh, no. I'm not in school, but my sister, um..."

*Focus Kayla. What's wrong with you?"*

"I'm more interested in the author. I'm inve..." she paused. "I'm researching Dr. Triton. He's quite interesting. Have you heard of him?"

"Oh yes, dear. He gives lots of money to help others."

"So I've heard."

"But giving just to show how good he is isn't necessarily a *good* thing."

"How so?" Kayla asked.

"Well," she explained, "only God knows what's in your heart. He always sees the truth. If you give because you want to, it doesn't matter who sees you. Everything Triton does warrants media attention, just the way he likes it. If people didn't worship him like they do, praising his every humanitarian effort, do you still think he'd help others?"

Kayla didn't know what to say. She just stared at the old woman.

"Ms. Rose, I know you are more than just interested in Triton. I feel there is more that you aren't sharing. Excuse me if I'm prying, but I think I can help you, dear."

Kayla was caught by surprise.

*How does this old woman have any idea what I'm doing here?*

"I know why you seek information on Dr. Triton. I saw your badge on your belt," Beatrice said, gesturing at Kayla's waist with her wrinkly fingers, "you believe he could be involved with those strange murders don't you? If you didn't, you may want to think about it."

Kayla looked down at her belt. Just behind her jacket, her badge was shining, her holster hung just next to it.

"Oh, well, actually, I can't discuss it, *it* being a current investigation and all," Kayla said hurriedly, stumbling through her words.

*You sound like a babbling idiot, Kayla. Get it together!*

"I understand, dear," Beatrice said, "but your sister's dreams won't stop simply by you reading this book, and it won't stop your dream from coming true either."

The old woman slowly tapped the cover.

"How?!" was all Kayla could respond, her mouth gaping, the word coming out as more of a gurgle than a question.

The librarian handed Kayla the book and a small slip of paper with an address on it.

"Please, go see this man," she whispered. "He's a very old friend of mine. If you believe what I've told you, you'll find him at this location. He'll be able to help you more than I can."

Kayla just stood there. Her shocked expression must have been obvious.

"Tell me child, why do you wear that?" she asked, pointing at Kayla's silver cross necklace. "Because if you don't know, then it's about time you straightened things out dear. Please be careful. Triton is not what everyone believes he is."

"Thank you," Kayla managed to utter awkwardly as she turned and headed towards the hall.

She looked at the scrap of paper, the name *Joseph* scrawled on it in shaky handwriting, below that, the words *Titicus Reservoir*. Kayla couldn't believe it. This was so strange. Heading around the corner toward the elevators, Kayla stopped and looked back at the Microform Room, the desk where Beatrice sat just barely visible. She was no where to be seen. A much younger woman was there in her place, quickly punching away at the computer's keyboard, all her fingers working in perfect, efficient unison.

Excited despite her confusion, Kayla turned towards the elevator and slipped the paper into her pants pocket. Ashley needed to hear this.

***********

"Here is fine," Triton smiled as they approached the stone pier.

The driver pulled the limo to the curb, the tires screeching softly as he stopped. Mayor Bradford looked ill.

"Leave the engine running," he ordered, stepping from the car. "We won't be long."

The two men made their way to the end of the pier. Their jackets fluttered in the cold breeze coming in off the Atlantic Ocean as they stood staring out over the glassy water.

There, out in the middle of the harbor, was Liberty Island, the Statue of Liberty standing tall, the torch in her right hand raised triumphantly as a beacon of hope to all who found her in their travels.

"Lady Liberty," Triton smiled; his hands deep in the pockets of his heavy wool dress coat.

"Uh huh," the Mayor replied, looking cautiously to the left and right, then, over his shoulder.

"She stands for the one thing this country knows so well, but cares so little about," Triton frowned.

"And what is that?"

"Freedom," he answered simply, "freedom to live, to work, to raise families, to *die* respectfully. It's something so many people take for granted."

Mayor Bradford shifted from one foot to the other impatiently.

"What do you see when you look out there, when you look at her?"

"Just a statue, a hunk of metal," Bradford mumbled. "It's getting cold, can we get going?"

"Do you know what I see, Mr. Mayor?"

"What?"

"I see Nebuchadnezzar," Triton said sternly. "Do you know who that was?"

"Neba who?" Bradford grunted.

"I didn't think you would," Triton replied sadly. "Nebuchadnezzar was a Babylonian king, strong and proud. He ordered a statue of gold to be erected, a statue over ninety feet high, and all the people of his kingdom were made to bow down in worship. He was a magnificent man, but his weaknesses are my strength."

The Mayor stared at his feet, not wanting to make eye contact as Triton stood gazing over the bay, as if reminiscing, thinking about an old friend.

"So, now can you tell me what I see?"

"Nebubukezer?"

"No, no, my good man," Triton laughed, "not *Nebuchadnezzar*, I see, me, or rather where I should be. I see people looking at that hunk of green metal for hope when they have me standing right here, right now. You see, they are all slaves to something, *someone*. Why not me? Tell me Mr. Mayor, how would it look if it had my face?"

With those words, Triton's voice changed. His tone grew darker. His arrogance echoed in every syllable as he savored each word that rolled from his tongue.

"What are you talking about?" Bradford asked as he turned to face Triton, a look of disgust growing in his eyes.

"I'm talking about the statue that people will erect of me someday," Triton said sincerely. "Maybe it's time Lady Liberty retired from her vigilant watch over this harbor. Maybe it's time they recognize the new guardian of this empire."

"Okay, okay," Bradford laughed, waving his arms, "you got me, very funny."

Triton glared at him, dead serious.

"This is a little much. Are you saying you want to replace the Statue of Liberty with a statue of, *you?*"

Triton stared out over the choppy water, watching the small waves break against the stonework at the edge of the pier.

"You know me," Triton chuckled, "I'm just a dreamer, always thinking larger than life."

Bradford relaxed and shared Triton's smile. Together they fixed their gaze at Ellis Island.

"You're right though," the Mayor chuckled, "for everything you've done for this city, some organization will have to make a memorial in your honor or canonize you or something when you die."

"Oh no," Triton grinned, putting a hand on Mayor Bradford's shoulder and leading him back to the limousine, "I'm not a saint, and I'll never die."

"You definitely are a dreamer!"

"Uh huh," Triton shrugged as he closed the door behind him, the limousine pulling away from the pier. "Let's get some coffee and I'll return you to your office."

"Sounds good to me," Bradford smiled as they headed back into the Financial District, thankfully watching the Statue of Liberty disappear behind the tall, gleaming buildings.

# V

## SATURDAY AFTERNOON

Ashley sat at Kayla's computer, searching, just as her sister had, for anything she could find about dreams and visions. Her phone rang, the bubbly ring tone breaking the silence.

"Hello?"

"Hey Ash," Kayla said almost too excited to talk, "you're never going to believe this."

Kayla spoke of the old woman at the library and Triton's book, her words gushing with unbridled excitement. Ashley tried to keep up, leaning back in the chair as she gazed out the window, staring at the New York skyline.

"So what do you think?" Kayla wondered, finally taking a breath.

"Well, it sounds *crazy*, but then again, with the dreams I've been having, who am I to judge crazy?"

"I'm going out to the address that old lady gave me."

"Are you sure?"

"Yeah, why?" Kayla laughed.

"Well," Ashley wondered, voicing her concern, "what if it's a trap, like in the movies?"

"Ash, who would try and trap me? I'll be fine."

"Alright, just be careful."

"I will," Kayla answered, hanging up her phone.

Ashley looked back at the computer monitor. An artist's rendering of a shadowy creature, a winged demon as the website described it, stared from the screen. Ashley glanced towards the kitchen, looking over her shoulder. She could have sworn she'd smelled something sour lingering in the air, sulfurous, putrid. Turning back to the computer, the image seemed to be laughing at her. A haunting whisper cried from somewhere in the room as she felt a chill sweep across her.

She closed the webpage and stared at the background on Kayla's computer: the picture of their family at the beach. It made her smile. A tear ran down her cheek as she rested her head on her arms. She still felt so tired.

*Hopefully Kayla will find some answers. Hopefully, everything will be alright.*

\*\*\*\*\*\*\*\*\*\*\*\*

Jamie knocked on the half-open door to O'Donnell's office.

"What have you got for me?" the Captain asked as Jamie walked through the frame.

"The histories on the victims."

Jamie tossed a stack of manila folders onto the desk. O'Donnell flipped the first one open and sorted through the files. Pictures of the victims were paper clipped to each corresponding bio providing background information.

One was a retired school teacher; another was a nurse at New York General Hospital. The list went on. There was a career foster parent, a Sunday school teacher, a student from the police academy, as well as a firefighter, an army reservist, a nun, and five college students all studying either theology or sociology.

"None of the thirteen had any criminal record or any blemishes in their history," Jamie explained, "except for one."

O'Donnell looked up from the papers.

"Who?"

"This guy," Jamie said, flipping open another folder and sliding it across the desk. "Michael Hampton: he has his own file. Twelve years ago, he killed an officer, three shots to the chest, but he got off at his trial. His lawyer motioned for a plea of insanity and the jury bought it. Otherwise, he was spotless, not even a parking ticket."

"Maybe he didn't kill the cop?" O'Donnell questioned in his deep, grunty voice.

"His prints were all over the gun and the officer's partner was a witness."

Suddenly, the Captain sat up in his chair, his eyes wide, his hand on his chin, "Hampton...Hampton..."

"What, you know him?"

"Matter of fact, yeah," he said, "I think I remember this case; actually, I'm sure of it."

"Well, it was in your department," Jamie answered.

O'Donnell stared at the photos dumbfounded. Jamie leaned on the edge of the desk, looking at the papers over the Captain's shoulder.

"Besides Hampton, these were all good people, people who shouldn't have died," O'Donnell said, pushing his memories aside. "What do they have in common?"

"Other than the fact that they all have positions enabling them to reach out to those in need, or are planning to dedicate their lives to helping or teaching others, I can't find anything relevant."

"What do you mean?"

"Well, they're all from different demographics. The school teacher was a sixty-seven year old black male. The nurse was twenty-four, a female, and white. The rest of them were just as different," Jamie shrugged.

He felt confident in his answer.

"What about religious affiliation? This seemed to be a cult style ritual. You think that plays in?"

O'Donnell was reaching, but Jamie knew where he was headed.

"I thought about that," he answered, "but they all came from either typical church backgrounds or had more secular beliefs. I don't think they took their lives in a ritual suicide, but I do believe the killer is telling us that he doesn't discriminate. Male, female, any race, any creed, he'll kill them all. He has no regard for social stereotypes. They're victims all the same."

Capt. O'Donnell sat back, resting his hands on his large stomach, "Let me talk to Dimitri and Jones. I'll see what they've found out and fill them in on what you've dug up."

The Captain flipped Hampton's folder shut and handed the stack back to Jamie.

"I want to apologize if I seemed gruff with you and Rose the other morning," O'Donnell mumbled, his weathered face softening. "You two have a good thing going, I just don't want to see either of you get hurt."

Jamie stared at him, his jaw flinching once again.

"Don't look at me like that, James. It's not like it hasn't happened before."

"You mean Gloria?"

"Of course! Look, I know you two were really close, and when she broke things off, well..."

"Well what?" Jamie pushed defensively.

"It broke me up inside," O'Donnell admitted, his hardnosed cop persona slipping away to reveal a sensitive side few ever witnessed. "You've been like a son to me. I hope you think of me the same way."

"Like a son?"

"You know what I mean," O'Donnell chuckled, "you and that smart mouth of yours; it's going to get you into trouble one of these days."

Jamie leaned in close to O'Donnell and grinned his mischievous grin, "Kayla is different: she *makes* me different."

"I know, Kayla's a good girl," he grunted, standing to put his chubby arm around Jamie. "Just don't you mess things up with her."

Jamie turned to head out the door. O'Donnell wasn't finished.

"By the way," he mumbled cautiously, clearing his throat, "about the case, *Hampton*, be a little sensitive when you tell Rose, she may not like what she hears."

"Why?" Jaime questioned.

"That cop he killed was her brother."

Jamie stood there frozen, his heart creeping into his throat.

"Okay, well, so far so good, Jamie, keep it up. Now get out of here," O'Donnell said, breaking the tense silence, a yellow toothed grin on his sweaty face.

Jamie headed out of the Captain's office and down to his car.

*I wonder how Kayla's research is going.*

He flipped on his stereo, as he pulled his car out into the busy line of traffic.

*I'll check in with her after I eat lunch.*

His heart ached for her, for her brother. He wanted to be there for Kayla. He wished he could have been there, to help her through the loss.

*Why didn't she ever tell me?*

\*\*\*\*\*\*\*\*\*\*\*\*

Kayla pulled her car off to the side of the road, the bright mid-day sun reflecting off the vast reservoir on her right. She scanned the tree line on the left, but found nothing that looked like a drive or a clearing of any kind.

"Well, I'm here," she said aloud, feeling lost, "where are you Joseph?"

She looked down at the note, then pulled back on to Rt. 116. Slowly, she hunted for a clue to where she was supposed to go. Finally, she spotted an intersecting road ahead. An SUV was stopped, waiting to turn. Kayla pulled onto the side road and rolled her window down. The lady in the truck did the same.

"Excuse me," Kayla smiled politely, flashing her badge as she spoke, "I'm looking for someone, a man named Joseph. Do you know where he lives?"

The lady thought for a moment, but shook her head, "No, I'm sorry. My husband and I live just back up this road. We know all our neighbors and there's no one named Joseph around here. Maybe try over in North Salem?"

"Thanks," Kayla shrugged, pulling a u-turn as the woman headed left.

Kayla turned right, deciding to give the search one more try before starting the long drive back to the city. She drove slowly, looking for something, anything, out of the ordinary. Her phone beeped; a text message from Ashley.

She pulled the phone from her pocket as she stopped again on the side of the road.

The message read: *hope you're finding something. i'm bored...still tired...btw, i ate the strawberry yogurt in your fridge...sorry. ash*

Kayla began to type a response, but was suddenly blinded by the bright sunlight reflecting off the cab of an oncoming semi. She looked away, her eyes settling on the darkness of the woods.

*That's odd?*

Something caught her attention: an old rusted mailbox peeking out from the overgrowth. Some scraggly bushes sat on either side of a very narrow, hidden drive.

*I think I found the place...I'll let you know what I find...don't worry about the yogurt! K*

Looking up and down the country road, she searched desperately for a sign or house, or something, anything, but it was just her, alone in the middle of nowhere, and a nondescript mailbox. Minutes passed as Kayla debated what to do. Each one felt like an eternity. She needed to make a decision. She looked at the paper one last time and finally shook her head apprehensively.

"Someone will probably find me in a ditch three weeks from now," she groaned as she put her car in gear.

Turning onto the path, Kayla used her cell to call Jamie. After a few rings, he answered.

"Hey," Kayla began, "I'm following a lead. I'll explain later."

"Where are you?" Jamie asked, "Your phone's all muffled."

"I'm way outside the city. You wouldn't believe me anyway."

"A wil goo chaz?"

Jamie's voice was a mish-mash of mumbles. Kayla shifted in her seat, an eyebrow raised as she tried to understand.

"What?!"

"I said, a *wild goose chase?*"

"Yeah, maybe...are you eating?" she laughed.

"Uh huh," he said, wiping sauce from his mouth as he sat at a small round table in a Mexican restaurant, a taco in one hand, his phone in the other.

"What about your meeting, you know, the all day summit you so valiantly saved me from?"

"Oh. I may have exaggerated, or O'Donnell did when he told us what to expect. Regardless, it was a waste of time, so I hope you have better luck."

"What do I need luck for?" she teased.

Jamie swallowed his bite and grinned.

"I just gave the Captain some great information: the history on our John Does," he teased back with a laugh. "I was up all night compiling them. Now you've got to catch up or it'll look like I'm doing all the work."

"We'll see. I think I've got something here, something big. I'll talk to you in a bit."

"Bye then." Jamie said, taking another bite of taco.

She smiled and closed her phone.

Kayla pulled around a small bend in the very long drive and came upon a clearing beautifully cut and maintained in the middle of the immensely dense woods. Gravel crunched beneath her tires. Birds chirped and sang their melodies somewhere in the trees above. Following the dusty path, Kayla found herself over shadowed by what looked like an old fort or castle. Large, gray stone-work walls supported a Spanish style red slate roof, while small square windows with wrought iron detailing and stained glass decorated the many ivy-covered, interconnected structures. A giant bell tower loomed at the far corner. A large, steeply pitched building stood just beside it, its peak rising above the tops of the trees. Shrubs and elegant plantings landscaped the villa's perimeter with an intricate fountain in the middle of the yard: a life size sculpture of an angel, its wings outstretched, hands clenched in prayer, eyes looking to heaven, an immense sword sheathed at its side.

Kayla parked in front of one of the smaller buildings and searched for what looked like an entrance. A stone arch led into a dark hallway, dimly lit with candle light. Stepping cautiously from the car, Kayla placed a hand on her holster.

"Hello?!" she called out.

Silence.

"Is anybody here?" she asked again.

Still, silence.

Slowly walking down the long corridors, a calm came over her, a peaceful sensation, something she hadn't felt in a long time. Removing her hand from her ready gun, she realized she was closing in on another hall. A cool breeze wafted through the pass, the smell of flowers from the gardens filling the air. No one seemed to be around.

*Quiet as a tomb.*

Dropping her guard, she began exploring the vast hallways. The layout was incredible, like a maze. Paths twisted and rejoined, spiral stone stairways climbed to the second floor. Sunlight cast glowing stories on the walls through the intricate stained glass windows. The compound was much larger than it had first appeared.

She walked along silently, taking in the beauty, reflecting. Childhood memories of the church she used to attend filled her mind. It was odd, the feeling around her, like a presence was watching, looking deep inside her, but there was no one there. It wasn't a scary or intimidating feeling: it just felt like something was tugging at her heart, like her conscience was trying to tell her something, maybe wake her up.

Rounding a corner, Kayla stopped. The most amazing window she'd seen yet glowed in front of her, simply beautiful. In the window, it showed a garden, full of flowers and light. In the middle, a glowing figure, his palms open and outstretched. Nail holes pierced the hands. Behind the image was an empty tomb, a giant round stone rolled off to the side.

A lump grew in her throat. *The Resurrection of the Christ,* the placard said on the frame. She stood there, taking it in.

"Miss!" a voice echoed down the hall.

Kayla nearly leapt out of her skin, her hand instinctively dropping to her holster, ready to draw.

"Welcome. Can I help you?"

The lump in her throat was replaced by her quickly beating heart as she turned to see who was there.

"I'm sorry," she explained, "I didn't think anyone was here."

A plump old man stepped from the shadows dressed in a tattered brown robe, a warm smile easing Kayla's fear.

"I'm Father Martin. This is our monastery," he explained softly. "We welcome any who come to pray or escape from the pressure of the world."

Kayla nodded, releasing the grip of her pistol as she relaxed.

"But I must admit: few find us here, and so well armed," he winked.

"Oh, thank you, and sorry, about the gun," Kayla said as she pulled the slip of paper from her pocket and handed it to Father Martin. "You are sort of in the middle of nowhere. I'm looking for Joseph."

"Yes. He's in the chapel. I'll take you to him," he said, motioning down the hall as he turned and headed in that direction.

Kayla followed the old man through the catacomb like corridors, feeling as though they were walking in circles. Soon, she couldn't remember from which way they'd come. Finally, he led her to a set of tall intricately carved double wooden doors with large bronze handles.

"Joseph should be just inside," Martin told her, turning back down the hall.

"Thanks," she said, reaching for one of the door pulls.

Just as her fingertips touched the heavy cold handle, the doors slowly creaked inward, pulled from the inside. Startled, she stepped away. Another old man walked through and pulled the doors closed behind him.

"You must be Kayla," the man said excitedly.

"How?" she asked stunned.

"Let's just say I've been expecting you for some time now," he grinned. "I'm Joseph. Please, follow me to my study. We can discuss matters there."

"Beatrice," Kayla whispered.

"Who, my dear?"

"Beatrice, the librarian, in the city: did she call you, tell you I was coming?"

"Beatrice...Beatrice? Oh!" he laughed, wagging his finger enthusiastically. "That is clever...Beatrice!"

Kayla watched him carefully, trying to read him, as he turned and headed off down the hall, still smiling, apparently amused by the name Beatrice, but never giving any sort of answer as to why, or even how he came to expect Kayla for that matter.

*Maybe I should have taken Ashley's trap suggestion a little more seriously.*

At every turn, Kayla thought they'd finally found where they were headed. But after several more confusing twists, they'd walked down yet another hall, this one a dead end, an old wooden door blocking their path.

"This way, Miss," he smiled, waiving his hand towards the room within.

Kayla stepped over the old wooden threshold and looked around. Fantastic old oil paintings decorated the walls. An antique bookshelf sat in one corner; a dust covered suit of armor guarded another. Joseph's humble wooden desk was centered between the two, a rickety chair sat just behind it. Another shelf hung from the wall behind her, small bottles and curious boxes filled the space. An old decorative cross hung to her right.

"Please, Ms. Rose, sit," Joseph told her, pulling a leather chair worn thin with age from its place in front of his fireplace, the burning wood crackling, spitting dancing sparks.

Kayla settled in, silently wondering what he could do to help. He was dressed like a friar as well. Joseph wore old, leather sandals and his hooded robe was belted with a hand-woven rope. Kayla glared at the hood with distrust, it being large enough to cover his head and most of his face if he wanted. His hair was thinning, nearly bald on top, a gray ring of shortly trimmed curls crowning his head. His wrinkled face looked kind and warm, what Kayla thought Santa Clause might look like, just without the beard. But he was quite thin, his robe draping over his body. He sat at his desk, his steady hands folded calmly in front of him.

"Now, my dear, tell me why it is you have come here?" Joseph asked, smiling as if he already knew the answer.

Kayla thought for a second, gathering her words, afraid she might sound foolish.

"Well, Father Jo..."

He interrupted her, "please, just Joseph. I'm not a priest, only a servant of God and there's no reason to be anxious."

"Sorry, I just figured with the robe and all, you were a priest or like a, like a monk of some sort."

"I understand. Peace be with you," he winked.

"Oh, sorry. Okay, peace, um..."

"It's alright, please go on," he encouraged.

"This morning, I stopped at the New York City Library," Kayla explained, courage welling up inside her, "and I met a woman."

"Beatrice," he chuckled.

"Right," Kayla paused, still confused as to why that was funny. "She said you could help me find out if Triton was involved in a crime I'm investigating."

"The thirteen dead," he stated matter-of-factly.

"Yes," she hesitated.

"What do you think, my dear?"

"Well, I don't really know for sure. See, my sister has been having..."

"Dreams," he smiled, finishing her sentence. "I know all about her, and the dreams."

"How could you?"

"I just *know*," Joseph said, his eyebrows shrugging intently.

Kayla stared at him in disbelief, her lips pursed speculatively. Joseph's words had caught her completely off guard, he could tell by the look on her face. She wasn't expecting to hear anything like this.

"This will sound strange, but you must have faith. I've been chasing Triton in one form or another for centuries," he began. "Please, listen to what I am about to tell you. If you truly believe your sister, then you will believe me as well. Triton is involved in your case, but not in the way you expect. He is not a criminal by definition. He is evil, like an incarnation of pure hate."

Kayla placed her hands on the thick arms of the chair, ready to stand.

"I'm sorry. I'm wasting your time," she said, preparing to leave. "I can tell you are busy here with your books and, *things*, so I'm going to go."

"Please, wait," he assured her, a slight smile on his kind face, "I can help you."

She stood, looking over his desk, not sure whether she could trust this old man. His story seemed so unbelievable; and yet, there was a peace about him that drew her near.

"Please, sit Ms. Rose. I want to help you, but you must first believe."

He hesitated for a moment, letting his words take effect.

"Tell me, have you ever been to church? I see you wear a cross."

Reaching up to her neck and touching the cross that hung from it, Kayla thought for a moment. Sometimes she almost forgot she wore it.

"I used to go with my parents. It was sort of a family thing. But now that I'm working, I haven't had the time."

"You haven't had time for faith?" Joseph asked.

"I wouldn't say that," she replied defensively. "I know what I believe."

"And what would you say that is, Ms. Rose?"

"I believe we should love our neighbors like we love ourselves. I think we should treat people the way we want to be treated," she answered sincerely.

"Ah yes, the 'Golden Rule'," he laughed, a wide smile across his wrinkled face. "I mean deeper. What do you know in your heart?"

"I know that I have a purpose. I know that I've been placed here for a reason. I know that I'm a good person."

"That is a good thought, very noble, but if you can't look inside yourself and see your need for salvation, then you are not ready to confront Triton. He is not a man in the way you understand a man to be."

"Then what is he?" Kayla asked, growing impatient.

"He's a threat to all who believe in a greater good, the one true God. He kills so that life can be granted to himself. He feeds on the pain and the blood of others, of good people. In the past, I could not stop him."

"*Past?*"

Joseph folded his hands and thought for a moment, then spoke, "What I am about to tell you will be difficult to understand, I know this, but please, listen to my words and have faith."

Kayla shifted in her seat, unsure of this seemingly eccentric old man, but he had her attention.

"Though I tracked Triton for almost longer than I care to

remember, he managed to slip away, century by century, as if he were a part of time itself."

"Century by century? That's impossible! You would have to be hundreds of years old."

"Time, like age, is of no importance," he grinned, "it is only man's measurement of the space between the rising and setting of the sun. With the Lord, a day is like a thousand years, and a thousand years are like a day. Let's just say I've seen much during my time on Earth."

Kayla couldn't hide her growing interest, her doubt was no match for the peace that inexplicably filled her. Joseph stood from the desk and walked to his old bookshelf, pulling a large leather bound book from its place, then sat once again, dropping the old book in front of her. A cloud of dust filled the air. He flipped open the old faded cover and sorted through the pages till he found what he was looking for. There was a large engraving of a bat-winged creature, its eyes closed, a bloody human heart in one hand, a sword in the other.

"What did you hunt?" Kayla asked, leaning forward in her seat.

Joseph's expression became intense, his eyebrows pointed sharply.

"I hunted demons, Ms. Rose," he said, pointing at the page, "and, for a time, accompanied a noble group of knights on a fierce and dangerous quest."

Kayla crossed her arms apprehensively. Even if this man ended up a delusional, old codger, years removed from reality, this could still be a great story, a story worth hearing.

"It was the year 1096," he began wistfully, "and Pope Urban II had declared war on the Muslims, a war to reclaim the holy city of Jerusalem. Six men met in secret at the yet unfinished Claremont Cathedral, just a shell of the beautiful church it would become. There, the Pope called upon them to wage a *unique* war upon an unseen enemy. It was then, that I stepped from the shadows and made my presence known. They drew swords against me, fearful that I was a spy, but the Pope stayed their hands.

'And who then are you,' he asked me."

"What did you say?" Kayla asked with feigned enthusiasm, playing along with the old man's story.

"I told him that I was a simple traveler and a servant of the Most High."

"So what happened next?"

"He ordered me to leave, that what he was asking of these knights was far too dangerous for the likes of someone such as me. I did as he requested, but waited within earshot, hidden in the darkness, listening to the purpose of their quest. When I heard it was to battle demons, I knew that this was why God had placed me where He had when He did. I made a vow to God that I would accompany these men and help them in their expedition, to protect them from their unseen adversary."

"And everyone lived happily ever after?"

"Not in the least, my dear, not in the least."

Joseph's sudden change bothered Kayla, his tone shifted from jovial reminiscence to regret. Though the story was so ridiculously fantastic, she found herself hanging on his words, now wanting to know what happened after Joseph made his vow.

"I approached the men as they left Claremont," he continued, "asking to accompany them as their blacksmith, a helping hand. They agreed and, in a matter of days, we set off for Jerusalem. The journey took weeks, traveling from Europe to the Holy Land on horseback, but as the crusades raged on around us, we avoided the battles, the bloodshed. You see, I believe the slaughter of the Muslims was wrong. It wasn't the Christian way, nor were the crusades. You see, there were those who saw the Muslims in Jerusalem and their beliefs as a threat, but the real enemy was of a different world, a different spiritual plane of existence, a world we cannot see. It surrounds us even now."

Kayla glanced around the room. She didn't see anything.

"When we arrived in Jerusalem, we found it to be a stronghold, not of Muslims, but of demons. The violence during the crusades was atrocious and the things we saw...well I'll never forget them. But we fought against the demons that surrounded us, breaking their line and driving them back. And one demon stood out to me in particular, a captain, it seemed, among the ranks. It was larger, more ferocious, and seemed to guide the waves of attacking demons. Soon, a battle between Muslims and crusaders spilled into the area where we were. The stone of the holy city had been tainted by blood-lust. It was then that I noticed that one demon as he crept away from battle. I drew my sword, as did the knights, and we made chase, away from the fighting and after the demon. He led us into a hidden passage, a tunnel mired in cobwebs and darkness. One of the knights lit a torch and we pressed on, deep into the bowels of the Temple Mount. Voices began calling out to us, confusing us as we moved through the claustrophobic catacombs, till we became separated in the darkness, the knights down one path, and I on my own."

Kayla listened intently, her imagination bringing his words to life in vivid detail, as if she were there herself. Joseph continued.

"I called out to the knights, but I was alone. Now feeling my way along the walls of the corridors, lost in the midst of pitch black nothingness, I came to a narrow junction where two tunnels intersected. A draft wailed through the halls. I put aside all thought and headed in the opposite direction, away from fresh air, from safety. It was then, that I finally came face to face with the demon who called itself Triton. He caught me by surprise, knocking me to the ground, his shadowy figure darker than the darkness, consuming even the faintest light.

Triton lingered for a moment, then hissed, 'Turn away and I will spare you. I came for the others, go now.'

I felt across the floor searching for my sword, my fingers finally clasping around the hilt of my blade. Desperately, I swung up at him, striking from the ground. But he was gone, his deep laugh echoing all around me."

Kayla was now enthralled, "What happened to the knights?"

"I decided to continue on in an attempt to reunite with my companions. I followed the tunnel that Triton had come from till it opened up, high above a large chamber bathed in candle light. The room was filled with rubble, but beneath the crumbling stone and rotten wood was pile upon pile of gold and jewels, the riches of Solomon. And there, in the middle of the room, stood the six knights, overcome by their greed, the forgotten treasure. I tried to call down to them, but my voice was silent. Then, I watched as a man, cloaked in black, his head hidden beneath a hood, entered from a side chamber.

'All this is yours,' he bellowed, 'the finest riches and wealth the world could imagine, a guaranteed legacy, and happiness beyond all you can imagine. But you must do as I say.'

'What do you request of us, my lord?" the knights asked, kneeling before the tall, slender figure.

'You will be the foundation of a new empire, a rising power. You will follow all that I tell you, but you must remain hidden till I say the time is right.'

'Can you grant us eternal life, my lord?'

'You will receive life by teaching others the things I will teach you. Select wisely those who will follow after you, for your legacy will become their legacy, and so on, for many generations to come. Keep these words secret and your oaths sacred, as you will prepare the way for the one, one who will come and lead my master's armies against this Earth.'

I watched from above as Triton conducted the ceremony. I watched as those men took an oath, their promise bound and sealed with their blood. When they concluded, the knights extinguished the candles and followed Triton out of the chamber. Again, I was alone in the dark. I never saw them after that, but history does reveal clues as to what may have become of them. Of course the legend of the Templar Knights is best known, but there are other secret orders, sects, and meetings, recognized by names like the Illuminati or the Bilderbergs, even the Free Masons. But, Ms. Rose, that is another story, for another time. The point of all this is to illustrate that a never-ending battle for our souls is waged all around us, angels and demons invisible to our eyes, locked in conflict: good versus evil. There are guardians and warriors as well as fallen angels, dark angels, demons, that want us to fail, to fall like they fell. I know this is hard to believe, not to mention understand. But this is why your sister has dreams. She is sensitive to this world. Something within her allows this unseen dimension to communicate with her."

************

Ashley sat up, her eyes wide, her heart pounding in her ears. She'd fallen asleep at Kayla's computer desk. Her dream was fresh in her mind. Ashley could still see Jamie, broken, beaten, the same dream as before. She had to call Kayla. Jumping up from the chair, Ashley glanced around the room, searching for her cell phone.

*Come on. Where is it?*

Finding her messenger bag, she dug through its pockets. It was nowhere to be found. Looking around again, she spotted it on the kitchen counter.

As she reached out to pick it up, it rang, its song startling her. She looked at the caller I.D.: *Kayla's Cell.*

"Hey," Ashley said answering the phone.

"Are you dressed?"

"I can be, why?"

"Call a cab and get here as fast as you can. I'm up on Titicus Rd; Rt.116, east of 684 North, across from the reservoir. Look for an old mailbox; it marks the entrance to a hidden drive."

"Is everything okay?" Ashley asked.

"Yeah, just hurry, it'll take you a while to get out here."

The phone went silent. Ashley headed to the bedroom to put on her jeans and grab her jacket. She had no idea what she was about to hear.

************

The cab driver stopped the car in front of the rusty mailbox, the car idling as he peered deep into the woods. Ashley grinned with excitement: she loved the adventure.

"I'm not going in there," the cabbie grunted. "There's nothing back there, just trees. And it gives me the heebie-jeebies. You know what I mean?"

"Just drop me off here then," Ashley decided, opening the door before he could argue.

She paid the driver then turned to scan the woods as he sped off. Somewhere, in the middle of all those trees, was the answer to all the questions she'd been asking, an explanation of her dreams.

Just a few yards beyond the overgrown entrance, the gravel drive opened into a well-manicured path. She followed it as it finally led into a peaceful clearing invisible from the road. There, she spotted Kayla's Honda, parked in front of the old stone monastery. The building looked like it belonged in Europe: it seemed so out of place.

"Hey!" Kayla called out from the stone archway that opened into the courtyard. "Follow me."

She turned and headed in the direction of her sister's voice.

"I would never have imagined a place like this anywhere near the city," she gushed as Kayla greeted her with a hug.

"I know. It almost feels," Kayla paused, "other worldly."

Kayla led her through the winding tunnels and into Joseph's study. Father Martin nodded as he left the room.

"Is there anywhere I can go to think while you two talk, someplace *quiet*?" Kayla asked, pulling Joseph aside. "I need to sort everything out."

"Wait just a moment, my child," Joseph said, turning to Ashley. "I'm going to show your sister to the chapel. It's easy to get one's self lost here. I'll return shortly."

Ashley smiled nervously as she sat down in the large leather chair and studied the paintings hanging on the walls. One looked an awful lot like the old man, or at least she thought it did.

Joseph placed his hand gently on Kayla's shoulder and led her back to the chapel. She felt like she was walking along with her grandpa: it brought back so many warm memories she'd long forgotten.

"Here is where I leave you to find what it is you seek."

"And what is that?"

"The truth, my dear, only the truth."

"Thank you," she said, taking hold of the old man's bony hand, "for everything."

"I've been in your place, Ms. Rose. But please understand, we cannot speak lightly of Triton. His messengers are everywhere; his ears hear all we say."

The heavy doors closed solidly behind her. She turned and looked down the center aisle of the chapel. Large pillars supported the high ceiling on each side. Beautiful stone and wood detailed the entire space. Two rows of deep-stained, high-backed benches stretched across the cold, gray floor, one on each side of her path. A large cross hung on the far wall, just behind the hand-carved pulpit. On the cross, a lifelike Christ stretched His arms out as if to hold any who reached out to Him, nails through his feet and wrists. His eyes were open, looking straight at her, as she walked slowly down the aisle, finally taking a seat in a pew at the very front of the room.

Kayla stared at the cross, taking in every detail: the crown of thorns, the bloody brow, the expression of love across Christ's face. Even in all that pain, He still cared.

*He died for us, for what He believed was right, for what He knew was right. He died for our salvation.*

Her thoughts raced through her mind. She wondered if she could do the same: give her life for others with unconditional love. That was her calling as a police officer, to serve and protect, to give her life if needed, to act without any thought of herself. There, alone, in silence, she sat in contemplation, still staring at the cross, her eyes filling with tears.

But Kayla couldn't see the world around her. She was not alone.

A chill filled the room. Flames danced and flickered on top of the candle stands. Watchers were all around. Some hid in the shadows; others climbed the tall stone pillars and hung from above. The demons that had tormented her for years, ever since her brother's death, were still clinging to her, even now, in the chapel.

As she prayed, they watched. They had come for her.

************

The return walk from the chapel was long, lonely. Even though she'd felt peace there, at the foot of the cross, a heaviness still consumed her, weighed her down as she made turn after turn down the dark, candle-lit corridors. At times it sounded as if someone might be following her, lurking in the shadows. But each time she turned, there was nothing. Yet an odd calm lingered as she listened hard, trying to decipher the eerie footsteps: the warmth of an old friend walking along side her. It made her forget her fear.

Kayla returned to Joseph's study. Ashley sat in stunned silence. Joseph had just finished his story.

"We've got to get going," Kayla said, leaning on the door frame.

"I know," Ashley answered thoughtfully.

Joseph stood to see them out. Reaching the courtyard, he slipped a tightly folded scrap of paper into Kayla's jacket pocket as they took one last look around, Ashley pausing to study the statue of the angel.

"God bless you and good luck," Joseph said, as he watched them drive off in Kayla's car.

# VI

## SATURDAY NIGHT

"So that was your big lead?" Jamie asked, his voice ringing with sarcasm. "That's impossible, Kayla, and you know it. Some old man tells you a convoluted story about *slaying demons*, an *ancient Pope*, and a *secret society* and you just accept it at face value?"

Kayla crossed her arms as she stared at Jamie. The coffee was almost finished brewing: the rich aroma filled the office there on the second floor of the police station.

"No offense, but I'm not buying it, and I can't believe you are either."

"It's okay," she answered softly, "I didn't expect you to believe him, but I hoped that you would believe *me*. Regardless of what you think, reasoning isn't going to answer the questions we're dealing with. You have to know that?"

Jamie thought for a moment, his pen in his mouth, the last week replaying in his head. She had a point.

"What's that?" Kayla asked, setting Jamie's mug down on his desk, steam rising from the freshly poured hot coffee that filled it to the brim.

Jamie shuffled through a pile of manila folders and quickly covered up the file that had caught her attention. Too late: she noticed how purposefully he hid that folder, hastily shuffling it into the middle of the others.

"They're the files on the John Does from that apartment building," he finally said, shifting his mug uneasily.

"Anything *interesting*?"

"Yeah, actually," Jamie answered, trying to think of a way to ease into the subject of her brother's murder. "Everyone was clean: they may as well have all been on a waiting list for sainthood, all except for one."

Kayla sat down at her desk and turned on her laptop, "And what did he do, tear the tag off his mattress?"

Jamie paused, "It was a little worse."

"Oh yeah?"

"Yeah," he said softly, "he gunned down an officer during a traffic stop."

Kayla's eyes glazed over. Every bad feeling she had ever felt tore at her insides as she watched Jamie's mouth move. She fought off the tears that tried to flood her eyes as she felt her throat tighten.

Gathering her thoughts, she tried to control her emotions; but as she did, a figure loomed unnoticed amongst the shadows. The demon laughed hysterically, its wings beating the air.

"What was the officer's name?" she asked, wiping her eyes, already knowing the answer.

"Jack Rose."

Jamie could hardly stand to look at her. She made him want to break down. But Kayla was strong, stronger than Jamie knew.

She choked back her tears and reached for the pile of folders, flipping through them till she came across a name she recognized: Michael Hampton. His file sat in front of her. For what seemed like an eternity, Kayla just stared at the name printed on the corner, silently wondering what she would find inside.

Jamie stood up, his still full mug in hand, and leaned over her at the desk, his hand resting softly on her shoulder, "I'm going to go get some more coffee, you want some?"

She didn't respond, maybe couldn't respond.

"Are you going to be okay?" Jamie whispered.

Still, she didn't answer, but, almost robotically, she reached up and squeezed his hand. He understood.

"I'll be back in a while," he said softly. "If you need me, I'll be in the lounge thinking things over."

She looked up at him with a weak smile. He let her go and headed towards the coffee pot.

Slowly, Kayla opened the folder, her heart pounding in her ears. Staring up at her from the page was a mug shot of Michael Hampton, middle-aged and balding. He didn't look like a killer: he looked like the school teacher that he was.

*They never look like killers.*

She flipped to the next page, more pictures paper-clipped together: pictures from the abandoned apartment. Turning ahead, page three of the file recorded his testimony and statements from his trial.

"Unexplained states of psychosis, mental fatigue, blackouts…" she read aloud.

The words blended together as she studied the page. Hampton's testimony echoed in her mind, like she could hear his voice even now.

*I felt like something was inside of me…*

The words haunted her, ringing in her ears.

*I felt like I wasn't myself, like I wasn't seeing through my own eyes. I remember the officer pulling me over and then I blacked out. When I came to, I was in the back of a cruiser and there were lights and sirens and, and all I know is that I didn't shoot that officer, I mean, I may have. But it's like I wasn't in my own body, like someone else was controlling me!*

Kayla couldn't read anymore: she expected to feel angry or sad, or something, but not indifferent. Whatever Michael Hampton claimed, her brother was still dead, taken violently from a world he promised to protect.

She turned to the last page in the folder. It was Hampton's education and employment histories.

She read aloud, "Attended Notre Dame, graduated with a double major in accounting and education, summa cum laud."

Kayla skipped to the next paragraph, "employed at *Tri-Corp...*"

"Jamie!" Kayla called out slamming the folder shut.

"Yeah," he said dashing around the corner, hot coffee sloshing over the top of his mug and down across his fingers.

"I need to talk to my brother's old partner," she said.

There was a fire in her eyes, and Jamie liked it.

\*\*\*\*\*\*\*\*\*\*\*\*

Ashley sat at a small round table in the corner of one of her favorite coffee shops. A leather journal rested in front of her, the pages scribbled full of quickly jotted notes in her very artistic, borderline sloppy handwriting. She had decided to record all of her dreams, as much as she could remember. This was her dream journal: therapy.

She wrote a few more sentences, then sipped carefully on her hot latte. A noisy group of college kids sat in one of the booths, laughing loudly at something only they found hysterical. To her left, a waitress wiped down a dirty table.

Looking back to her journal, Ashley began to write again. She was halfway through a thought when she heard someone call her name. Her eyes shot around the room, no one seemed to be paying any attention to her. The college kids were still laughing and the waitress had moved on to another table.

Then the voice called again, this time from just over her shoulder. It made the hair on her arms tingle. Hot breath tickled the back of her neck. Quickly she turned around in her chair, but no one was there.

Glancing at the clock on the wall behind the counter, she realized the time.

*Oh no, I'm late for work!*

Burning her tongue as she took a bigger gulp of her coffee, she stood and slipped her journal into her messenger bag. As she did, she caught her reflection in the window. For a moment, she wasn't sure, but she could have sworn she saw the silhouette of a shadowy figure standing behind her. She shook the thought from her mind and walked out the door.

\*\*\*\*\*\*\*\*\*\*\*\*

Thirteen walked down Fifth Avenue. No one noticed him as he passed by, whispering curses and grinning to himself. It was like they couldn't see him. With every step, his confidence grew. He was reveling in his new found power.

"This city will never know what hit them," he laughed.

\*\*\*\*\*\*\*\*\*\*\*\*

Kayla put her car in park and took a few deep breaths. It had been an awkward, silent drive. The sun was slipping slowly behind the rooftops as they scanned the street, a quant neighborhood in New Rochelle.

"Are you sure you want to do this?" Jamie asked as he unbuckled his seatbelt and reached for the door latch.

"I'll be fine," she smiled, reassuringly.

Before they could make it to the front door, they spotted a heavyset, graying woman standing on the porch, her hands on her hips, her lips curling into a Southern smile.

"Well! If it isn't little Ms. Rose," the woman said with a sentimental inflection.

Kayla and Jamie walked up the pathway through the perfectly manicured lawn and past the exquisite flower bed.

"Hello, Mrs. Richards," Kayla said stepping onto the porch, her hand extended in greeting.

Mrs. Richards ignored Kayla's hand and wrapped her large arms tightly around her. Jamie introduced himself and reluctantly received the same hug.

"Kyle is just inside, darlin'," she said, her cheeks red with excitement. "It's good to see you."

"You too," Kayla forced out with a smile.

"I'm going to put some tea on," Mrs. Richards planned aloud. "Follow me inside and you can talk with Kyle. I was so surprised when you called, and so late too, but don't worry."

Jamie followed Kayla through the door. He hoped this would go well.

Kyle smiled as they entered and invited them to join him at the kitchen table. They pulled out their seats as Mrs. Richards hummed and bustled in the background.

He looked nothing like Kayla remembered. Then again, she hadn't seen him since her brother's funeral. Years ago, Kyle was tall, strong; now, he seemed older than he really was. He sat partially slumped in his wheelchair; his wrinkled hands folded one on top of the other.

Mrs. Richards was as pretty and cheery as ever: an exact opposite of her husband. Jamie smiled to himself as he thought of what an odd couple they seemed.

"Before we go any further," Kyle began in an ominous tone, "I want you to understand that this is going to be strange for you."

Kayla nodded. Jamie did too: his attention was drawn to a painting of an angel on the wall, its wings wrapped around two small children as it kept them safe from a raging storm, a shadow of a cross in the background. It was already strange.

"Alrighty then," Mr. Richards said gruffly, "why don't you tell me what you know."

Jamie and Kayla shared a quick look and then slowly began to unwind the ball of yarn they'd become entangled in. Mr. Richards furrowed his brow with interest.

"It may be nothing more than coincidence that brought us here today," Kayla explained, "but we've been investigating the murders from last Thursday night, the ones at that old apartment in Harlem."

"I heard about them on the news," he said shaking his head in disgust, "terrible, terrible. Go on."

"We have reason to believe that Dr. Maurice Triton, founder of Tri-Corp, may be involved at some level." Jamie continued.

Kyle's brow wrinkled even more. He looked almost comical lost in his deep thoughts.

"And what brought you here?" he asked.

Kayla answered softly, almost in a whisper, like the walls were listening, "I believe you might have known one of the victims: Michael Hampton."

\*\*\*\*\*\*\*\*\*\*\*\*

Ashley quickened her pace as she looked for the first cab she could find. The sun had almost set. She felt like someone was on her heels, watching her every move. She was right.

As she stepped into the taxi, Thirteen stood on the sidewalk just behind her. The car sped away. With a burst of light, he was gone as well.

************

Kyle Richards sat in silence, pondering what he'd just heard. His mind was reeling.

"Hampton's dead?" he asked in shock.

"Yeah," Jamie answered quickly, "and we think that's possibly more than just a coincidence."

"I think you're right," Kyle admitted. "What I'm about to tell you is something I haven't talked about in twelve years, Ms. Rose. But it's time you knew."

Jamie loosened his tie and pulled his iPhone from his pocket. He selected an audio recorder app and placed the phone in the center of the table. Kayla grabbed Jamie's hand.

"Twelve years ago, Jack and I were investigating a murder involving a pastor from a small church that met in the basement of a building owned by Triton, over in Astoria. Members of the church used to say that strange things would happen in that building, odd noises, other spooky *things*. Look, I'm not one for the religious stuff myself, but your brother, he dove in head first. When the pastor was found dead in his office, an apparent suicide, reeking of foul play, Jack made it his personal quest to find out who was behind it. He dug deep, snooped too far. The Commissioner closed the case sighting lack of evidence and made sure the official autopsy stated suicide as cause of death. But your brother didn't let it go. Next thing I knew, he was rambling about Triton and a cult group, stuff I found hard to believe."

Kayla wasn't sure what to think of what she was hearing. Her brother was involved in a similar investigation, one that ended in conspiracy, and his death.

"Jack confronted Triton with some evidence, some pretty strong stuff. He built his case on faith, which is hard to prove in court, but it seemed at the time that he had good leads."

"What kind of evidence?" Jamie wondered as Mrs. Richards set four cups of hot tea on the table and took the chair next to her husband.

"Cassette recordings of strange meetings, séances, chanting mumbo jumbo, all through a contact that Jack made on the inside," Kyle explained.

"Who?" Kayla and Jamie nearly asked at the same time.

"Michael Hampton," he answered grimly. "He said he was suckered into Triton's little *club* and wanted out. He thought helping Jack would be a good place to start. After your brother had the recordings, he tried to use them to corner Triton. A week later, he was dead, killed by his own informer."

"I thought he was shot making a traffic stop?" Jamie frowned confused.

"He was," Mrs. Richards replied sadly. "Hampton was driving recklessly and by chance, Jack pulled him over, almost too incredible to believe, the wrong place at the wrong time."

"So what happened to the tapes?" Kayla wondered.

"Triton took them and destroyed the very evidence Jack used to confront him with."

"What about you?" Jamie prodded. "Why didn't you speak up, share what Jack uncovered? He was you partner."

"Are you serious, boy?" Kyle chuckled, a slight wince in his eyes. "How do you think I ended up in this chair? Triton tried to kill me too. Someone shot me in the back. The bullet severed my spine at the waist, haven't taken a step since."

"I'm sorry."

"That was enough to shut me up. But, Jack's death did wake something inside me. Even in my pain, I found God."

"It's too bad we couldn't hear what was on those tapes," Jamie said, awkwardly changing the subject, his eyes again fixed on the painting of the angel, contemplating what Kyle had said.

"That's the kicker," Kyle laughed. "Just before your brother died, he made copies and told me to hide them, keep them safe. He said he didn't know why, but he felt that he was part of something, something...*bigger*, something that he alone couldn't stop. He said he wanted me to give the tapes to you when you were older. It never made much sense then, but I guess now's the time: somehow he knew this day would come. Just be careful. Triton killed your brother over these tapes. I'd hate to see what would happen if he found out there were copies."

A sudden rustling outside the kitchen window followed by the sharp sound of scratching on glass broke up their meeting. The curtains billowed as if the wind had blown them, but the window was closed, latched and locked. The four shared an odd silence, each one trying to read the look in the others' eyes, the details of their conversation sinking in.

Jamie thanked Mrs. Richards for the tea as he received another big embrace. Kayla headed back to the car, a small package tightly wrapped with brown paper in her hand.

"Are we getting in too deep?" Jamie asked as she pulled away from the curb, Mrs. Richards still waiving from the porch.

"I think we'll know when we hear these tapes," she said tightly gripping the steering wheel, her voice calm, her eyes fixed on the road ahead.

*************

The black night sky lit up with flames. Smoke poured from the windows of the old apartment building in Harlem. A gas line exploded beneath the street, engulfing the brick structure in fire, glass shattering, wood crackling, as a lone dark figure emerged from the hazy doorway. Slowly, he straightened his black suit coat and brushed ash from his sleeves. His eyes glowed white and vibrant beneath the black mask that shrouded his face, its mouth stitched up into a horrid grin. He was one of Triton's Tri-Six and he had one job, one task to complete: destroy the evidence of the sacrifice.

As sirens echoed off the surrounding buildings and fire trucks roared down the street, he leaned against a trash dumpster hidden in the shadows of an alleyway. He chuckled to himself at the beauty, the completeness of his work. Watching fire fighters scramble about, their hoses heavy and dragging on the sidewalk as the heat of the blaze licked at their faces, the smoke covering them in sooty ash, Triton's soldier slipped away into darkness.

\*\*\*\*\*\*\*\*\*\*\*\*

"Sorry I'm late," Ashley said as she arrived at work, racing through the front door, the words *The Wanderer's Gallery* etched in the glass, the bell on the door jingling as it swung shut behind her.

Her boss stood behind the tall wooden counter, his fingertips tapping impatiently on its surface. He stared at her through his thick glasses, the lenses reflecting the fluorescent lights above, the veins in his forehead protruding.

She worked a modest job at an immodest gallery in Manhattan. Some of the art was quite good, but work was still work.

"Come on, Rose. It's a Saturday night, one of our busiest. I've got a dozen canvases that need wrapped in the back and three buyers picking up pieces before we close," he barked, pausing for a slight, raspy cough. "So, if you can find the time to do your job, I would appreciate it."

"Yes, sir," she smiled politely as she headed through the door marked *employees only* and dropped her bag off on a small table.

"I do believe I told you to be here at five, not seven thirty," she heard him saying, his voice growing softer as she left the sales floor.

As soon as the door closed and her boss was behind her, the smile disappeared. If he hadn't paid her so well in the first place, she'd have been long gone, but he wasn't usually this gruff. Otherwise, the hours weren't too bad and he'd even let her display a few of her choice pieces.

"He must be having a bad day," she decided, almost feeling sorry for him.

Quickly, she went about her work, wrapping frames in canvas, stapling the edges, making sure they were tight, ready to paint. Ashley placed the completed canvases on a shelf in the storage room and headed out to check the purchase log. She stopped by the holds to pick up the pieces that were ordered, ready for pick-up, and set them on her work table.

As she prepared the first picture, the lights flickered. A soft hum echoed within the thickly plastered walls. Ashley finished wrapping the artwork in brown paper and taped down the corners, then, slowly moved towards the light switch. Flicking it off then back on, she tested the lights. A cold chill filled the room and the hum grew louder, but the lights seemed to be alright.

Ashley went back to her work, wrapping the second and third pictures, ignoring the sound. But as she finished the last one, the lights went out completely. She felt along the wall for the switch. It was still in the *on* position. She flipped it off, then quickly back on, but nothing happened. Suddenly, she heard her boss shout from the sales floor. She hurriedly ran down the dark hall, nearly tripping over a pile of boxes hidden in the shadows. The hallway felt like it went on for miles, like in a bad dream where she could see the end, but it was always just beyond her reach. He yelled again, this time in agonizing pain. She ran faster, but felt like her feet weren't moving.

Finally, she made it to the door ahead, light leaking in faintly beneath it. Ashley swung the door open. As she did, the lights in the hall, the work room, everywhere, flicked on.

"You okay?" her boss asked as he looked away from the customer he was schmoozing.

Ashley stared at them, wide eyed and breathless. The customer glared at her from behind his trendy wire framed glasses. His look showed disgust, like she was out of her mind, an inconvenient little person. Without waiting for an answer, her boss attempted to pull the customer's attention back to the sale. Confused, she turned and headed back to the workroom, the humming sound now gone.

"Well, he's definitely not going to buy anything," a voice laughed from behind her, "at least not tonight anyway."

It was her boss, in all his skinny, tight-pant, wide-tie, suspender-wearing glory. Ashley was sure he was really going to tell her off good, so she put on her most polite smile and readied herself for her usual talking-too.

"Did you get those canvases wrapped?"

"Uh huh," she answered, still smiling, bracing for his outburst.

"And the pictures are ready for pickup?"

"Yep."

"Well then," he shrugged, "you got that all done sooner than I expected. If you're having a bad day, you can go ahead and get out of here."

Ashley was taken aback. He'd never offered to let her leave early.

"It's okay," she replied, still smiling. "I really need the money."

"Come on, it's the weekend; you're young, go enjoy yourself."

"No, seriously," she said, trying to sound convincing.

"Actually, you're doing great, kid. I'll just pretend you worked your whole shift."

He smiled and turned around slowly, then walked down the hall and back out onto the sales floor. Ashley stood there for a few moments, taking it in, still confused.

His smile was a smile, but there was something sad in it, something that she'd never seen before. It made her forget that only moments ago she had been panic stricken.

Ashley picked up her bag and headed out onto the sales floor. Her boss was staring out the front window, his hands in his pockets, lightning flashed. She could see his sad expression reflecting in the rain streaked glass.

"Is everything alright, Mr. Barry?"

Mistily, he looked down at his left hand and then at Ashley.

"My wife left me today," he said, smiling that same sad smile, "after twenty-two years."

"I'm so sorry."

"Don't be," he replied as he took his wedding band off and set it on the counter. "I just hope I can keep this place open."

"If you don't mind me asking, Mr. Barry, what happened?" Ashley wondered.

"Truth is, I don't completely know. I think my wife believes I love this shop more than her. Maybe I do?"

Ashley tried to think of something to say, but no words seemed to fit.

"You know, it's very important what you believe," her boss said as he stared out the window, lost in his thoughts. "Always know what you believe."

"Thank you, Mr. Barry."

Ashley smiled what she hoped was an encouraging smile and headed out the door and into the rain, her messenger bag slung over her shoulder, the bell on the door jingling goodbye. She was beginning to think she was going crazy. Between her dreams, and now this, she wasn't sure what to think, let alone believe.

************

"So what do you have to say for yourself," Triton growled in his deep, gravelly voice as he gazed out over the cityscape from his office on the one hundred and thirteenth floor of the Tri-Corp building.

Silence filled the room. Rain spattered against the window.

"What do you mean, Sir?"

"You know perfectly well what I mean!"

"I did what you asked of me?" the Tri-Six soldier said in confusion.

Triton turned and pierced into the man with his cold gray eyes. The room grew darker as the rain outside turned into a storm.

"But I asked you to do it two nights ago. Now, the police have been there, they have seen the remnants of the sacrifice, *and* you did it all with the bravado of a madman. I asked you to destroy the evidence, not burn down a city block and make your brothers look like fools."

"I don't know what you wanted me to do?" he pleaded, his mask shifting as his eyebrows furrowed beneath it.

"You make it sound so much more difficult than it really was," Thirteen laughed from the shadows, his eyes two small white slits floating in the dark.

"What are you doing here?!" the soldier cried out, taking a step back, gauging the distance between himself and the door.

"Silence!" Triton commanded, stretching his hand out towards Thirteen while keeping his gaze fixed on the Tri-Six. "Were you trying to impress me? Did you think you could match Thirteen's power? Are you jealous of him?"

Thirteen walked over to the window and leaned against the frame, half of his body still hidden as if the shadows moved with him. The sound of knuckles cracking echoed in the darkness.

"I'm not jealous!" the man grunted in defense. "I did what I thought you wanted."

"Well," Triton grinned, "when I ask you to do something, I expect it to be done without hesitation, without failure. Don't think for one moment that you are special simply because you wear that mask. I *made* you and I can *break* you."

"I'm sorry, Sir."

"No. It's too late for that," Triton replied solemnly.

The sound of a metal blade sliding from its sheath rang out, as the soldier caught a glimpse of cold, sharp steel reflecting a bright burst of lightning. Thunder rumbled, shaking the glass in the window sills.

"Put that away. There is no need for your theatrics tonight. I will handle this myself. Besides, he's *sorry*."

Slowly, Thirteen slid his blade back into its sheath, his mask contorted in disappointment, all the while glaring at Triton with disdain. He leaned once again on the window frame.

With an overbearing smile, Triton approached the man. His arms open, his hands outstretched in what looked like a forgiving embrace.

"Take off your mask. I want to see the shame in your eyes."

The Tri-Six soldier reached up with his black gloved hand and sadly pulled the mask off, placing it in the inner pocket of his jacket, his hair messy and matted. Taking a step forward, he reached for his master, tears filling his eyes.

Triton stepped purposefully closer. And as the man readied for the warmth of redemption, Triton thrust his hands tightly around his soldier's neck.

As the man felt his master's hands choking him, he panicked and grabbed Triton's wrists, flailing, trying to free himself from death's grasp. Triton tightened his grip, his knuckles white. He could feel the last attempts for air as the man struggled and shook in his strong clutch.

For a moment, they stared into each others eyes. Triton savored it. The man trembled: he had seen the face of death.

The soldier's limbs fell limp. His master had choked the life from him, even as he stood faithful, repentant.

Triton dropped the body to the floor and straightened his tie. With a certain air of satisfaction, he turned to Thirteen, "Select a capable replacement from among the servants."

"As you wish."

"And clean this up."

"What?" Thirteen questioned in surprise, his head cocked angrily to one side. "That's what the servants are for. Summon one of them."

"You will not question me." Triton demanded, "Yes, I have chosen you from among the other Tri-Six. You are strong, but you are not as strong as I am. Do what I ask, without hesitation, and I will reward you. Disregard my words, and share his fate."

Without reply, Thirteen raised the body onto his shoulder and carried it to the elevator. After a moment, he disappeared from Triton's view behind the gold doors as they closed together smoothly.

Triton slid into his high back leather chair and faced the window. It was still pouring. He could see his reflection staring back in the glass, a broad grin across his face. It pleased him and he smiled all the more.

# VII

## SUNDAY MORNING

Captain O'Donnell stepped off the elevator, the sterile smell of hospital filling his nostrils. Turning left, he headed down the corridor towards the nurses' station.

"Can I help you?" a young woman asked sitting on the other side of the counter, color coded files labeled *I.C.U.* lined neatly in front of her.

"I'm here to check in on Officer Gary Keller," he said, flashing his badge.

"Oh. *Okay*," she answered hesitantly, "down the hall...room 308."

The room wasn't just *down the hall*: it was also at the end of a right followed by another hall and an immediate left, but, after much walking and examining each door placard, he finally found it. Now that he stood in front of the door however, an odd sensation came over him. He wasn't sure if he wanted to enter. Reaching for the handle, he rested his hand on the door thoughtfully and peered through the glass.

Officer Keller was alone, lying in his bed, the curtains drawn. The room seemed dark, sad. Flowers from well-wishers were lined up on a table sitting in the corner, but they were dying, the petals fluttering to the floor.

After what felt like an eternity of debate, he grabbed the handle and pushed the door open. A long solid beep echoed inside the room. It took O'Donnell a moment to place such a familiar sound, a sound he'd heard in movies and cheesy cop dramas on television, but finally, it hit him. His arms went limp.

Keller's heart had stopped. The monitor was crying for help.

The Captain grabbed an orderly that was passing by, pushing a cart, taking no notice of the sound. O'Donnell scared him to death, nearly causing him to spill his cart.

"That man's dying in there!" he yelled. "Get a doctor!"

The orderly nodded, walking off around the corner. He didn't seem to be in a hurry.

O'Donnell turned back to the room and ran his fingers frantically through what little hair he had left. Keller was a good cop. He hated to see this happen. Finally, he felt a hand on his shoulder. A graying doctor stood next to him, a chart at his side.

"I'm Dr. Ramsey," he said calmly. "Why don't we step inside?"

O'Donnell couldn't find the words to answer as the doctor led him into the room, the door clicking behind them. They stood staring at Keller, the monitor still flat lining. After a few more awkward moments, Ramsey walked over to Keller's bed and switched the heart monitor off.

"What are you doing?" O'Donnell spit out, his face furiously red.

Dr. Ramsey turned toward him slowly, a grim expression across his face, "he's still alive. It's just that his heart has *stopped*. It stopped two days ago."

The Captain flopped into a chair as he wiped the sweat off his brow with his handkerchief. Ramsey pulled another chair over next to him. He flipped through the charts in his hands, then closed them crossly, as if they defied everything he'd ever seen in all his years of medicine. O'Donnell was speechless.

"It's the most bizarre thing I've ever dealt with. Clinically, this man has been dead for days. His heart has stopped, but his brain activity is off the charts. When we first admitted him, he was suffering from severe swelling, but that has passed. Now, his finger nails have turned black and his eyes have done the same; not just the retina, the entire eye. Not to mention, the last time we drew his blood, it looked like motor oil. Also, his muscular structure has changed dramatically. His body fat has decreased and his muscle fiber has more than quadrupled. As of yet, however, he has remained comatose. But like I said, with his brain activity, there's a good chance he could wake at any moment. It's the most bizarre thing I've ever seen."

O'Donnell gathered his wits and walked over to Keller's bed. There was a peculiar odor in the room: rotten eggs. He reached down and poked at Keller's exposed arm, a bloody bandage was visible just above the wrist where the woman had bitten him.

Keller's skin was dry and leathery; a black crust had formed around the edges of the bandage. O'Donnell noticed his eyelids flinching, but they remained tightly closed.

"He looks like he's dreaming."

"That's the constant brain activity I mentioned. Like I said, it's very odd. It's as if he's in the middle of a REM cycle, but remains in a coma."

O'Donnell turned and headed towards the door. Dr. Ramsey followed.

Neither man noticed the two winged figures crouched in the dark corner, wisps of sulfurous yellow smoke swirling from their nostrils. They remained hidden in the shadows, watching, their green glowing eyes fixed on Keller.

\*\*\*\*\*\*\*\*\*\*\*\*

The cassette player clicked to a stop, leaving Kayla and Ashley staring at each other blankly. For the last hour and a half, they'd listened, fast forwarded, rewound, and listened again through tape after tape, Triton's propaganda ringing in their ears.

Kayla picked up the final case. It was labeled "Jack, 10/17/91."

"That was about a week before he was murdered," Kayla thought aloud.

Ashley took out the tape they'd just finished and put in the last one. She pressed play and then leaned her elbows on the table, her hands under her chin.

The sound of their dead brother's voice brought tears to their eyes. It was difficult to listen to:

*After the last three years, I've come so close to tying Triton into all of this, all the murders...all the lies. I'm just missing the final piece to the puzzle. Hampton has done so much for me on the inside, gathering so much information. But still, something's just not adding up. Triton's not who he says he his. Still, I'm so close...*

Kayla stopped the tape. Ashley wiped her eyes. Jotting in a notebook, Kayla began adding up all she had on Triton. The evidence was staggering, except for Jack's missing piece. Her pencil hit the table. She had an idea. Kayla reached for her phone and dialed Jamie. It rang a few times before he answered, his usual blend of *hello* and *yellow* that always made her smile.

"What are you doing right now?" she asked.

"Just standing in line to order a coffee."

"Can you come over?"

"On my way," he smiled, hanging up his phone.

************

"I want you to wait till it's completely dark," Thirteen commanded one of Triton's followers as they stood over the body of the dead Tri-Six, "dump him in the park, somewhere where he's sure to be found."

"But why would you want him found?"

Thirteen arrogantly pulled a handgun from a holster under his jacket and clicked the hammer into place, the barrel pressing against the servant's forehead.

"Do what I say and you will be rewarded. Fail me, and well, you can figure it out."

The man swallowed the knot in his throat and gathered himself, "Should I wipe the body clean, make it look like a robbery gone bad?"

"No," Thirteen replied smugly, "leave the body as it is. I want to send a message."

\*\*\*\*\*\*\*\*\*\*\*\*

"We should talk with Joseph again," Kayla told Ashley, as they waited for Jamie. "I want to play these tapes for him and see if he understands any of the strange languages they're speaking."

A knock at the door startled them. Kayla peered through the peephole. Jamie was standing in the hall wiping spilled coffee off his white dress shirt with his tie.

"Do you ever wear anything but a suit?" Ashley teased as he walked into the apartment. "Can I get you anything, maybe a sponge?"

"Shut up," Jamie grinned, heading into the kitchen and flipping on the faucet after laying his suit jacket over the back of her couch.

He pulled off his navy blue tie and unbuttoned his shirt, slipping his arms out of the sleeves. Soaking the stain in hot water, he turned and leaned against the counter, crossing his arms.

Kayla smiled. Jamie stood in his tight-fitting undershirt, his muscular arms exposed. Ashley grinned as well, giving her sister an approving look.

"Hit rewind, Ash," Kayla said, heading over to the counter and resting against it, next to Jamie. "I want him to hear these."

They listened to the tapes. Jamie stared at the cassette player, watching the reels turn as he rubbed his chin. Ashley sat down on the couch and tried to ignore Jack's voice. She didn't know if she could handle hearing him again.

Jamie glanced at his watch and rubbed his eyes, the last tape clicked to a stop. Kayla looked at him, trying to read the pensive expression on his face.

"What do you think?"

Jamie squeezed Kayla's elbow and walked to the window. He looked down at the busy street below.

"I can't believe it. Your brother's investigation was so similar. It's almost like déjà vu!"

Ashley and Kayla glanced at each other.

"I need some coffee," Ashley yawned.

"I've looked through Luke's notes. He didn't try very hard on this one. He didn't even collect any statements from the S.W.A.T. team. I need to make up for his mistakes, and now I feel like we're getting behind."

"So what are you going to do?" Kayla wondered.

"I'm going to pay Lt. Sykes a little visit," he shrugged. "I need to hear what went on down there for myself. I don't think Bradford told the whole story."

"You know Sykes took a leave of absence right?"

"Yeah, but I'll give him a call, see if he doesn't mind talking, maybe get something to drink."

"Well, I was thinking, Joseph should hear these as well. Maybe he'll have a different perspective, some insight, catch something we missed. We'll go see him and we can meet up with you afterwards."

"You really trust that old man?"

"Should I have any reason not to?"

"How about he's *crazy* for starters!"

"You'll see," Kayla smiled, "he'll prove you wrong."

"Alright, be safe driving out there. Those are narrow lanes," Jamie warned jokingly as he headed out the door, pulling his suit coat on over his t-shirt.

"What about your shirt and tie," Ashley laughed.

"I've got back-ups in my trunk," he hollered as he disappeared into the hall, pulling the door shut behind him.

"Let's go," Kayla said, picking up her purse and gun.

Ashley yawned again, still wanting a cup of hot coffee, as they headed down to the garage and jumped in Kayla's car. It was going to be a long day.

************

"What am I doing in Jersey?" Jamie mumbled as he slowly passed by a row of three bedroom homes on a quiet neighborhood street, carefully checking the house numbers.

Finally, he found the address he was looking for. Jamie pulled up to the curb in front of the house and unlatched his seatbelt. Walking towards the porch, he stopped and smiled. In the next yard, a couple of kids were playing catch, the ball thwapping against the palms of their baseball gloves. The front door creaked open, drawing his attention back to the house. Lieutenant James Sykes was standing on the porch. Jamie turned and walked towards him, his hand outstretched as he bound up the front steps.

"How are you today, Detective?" Sykes smiled.

"I'm good, you?"

Sykes looked tired, like he hadn't slept in days. His hair was disheveled and thick stubble covered his chin. He wore an old pair of sweats, beat-up running shoes, and a musty smelling white t-shirt, *N.Y.P.D.* screened in black on the front of it.

"Fine, I guess" Sykes said, his smile fading, "let's head inside."

They walked through the front door and into a neatly decorated suburban living room. Sykes motioned towards the blue upholstered couch that stood against the wall, just under a large picture window. Jamie took a seat. Flopping down in a leather recliner, Sykes pulled a cigar from a humidor on the end table and held it to his mouth. He bit off the end, spitting it onto a plate with a half-eaten roast beef sandwich on it, lit it, then took a long pause. Slowly, he blew out the thick gray smoke.

"So," Jamie smiled, his eyes burning from the cloud forming around their heads, "How long is your leave of absence."

"A couple of weeks," the Lieutenant shrugged as he offered a cigar to Jamie.

"No thanks. I don't smoke."

Sykes set the box of cigars back down and leaned forward in his chair, his elbows resting on his knees, the brown leather seat squeaking beneath him.

"What brings you all the way out here, Branson?" he asked, seriousness washing over his pale face. "I know this isn't a social visit."

"I thought we could talk a little, about what you found in the basement of that apartment building a few nights ago, if you're alright with that."

"Actually, it might be good for me." Sykes grunted. "I can't get it out of my head. But I'm sure you've read the notes, seen the photos, the evidence Detective Bradford collected."

"That's just it," Jamie frowned, "Bradford didn't collect anything. He said the place was clean."

"No way! There had to be something there. Something he missed. I'd never seen anything like that night, not in the thirty years I've served the city of New York. I mean, I've seen some pretty grizzly stuff, you know, but nothing like that."

"That's why I need to talk to you, to get a firsthand account, talk to someone who was there."

"What about your buddy, Keller?" Sykes asked, flicking the ash from his cigar into a glass dish on the coffee table.

"We haven't really talked in years...besides; O'Donnell says he's in a coma, or, *something*."

"There's nobody else, any of the other guys from that night? I had an eight man crew, ten counting Keller and myself."

"No one I trust like you. I know you and the Captain go way back, you're close. That's why I'm here."

"Yeah."

Sykes looked at a clock on the wall that hung above the fireplace. He mashed the tip of the cigar into the ashtray.

"My sister and her husband will be home from church soon: they like to take their kids to Sunday school. They're considerate enough to let me stay, but she wants me resting, not talking about that night. She says it will keep the memories fresher, that it'll make them harder to forget. They won't be happy finding you here."

"Alright, where do you want to go?" Jamie asked, standing as Sykes led him out the front door.

"There's a park, with a jogging path, some nice benches, about a mile from here. It'll be a quiet place we can talk."

Jamie pulled his car away from the curb and followed Sykes's directions. After a little over a mile and a few nearly-missed turns, he found the park. Silently, they headed through a pavilion and across the jogging path. Jamie followed Sykes as he walked towards a bench that sat in a small cluster of trees. Leaves crunched beneath their feet, the bench was damp from the seemingly constant rain.

"So," Jamie said, rubbing his hands together, then reaching into his pocket to retrieve his iPhone, "what can you tell me?"

"No, no, Detective," Sykes urged when he saw the device. "If I tell you anything, it's strictly off the record. You take my words and make them yours. Got it?"

"I got it," Jamie grinned, tapping several times on the touch screen before slipping it back into his pocket. "I put it on vibrate so we won't be interrupted."

"Good," Sykes began. "What I'm about to tell you, I haven't told anyone; not O'Donnell, not my sister, the department shrink, no one. Capiche?"

Jamie nodded in understanding. Sykes lowered his voice and looked around carefully, making sure no one was watching them.

"That night, dispatch got a call from an officer on patrol who noticed something peculiar. A large number of people had gathered in front of that old apartment building. It looked like a party in the street. They were celebrating something. Several of them seemed pretty drunk: hooting and hollering. Anyway, as he passed by, he said he felt like they were watching him. He tried to act like he didn't notice they were there, but how could he, there were so many, and the racket. You follow?"

Jamie nodded.

"So he figures he's like twenty paces from his cruiser. The officer doesn't make any eye contact. He just keeps walking for his car. Once there, he was going to call it in and hang around to see if anything went down."

"Go on," Jamie encouraged, his brow furrowed as he listened intently.

"The officer almost made it to the car door when he heard a gunshot ring out. Instinctively, he dropped to the ground and crawled the last couple feet to the car. He popped open the door, reached for his C.B. and called for help. Once he was in the car, he noticed that all the people were pulling out guns and waiving them around, then they disappeared into the apartment."

"What happened then?"

"Well, the officer pulled his gun and waited for a response on the radio. He went to stand and doubled over. One of the bastards had shot him, right in the lower back. He didn't even realize it till then. I guess it was all the adrenaline. So now, he's looking down at the blood on his hands, the blood soaking through the front of his shirt from the exit wound."

Sykes pulled another cigar from his pocket and lit it, puffing away as he stared off into the distance. Jamie shifted uncomfortably on the wet bench.

"He calls in that he's been shot and describes the number of perps and the dispatcher calls for backup. We get the green light, time to roll. We get down there and block off the road with our S.W.A.T. vans and take cover. The place is silent, no one to be seen. I head over to the officer, make sure he's okay. He tells me everything I just told you, then dies in my arms."

"No way!" Jamie exclaimed.

"I swear it's the truth. Anyway," Sykes continued, "I give the order and we bust down the front door. It's a mad house in there, guns blazing; plaster flying off the wall, smoke everywhere. But then it hits me: my guys are good, real good, but they're dropping the shooters like it's nothing. And the perps, they can't hit anything. They're shooting away, spraying bullets, but my guys tear right through them. Not a single injury till Keller got himself bit up on the third floor."

"Incredible," Jamie said thoughtfully. "Maybe they were druggies, no real experience. You guys walked in on their party; just a bunch of low level thugs flashing guns, thinking their tough?"

"I doubt it," Sykes grinned, shaking his head. "They were too quick with their weapons, I mean to say, they reloaded *so* accurately, so efficiently. They were trained, *well*. And on top of that, they were well armed too. They had expensive semi-autos and a couple submachine guns. That means they were well funded. Doesn't sound like low level criminals to me."

"So you go through the building. You clear each room," Jamie recapped, "then what?"

"We head for the basement. The stair well is dark, we're used to that: we've got our flashlights. We hit the hallway, and I freeze. My two-way goes out, and get this, I can swear I see someone, or some...*thing*, moving at the end of the hall, but its pitch black down there. Everything looks like a shadow, so I figure no big deal. We make it to the door. It's big, heavy, sealed from the inside, so we bash it down. And then..."

"What?"

"I'll never forget that smell."

"What did it smell like?"

"Blood and uh, uh, sulfur," Sykes said with a snap of his fingers as he found the right words, "it smelled like death."

"Did you notice anything about the room when you first entered, anything that didn't seem to fit the crime scene?"

"Come on, Branson. I don't think like you. We're trained to be quick in, quick out. We find bodies, especially something like this, we call homicide, and they send you to put the pieces together."

"Well right now," Jamie said calmly, "I'm missing a few pieces and you're the key to unlocking the puzzle."

"It's funny you would say that," Sykes chuckled, as if he just remembered something that he hadn't before. "In the room, there was a table, covered in candles and melted wax. After I got my stomach settled down, I cleared my men out and took one more glance around the room. I thought it was odd that on that table, there was an old rusty key. It stood out to me because it was too old to be useful in a building of that age. I mean, this thing had to be at least, I don't know, a couple hundred years old. I'd completely forgotten about it till now!"

Jamie leaned back and rested his hands on the back of his head. He pictured the list of items in the room that Detective Bradford had noted. Everything was accounted for, except a key.

Sykes jumped, shaking the bench, his eyes locked on the pavilion. Jamie tried to look in the same direction, hoping to see whatever it was that Sykes saw.

"What's up?" he asked, still trying to figure out what he was looking for.

"I just saw the same shadow I saw that night, at the end of the hallway in that basement, just outside of the room!"

"Where?!"

Sykes pointed towards the wooden arch they had entered through. There was no one there. The sun was hidden behind clouds. There was nothing to make a shadow.

Jamie looked at his watch. Sykes still sat panic stricken.

"We've been here for an hour already," he said, trying to bring Sykes back to reality. "You need to rest. Let me take you back to your sister's."

Slowly, Sykes looked away from the pavilion, the color returning to his face. Light rain drops began to fall.

"Don't worry about me, Detective. I'll jog home. I need the exercise and the fresh air will do me good, help me clear my head."

"You sure? It looks like this rain could pick up."

"No, Detective. I'll be fine."

With those words, Sykes looked at Jamie with an unsettling calmness in his eyes, then took off onto the jogging path at full stride.

*He can definitely use the time off,* Jamie thought to himself. *He is way too high strung.*

Jamie closed his car door and ran his fingers through his hair. Pulling his iPhone from his pocket, he stopped the app he'd left running and listened back to a small clip. Parts of it were muffled, but he had managed to record the entire conversation without Sykes noticing.

"Jamie Branson," he laughed, starting his car and backing out of the parking space, "you are a genius."

*************

Joseph listened to the last tape, an expression of dismay across his care-worn face. Ashley and Kayla looked on intently as they waited for him to give them a profound revelation or some other word of insight, but he just sat there, staring at the cassette player long after it had stopped, an old man lost in thought.

"Well?" Kayla finally asked. "What do you think?"

"I'm not sure what to think, Ms. Rose," he explained. "I mean to say, I know what I believe and the tapes all seem to support that, though I now feel that, after hearing all of Triton's thoughts, he is not working alone. He has his army, but I fear he is grooming another: one who will take his place, possibly lead his army. If this is so, then I may not be the one to help you."

"What about the strange language?" Kayla questioned.

"Aramaic, spoken during the days of Christ: I don't know of anyone today who would use it. It's not a common tongue," he thought aloud. "I don't recall hearing it spoken in centuries."

"So what do we do now?" Ashley wondered, sitting back in her chair, her arms crossed.

"I want more time to think," Joseph answered. "The last thing we need is to be caught with our hands in our pockets."

"So we just wait for Triton to do whatever it is he's going to do?" Kayla questioned as she began to grow frustrated with the old man's lack of urgency.

"I'm saying that time will expose the truth, lead us in the path we should follow. Do not lose faith. This is far from over. Besides, look on the brightside."

"Brightside?" Kayla asked crossly.

"Yes," Joseph grinned with a wink, "It's Sunday, and you're here...at church."

\*\*\*\*\*\*\*\*\*\*\*\*

Sykes jogged back to his sister's house. He huffed along at a steady pace.

"Boy am I out of shape," he laughed aloud.

Glancing up at the red glow of the setting sun as it passed behind a cluster of rain clouds, it was such a relief to get his thoughts off his chest and now, not even a little rain would slow him down. He smiled as he ran, thinking of the new day that was coming. Maybe he could even return to work soon. He turned the last corner; he could just begin to see the roof of his sister's house in the distance.

Suddenly, a voice called his name from behind. Breathing hard, Sykes stopped in his tracks. Before he could react, he heard a loud clap like thunder and looked to the sky. The world grew silent. An agonizing burning in his stomach dropped him to his knees.

Looking down at his shaking hands, he saw the red stain soaking through his sweaty shirt. Then, another loud shot rang out. Sykes slumped over on the cool concrete, his head landing in a puddle.

A final crack of gun fire echoed off the houses. He wheezed heavily, coughing up blood.

"You!" Sykes stammered, blood dripping from his lips. "I saw you in the park, and in the basement!"

His body went limp as he drew his last breath. The sidewalk was stained in his blood as his motionless body rested doubled over, clutching his stomach.

Thirteen stood over him, light wisps of smoke sweeping from the hot barrel of his gun as he watched Sykes die, staring into his blank lifeless eyes. Rain began to pour down on them, sending the blood streaming off the curb and into a nearby sewer grate. Thirteen spread his arms and turned his face towards the sky, the cool rain soaking his mask. With a sudden, bright flash of lightning, Thirteen disappeared, leaving Sykes dead on the sidewalk.

# VIII

## SUNDAY NIGHT

The sun sank deep into the West. Another day had gone. Darkness would soon blanket New York in shadows.

Triton enjoyed his favorite meal at his favorite restaurant, sitting at his favorite table: his private table. Across from him were the Mayor and the Police Commissioner, next to him, the city's District Attorney. Softly, they discussed Wall Street, opera, and fund raisers, till the conversation finally turned to more serious matters.

"Gentlemen," Triton bellowed, "this is a brave time for our fair city."

The men nodded in agreement, sipping at their drinks.

"But," he continued, "I have a thorn in my side. Detectives Rose and Branson have been making allegations, spreading rumors. Capt. O'Donnell is beginning to take notice."

"Maybe we can pay him to shut them up," Mayor Bradford grinned, rubbing his hands, "make them forget about certain *details* of their investigation?"

"No," Commissioner Johnson frowned, "O'Donnell's clean. We can't get him to do something like that."

"If they are allowed to continue, they could implicate all of us," Lister, the District Attorney, added, filling his glass with more wine.

"Mayor," Triton said thoughtfully, "your nephew is a detective, is he not?"

Bradford shrugged and lit his cigar, "Yeah, you told me to put him on the case, remember?"

"Do you think he has aspirations to be a police captain?" Triton asked.

"Absolutely," the Mayor coughed a slight laugh followed by a cloud of gray smoke, "how?"

"Don't worry yourself with details," Triton smiled coolly. "Let's just say it's already taken care of. Just remember who's in control here."

************

"I was really hoping Joseph would say something encouraging," Ashley frowned, shaking her head as she stared out the car window, watching the passing blur of fall colored trees glowing in the sun's last light.

Kayla didn't respond. She couldn't shake the bad feeling that was creeping up inside her. They hadn't heard from Jamie all afternoon, and now, it would be dark soon, another day passing with no new answers to the questions that plagued her mind.

The silence was broken by the shrill ring of Kayla's cell phone. She pulled it from her purse and looked at the screen with a sigh of relief.

"It's him," she said aloud as she answered the phone, "Hey, Jamie."

"...Ye...sor...ry...<*crackle*>...the...ust...be...so...int...ference...<*crackle*>...." his broken voice faded in and out.

"Jamie?"

Her worrisome thoughts were overwhelming as her mind jumped to the worst possible scenario. All she could envision was the masked face from her dream and it fed her fear. She continued calling out to Jamie, but there was no reply.

"The call was dropped," she said, turning to Ashley, "but my signal is still good."

Deep down, Kayla doubted that reception was the real problem. Determined, she pressed the call button and looked back at the road ahead.

\*\*\*\*\*\*\*\*\*\*\*\*

"Well then, gentlemen," Triton grinned, his wine glass held high above their table, "a toast, that we may share in the spoils of our impending success."

The men raised their glasses, the rims clinking, followed by laughter. Together, they drank, their dark plot twisting into reality.

\*\*\*\*\*\*\*\*\*\*\*\*

"Come on, Jamie," Kayla groaned impatiently, "answer."

The phone beeped as it hung up again. She redialed, but this time Jamie's phone went straight to voice mail. She wasn't getting through.

"Hey Jamie, it's Kayla. Give me a call as soon as you get this. You've got me worried, so it would make me feel better if I knew you were alright. Ashley and I are heading back from the monastery now. Let's meet up at my place. Okay, bye."

Kayla flipped the phone closed and placed it back in her purse. Ashley gave her sister a concerned look then went back to staring at the trees.

\*\*\*\*\*\*\*\*\*\*\*\*

A handsome young man, clothed in a black, rain-soaked suit, strode towards Triton's table. His wet hair was slicked back and he stood with his head cocked to one side as he watched their celebration. Triton noticed him approach, as did the other men, and the table fell silent.

"What are you doing here?" Triton wondered as the man pulled a chair over from another table and sat down, his arms and legs crossed in exuberant confidence.

"I just came to tell you," he sneered, "all the arrangements have been made. The body has been disposed of and one of the servants is being promoted as we speak."

Triton looked around at the other tables. Everyone was eating and laughing, drinking, enjoying the good life. They didn't seem to notice as the man pulled a black piece of cloth from his pocket and stretched it down over his face.

"What's this all about?" Bradford chuckled, staring at the oddly stitched mouth on the mask. "Who is this guy?"

"Yeah, I don't think we should be seen in public with one of your clowns," Lister scoffed.

"*Clowns*, huh?" the man in the mask grunted disapprovingly.

"Thirteen," Triton reprimanded. "They're right. You shouldn't be here."

"But I'm not," he laughed, disappearing into thin air.

The men stared at his empty seat, casting glances around the room. All the other tables were minding their own business. They hadn't seen him.

Triton pulled the richly woven napkin from his lap and threw it onto the table, his face red. The other men quickly finished their wine.

"I think this meeting is adjourned," he said, standing and heading for the door.

\*\*\*\*\*\*\*\*\*\*\*\*

Kayla's cell phone buzzed to life. It was Jamie.

*Finally.*

Quickly, she answered, her heart racing. Ashley glanced at her, her lashes fluttering, her eyes growing heavy.

"Hey Kayla, sorry about earlier, when you couldn't reach me. I was driving in from Jersey, through the Lincoln Tunnel. My signal was no good. I didn't mean to give you a scare."

"That's alright," she replied, relieved to hear his voice.

"I stumbled on a gold mine this morning," he continued. "I spent the rest of the day verifying and re-verifying new information. I'll tell you all about it when I get to your apartment. You two hungry?"

"Are you hungry, Ash?" Kayla asked.

Ashley nodded her head sleepily and shifted uncomfortably in the passenger seat of Kayla's car.

"Yeah, we're hungry," Kayla smiled. "How about Chinese takeout?"

"Chinese it is."

\*\*\*\*\*\*\*\*\*\*\*\*

The heavy glass door to Triton's office slammed shut. The lights were off. The sun had set. Blackness engulfed the room.

"Where are you!" Triton barked into the darkness.

An odd clicking sound, followed by a soft thump echoed from the corner, then, silence.

"What are you doing back there? Answer me!" Triton commanded.

Thirteen stepped from the shadows, a brown leather bound book in his hand.

"Just reading," he replied smoothly.

"Was your little stunt at the restaurant tonight really necessary? How dare you appear in public, with me, in that *mask!*"

"I'm sorry, Master."

"Yes, well, just be glad none of those people at the restaurant saw you. You could have ruined everything. It would have been one thing if you'd left your mask in your pocket, but you had to do that, in front of the mayor, *and* the commissioner, *and* the district attorney!"

"Ah, yes," Thirteen grinned, "*Lister...*"

"It took a lot of convincing to get that man on my side," Triton scowled, "and you risked undoing that tonight."

"Well, it won't happen again," Thirteen said sweetly as he took a low, gracious bow, "I can assure you of that, my Master."

\*\*\*\*\*\*\*\*\*\*\*

A scream cried out from the house of District Attorney Dennis Lister. His wife stood in the doorway to his office. Lister sat at his desk. The green glow from his computer monitor illuminated his face and the thin trickle of blood that ran from the bullet hole in the center of his forehead. On the desk, carved deeply into the wooden surface, was a roman numeral: XIII.

\*\*\*\*\*\*\*\*\*\*\*

Jamie, Kayla, and Ashley gathered around the small island counter top in the kitchen. Sitting on stools, chopsticks in hand, they ate from little white carryout boxes covered in artsy, red Chinese writing and dragons. Jamie explained his meeting with Sykes between bites. The girls listened intently, Ashley sipping on a bowl of wonton soup.

"So do you have any notes on your conversation?" Kayla asked, picking at a pint of steamed rice with her chopsticks.

"Better," Jamie grinned. "I recorded it on my iPhone. It's okay, don't thank me all at once, but this is a very solid lead."

Ashley finished her soup and started on her governor's chicken. Kayla put her chopsticks down.

"I want to hear it!"

Jamie slipped his phone from its leather holster and pulled up the audio file named "Sykes 10-12-07." Pushing a carton of lo mein aside and setting the phone down in the middle of the counter, he hit *play*. Jim Sykes rough voice talked excitedly.

Eating, they listened on in silence. After an hour or so, the recording ended and they sat staring at the nearly empty cartons of food. Jamie burped.

"Excuse me," he grinned as he scratched his full stomach.

"I don't see how that was any real help?" Ashley questioned, standing and taking a bottle of water from the fridge. "Isn't that all information from the original reports?"

"Everything, except the business about a *key*," Kayla replied, pulling her hair into a ponytail.

"Exactly!" Jamie exclaimed with a smile.

"But you don't even know what the key looks like, other than it was *old* and *rusty*," Ashley argued, recalling Syke's words.

Jamie and Kayla looked at each other, reading each others' faces. Ashley had a point.

"Okay. So let's summarize everything we know so far," Kayla said as she walked over to her computer desk and returned with a pen and yellow legal pad.

"Well," Jamie thought for a moment, "we'll start with the murders at the old apartment: Thirteen dead bodies found in a perfect circle, a pentagram drawn with their blood..."

"...then, the footprints burnt into the sidewalk on Park Avenue," Kayla interjected.

"Don't forget about the librarian," Ashley added, sipping at her water, suddenly feeling wide awake, the investigation exciting her.

"We're only looking at hard evidence here," Jamie said thoughtfully. "We need to focus on physical proof that will substantiate our case."

"Like Jack's cassette tapes?" Ashley replied.

Jamie nodded.

"So we've got the murders, the footprints, the tapes," Kayla recapped, adding them up on her fingers, "anything else?"

"Yeah," Jamie grinned, "Michael Hampton, our link to Triton."

Kayla counted Hampton on her pinky.

"So that makes four pieces to the puzzle," Ashley smiled.

"Right," Kayla replied. "But what do the footprints have to do with any of it. Jack's tapes corroborate that Triton was involved in weird, ritualistic experiments. Still, they don't directly connect him to the murders."

"What about Jack's killer, that Hampton guy?" Ashley asked. "He's dead and he worked for Triton. Doesn't that seem like too big a coincidence?"

"Correction: Hampton *worked* for Tri-Corp, not exactly Triton. With thousands of employees all across the country, Triton couldn't have known each and every one." Jamie answered, running his hands through his hair. "I mean, if someone worked for Microsoft and was mysteriously murdered, it wouldn't naturally link Bill Gates to the crime."

"No," Kayla replied, "*but* recordings made by an insider with the suspected murderer's voice all over them would help to draw some conclusions."

"So what about the footprints then?" Jamie said, revisiting that day in his head. "What links them to Triton?"

Kayla thought for a moment, trying to see past all the distractions.

"Joseph said that he thought Triton was grooming another," Ashley said, her eyes wide and bright.

"Like I said," Jamie grinned, "hard evidence."

"Sorry."

"I can't come up with anything," Jamie frowned, shaking his head. "The footprints make absolutely no sense."

The loud ringer on Jamie's phone startled them. He reached for it on the table and answered.

"What's up, Captain? Uh huh, are you kidding? When? Tonight! We'll be there."

"What?" Kayla asked.

"District Attorney, Dennis Lister," Jamie replied deep in thought.

"What about him?"

"He's dead."

\*\*\*\*\*\*\*\*\*\*\*\*

Jamie stopped his BMW at the foot of Lister's driveway. Three squad cars sat parked at the curb. An ambulance was in the drive. Two officers guarded the front door and yellow police line cordoned off the yard.

"Look at this place!" Ashley exclaimed from the backseat. "So this is how the other half lives."

"*Lived*," Jamie grunted, stepping from the car.

"You stay here." Kayla said, looking at Ashley in the rear view mirror. "We won't be long."

Jamie and Kayla approached the front door.

"Evening, officer," he smiled as they stepped into the spacious entry hall.

Jamie turned to close the door but paused, looking at the lock and heavy wood frame. He ran his fingers curiously over the deadbolt, checking the door frame for splintering.

"No sign of forced entry."

Kayla shrugged and headed towards the next door, an officer busily scribbling on a small notepad.

"He's in there," the officer said matter-of-factly as they walked past him into Lister's study.

Kayla slipped her digital camera from her pocket and began snapping pictures, the bright flash illuminating the dark room, "Looks like one shot, directly to the head; a professional?"

"I would guess," Jamie said, pulling on a pair of latex gloves.

Kayla continued photographing the body as Jamie walked the perimeter of the room.

"Hey, Kayla," he called out, bent over underneath a tightly closed window, his flashlight aimed at something on the hardwood floor.

"What's up?"

"Take a picture."

Kayla stood directly over his flashlight beam and snapped several photos.

"What does it look like to you?" he wondered.

"Muddy footprints?!"

Jamie took a ball point pen from his pocket and placed it next to the mess on the floor, then stood and checked the window. Kayla snapped another photo, this one for size reference.

"It's locked," he observed, clicking the switch on top of the window open then shut, "from the inside."

"That's a neat trick," Kayla grinned.

"Officer...*you*," Jamie stammered, not knowing the man's name, "check all the rest of the windows in the house."

"Spidowski, Officer Spidowski, Sir."

"Okay, *Spidowski*; check the windows."

"Yes, Sir."

"Hey," Jamie called, looking at another officer who was in the next room, consoling Lister's wife, "was this door locked when you got here?"

"Yes," he replied. "She opened it for us when we arrived."

"Are there any other doors on this level?"

"Yes Sir, two more, one leading from the kitchen to the patio out back, the other into the garage. I checked both of them. They're locked as well."

Jamie headed back over to Kayla. Now she was photographing the desk.

"Find anything?"

"Yeah," she said, pointing at the corner of the finely crafted top.

Jamie ran his finger over the etching.

"Detective Branson..."

He jumped. Officer Spadowski stood in the doorway, motioning for Jamie.

"Yeah?"

"All the windows are locked."

142

"I figured. Thanks, Officer."

Jamie turned back to the desk and looked closer, tracing the marks in the surface with his index finger.

"It looks like a roman numeral thirteen," Kayla commented, flipping off her camera and returning it to her pocket.

"Yeah," Jamie grunted, "like the one in that basement."

He continued to stare at the carving till he stood straight up, a puzzled look on his face.

"Did you see any other footprints?"

"No," Kayla replied.

"So how did the killer get from there to here without leaving a trace? It's a good fifteen feet."

Jamie stepped back over to the footprints and stood next to them, his feet aimed in the same direction as the mud on the floor, the locked window at his back. Straight ahead was Lister's desk, his dead body facing directly at him.

"So," Jamie deduced, his arm raised, his fingers pointing like a gun, "the killer stood here and fired one round to the head..."

His train of thought was interrupted by a squeal from the living room followed by heavy sobs. Jamie cleared his throat. The officer sitting with Lister's wife led her out to the kitchen, far from the reach of Jamie's voice.

"But that's just it then," he said as he rubbed his brow, "one shot, then what? No more footprints, no sign of escape."

"Maybe the killer is still here?" Kayla wondered aloud. "Where was the wife? Maybe she killed him?"

"But this is a really accurate shot. Even within fifteen feet, to place a bullet dead smack between the eyes? It would take a very experienced marksman to make that shot," Jamie noted, spotting a spent shell under the corner of an armchair that sat just beside the window.

Kneeling, he picked it up between his gloved fingers. *9mm Luger* was imprinted on the casing.

"We'll have ballistics do a search for the bullet, and see if we can match it up to a gun," Kayla said, watching Jamie drop the casing into a plastic evidence bag. "Let's go talk to his wife."

\*\*\*\*\*\*\*\*\*\*\*\*

Ashley sat in the back seat of Jamie's car, patiently waiting for them to return. She played a handheld video game to pass the time, the bright colors on the dual screens flashing, reflecting in the windows of the dark car. Ashley huffed in frustration as her red clad plumber missed a jump and went tumbling off a cliff.

*It's his stupid mustache. I swear! It weights him down so much he can't jump right.*

Suddenly, the screens flickered, then went black. She'd just charged it that afternoon. The battery should be full.

She caught a glimpse of movement from the corner of her eye, outside, just across the street from Lister's immaculately manicured lawn. It was too dark to see, the street lights had gone out as well, but it looked like there was a man standing with his arms crossed, staring up at the house. He seemed to be wearing a dark colored suit. Ashley squinted, but she couldn't see his face, just two white, glowing eyes.

Turning to see if the officers guarding the door had spotted him, she saw that they were talking, one sipped at a travel cup of coffee, the other laughed at what must have been said. They hadn't seen the man.

Ashley quickly looked back to the shadows across the street. He was gone, the streetlights were back on, illuminating where he had stood, a muddy puddle where his feet would have been. Her video game beeped to life. She looked down, the screens flashed images of a princess and a castle.

*What is going on?*

\*\*\*\*\*\*\*\*\*\*\*\*

"Mrs. Lister," Kayla asked gently, "if there is anything you could tell us that would help us better understand what went on here tonight, it would be much appreciated."

Jamie found a copper tea kettle on the counter and started a burner on the top of the stove. Filling the pot with water, he set it down to boil.

"Ma'am," he said pulling a chair out from the kitchen table Mrs. Lister sat at, "I know this is hard for you, but we want to find whoever did this, bring them to justice."

"I...I...I...don't know what happened," Mrs. Lister sniffed. "He came upstairs and kissed me goodnight, then told me he had some work to do on his computer. That was the last time I s-s-saw him."

"Did you hear anyone downstairs with him, a conversation, an argument?" Kayla wondered, touching Mrs. Lister's shaking hands empathetically.

"No, I didn't hear a thing."

"You didn't hear any noises like a door opening, maybe a window?" Jamie asked. "How about footsteps, or someone walking around?"

"No, nothing."

The kettle whistled, steam shooting from the spout. Jamie stood and headed for the stove. He returned with a cup on a saucer, a tea bag soaking in the hot water, and placed it in front of Mrs. Lister.

"Thank you," she said, trying to smile.

"So what brought you downstairs, Mrs. Lister?" Kayla asked.

"It was odd," she answered slowly, "like something woke me, whispered in my ear. I sat up, thinking it was Dennis coming to bed, but he wasn't there. I put on my robe and stepped into my slippers; then, everything went black. When I came to, I was standing in the doorway of his office. That's when I saw him, and..."

"It's okay," Kayla said comfortingly.

"I'm sorry I have to ask this," Jamie began carefully, "but I have to, it's our job. Did Dennis own a gun?"

"Yes. It's in a box on the top shelf in the hall closet. He wanted it kept up high, where the kids couldn't reach it."

"And where are your kids now?" Kayla wondered.

"They're at my parents' house. It's our wedding anniversary and we were going to celebrate," she said, casting a glance at a bottle of wine and two unused goblets on the counter.

Jamie headed for the hallway, as Kayla sat consoling Mrs. Lister. The closet door was ajar. Cautiously, he reached up, feeling for the box. It was too dark to see. He grabbed his flashlight and aimed it up. The box was pushed deep into the far corner of the closet.

Standing on his tip-toes, he pulled it to the edge of the shelf, then brought it down to look inside. A box of 9mm ammo was spilled open on the bottom of the box, the rounds rolling to one corner as he held it. No gun was to be found. Jamie picked up one of the bullets and examined the casing: 9mm Luger.

He pulled another evidence bag from his pocket and dropped the bullet into it, then placed the box back onto the shelf. Comparing the spent casing he'd found in Lister's office with the bullet he took from the box, Jamie shook his head sadly. They were a match. It looked like the killer may have used one of these rounds, or at least, the same brand.

Reluctantly, Jamie stepped back into the kitchen, the new evidence bag still in his hand. Kayla looked at him inquisitively as he entered.

"Mrs. Lister, have you ever fired his gun?" he asked, placing the bag with the bullet on the table.

"Never," she said, tears in her eyes. "I hate having it in the house."

"Mrs. Lister," Jamie said calmly, "the box only held bullets. There was no gun."

"What? No, no, that's not right. He always kept it there, in the hall, the closet," she stammered, pointing in that direction.

Jamie turned back towards the hallway and examined the area. Several paintings hung on the wall, a potted plant sat in the corner. A tall table rested against the wall next to the closet, a lamp in the middle, a lace doily underneath it. Family pictures sat in frames on either side of the lamp.

Jamie pulled open a long drawer that ran the length of the table. At first, nothing seemed out of place, just a few domestic odds and ends. But then, he noticed something peculiar pushed to the back. Slowly, he pulled it from the drawer. It was a newspaper clipping folded in half, a picture of Dennis Lister shaking hands with Mayor Bradford. "City Welcomes New D.A.," the headline read.

*Odd*, he thought, *that's the kind of thing someone would usually frame and hang.*

Placing the news clipping back in the drawer, his fingers touched something cool, metallic. Slowly, he wrapped his fingers around it. It was a 9mm handgun. Jamie ejected the magazine and inspected the first round. It matched the casing he'd collected as evidence. Examining the barrel, he smelled gun powder. It had been recently fired.

"Spadowski," Jamie said softly, placing the gun in another bag, "I need this checked for prints."

The officer brought Jamie a finger print kit from the entrance hall. Jamie flipped open the lid and pulled out the items he needed. Carefully, he dusted the hand grip on the gun, then placed a strip of adhesive across it. When he pulled it off of the gun, a pattern of fingerprints was visible.

"Spadowski, go take Mrs. Lister's prints."

After several minutes, the officer returned, a fingerprint card in his hand. Jamie pulled his phone from his belt and snapped a picture of Mrs. Lister's fingerprints, then the fingerprint he'd taken from the gun. Using a photo editing app, he resized the images, then made quick comparisons and overlaid the two prints searching for a similar papillary pattern.

*Bingo.*

They were a positive match.

"Kayla," he called from the hallway.

"Yeah, Jamie?"

"Come here a second."

"I'll be right back," Kayla assured Lister's wife.

Jamie handed her his phone as she stepped into the hall, "take a look."

She studied the prints as Jamie grinned.

"See this whorl," he said, pointing at the print, "it's exact. And this branch and this delta, the same as well."

"I don't believe it," Kayla shrugged, "she seemed really, genuinely upset."

"Officer Spadowski," Jamie called, "take Mrs. Lister into custody for further questioning. Her prints match the ones found on the murder weapon."

\*\*\*\*\*\*\*\*\*\*\*\*

Ashley looked on as two officers escorted Mrs. Lister out the front door and down the walkway, her hands restrained behind her back. Jamie and Kayla followed with another officer.

"I'll write up the report," Spadowski said solemnly, watching as the officers guided Mrs. Lister into the backseat of their cruiser, her pale, tear-marked face staring out blankly from behind the glass as the car door slammed shut.

"Thanks," Jamie replied rubbing his eyes. "It's getting late. I'll prepare my statement tonight and file it in the morning."

"Alright, Detective."

Jamie and Kayla sat down in the car. Ashley leaned forward between the seats, her excitement obvious.

"What?" Jamie asked as Kayla fastened her seatbelt.

"I saw a man!" Ashley blurted.

"Where?"

Ashley pointed at the light post across the street, her eyes sparkling with enthusiasm, her video game bleeping and blurping in the background. Jamie reached for Kayla's digital camera, his hand disappearing into her jacket pocket.

"Hey!" she complained, watching as he raced over to where Ashley had directed, his car door left standing wide open in his haste.

At the base of the light post, he found a set of footprints pressed deeply into the mud, a small puddle formed around the impressions. He snapped a few pictures and sprinted back to the car.

"I'm willing to bet that these prints will match the ones from inside the house." he grinned, handing Kayla the camera.

\*\*\*\*\*\*\*\*\*\*\*\*

Jamie sat down at his computer and placed the memory card from Kayla's camera into a card reader on his desktop. The hard drive whirred along as he pulled up the evidence photos Kayla had taken that night and dragged them into the main file folder from their investigation.

Clicking open the file for the pictures, he searched till he found the ones he was looking for. Jamie pulled up the photos of the footprints taken inside the house and placed them side by side with a picture taken from beneath the light post. The imprints looked like they matched. The heels were worn similarly, and a scuff across the forefoot on the left shoe was identical.

Jamie leaned back in his chair, his hands resting on the edge of his desk. Staring at the pictures on the screen, a thought came to him. Searching through the rest of the files, he found the pictures they had taken the previous Friday morning, the accident downtown. Jamie scrolled through the pictures for the footprints burnt into the sidewalk. The heels were worn in the same places as the muddy prints, and the forefoot scuff matched as well.

*No way!*

\*\*\*\*\*\*\*\*\*\*\*\*

Joseph sat alone, reading in his study. His Bible lay open on his desk in front of him. He closed his eyes and prayed for guidance, for the protection of Kayla and Ashley, and for strength for the hardships to come.

"Lord, I don't understand what You have planned," he prayed aloud, "but I trust You and I know my time has come."

\*\*\*\*\*\*\*\*\*\*\*\*

"Pick up," Jamie mumbled as he called Kayla on her cell.

"Hello?" she answered sleepily.

"You aren't going to believe this," he chuckled, astonished at what he discovered.

"This better be good!" she managed through a yawn.

"The footprints at the Lister house match the burn marks on the sidewalk."

"Uh huh?"

"Did you hear what I said?"

"Uh huh."

"It was the same guy, Kayla!"

She sat in silence, her mind lost somewhere in a foggy state between sleep and awake, making it difficult to process this new information. Ashley stirred next to her on the couch, but never woke. A movie they had left on flickered in the darkness as her tired eyes adjusted to the light.

"Kayla?"

"Yeah, I'm here. I was just trying to make sense of it."

"We'll get to the bottom of this," Jamie replied confidently, "I promise."

# IX

## MONDAY MORNING

Jamie's BMW dodged through traffic as he raced up Broadway. Kayla watched the rain run across the passenger side window as they sped through the streets.

"So where'd they find this guy?"

"Face down in a puddle," Jamie frowned, "just inside the West 72nd St. entrance to Central Park, you know, that small stone bridge with the path that runs beneath it? A jogger came across him early this morning."

Kayla shifted curiously, "You mean *Riftstone*?"

"What?"

"That's the name of the bridge," Kayla said matter-of-factly, "the one by the Lennon Memorial, Strawberry Fields."

"How do you know that?" Jamie chuckled in amazement.

"I don't know, I just heard it somewhere and it stuck."

"Um, okay, nerd," he teased.

Kayla straightened in her seat, carefully hiding a slight smile, rather proud that she knew something her partner didn't.

Quickly, her thoughts landed on more pressing matters, "Why'd they call us? Don't we have enough on our plate with the apartment murders?"

"Remember the accident the other day, the explosion downtown," Jamie grinned, "the one with absolutely no leads but the footprints on the sidewalk?"

"Yeah?"

"The body they found matches several eye-witness accounts of the man who may have left the prints."

"What a coincidence..."

"Yeah, well," Jamie chuckled, "the D.A. passed an order on to O'Donnell telling him to close that case, that it was some freak of nature accident. Now, Lister's dead and this guy pops up."

"Jamie, we can't take on two or three investigations all at once!" Kayla reasoned. "We don't even have anything on the first case yet!"

"From where I sit, I'd say these are all starting to look like the same case. We just didn't know it. Besides, O'Donnell trusts us to figure things out. He wouldn't have asked if he didn't think we could handle it."

Jamie pulled his car into the park and stopped next to the cruisers that blocked the main road, their flashers blinking, glistening in the rain. Yellow tape closed off the path below, officers walked back and forth, pushing curious onlookers away from the crime scene.

Quickly taking in their surroundings, Jamie slid from his driver's seat, then walked around the front of his car and opened Kayla's door, taking her hand as he led her towards the path that ran beneath the road. Kayla followed after him, an umbrella open over her shoulder, rain spattering off it, dripping from the edges.

Carefully, they made their way down the steep bank. Reaching the bottom, Jamie held the yellow police-line up for her to walk under.

"Good morning, Detective," an officer greeted as Jamie flashed his badge.

"Give me a rundown on what we've got," Jamie said sternly, getting down to business, as they stood at the mouth of the tunnel.

"6:30am," the officer explained, "call came in from a jogger, found the body under the bridge, laying flat in the shadows next to a storm drain, looks like he's been here all night, Detective. Forensics is on the way."

Moving slowly into the tunnel, they began to make out the shape of the body where it lay, not more than a foot away from the wall on their right. The soft sound of trickling water echoed nearby. Jamie walked around the body, viewing its position from every angle.

"Has anybody touched the body?" Kayla wondered, noting the plethora of footprints in the surrounding dirt.

"No. We'd just finished cordoning off the area when the Captain called in, said he wanted you two to get the first look."

"Alright," Jamie replied as he pulled a pair of latex gloves from a small leather pouch on his belt, "try and hold forensics off as long as you can, and get these people back."

They moved carefully in the darkness under the old stone bridge, not wanting to disturb any unseen evidence. The officers began pushing back the crowd that was quickly gathering, hoping for a glimpse.

Kayla pulled out her digital camera and began snapping photos. Jamie flipped on his flashlight and scanned the walls of the tunnel and the area directly around the body. Nothing seemed out of place.

"No sign of a struggle," Jamie observed, kneeling down next to the body.

"What about the footprints?"

"There're too many here to decipher, plus they're not concentrated around the body in particular."

Kayla listened intently. Jamie's hands motioned along to convey his thoughts.

"If you look, they all lead in two general directions, in and out, so I'd say these are mostly irrelevant, just joggers or walkers making their way through the tunnel on their route, some are possibly days old."

Kayla smiled, she loved how his mind worked.

"These prints here though, by the shoulder," he pointed, "these aim towards the body and then look like they turn, blending in with the other impressions."

Jamie pulled out his iPhone and tapped on the audio recorder. Kayla continued to photograph the body, starting with the shuffling footprints, then snapping shots of the body's positioning.

"Male...Caucasian...late twenties..." he said, first checking around the body, then underneath it, finally rolling it onto its side to take a look at the face."

The man's eyes were wide open, a hazy white film seemed to cover them. He was dressed in an expensive black suit. His white dress shirt was muddied from where he laid: his tie was pulled loose, but still knotted.

Jamie checked the man's pants pockets. His wallet was still there.

"We've got a wallet, brown leather, found in the right rear pocket," Jamie dictated, "doesn't appear to be a mugging."

Flipping open the wallet, he found the man's driver's license, some large bills, a couple credit cards, nothing suspicious.

'George Bisson...ID number: 931 686 902...date of birth: 03/18/79..."

"Are those bruises on his neck?" Kayla asked leaning over the body as Jamie slipped the wallet back into the man's pocket.

Jamie pulled the collar away to get a better look. It was definitely bruises.

"Contusions on and around the neck...heavy bruising on the

posterior side as well as swelling near the jugular...a small abrasion, on the left hand side surrounded by several small lacerations...no ligature pattern, but these marks do infer fingernail scratches...looks like he was strangled."

Jamie lifted each hand and checked the nails for hair, fibers, anything that could give them a lead. But nothing stood out. The body was clean.

Voices began to echo in the tunnel. Kayla stood and watched as the forensics team made their way past the yellow tape.

"I'll stall them," Kayla said, straightening up and handing her camera to Jamie, then heading their way, greeting them and filling them in on the crime scene.

Jamie stopped the recording and did one more quick check of the body. Reaching into the jacket's right breast pocket, he found a finely crafted, very expensive French-made ball-point pen, the name *Tri-Corp* engraved on the brushed aluminum casing. From the left pocket, he pulled out a small neatly rolled piece of black fabric. An odd uneasiness coursed through him as he unfolded it. His stomach churned as he stared intensely at the cloth.

Shining his flashlight on it, he stood. This body wasn't just a body.

Two black slits marked where the eyes would have been. The mouth was stitched into a sickening grin. It was a mask. Jamie could have sworn he heard a mocking laugh echo off the stone walls.

Quickly, he stuffed it into his pants pocket along with his phone and the pen as he turned and watched forensics push past Kayla. She shook her head at them angrily, but they didn't care.

He started to exit the tunnel when a thought hit him. Flipping on Kayla's camera, he moved hurriedly back to the body, carefully snapping a few shots of the soles of the shoes, then stood and turned on his heals nonchalantly as forensics approached.

"He's all yours," Jamie said, pulling off his gloves, the rubber fingers snapping as he passed the team.

Kayla and Jamie watched as the group went to work. One of them set up bright spotlights and aimed them at the body while another began snapping photos. The other two knelt down and opened up black cases they carried filled with gloves, tweezers, ultraviolet light emitters and other tools of the trade.

"Let's get going," Jamie said, opening the umbrella and handing it to Kayla.

They made their way back to the car slowly, softly discussing the crime scene in hushed voices. Sitting down in Jamie's car, they stared out the front window, the wiper blades flitting back and forth in a perfect arc.

"So what do you think?" Kayla asked as Jamie reviewed the pictures on her digital camera.

"Whatever happened to him didn't happen here. The body was dumped," he said, flipping from photo to photo, "and whoever did the dumping didn't seem too concerned about cleaning up either. They left all his belongings: his wallet, a very expensive pen, his wristwatch."

"Yeah," Kayla agreed.

"Check this out," Jamie chuckled, pulling the pen from his pocket."

"Tri-Corp," she read aloud.

Jamie hesitated, his thoughts turning to the mask. He looked into Kayla's eyes, reading her expression, the way she stared back longingly, but as if she tried to hide it.

"What is it?" she asked as she leaned in closer to him.

Jamie smiled. She smelled wonderful, like vanilla. If only they were together, alone, under better circumstances.

Gathering his thoughts, putting his feelings aside, he cleared his throat and again reached into his pocket, this time pulling out the jumbled handful of black material and slowly unfolding it in his lap.

"I found this on him." he said, staring nowhere in particular. "I didn't want anyone else to see it till we had a good chance to really look at it."

Kayla felt her hands shaking as she reached for the crumpled cloth, the stitches grinning at her. As her fingertips came into contact with the mask, at the slightest touch, a surge of electricity shot up her arms.

Tears formed on her lashes as she clenched her eyes tightly shut. Kayla suddenly thought of her dream; the nightmare about Jamie. And then, that face, that horrible, evil grinning face, laughing at her from behind a black mask as it leaned into the dim light.

She pulled her hand away sharply, her eyes flipping open, a tingle in her fingertips. Tears streamed down her cheeks.

"Hey, you okay?" Jamie asked, reaching out to her, one hand gently touching her arm, the other wiping the tears from her cheek.

Kayla stared at him, trying to forget her dream. She didn't want to tell him, at least not now. It was bad enough that her sister was seeing things, he half thought Ashley was crazy, but what would he say if he knew she was having them as well?

"It's nothing," she said, wishing she could tell him everything, "it just caught me off guard. That, and when I touched it, it shocked me. I'm sure this'll sound crazy, but it was kind of like when you take your shoes off and rub your feet on thick carpet and then touch a doorknob, only much stronger."

"Like static electricity?"

"Yeah."

"I don't feel anything," he said curiously, stretching the mask out in his hands. "Don't you think I'd notice something as well?"

"I don't know, maybe I'm crazy?"

Jamie tried to smile reassuringly as he watched sadness wash across her sullen face, then he tucked the mask back into his pocket and put the car in gear. Kayla rubbed her hands together. Her fingers were still tingling.

"Let's check in with O'Donnell," Jamie thought aloud. "I'm sure he'll want to know what we've found."

Kayla crossed her arms. Maybe it was just a chill from the cold fall rain, but for some reason, she felt like she'd never be warm again. After touching that mask, it was like every happy memory she had was stripped from her. Kayla looked over at Jamie, wanting to tell him the truth, tell him everything, but she was afraid that things would never be the same.

As they drove back to the station, Jamie reached over, his eyes still fixed on the road, and took a hold of her hand. He didn't have to say a word, not one. She understood. In silence, they shared a moment, and without words, Jamie said everything he wanted to say.

************

Ashley sat on the couch in her apartment. It felt strange to be home again, the last several nights being spent with her sister, and now that she was alone, her thoughts were haunted by strange visions and dark figures. She picked up her graphite pencil and a small cylindrical sharpener, then began sharpening the pencil, watching the spiral of shavings grow in the plastic tube as she twisted the pencil round and round. Ashley pulled her legs up onto the couch and sat Indian-style, resting her sketch pad down between her knees. Closing her eyes, she imagined the image she would draw, all the details of the face coming together before a single pencil stroke. Finally, she opened her eyes and began sketching, filling the blank page with sure, defined lines. Wicked teeth and a ghoulish smile began to take shape; an evil face with hollow slits for eyes was staring up at her from the page. She stopped after shading in the black pupils. Why couldn't she get this image from her head?

************

Kayla laid a note on Capt. O'Donnell's desk and headed back out the door. Every thought still collided as she balanced reason and doubt. But, for the first time, she felt they had Triton right where they wanted him.

"What was that?" Jamie asked as he watched Kayla sit down across from him at her desk.

"Nothing," she smiled, staring longingly into his face as they sat in the empty office, "just a note for the Boss."

159

Jamie continued typing. The clatter of the keyboard was exaggerated by the silence of the room.

"Where is everybody?" she wondered aloud, glancing at all the vacant desks.

"You're guess is as good as mine."

Jamie finished typing then held down the control key and clicked "s", saving the file. Kayla sipped at her steaming cup of coffee.

"My reports from this morning are all done and I just finished my statement from last night," he said, leaning back in his chair, his arms stretched high above his head, the hinges in the chair creaking beneath his weight.

Kayla stood from her desk, then sat down on Jamie's lap and kissed him.

"Wow," he smiled, a bit surprised, "how did I get so lucky?"

She shifted and rested her head on his shoulder, speaking softly, "I was watching you work and thinking about everything that's going on and..."

"And what, Kay?"

"And wishing that we weren't caught up in all this, that I could just leave what happened to my brother in the past and move on, that we could be together the way I want to, like it was before this. I miss you."

"You'd better believe I miss you too."

Kayla kissed Jamie again, her hands behind his head, cradling him as he wrapped his arms around her. Her lips were so soft. All he could think about was taking her pain away, to make her happy, if only for a moment. Gently, he touched her knee, then softly caressed her thigh, slipping his hand higher and higher.

"Jamie!" she laughed, jumping up from his lap and straightening her skirt.

"What?!" he asked in a hard-breathing panic.

"It's O'Donnell," she blushed, sliding back into her chair as she fixed her hair and composed herself, "he just came out of the bathroom!"

He glanced over his shoulder and watched as the Captain clomped across the office, then stopped, looking inquisitively at Jamie, "where is everybody?"

"No clue, Boss." Jamie grinned.

"Did you file your report?" O'Donnell grunted.

"Yep," Jamie replied, trying to look natural.

Kayla stared at her blank computer screen, embarrassment plastered on her face, *Did he see us? Oh, I hope he didn't see us.*

"What's wrong with you Rose, your face is all red?"

"Nothing, Sir...just hard at work."

Jamie shot her a sideways glance. She bit her lip and smiled.

"We were just getting ready to go," Jamie said, jumping up from his chair and slipping on his suit jacket, "right, Kayla?"

"Yeah," she said, following Jamie's lead, "we have something we need to check up on."

"Alright," O'Donnell frowned as he headed for his office while the detectives raced for the door. "Oh, and Branson..."

"Yes, Sir?" Jamie answered, sliding to a stop at the end of the hall.

"One more thing..."

"Yes, Sir?"

"Wipe that lipstick off your face before anyone else sees it," O 'Donnell grinned. "Now get out of here."

\*\*\*\*\*\*\*\*\*\*\*\*

Thirteen paced along the edge of the rooftop at New York General Hospital. A pair of demons flanked him, one on each side, their wings beating in the crisp morning air.

"Everything is going according to plan," he laughed from beneath his mask.

\*\*\*\*\*\*\*\*\*\*\*\*

Kayla barely closed the door to her apartment before Jamie pinned her against the wall, his lips pressing into hers. She tossed her purse onto the floor, quickly followed by her jacket and his suit coat. Slipping out of her heels, she loosened his tie as he began unbuttoning his shirt. Jamie held her, his hands rubbing the small of her back. She loved his touch, his strong fingers. Grabbing his hand, she led him to the couch. They sat for a moment in silence, then kissed again.

The world they knew ground to a halt. As they embraced, there was no investigation, no mysterious murders, no haunting clues. The complexity of life disappeared. All they could see was each other.

Kayla wrapped her arms around Jamie, pulling him close, the muscles in his back and shoulders flinching as she held on to him. Jamie ran his hands through her hair, teasingly grazing her ears and neck. In that moment, they were all that mattered. For that one moment, everything made sense.

Jamie ran his hand down her back and stopped at her waste, his fingers grazing the skin just above her skirt. Then slowly, he pulled up on her shirt.

"Jamie, wait..."

\*\*\*\*\*\*\*\*\*\*\*\*

Capt. O'Donnell finished his cup of coffee and threw the Styrofoam cup into the trash can along the side of his desk. Nervously, he stuck a cigarette between his lips and raised a lighter with his shaking hand. Smoke filled his office, though he hadn't lit his cigarette yet. Three shrouded figures stood behind his chair, but he couldn't see them. Their bodies were hidden behind leathery wings and their eyes glowed red just above their large jagged shark like grins. They were laughing at how scared O'Donnell was, and rightfully so. They'd followed him since he'd left the hospital, whispering taunts, helping him relive every bad moment of his life. Finally he was able to get his thumb under control enough to make a flame.

*Nicotine...nic...o-o-o...tine,* he thought, puffing away at his cigarette.

He was still spooked from his visit to Officer Keller's hospital room, but that was just the beginning. He'd tried to look through the victims files from the murders, but as he flipped through them, each face seemed to be smiling at him. O'Donnell thought he was going crazy.

Now, he could even hear the laughter: it echoed in his mind. Clenching his fists, he slammed his hands down on his desk, his mug full of pens and pencils spilling onto its side.

"Get out of my head!" he growled.

Yelling made him feel better. Calming down, O'Donnell noticed the folders in front of him. A post-it-note was attached, Kayla's handwriting scribbled quickly across the yellow paper.

*Captain,*

*This might sound crazy, but Jamie and I have found evidence linking Dr. Maurice Triton to the murders. We need a warrant to enter Tri-Corp and bring Triton in for questioning. It all started with Jack, Sir. He knew. You've got to trust me.*

*Please call the courthouse. Let's bring Triton to justice. I'm counting on you.*

*Thanks,*

*-Kayla*

"Oh boy," he mumbled, his cigarette hanging from his mouth.

Pulling a black labeled bottle of whiskey from one of the drawers on his desk, he picked up the mug he used as a make-shift desk organizer, dusted it out, poured a shot and swished it around the bottom of the mug, then drank it down and poured another. O'Donnell stared at the note for a while, then finally picked up his phone and punched the number for the courthouse. He couldn't believe he was doing this. The line was busy. He waited and dialed again: still busy. As he hung up the phone, he heard a firm knock at his door.

"Come in!" he barked, rubbing his cigarette in his ashtray.

The door swung open. It was FBI agents Dimitri and Jones.

\*\*\*\*\*\*\*\*\*\*\*\*

``We can't do this right now." Kayla said, flustered, red in the face, as she jumped up from the couch and straightened her shirt. "I want to, I *really* want to, but we can't lose focus now. I know we're getting close to solving this case. Everything, even the stuff that hasn't made sense, is beginning to line up."

Jamie leaned against the back of the couch, his arms resting behind his head, and let out a deep sigh. As much as he hated to admit it, as much as every ounce of man in him regretted stopping, she was right: this wasn't the time to get carried away.

"Maybe I should just go talk to him?"

"Who?"

"Triton," Jamie grunted. "Maybe everything does point to him. Maybe if we put some pressure on him, he'll give something away."

"First of all, you'd need a warrant. Right now all we've got is suspicion. Second, do you honestly think he's someone that can be intimidated? Jamie, come on. He had my brother killed, Hampton murdered, gosh," she paused, "maybe even Lister!"

"Hold on," Jamie reasoned, "why would he murder the District

Attorney?"

"I don't know, Jamie. But it can't be ruled out!"

"His wife's prints were found on the murder weapon," he scoffed.

"So?!"

"It's airtight, Kayla. She did it."

"What about a motive then?"

"She told you they were going to 'celebrate' their anniversary. There were perfectly clean wine glasses, an unopened bottle, and Mrs. Lister in a sleazy negligee. Dennis Lister was a workaholic. He put his work before his wife and she took it personally. Obviously, a disappointing date night was the last straw."

"Yeah, maybe," Kayla shrugged, seeing Jamie's point, "but what about the muddy footprints and the etching on Lister's desk?"

"I don't know, Kayla," he said thoughtfully, "I don't know."

************

A young nurse cautiously peered around the corner in a dark hall on the second floor of New York General Hospital, the fluorescent lights above flickering as screams echoed all around her. She had to find a place to hide.

Security guards sprinted past, batons in hand, their walkie-talkies screeching. More screams filled the air as several nurses ducked into a nearby maintenance closet, the lock clicking behind them. She hurried to the door and pounded on it with her fists, crying for them to let her in, but they wouldn't open the door. She beat harder. Still, they ignored her. The ear-splitting bangs of gun shots bounced down the hospital corridors, then the sound of footsteps coming her way. She whispered a silent prayer to whoever she hoped was listening.

Quickly, she raced down the hall and dove into a laundry cart filled with dirty bed sheets. She wrapped herself up in them trying to hide, burying herself down in the corner of the cart, leaving just enough of an opening so that she could peek out. The halls were quiet now. The screams subsided. She held her breath. The soiled sheets smelled awful. But this was the only place she had to hide.

*Whatever's out there is much worse*, she reminded herself.

Heavy footsteps were coming slowly down the hallway; then, raspy breathing. She strained, trying to see. The massive figure of a man was approaching. His eyes were completely black. His skin was pale, leathery. He looked dead, but he was very much alive. In his left hand, he carried a gun; in his right, a severed arm, torn off at the shoulder. His face was hollow, expressionless; his chest riddled with bullet holes, but no blood, just black smears on his white gown. The nurse realized who this man was: Officer Keller.

\*\*\*\*\*\*\*\*\*\*\*\*

"Well regardless of his involvement in Lister's death, I'm definitely not going to sit around and wait for Triton to commit another murder," Jamie said, standing up from the couch. "I want to go talk to him now, get to the bottom of this. Warrant or not, we're going to bring him down."

Kayla walked over to the mantle and stared at the empty picture frame. She'd felt so many emotions in the last hour, her head was spinning.

"No, Jamie. We're still waiting to hear back from O'Donnell. We *need* that warrant before we can do anything," Kayla reminded him.

"Ever heard of reasonable suspicion?"

"It's still just suspicion," she frowned.

"I'm going down to the Tri-Corp building. Triton's going to answer for what he's done," he said, checking his gun and heading out the door.

\*\*\*\*\*\*\*\*\*\*\*\*

As soon as Keller was out of sight, the nurse scrambled out of her hiding place and ran to the nearest exit she could find. The hospital looked like a battlefield, bodies everywhere. All the guards were dead, pieces of them scattered about. Keller literally tore them apart. She passed nurses and doctors, orderlies and patients, some mangled like the guards, others with bite marks on their arms, necks, or even faces. The nurse began to cry.

*What a monster!*

Running around the last corner, she came to the doors that led to the emergency room. She'd almost made it out.

*Just a little further.*

"Oomph," the nurse hit the ground with a thud, she'd tripped over a body.

Rising up off the floor, she looked at her skinned elbow, then at the pretty young woman lying at her feet. The fearful expression on her face turned to sadness. Her best friend, a fellow nurse, someone she'd known since high school, was lying dead on the floor. She bent down and checked for a pulse.

*Nothing.*

She skewed her head to one side: the dead woman's chest moved, slowly, deeply. The nurse cautiously put her head down close to her friend's mouth. Hot breath wisped along her neck. She could hear her breathing. Suddenly, the girl's eyes blinked open, black as night. The nurse jumped back in horror.

Turning, she flung the emergency room doors open, but stopped short of entering. A dozen bodies stood deathly still, hungrily staring at her; glazed pale expressions on their gaunt faces, her face reflecting back in their hollow black eyes. Thirteen paced in the midst of them, his arms crossed, his mask grinning wickedly. The nurse screamed; her face twisted in pain, her arm burning. She strained against her tears, trying to clear her vision as she looked down. Swollen teeth marks cut deep into her skin. Standing next to her was the nurse, her best friend, a vacant stare, red blood dripping from the corners of her pale mouth. All she could do was cry as she slumped to the floor, a surge of heat coursing through her body.

\*\*\*\*\*\*\*\*\*\*\*\*

Ashley cautiously opened the door to her apartment. She'd fallen asleep on the couch and someone's knocking had woken her.

"Kayla," she yawned, stretching, her colorfully striped bathrobe hanging open, hardly hiding a pair of very short flannel boxers and a well-worn baggy Penn State t-shirt, "what's up?"

"Get dressed, we're going to see Joseph."

"Okay," Ashley said, bounding excitedly for her bedroom.

Kayla walked around the small apartment. She recognized most of the furniture: their grandmother's old sofa, her parents' plaid armchair, and other hand-me-down decorations. She smiled, recalling the memories attached to each item, some trivial, mostly sentimental.

Picking up her sister's sketch pad, Kayla leafed through the pages. She'd always admired Ashley's creativity. The pictures were so tranquil, fantastic, an escape from the doldrums of this life. Kayla paused on the sketch that Ashley had just finished. The black eyes were piercing; the toothy grin and serpentine nostrils gave her chills. It was nothing like the others.

"What's this you drew?" she asked.

"What's what?" Ashley asked popping out of the bedroom as she pulled a green polo shirt down over her head and buttoned up her cargo khakis.

Kayla held up the sketch book, the evil face glaring at Ashley, "this."

"Oh," Ashley said, sitting down on the couch to tie her tennis shoes, "I can't get that out of my head. I see it when I close my eyes. Sometimes, when it's dark, I feel like I can almost see it in the shadows, like it's some sort of monster."

"Well, I'm taking it with us. We'll see what Joseph has to say about it. Come on."

\*\*\*\*\*\*\*\*\*\*\*\*

168

Jamie stood in the lobby of the Tri-Corp building as the receptionist called up to Triton's office, awaiting a reply to his availability. Placing her phone on its receiver, she looked up at him with a flirtatious grin.

"Dr. Triton will see you now, Detective," she said smiling, the elevator doors behind her quietly opening as if on cue.

Stepping into the elevator, he gathered his composure, trying to forget that he had no idea what he was going to say, as the doors closed and the elevator began its ascent. With a smirk, he listened to the ridiculous music softly playing in the background as each level passed. The long ride was nerve-racking: it went on forever. All Jamie wanted to do was get in there, poke around, and get out.

*Kayla was right, with no warrant I have no business here. This is stupid, so stupid.*

The elevator finally stopped on the one hundred and thirteenth floor. Two large men in black suits silently greeted him with brawny nods, then led him to the double frosted-glass doors of Triton's office. Confidently, Jamie nodded back, putting on his best business face. The doors opened into a small room with another set of identical glass doors. Two Italian leather chairs sat opposite each other in the small space. Small plantings decorated the off-white walls of the little room.

"Sit," one of the men commanded Jamie, the other walking through the next doorway.

*What am I, a dog?*

The man stood looming over him, a stone expression on his face. After a moment, the other man returned.

"This way," he said, holding the door open.

"Thank you."

The office was amazing. Jamie had been in nice places, was used to really expensive things, but this was beyond imagination. The outer wall was nothing but one large window. An enormous glass desk sat near the windows straight ahead, a high-backed leather chair faced the cityscape. A mish-mash collection of globe-spanning artifacts filled the rest of the space, some ancient, some modern, almost artistic, yet intricately mechanical. A long series of bookshelves stretched across the far wall, wrapped around the corner, then turned into a beautiful wooden curio filled with various oddities and curiosities. He wished he had more time to simply look around: this wasn't an office, it was a museum.

Jamie's dress shoes clicked against the marble floor as he slowly approached the desk. The two men walked closely behind him, one on either side.

"What can I do for you today, Detective?" a deep voice called out from behind the desk.

Jamie paused, choosing his words carefully, *here goes nothing!*

"I was wondering if you could give me a few moments of your very valuable time."

"Anything for New York's finest," Triton said, spinning around in his chair, then standing to face Jamie with an outstretched arm.

Jamie shook his hand and took the seat that was offered to him. Triton, though intimidating, seemed cordial as he returned to his fine, leather chair.

*Maybe this won't be so bad.*

"Please, Detective, go ahead."

Jamie suddenly felt uncomfortable, something he wasn't accustomed to; and worse, Triton's guards still hovered over each shoulder. He'd started out strong. Now wasn't the time to back down.

"I have some questions about an old, run down apartment building in Harlem, a property you own, if I'm not mistaken."

"I'm sorry, Detective, but I own many buildings in this city," Triton smiled, "Could you be more specific?"

The smile on Triton's face was sickening, fake. It did nothing but aggravate Jamie.

"The only building you own that has been involved in a mass murder, I'm sure," Jamie replied coyly.

"Oh," Triton chuckled, "*that* building."

The guards echoed Triton's laugh. Jamie could feel their eyes boring into his back.

"It seems one of the victims was employed by Tri-Corp."

"That's interesting," Triton stated calmly, his hands resting on his desk. "But once again, you'll need to be more specific; I employee many hard working Americans."

"Michael Hampton."

"I've never heard of him."

*Yeah right.*

Triton was polite to the point of frustration and he had the home court advantage, but he still had to have a weakness. Jamie decided to try a different angle.

"Fair enough. Can you account for the explosion that took place there two nights ago? I spoke with your building superintendent he said you were planning on demolishing the building. That would be a rather unorthodox, but effective way to take care of the building, not to mention destroying a crime scene linked to you."

"The property was a danger, Detective, very unsafe, and the explosion would seem to prove my point," Triton reasoned, a slight wince in one eye. "Besides, it had already been condemned before I purchased it."

"I suppose. But just imagine all those shiny new apartments that could be built in its place, in fact, why not demolish the entire neighborhood while you're at it. Just think of the rent that would come rolling in, not to mention your name across every news headline for such a great act of civic restoration," Jamie smiled, digging in deep.

*Bingo.* Triton sat up stiffly, the vertebrae in his neck cracking as he twisted his head to one side.

"Like I said, the building was already condemned when I acquired it. And, as a matter of fact, we were planning on having it demolished to break ground on a new complex as early as this coming November. But that hardly has anything to do with what you're implying, Detective."

Jamie thought he had him, but Triton recovered quickly.

*This guy knows how to play.*

"It is a shame though, the way the bodies were found," Triton said, an odd expression filling his face, his brows raised. "I find it quite interesting, actually."

"I'm not following what you mean, Doctor," Jamie questioned. "The crime scene photos were never released to the public. How could you know what we found?"

Triton's demeanor changed, as if another man took his place in his chair.

"You have your sources, I have mine. Come now, Detective. Do you honestly think that I wouldn't have access to that kind of information? I own half this city and the other half will be mine soon enough," Triton blustered arrogantly, his lips curling into a sneer.

"I know why you're here, Detective. I knew before you walked through the lobby doors this morning. I saw you before you even woke," he bragged, raising a hand and pointing out the window.

"Take a look outside, Detective Branson," Triton said, standing and gesturing for Jamie to follow.

Jamie stood and cautiously stepped towards the window.

"What are we looking at, Doctor?"

"We're looking at a world of lies, a city crawling with filth and decay. You do your best to clean it up, but when you arrest one drug dealer, three more take his place. I buy property and I make it new. We are very much alike, Detective. We want the same thing."

"And what is that?" Jamie asked, sarcasm echoing in his voice.

"Peace," Triton answered, a faint smile on his face.

"Peace?"

"Yes," Triton said, leaning forward, resting his hands against the window frames, "but we will never have peace, not with so many who disregard the future."

"And what is the future?"

"The future is what we make of it, Detective. What *I* make of it."

"What about George Bisson?" Jamie pushed, maybe too hard. "Did you decide his future as well?"

Triton, his face burning red with anger, turned to face him. Jamie immediately felt regret for every stupid thing he'd ever done, like walking into Triton's office that day. Then, without a word, Triton returned his gaze to the window, the definition of calm and cool.

"For my part."

"I think I've heard enough," Jamie said as he turned towards the door. "Thanks for your time, Sir."

The two large men stepped together, blocking Jamie's path. Jamie watched as the glass doors disappeared between their wide shoulders.

"This is my empire, my Rome, Detective," Triton boasted as he looked out across the bustling city below, ignoring Jamie's attempt to close their conversation.

Jamie didn't know what to do. He was stuck.

"Now, gentlemen, if you please, he seems to know too much."

*Uh oh...*

The guards grabbed Jamie by his arms. Triton looked on, a fiery excitement in his eyes.

"Your questions are too pointed, Detective Branson. I can't have you continuing your investigation. We will deal with your partner: *the* woman. *Her* fate will be the same as yours. Take him downstairs," Triton ordered, sitting back down at his desk and straightening his tie as he watched them drag the struggling detective out of the room.

"What about your book," Jamie shouted, "'The Fall of Man'?!"

"Stop!" Triton commanded, surprise in his voice, his interest peaked. "What about my book?"

The men loosened their grip. Jamie straightened himself up, his disheveled hair matching his now wrinkled clothes.

"What's your book about? Is it about peace?"

Triton thought, then replied, "My book is about the destruction of peace, something I have studied my whole life. You see, Detective, you could say I know firsthand how mankind fell, what has led us to this point, a world full of sin and hate. I stole compassion away, and I can do it again. Everything that happens, happens for a reason. Now, my friend, you must figure out what that reason is. Take him."

The guards forced Jamie into the elevator. He couldn't get away.

\*\*\*\*\*\*\*\*\*\*\*\*

"Gracious, what are you doing here child?" Joseph wondered, the door to his study creaking open. "How's your investigation going?"

Kayla stared at him nervously. Ashley mustered a smile.

"Well, come in, come in."

\*\*\*\*\*\*\*\*\*\*\*\*

"So, what can I do for you guys?" O 'Donnell asked.

"Well we actually came down to see what kind of progress you've made in your investigation, Captain," Dimitri grinned.

"If any," Jones added under his breath.

O'Donnell didn't seem to notice.

"Sure I have," he laughed, lighting another cigarette. "I've got the best detectives in the city working on this case."

Dimitri and Jones looked at each other through their dark tinted glasses.

"So what about those puncture wounds on the victims?" O'Donnell continued, holding out his pack of cigarettes, offering the men a smoke.

"They are of no consequence" Jones explained aloofly, ignoring the Captain's gesture.

"They look like frickin' bite marks!" he argued.

"A coincidence, I assure you," Dimitri countered.

"Well I'll be!" O'Donnell shrugged as he leaned back in his chair. "And how'd you boys figure that one out?"

"We spent some time at the hospital, asked around," Dimitri said. "We *know* some people there."

O'Donnell had to keep from laughing, "You *know* some people there? Well, I'll have *my* people call *your* people and we can discuss this another time."

He stood to walk them to the door. Maybe he had caught Jones' sarcasm.

"That won't be necessary," Dimitri grimaced, removing his glasses, his eyes glowing white. "You're investigation is over."

************

*Thud!*

Jamie's body hit the floor. The men stood over him, kicking him repeatedly, mercilessly. He was their personal punching bag. The elevator dinged with each passing level. Jamie could no longer hear the music over the sound of the men yelling at him to get up, to fight back.

As the doors popped open, Jamie was thrown into the hall, striking his head where the wall met the floor. Bracing himself, trying to climb to his feet, he could feel the sticky blood running from his battered forehead.

Looking up, anticipating the next swing, he watched as the guards stepped from the elevator, their gloved hands reaching inside their inner jacket pockets. Jamie cowered slightly, a hand raised shakily to protect his face, not sure what they were going to do, thinking they might be reaching for guns. Slowly, each man pulled out something black, cloth-like and tightly wrapped, then unfolded them and pulled them down over their heads. They were masks, black masks, the mouths stitched closed. Their white eyes seemed to float in the darkness of the empty hallway. One of the men reached down and grabbed Jamie by his hair, pulling him sharply to his feet as the other man hit Jamie once again, a hard shot to the stomach, doubling him over.

"Clean yourself up," the man mocked from beneath his mask, handing Jamie a handkerchief as he raised him back up to look him in the face. "You look horrible."

The threats Jamie wanted to make wouldn't come out as the metallic taste of blood in his mouth brought him back to reality. All he could do was cling to the handkerchief as they drug him down the hall and threw him into a small dark room.

*This is it, I'm dead.*

A dim light bulb flickered, dangling from a cobweb covered cord that disappeared into the ceiling. The men stepped into the room behind him. Jamie hobbled around to the far side of an old wooden table that stood in the middle of the four cracked, dirty cinder block walls, trying to put as much space between himself and them. With his makeshift bandage in hand, he remembered his gun. Reaching under his jacket, searching in his holster, he found nothing. A clicking sound echoed in the room. Jamie looked up, his gun barrel staring back at him.

"It's right here," his attacker said smugly. "Have a seat and get comfortable. You'll be here a while. Better hope your partner makes the right choice."

"Kayla!" Jamie yelled. "Leave her alone!"

No one was there to hear him. The men had gone, locking the door from the outside. Looking through the small, dirty window in the door, Jamie could barely make out the shadow of one of them standing close by.

He was alone. He couldn't remember the last time he prayed or even if he knew how, but silently, he whispered words hoping that Kayla would be safe.

************

*I wonder how Jamie is getting along*, Kayla thought as she paced back and forth in Joseph's study. *Questioning Triton was a bad idea.*

Joseph sat in the corner, his eyes closed tightly. Ashley looked uncomfortable: between her dreams and the constant feeling of being watched, she had every good reason to fidget.

"Do you think he's praying or asleep?" Ashley joked, pulling a stick of gum from her pocket, trying to ease the tension in the small stone-walled study.

"We should all be praying," Kayla said seriously.

"When did you get so religious?" Ashley teased, tossing the crinkled wrapper over her shoulder.

"I don't know," she answered, replaying the last couple of days in her head. "I guess it's got a lot to do with everything that's going on."

"I know what you mean," Ashley smiled. "I guess I'm sort of fighting it."

"Don't," Kayla said reaching over and grabbing her sister's hand.

Joseph sat up, definitely awake. The girls jumped as he raised his hands high over his head.

"Something terrible has happened, something I haven't foreseen."

"What?! What is it?" Kayla said her hands shaking.

"A young woman, in pain." Joseph cried, looking down at Ashley's drawing. "Darkness, real darkness, has come."

# X

## MONDAY AFTERNOON

Kayla's car streaked across the empty two-lane highway leading back to the city. Neither of them knew quite what to say. Joseph's words: *real darkness has come*, kept replaying in Kayla's head. She tried to drown it out. Ashley stared out the window, at times acting as if she had something to say, the words never passing her lips. Silently, they sat, listening to the hard rock music that pulsed from the speakers.

"Is this your CD?" Ashley mused, turning it up, her countenance brightening as a new song began to play.

"No. Jamie left it in my car. I put it in my disc-changer, but haven't remembered to give it back."

"I like it! What's the name of the band?"

"I don't even know, but the music reminds me of Jamie, so I've sort of been listening to it over and over, and..."

"Obsess much?" Ashley laughed, then trailed off, her thoughts returning to whatever it was that was eating away at her.

She felt so uncomfortable. Something inside her tugged at her heart, whispered in her head. She needed to say something, get it off her chest.

"I haven't been able to find a good time to tell you, but I guess now is better than ever," Ashley said reluctantly, flipping off the CD player. "I had another dream."

"Really," Kayla said attempting to sound calm, though her knuckles whitened as she wrung the steering wheel. "Any idea what Triton's going to do next, is it about Joseph's young woman?"

"No, not the girl, Kayla. He, I mean Triton, already *did* something," Ashley said, staring out the window once more, avoiding eye contact. "He has Jamie. I'm sure of it."

Kayla focused intently on the road ahead, gripping the wheel even tighter as Ashley's words sunk in. She felt her heart beat as it pounded in her ears.

*I knew he shouldn't have gone down there. I just knew something like this would happen!*

The sisters remained in awkward silence, Kayla wrestling with her emotions, Ashley not giving in to her own. The car cruised along steadily, the wheels thumping over cracks in the weather-worn paved road.

"Tell me what happened, tell me what you saw?" Kayla finally managed to ask, her face growing pale.

"Well, I had the dream Saturday afternoon when I was at your place. I fell asleep at the computer, then you called me and I came and met Joseph. I completely forgot till today, with everything going on, I guess it just slipped my mind."

"That's crazy! How could that slip your mind? Why didn't you tell me sooner?"

"Since I remembered, I've wanted to, but you had the dream as well, and I know how much he means to you. I was afraid you would worry too much about Jamie and lose focus. Plus, I dreamt it after you, and I thought maybe it was influenced by yours, you know?"

"Well, I still wish you would have told me," Kayla said sadly. "I would never have let him go crusading off this morning."

"I know," Ashley said, carefully choosing her words. "I saw a man in a black mask in my dream, he was holding Jamie hostage. And, when Joseph and I were alone, that first time I met him, he told me he had the same dream as well: three different people, all the same dream."

"Why is this happening?" Kayla gave in. "I thought dreams were just dreams, imagination, random thoughts, nerves firing blankly as we sleep. Why are they coming true?"

"I don't know the answer, I'm not even sure Joseph does, but after all this," Ashley reasoned, "I don't think I'll ever believe a dream is *just* a dream. I'm sorry, Kayla, but I know Jamie's in trouble."

Turning back to the window, Ashley glanced in the passenger-side mirror: two shiny black sedans were quickly approaching, weaving back and forth across the double yellow line. They moved fluidly, in perfect sync.

"We may be in trouble too!"

"I see them, hold on."

Kayla pressed the pedal to the floor, the engine roaring as they raced ahead. But the black sedans kept up effortlessly. She looked in her rear-view mirror, trying to catch a glimpse of the drivers, but the windows were tinted too darkly. All she saw were the emblems on the cars' hoods: Mercedes Benz.

"I don't think they're headed for the country club," Ashley moaned.

Every bend brought them closer to the city. Car horns blared as Kayla wove through the lanes of growing traffic, back and forth over the double yellow lines that ran down the center of the crumbling asphalt.

"Someone's going to get killed!" Ashley exclaimed, anxiously peering around her headrest.

"Just pray it's not us!" Kayla replied as she swerved out of the way of an oncoming eighteen wheeler, avoiding what was nearly a devastating head on collision.

Kayla tried to out-maneuver their pursuers as the chase wound through the twisty roads, dodging in and out of traffic, trees flitting past, green blurs in the corners of their eyes. Ashley turned the CD player back on. She needed a distraction. Loud music filled the cabin of the car.

No matter what Kayla tried, the black sedans still sat on her tail. She came up on a slow moving pick-up and followed it into a blind turn. As Kayla drifted left of center, anticipating the pass, she spotted another car coming head on. Kayla hit the throttle and jumped back into the right lane, nearly clipping the front bumper of the old truck. The black sedans followed, pushing the oncoming car off the road, sending it disappearing into a sideways skid of dust and tire smoke. Ashley stared frantically ahead. The road curved sharply back to the left. A silver guard rail was all that stood between them and the deep valley beyond.

"Are you going to be able to make that turn?"

Kayla glanced down at her speedometer: 85mph. She was going too fast. Hitting the brakes, turning the wheel hard, she tried to slide through the turn, but the rear tires caught gravel on the side of the road and her car spun wildly, finally coming to a stop in a cloud of dust, her rear bumper just inches from the steel guard rail.

The two Mercedes pulled up next to her, one aimed at the side, the other at the front of Kayla's car, blocking any hope of escape. Three men stepped from each car, all in matching black suits, masks covering their faces. Only the whites of their eyes could be seen, the holes where the mouths would have been were stitched closed. In their hands, they carried handguns, .45 calibers by the look of them, all with long silver barrels, the cold metal flashing in the pale fall sunlight. Slowly, the men approached the car, gravel crunching beneath their patent leather shoes.

"Stay put," Kayla ordered, cautiously opening her door and stepping out.

"Uh huh," Ashley mumbled, her wide eyes fixed on the men.

Kayla slipped her hand to her side and flipped the safety off on the gun holstered on her belt. She didn't want to make a sudden move and set these guys off.

"Please, Ms. Rose," one of the men spoke, his voice commanding yet calm as he stepped ahead of the others, "that is far enough."

Kayla froze, her hand still under her jacket, ready to pull the gun.

"What do you want from me?"

"We want you to stop your investigation," the apparent leader of the men grunted, his head cocked arrogantly to one side.

"I can't do that," she said defiantly, the wind blowing her blonde hair across her shoulders.

"Then your partner will die."

"I don't believe you!"

Reaching inside his suit coat, his head finally rising to a normal position, he pulled something small from his pocket and tossed it onto the ground at her feet. Kayla bent down and picked it up. She didn't want to take her eyes off of them. Flipping it open as she stood, Kayla recognized it instantly: Jamie's wallet, his badge inside. Blood was dried on the leather.

"He's a cop!" she threatened. "You can't kill a cop! The entire New York City police department will come after you, *and* Triton!"

The confidence in her voice was questionable. The men could tell.

"Do you honestly think the police are of any concern to us?" he laughed. "If you want your partner to live, then you will make a statement calling your investigation a mass ritual suicide and claim the cult leader was also one of the victims: Michael Hampton."

"I'm *sure* you *know* the name," another man added sarcastically.

"Report Hampton committed suicide with his followers. You will make no mention of Triton," the man continued, his jaw flinching beneath his black mask, "or us. As soon as you do what we ask, your partner will be released, slightly...*used*."

"Triton is evil! I can't let him continue what he's doing!" Kayla said, pulling her gun from its holster and aiming at the man standing in the forefront.

In unison, the six men raised their guns, their sights fixed on Kayla, the hammers clicking into place. After a moment, she lowered her arm.

"You have a choice to make, Ms. Rose," the leader asked patiently. "What will it be?"

Kayla stared at them blankly. Her head was spinning. She couldn't take on these men alone. Joseph was right: this was Triton's army. If only Jamie were there. He would know just what to do. She glanced back at her car. Ashley sat in fear, stunned, watching every move the gunmen made. Kayla turned and looked again at the black masks grinning back at her, she couldn't think straight. The hair on her neck stood on end.

"Ms. Rose?" he asked again, wanting an answer.

Kayla stood firm, her eyes closed, asking an unfamiliar God for help. Gunfire rang out across the valley below. Birds scattered from the surrounding trees. Echoes rumbled in the distance. Then, *silence*.

************

Jamie sat alone under the dim, flickering bulb that hung above him, an eerie glow casting shadows about the room. Even in these circumstances, at the mercy of a madman, he worried for Kayla, hoped she would be alright. Slowly, he wiped the blood from his brow; his shirt collar stained a deep red. He tried to clear his head. He had to find a way out.

He scanned the walls, his eyes jumping from side to side as he searched for a sign of escape.

*Nothing.*

Jamie turned and glared over his shoulder: a shadow black as night loomed in the corner. A faint scratching noise startled him. He felt as if something was staring at him. Then, he heard the sound again, louder this time. But, as he squinted into the darkness, he couldn't see a thing. It was like that corner was sucking up the light and warmth in the room.

A lump grew in his throat. Memories of his past began to flash through his head. Jamie closed his eyes and tried to force the images away, but all he could see was glimpses of himself as a boy, his mother lying dead in his arms.

He reached into his pant's pocket and pulled out a small silver box.

Pausing for a moment, Jamie looked at it sadly, his eyes glazing as he traced his index finger across a set of initials engraved on the antique lid: *I.L.B.* Flipping it open, he dumped two oval white pills into the palm of his hand and popped them into his mouth, then tilted his head back and swallowed. In agony, he leaned forward, resting his pounding head on his arms, waiting for the pain to go away.

************

Kayla was still shaking as she sat down in the driver's seat of her car and tossed Jamie's bloody wallet on the center console. Ashley stared blankly at the dash.

"What just happened?" she asked in a stupor.

Kayla closed her eyes and took a long, deep breath, "It was just a warning."

"I thought we were dead."

"Me too," Kayla replied, her hands beginning to steady. "But if they wanted us dead, we would be."

"Is that really Jamie's wallet?"

"It looks like it, that's his badge number. If it's not real, it's a lot of work just to make a fake," Kayla reasoned, pulling her cell phone from her purse and dialing Jamie.

His voicemail answered, but she didn't bother with a message. She hung the phone up and dropped it back in her purse.

Standing back up, Kayla surveyed the damage to her car. The left rear tire was flat, the car now resting on the rim.

"They shot out the tire," Kayla moaned.

"So we couldn't follow?"

"Yeah, they wanted to slow us down," Kayla said, leaning back through the door frame. "Ever changed a flat?"

"Yeah," Ashley answered, waking from her daze as she got up to help.

The two began the tedious task of jacking up the car to remove the tire. Kayla pulled the spare from the trunk and leaned it against the bumper. Ashley went to work with the tire iron. As she finished loosening the lug nuts, she handed them to Kayla, who dropped them into her jacket pocket for safe keeping. Finally, they placed the spare on the wheel hub.

"Ready for a lug, Ash?" Kayla offered, reaching into her pocket.

"Yeah."

Kayla pulled the lug nuts from her pocket with a quizzical look. A piece of paper lay in her palm, nestled amongst the silver nuts.

"What's that?" Ashley asked, setting down the tire iron and taking the paper from Kayla's hand.

"I don't know?"

Ashley unfolded the scrap, finding a name scribbled on the faded parchment, a phone number written just below it.

"What's it say?"

"A name, *Gavin*," Ashley smiled curiously. "You know him?"

"No," Kayla laughed in admission.

"There's a number too."

Kayla took a look and reached back in the car, retrieving her cell phone, then dialing the number, "It's ringing!"

"Hello?" a tired sounding male voice answered.

"Um, hi," Kayla said hesitantly, "is this Gavin?"

"Yeah," he yawned.

"Sorry, did I wake you?" Kayla asked curiously.

"Yep, so this better be good."

Kayla rolled her eyes and covered the phone with her hand, "He says he was sleeping, who sleeps at five in the afternoon?"

Ashley shrugged, "Maybe he works nights?"

"Okay, here's the deal," Kayla explained, turning her attention back to the phone, "You'll never believe this, but here goes. I'm not sure how I got your number. I found it in my pocket and, well, I felt like I should call you."

"That's the worst pickup line I've ever heard," he chuckled. "That wasn't even worth me getting out of bed."

Kayla wasn't in the mood for this guy. She'd been chased, shot at, and now laughed at.

"Sorry I called," she said, readying to hang up the phone.

"No, wait!" the voice urged apologetically. "Hold on, you're Kayla, right?"

She froze. Ashley stood in the background, silently mouthing exaggerated words, wondering what was going on. Kayla did her best to ignore her.

"How do you know my name?"

"Joseph: he told me to expect your call."

Kayla slumped into her driver's seat, confused, trying to figure things out.

"Are you a friend of his?"

"Something like that," the voice replied. "I take it you've already spoken with Joseph?"

All she could do was listen.

"You could say he's my mentor. I've been learning his, um...trade. Meet me at the address on the note. It's a warehouse, in the old docks district, West Side."

"What address?"

"Look."

Kayla raised the slip of paper and nearly dropped it. An address was now scrolled boldly across the bottom of the note.

"Oh," she stammered, staring at the writing that was just a blank spot on the paper a moment ago, noticing that that the new penmanship was different than what must have been Joseph's.

"*So* how do I know I can trust you?" she asked.

"You can't."

The phone went silent. Ashley had just finished tightening the last of the lug nuts and lowered the jack. Kayla set the flat in the trunk and closed the lid.

"Things just keep getting stranger," she said, shaking her head as they got into the car.

\*\*\*\*\*\*\*\*\*\*\*\*

Jamie stood from the rotting, old wooden chair and paced in the small, cell like room. The bandage wrapped around his head was dry and sticking to his brow. Carefully, he picked at a spot of dried blood on his temple.

As he wandered aimlessly back and forth between the grimy walls, voices echoed in his head. It was maddening, alone in this hell, wondering if he'd ever see the woman he loved again.

\*\*\*\*\*\*\*\*\*\*\*\*

Kayla's car squealed to a stop in front of an age-worn warehouse. She looked down at the address on the paper, then back at the rundown steel-walled building.

"Is this the place?" Ashley wondered, staring apprehensively at the rusting front door.

"I guess," Kayla replied, pulling her gun out of its holster as she stepped from the car. "Stay close."

Kayla peered into the dark warehouse through a small window in the door. Ashley leaned against the wall next to her.

"Can you see anything?"

"Nope," Kayla said, shaking her head as she turned the knob.

She felt the lock click out of place as she pushed, the rusty door creaking open. Raising her gun, stepping carefully into the large room, she searched for any sign of life.

"Maybe that guy on the phone was one of the gunmen," Kayla whispered. "Maybe this is a trap."

Once inside, the girls were surprised by what they found. Two clashing-patterned couches made an L in the middle of the concrete floor, an armchair, stuffing protruding from its back, sat on the opposite corner. An ancient-looking console television stood to the right of the decomposing chair and a few small wooden crates made due for a coffee table. An oil-stained oriental rug was placed underneath it all, tying it all together.

The right side of the room was made up of a small dirty kitchen, a loft above it filled with cardboard boxes. Just beyond that, a small room caged in with chain link fencing could be seen, from there, a door which led who knows where.

On the opposite side, a flight of metal stairs led to an elevated area surrounded by a darkly painted metal railing. Kayla could just make out a set of doors. One had a faded restroom sign hung crookedly on it, the other led to a room with four large plate-glass windows that lined the walls, all with dusty, cream colored retractable blinds hanging in them. A small placard on the door marked it as an office. An aging rusty, black conversion van sat at the far end of the room, just in front of a large automatic garage door. Heavy chains hung from pulleys above. Small windows lined the room all the way up where the walls met the ceiling. Deep gouges in the cracked cement floor showed were machines must have been placed at one time. It was odd, but it seemed like someone had actually made this their home.

A rustling came from the office up the stairs as a shadow moved across one of the windows. And then, the door popped open as a man emerged, straightening the black hooded sweatshirt that hung loosely over his tall, athletic frame.

Kayla trained her gun on him, "Stop right there!"

"Whoa, take it easy!" he said, his hands in the air. "I'm Gavin, we talked on the phone?"

The two girls didn't take their eyes off him as he made his way down the stairs. Cautiously, Gavin headed towards them, his right hand outstretched in a friendly greeting, his left still raised above his head. Kayla didn't move, her gun still fixed between him and them.

"Why are we here?"

"This is where I live," he laughed, noticing their disapproving expressions. "You're safe here, I promise."

"Fine, but that doesn't answer why we're here?" Kayla argued.

He stood in front of them, his hand still offered in welcome. Kayla lowered her gun reluctantly, finally shaking his rough hand. Gavin smiled and then nodded at Ashley before turning excitedly towards the fenced-in room near the back of his makeshift home.

"I want to show you something," he said, a mischievous look on his face, a scruffy, shortly trimmed beard covering his cheeks and chin.

The girls followed apprehensively as Gavin disappeared into the shadows of the room. Despite his rough appearance, there was something about him that was comforting, something that reminded them of Joseph.

Kayla's jaw dropped as she stepped through the door, finding herself standing in the middle of an arsenal that would have made a military black ops unit proud. A collection of guns hung from the pegboard covered walls, dozens of them, perfectly organized, each in its place. The wall straight ahead was filled with submachine guns and Uzis as well as a broad selection of handguns of all calibers. Another door led through that wall and into a long sound-proofed room Gavin used as a firing range. The right wall housed various rifles and shotguns. To their left, the final wall was encased in shelves stacked high with grenades and odd-looking bomb-like devices as well as Kevlar vests and tactical knives. That wall was capped off by a steel cabinet in the far left corner, packed with ammo cans, boxes of rounds, and magazines, all preloaded and ready. A table stood in the center of the room. Its top was covered in old books like the ones in Joseph's office, an old map of New York City's subway system hidden underneath the dusty clutter.

"Do you have a permit for all this?" Kayla joked; her voice mingled with disbelief as she peered down at the targets at the end of the long gun range.

He just smiled as he sorted through the books, searching for one in particular. Ashley walked around the room. Kayla seemed to be relaxing.

"This is amazing," Ashley mused, "I've never seen anything like this before. It's like something in a movie!"

"Don't touch anything," Kayla warned, as if the whole room was crawling with disease.

Ashley smiled and continued exploring. Coming from a family of cops, she'd been around guns before, was comfortable around them, but this was extraordinary.

Gavin found the book he was looking for and flipped it open to a dog-eared page, an engraving of a man leaning against a stone fireplace, crossbow in hand, the picture inset among the seemingly hand-written words. He handed it to Kayla excitedly, then slipped his hands into his pockets, a grin of anticipation across his face.

"Look familiar?" he asked.

"It looks just like, just like...Joseph," she observed, "but much younger!"

"That's because it *is* Joseph," he smirked, closing the book, then flipping it over to show Kayla the hand etched date on the back of the book, *1492*.

"I can help you," he said, pulling a pair of stools out from under the tall table. "Joseph has trained me to *deal* with these guys."

"*Deal?*" Kayla wondered.

"Fight," Gavin restated. "But there's more to them. They aren't completely human: they have powers, demonic powers. I've been watching them, studying them. I think it has something to do with their masks."

"Their masks?" Kayla laughed.

"Well, it's something that me and some of the others have discussed, at least had discussed when there were more of us," he said scratching his beard.

"There are more like you?" Ashley asked, leaning next to him on the table.

"Well, not *just* like me," Gavin smiled. "The guys in the masks are no joke, and the demons that walk with them are pretty serious too. It takes strong faith to go up against them and come out on top. I'm what Joseph calls a Hunter. There are others, in other cities, trained by mentors just as I was trained by Joseph. But I've never met them. As for the men in the masks, they've always kept to the shadows, now something has changed. They're growing bolder."

"So are you an assassin?" Kayla wondered, trying to make sense of his story.

"Well," Gavin though a moment, "yes, and no. I guess you could say that I'm an assassin in the sense that I hunt and kill targets, but not human targets, understand? You must separate the physical from the spiritual."

"What makes you think you can help us? I just want Jamie back, I just want...Jamie," she said, trailing off into a sad whisper.

"That's it though, see? His kidnapping, you meeting Joseph, your entire investigation: they're all missing pieces to the big picture. I don't know what God has planned, but we have come together for a purpose, a singular, unified purpose."

"And that is?" Ashley questioned.

"I don't know," Gavin admitted, "I don't know."

Kayla and Ashley stared at him with doubt. The three stood for a moment in silence.

"Okay, well, I've been a terrible host. Let me get you ladies something to drink. I'll let the two of you talk," Gavin said with a wink, rubbing his hand across his shortly buzzed hair and smiling at Ashley as he headed for the kitchen.

"What do you think of this guy?" Kayla asked.

"I think he's cute," Ashley gushed, taking a handgun down off the wall and sitting on the stool next to Kayla.

"I mean do you think we can trust him?"

Ashley nodded her head, "I have a good feeling about him."

Gavin walked back in, precariously holding three cans of Diet Coke. Handing one to Kayla and tossing the second to Ashley, he popped the top on the third and took a long drink. Kayla continued to look through the books on the desk, sipping on her soda.

*A good feeling indeed*, Ashley thought, watching Gavin as he moved about the room.

"So, are you from New York?" Ashley asked him as she raised her pop can to her lips.

Kayla gave her a glare, then went back to her books.

"I was born in Ohio," he said, "Cleveland actually. I never knew my parents. I grew up in a foster home. They changed my diapers, fed me, took me to school, church. They were my real mom and dad. Finally, they adopted me. After that, we moved to a much smaller city in Ohio called Massillon. I was almost too young to remember."

"Do you ever see them?"

"Not really," he said sadly. "I know they love me, but they don't completely agree with my, *career.*"

"What career is that?" Kayla asked, eyeing the guns on the wall, "I still don't think I completely understand what it is you do."

"It's a long story: it started when I was young. I really don't think it matters," he said, finishing his pop, crunching the can in his fist, "you just need to trust me."

"I want to hear it," Ashley smiled.

Gavin liked her. It had been a while since he'd seen a pretty face. He never really had the time, or at least allowed the time.

"Well," he thought a moment, leaning against the metal shelving, "when I was about five, I began having dreams and nightmares: horrible monsters lurking in the shadows, waiting for me to wake. It really scared my mom. Then, I started seeing them in broad daylight. A shadow would move, or I'd catch something out of the corner of my eye. I'd even seen them in the church where my family attended. Finally, one night, when I was about fifteen, I was praying before bed. I'd just finished reading Ephesians 6, the Armor of God, and I saw an angel. It told me that I was set apart for something, *special*, when the time was right.

My parents were really concerned. My dad was afraid I'd imagined it, but my mom believed me. She talked to some friends at church and that's when the name Joseph was mentioned. He was a specialist on angels and demons, as well as dreams and visions, someone told her. She took me to see him."

"Out in the woods?" Ashley asked intrigued.

"The woods? No, Jersey," he answered, confused, "we drove seven hours to a church in Sussex."

Kayla stifled a laugh.

"Anyway, Joseph told me I had a special gift, like many before me. I continued to pray, study my Bible, and see angels and demons. I could walk down the street and feel the presence of demonic spirits. I'm used to it now, but when I was younger, it was scary.

When I was eighteen, I tried college, but it wasn't for me, neither was the military: my dad's choice, not mine. After my time in the army was complete, I went back to Joseph and he began training me to fight the demons, and the *Sleepwalkers* as he calls them, men like Triton. That is how I know I can help you. We were supposed to meet. It was all in God's plan."

Ashley was enthralled. She leaned on her elbows as she listened intently. She'd never heard anyone speak so passionately about what they believed, not even in church. Maybe that's why she stopped going. This man had a fire inside him and she wanted it too.

"Anyway," he laughed wistfully, "that's my story."

He pulled his sweatshirt off over his head and tossed it onto the counter behind him.

*Wow,* Ashley thought as she looked at him now.

She wished she had her sketchbook. She studied the creases, dirty patches, and grease stains on his baggy blue jeans, the waist cinched tight with a thick black leather belt. A handgun was holstered on his right hip. His worn pant legs shrouded tattered steel-toe boots: the laces undone, hanging across the sides of the black, cracking leather. A tight white tank top was accented by rock hard, chiseled arms that were covered in tattoos, from his wrists, to his shoulders, and across his back. Around his neck hung a silver cross and a scar could be seen disappearing somewhere under the collar of his shirt, down across his collar bone.

He smiled at her as he paced the room, his arms crossed. Kayla continued studying the books intently. Ashley didn't miss a detail. She wanted to draw him. He looked like he walked right out of a comic book. He was their super hero, or so they hoped.

# MONDAY EVENING

The phone in Capt. O'Donnell's office rang and rang. Kayla sat with her cell phone pressed against her ear, her fingers tapping on the top of Gavin's table.

"Pick up, pick up," she said anxiously, eagerly waiting for O'Donnell to answer.

The line clicked. She could hear the sound of heavy breathing.

*Finally!*

"Hello? Captain?"

The breathing slowed, "No, no it's not."

Kayla didn't know what to say. Confusion flooded her mind as every possible answer as to whom it may be flashed before her eyes, but she came up blank. She'd never heard this voice before.

A man in a black suit stood at O'Donnell's desk, the phone in his hand, a very serious look on his face. Just behind him, O'Donnell struggled on the floor, his hands and feet bound, a gag in his mouth.

"Captain O'Donnell is, tied up at the moment. Can I help you?"

"Who is this?" Kayla asked.

"Special Agent Dimitri, FBI. *Who* is this?"

"This is Detective Rose," she answered, relieved to hear a good guy on the other end, "My partner has been kidnapped by Dr. Triton, Dr. Maurice Triton, and..."

"We are well aware of your partner's situation, Ms. Rose," he said, cutting her off, "but it's hard to believe that someone as fine as Dr. Triton would be involved in such a scandal. Why don't you report back to the station? Bring your sister. We can talk about, *things*."

*What?*

Kayla shot a look Ashley's way. How did an FBI agent she'd never met, never heard Jamie, or O'Donnell for that matter, mention, know anything about her sister.

"What *things* would we talk about?" she frowned, thinking carefully for a moment before she answered.

"We need to sort through the evidence and talk to all witnesses. Your sister is a *witness*. She has seen things we need to know about, hear in person. We need..."

Dimitri was interrupted by the sound of O'Donnell cursing at him from the floor. His gag hung loose around his thick neck. Slamming the phone down on the desk, he gave him a swift kick in his stomach. O'Donnell winced from the blow.

"Kill him," Dimitri ordered. "He is expendable."

Special Agent Jones nodded and grabbed O'Donnell's arms. Dimitri turned back to the phone and hung it up with his finger, gently laying the receiver on the desk, leaving it off the hook. He took off his dark sunglasses and dropped them in the trash can, then pulled a black mask from his pocket and slipped it down over his head.

\*\*\*\*\*\*\*\*\*\*\*\*

Kayla quickly redialed the number to O'Donnell's desk. It was busy.

"They've got the Captain too," she said, turning to Gavin and Ashley. "The FBI has been in on it the whole time."

"What are you talking about?" Gavin laughed. "You honestly think the Feds would be in on something like this? I know the conspiracies and rumors, but this is a bit dirty, even for them."

"He said his name was Special Agent Dimitri, FBI."

"And you believe him?"

"Shouldn't I?"

"I think this is bigger than you're thinking," Gavin smiled.

"True," Kayla answered thoughtfully, trying to separate her emotions from the situation. "He mentioned Ashley. I can't see any way the FBI would have any knowledge of her, especially hinting at things she'd *seen*.

Ashley stood up and headed for the little sitting area in Gavin's warehouse. She felt like crying, but her eyes were dry, like her tears had run out.

\*\*\*\*\*\*\*\*\*\*\*\*

Jones tightened the gag and drug Capt. O'Donnell past the rows of detectives' desks. The thudding of his large body echoed through the precinct as the agent shoved him down the stairs and then into the lobby of the station.

Taking hold of O'Donnell's arm, Jones pulled him across the cold floor and forced him into a large maintenance closet, leaving him lying there, kicking and struggling, brooms and mops clanking to the floor.

"I'll tell Detective Branson you said goodbye," Dimitri mocked.

He flipped the safety off on his pistol and watched as Jones pulled out his mask and put it on. Two shots rang out, the spent shells tinking as they bounced off the granite floor. O'Donnell lay silent. Jones closed the closet door, nodding his head at Dimitri in approval and the two of them walked away silently, their masks crinkled in satisfaction.

\*\*\*\*\*\*\*\*\*\*\*\*

"Have you ever fired one of those?" Gavin asked, watching Ashley hold the gun.

She grinned at him innocently. Kayla sat deep in thought.

"What do we do now?" she questioned. "The FBI's involved, or at least a couple of dirty agents for what it's worth. On top of that, the Captain is their hostage. Can we even trust anyone at the station? We don't even know where Triton's men have taken Jamie. Who knows how deep this goes."

"We don't need back up," Gavin laughed, taking the gun that Ashley'd been holding and sliding a magazine into the grip. "You've got me. The cops wouldn't know how to handle Triton even if they could help."

"What do you mean?" Kayla frowned.

"You still don't get it. Do you think Triton is doing all of this alone? Remember those guys that shot out your tire? They weren't Feds and I'm sure the *Dimitri* guy you talked to on the phone is a fake as well. Triton's got his own army. We have to get past them to get to him."

"A few more guns wouldn't hurt," Kayla replied.

"We don't need them," he insisted.

Gavin sounded so convinced that they could handle this on their own, Kayla was beginning to feel better about their chances, even if only a little. In silence, she prayed, still feeling they needed help. She hoped God would understand.

Opening her eyes, Kayla looked back at Gavin. He was showing Ashley how to load and unload the handgun.

"It's an HK USP," he smiled flirtatiously, "9mm. I carry one just like it every day, but it's a .45 caliber."

Ashley laughed, flipping the safety on as she set the gun down on the messy table and double checked the breach, making sure no round was chambered.

"How'd you know to do that?" he asked, impressed to say the least.

"Cop granddad, cop dad, cop brothers, cop sister...dad used to take us to the range to practice gun safety and defensive shooting."

Gavin grinned. Now he really was impressed.

"Here," he said, pulling a set of red colored shooter's earmuffs off his shelf and handing it to her, "I want to see you shoot."

Gavin grabbed another pair for himself, then took her by the hand, leading her into his shooting range. Kayla quickly snatched another pair as well and hurried in behind him. She wasn't going to let Ashley out of her sight, especially with an armed stranger.

He closed the thick, heavy door and pulled on his earmuffs. The girls followed suit. Kayla leaned against a table that stood on their right. The room was long and narrow, about fifty feet end-to-end, but only ten or so feet wide Kayla estimated. She watched as Gavin clipped a cardboard-backed paper target on an electric pulley and held down a switch on the wall till the target had traveled about twenty feet. He then unholstered his weapon smoothly, slowed his breathing, aimed, and fired twelve quick rounds into the target, the bullets punching small tightly grouped holes. He released the slide on the pistol, flipped the safety lever, and reholstered.

Kayla's eyebrows rose. He was pretty good.

"You're turn," he grinned, looking at Ashley.

Ashley stepped up to the white shooting line Gavin had painted on the concrete floor and raised the pistol. She peered down the top of the gun, lining up the front sight with the rear. She held her breath and fired a shot. It had been years since she'd been to the range with her family. The bang startled her. She missed the target completely.

"Try again," Gavin urged.

Kayla watched her sister sight up again and fire. This shot hit the paper, but not within the black rings of the target.

"That was better," Gavin said, "but try this."

Kayla sighed as she watched Gavin give Ashley a lesson in stance, grip, and body control. Maybe this guy wasn't so bad after all.

"Move your feet a little further apart," he explained, tapping her left heel with the toe of his boot.

"Okay," she said, biting her lip.

Gavin placed his hands on her hips and twisted her slightly, her right leg shifting rearward. Ashley blushed.

"Now," he said, standing close behind her, his body brushing against hers as he reached around her and straightened her arms, then placed his hands on hers, "hold the grip like this and line the sights up again, just as you did before, but this time, don't pull the trigger too quickly. Pull it back slowly and stop when you feel resistance."

"Like this?" she said, her finger slowly pulling back.

"Yeah, now, exhale and pause. Pull the rest of the way and let the trigger fall surprise you."

Ashley could feel his chest against her back. His arms were warm, his skin soft. Gavin's beard tickled her neck. She took her time, not wanting this moment to end.

The bang of the gun echoed down the range as Gavin and Kayla spotted Ashley's hit on the target. The hole was inside the outermost ring.

"Very nice," he encouraged, "try again. Line up with the bulls eye and finish the magazine.

Gavin stepped away from Ashley and headed over to the table. Kayla smiled at him as he stopped next to her. Ashley fired another fifteen shots, the slide locking open after the final round. All her bullets hit within the target's circle, several nearly marked the bull's-eye.

Ashley checked the chamber and released the slide, then turned and headed for the table, "how was that?"

"Not bad," Kayla smiled, "I'm surprised."

"Are you going to take a turn?" Gavin asked Kayla.

"No thanks," she said, shaking her head, "I'm good.'

"We'll see," Gavin winked, opening the door and leading the girls out of the range.

Kayla took their earmuffs and placed them back on the shelf. Gavin pulled out a stool at the table and quickly removed the slide on his gun. Ashley sat down next to him as he pulled the guide rod loose and slipped the barrel free. Gavin then picked up a rod with a brush on the end of it, cleaned the barrel, and reassembled the gun, then swapped the brush out for a smaller one and did the same thing to the pistol Ashley had fired.

"We didn't shoot very many rounds," Ashley observed, "do you need to clean them?"

"One round or a thousand," he said, holding the barrel up in the light so he could see the rifling, "I clean every time."

Kayla sat down on the other side of the table and began leafing through the old book Gavin had shown her earlier. Ashley watched as Gavin reassembled the gun and set it down in front of her.

"So what got you started with all the tattoos?" she asked, tracing the ink on his forearm with her finger.

Gavin leaned closer to her, the corner of his mouth raised with enthusiasm, "Every tattoo is very important to me. They all have very deep personal meanings."

He looked down at the inside of his left forearm, a detailed image of Christ. Nail wounds marked His wrists as He clutched a collapsed man in His arms. The man held long nails in one hand, an old rusty hammer in the other.

Ashley studied the rest of his tattoos. She loved the art, the symbols. His right shoulder was covered by the face of a lion, regal and strong. The left shoulder was the face of a lamb. They symbolized the duality of Christ, gentle, yet kingly. His biceps were covered in beautifully detailed clouds, angels, and sunrays. The backside of his left forearm was a cross wrapped in thorns, ivy, and roses, the backside of his right, an archangel, fierce, ready for war, its wings wrapping around, framing a piece of intricate text on the inside of his arm. An eagle with outstretched wings sprawled across his back, from shoulder to shoulder, flowing parchment clutched in its talons, *Isaiah 40:31* scrawled in a version of Old English.

"What's that writing there?" she asked, pointing at the text on his right forearm.

The lettering ran from his wrist to the inside of his elbow.

"It's Ephesians 6:12," he said, looking her in the eyes. "For our struggle is not against flesh and blood, but against the rulers, against the authorities, against the powers of this dark world and against the spiritual forces of evil in the heavenly realms."

He didn't need to read it, he knew it by heart. Ashley shivered. She'd never remembered hearing that verse in Sunday school.

"It's kind of what I've come to live by, the definition of Triton, what we're really fighting," Gavin said, putting his arm around her. "But, most people don't appreciate them. I get a *lot* of dirty looks."

"I think they're great. There's so much passion behind each one. That makes them unique."

"I can't believe you see that. You must be a very artistic person," he grinned, his arm still resting across her shoulders.

"I guess," she said humbly, "I'm in art school. I love to draw.'

"Is it your passion?"

"Yeah."

"Maybe you could draw my next tattoo for me. I'll tell you what I want and you can bring it to life."

Ashley blushed and smiled at Kayla. She couldn't help but smile back. Kayla hadn't seen her sister look this happy since they'd lived at home in Pennsylvania, but watching them brought up feelings of Jamie. She missed him. She wished he could be there as well, his arm around her too.

"So where do you think they're holding Jamie?" Kayla wondered.

Gavin cleared his throat and let go of Ashley, then stood up from the table. Confidently, he crossed his colorful arms, a wide grin stretching across his scruffy face.

"Every king has a castle."

\*\*\*\*\*\*\*\*\*\*\*\*

Joseph sat at his desk, his wrinkled hand clutching an old ink pen. He scribbled notes as fast as he could. Thunder clapped outside. He paused, listening intently, focusing on a distant noise.

The old man's thoughts returned to Kayla and Ashley. He wondered if they were ready for what laid ahead, but whether or not he thought so, he knew it wasn't for him to decide. Besides, he had sent them a helper: they were with Gavin.

Joseph turned his attention back to the papers in front of him. His nerves were not what they used to be. His hand shook as he wrote:

*I've been so careful, for so long, and now you've finally found me. But it's too late for you. You will not win this war.*

*Joseph*

Nervously, he signed his name. A black gloved hand reached over his shoulder and took the paper from the desk.

"After all these years, this is all you have to say to our master?" a voice whispered in Joseph's ear.

"Tell him it is his time to die," Joseph said, closing his eyes.

"No speech? No condemnation?" another voice spoke.

"No. Your master knows his crimes. I am not his judge, only the hand of his executioner. And I have failed. But where I have failed, another will find victory."

"You speak of your apprentice," he whispered again, "the tattooed man. He is no match for us. We have a new champion. He will protect our master. There has never been one as powerful as him."

"Your faith will falter, old man, as will your disciple," the other man growled as he straightened his suit coat, his face hidden behind his mask.

The sound of a gun hammer clicking back echoed in the small dusty room. Joseph, his eyes still closed, whispered something unintelligible, his hands clenched in prayer. The two men began to laugh.

"Where is your God now?" the man holding the gun asked mockingly.

"My God is doing what He knows is best. He will always be in control," Joseph answered confidently. "I am not scared of death because He is life."

"Then here's to life," the man toasted, his finger pulling the trigger.

A loud bang bounced through the halls of the monastery. Joseph's body slumped onto his desk, a pool of blood forming, covering his books and notes that had been scattered haphazardly around him. The men walked from the room, wiping spatters of blood from their sleeves.

"The master will be pleased," the shooter said, sliding his gun into his shoulder holster, then buttoning his jacket closed over it.

"No, he won't," the other man said cocking his head to the side, walking just beside him, the driver starting the engine as they approached the black sedan. "There is still another."

************

Kayla leaned on the table. Ashley sat just beside her, watching Gavin as he raced around the room, talking to himself, pulling a gun off the wall, shaking his head uncertainly, then placing it back. Ashley picked up the gun he gave her and began pointing it at the wall and other parts of the room, practicing her aim.

"Are you sure you want a gun?" Kayla asked her sister.

"It's an HK USP 9mm," Ashley smiled.

"*Okay.* Are you *sure* you want an *HK USP 9mm?*"

"Do you get a gun?"

"Of course, I *am* a cop," Kayla laughed.

"Then so do I, right Gavin?"

Gavin smiled boyishly, "Don't put me in the middle of this."

Kayla frowned at Gavin as Ashley smirked with a told-you-so sort of smile. Gavin was still grinning as well, but it quickly faded as he took a more serious tone.

"Ladies, we are headed down a very dangerous road. We have to be ready. What's our plan?"

"Well," Kayla thought, "we have to get into Tri-Corp, but I'm sure they'll be expecting us. So, guards will be everywhere."

"True. I've done some research," Gavin said, unrolling a set of blueprints on the messy table. "Besides guards, the Tri-Corp building also has some of the most advanced security systems I've ever seen. The ventilation ducts are protected by laser triggered surveillance that will pick up anything larger than a rat caught in the maze of shafts. On top of that, cameras cover the roof and elevators, and the only way into the parking deck is through a three-inch steel bomb-proof door."

"When did you do all this?' Kayla asked, her lips curling into an impressed smile.

"I started working on this a few weeks ago. I never would have thought we would need it this soon, but, time has proven otherwise."

"A few weeks ago?!" Kayla laughed.

"Actually, it was Joseph's idea. I told you, I've been watching them."

The three of them sat silently for a moment, studying every detail of the drafts.

"So how are we going to get in there?" Ashley questioned. "What are you thinking?"

Gavin pulled a bullet proof vest over his shoulders and his usual grin returned as he placed his finger on a spot on the blueprints.

"I'm thinking front door."

\*\*\*\*\*\*\*\*\*\*\*\*

Gavin's old, black, rust-eaten van turned down a narrow alleyway littered with garbage and overflowing trash dumpsters. Pulling to a stop, the side door slid open. Kayla stepped out and looked up at the rear of the police station. Ashley followed just behind her as Gavin climbed out from the driver's seat.

"So remind me again why we're here?" Gavin wondered with a sarcastic smile. "I thought you heard me we when I said we *didn't need back up*. We can't waste any time."

"We're not here for backup and we're definitely not wasting any time. I want to find the Captain before we head to Tri-Corp," she said, pulling an ID card from her pocket, and swiping it through the security reader, the lock on the door clicking open. "I know he would want to help us find Jamie."

Kayla peered into the dark hallway leading up the back steps. No one was around.

"We have to get up to his office. That's where Dimitri probably has him," she said, motioning them to follow.

Silently, they approached the back stairwell. Kayla took the lead, Ashley and Gavin close behind, guns drawn and ready.

Reaching the second floor, they quickly checked the surrounding rooms. Still, no one was to be found. Kayla could see O'Donnell's office from where she stood at the end of the hall. The door was wide open.

Slowly, they stepped into the main office, detectives' desks neatly lining the wide open room. It was empty as well. The smell of burnt coffee filled the air.

Reaching the door, Gavin stepped into the office, his gun in hand, scanning for any movement. No Captain, only the faint beeping sound of the phone off the hook.

Kayla headed for Jamie's desk. Pulling open the drawers, she searched for the files from their investigation, but all she found was empty folders. She flipped through the paperwork on the top of the desk as well, still nothing.

"Everything is gone," she exclaimed, "the evidence records, statements, photos; everything!"

"It looks like those FBI agents took more than just your boss," Ashley said as she picked up a framed picture of herself and Kayla.

They turned and headed for the main flight of stairs, still watching for any signs of life as they walked down to the lobby. Ashley put the picture back down on Kayla's desk and followed them to the stairwell. Cautiously, they made their way back to the first floor, finally easing into the lobby.

"This is nuts," Kayla sighed.

The normally bustling room was dead silent, no phones ringing, no yelling detainees, just the clicking of their shoes on the granite floor.

"It's like a ghost town," Ashley mused, half expecting to see tumble weed rolling by the tall glass front doors.

They circled the room. Gavin peered through the window in the door leading to the holding area. Kayla picked up a phone sitting on the main desk. The line was dead.

"Where is everybody?" Gavin asked, his gun hanging at his side.

"I don't know," Kayla said, dropping her guard as well. "This can't be good."

Ashley had been enjoying every minute of their adventure, stalking through the station, her gun aimed at every shadow, just waiting for a reason to pull the trigger. But she stopped cold in front of a door in the far corner of the room.

"Hey guys!" she called out, her enthusiasm waning. "You better take a look at this."

The sound of their shoes echoed across the tall ceiling as they hurried over to Ashley. Kayla looked at her sister's horrified expression and then followed her gaze to the floor. A pool of blood was flowing out from under the door.

Gavin looked to the left, then the right. On each side of the door was another door, one marked "Men," the other "ladies."

"What's in here?" Gavin wondered, kneeling to get a closer look at the blood, then pressing his ear to the door.

"Supplies..." she answered, trailing off.

Kayla tried the knob. It was locked. Gavin moved her aside and kicked open the door, splinters flying around them. Ashley gasped. Capt. O'Donnell's body lay bound on the floor, mops scattered about him, a gag in his mouth, a bullet hole right between his lifeless eyes, a second wound in his chest.

Ashley was no longer enjoying herself. She thought she was going to be sick as she headed over to a bench and sat down, her head between her knees.

"I'm sorry," Gavin said to Kayla as he watched her eyes fill with tears. "We'll get these guys."

"Not as sorry as Jamie's going to be," Kayla whispered, lowering her head and wiping the mistiness from her eyes. "He was like a father to Jamie."

Then it hit her. The men they were dealing with, Triton's men, they had no respect for life. They were ruthless to the core. They were killing innocents with no regard for the consequences, no explanation of why. Standing there, looking at O'Donnell's bloodied body, all she could hope was that they wouldn't find Jamie the same way; that they wouldn't be too late. Gavin put his arm around Kayla and led her away from the closet, sitting her down next to her sister.

"You okay?" Gavin asked Ashley.

"Yeah," she answered, "it just caught me off guard, that's all."

"I know what it's like, Ash; your first dead body," Kayla remembered, "it got me too."

"You don't have to come along with us. Your sister and I can handle everything. You realize you may have to use your gun? It's one thing to think about, another thing to actually *do* it," he explained. "I need to know that if you had to, you could pull the trigger."

"No, Gavin, I can do this: I *want* to do this. I want Triton out of my dreams."

Ashley stood and wrapped her arms around Gavin's neck. He held her close, promising that everything would be alright.

"I think we're done here," Kayla said, pulling her hair into a ponytail as she stood, now fiercely determined. "Let's go find Triton before he finds us."

The front door clanked shut. Three men in black suits blocked their exit.

"I think he already found us," Gavin said, positioning himself between the girls and the Tri-Six.

The man in the middle spoke first, his white eyes glowing, "We knew you would come here. We knew you would want to rescue that fat slob of a man, too late."

Kayla recognized his voice, "Special Agent Dimitri, huh?"

"Guilty as charged," he grunted.

The other men laughed, pulling guns from beneath their suit coats. The man on the left stepped closer. Kayla readied her aim. She had him in her sights.

"Please, let's make this simple. You don't have to die. You can still save your partner, if you decide to. Oh, and I hope you didn't believe that pathetic old man either. He's deceived your friend here, taught him lies and called them truth. Do you honestly think that any one man could escape death, so many times, just to die at our hands now?"

"What are you talking about?!" Kayla exclaimed. "Joseph is too smart for you."

"Yeah, if Triton could never kill him, how could you?" Ashley added.

"There's no way he's dead," Kayla laughed.

Gavin remained silent.

"Well, Ms. Rose, I can assure you, he is quite dead. In fact," the gunman taunted, "I think the old man would have wanted you to have this."

The figure on the right moved in their direction, his hand outstretched, something small, shiny dangling from his fingers. Kayla stepped around Gavin and cautiously reached for what he was holding: a small, simple cross dangled from a chain. Kayla remembered seeing it before, around Joseph's neck.

"Where did you get that?!" Gavin grunted.

"I already told you," he said with an exaggerated huff, "we killed him. So, I didn't figure he needed this little trinket anymore."

Outraged, Kayla fired a round right into his chest. She'd caught the man off guard. He toppled backwards, blood soaking through the front of his shirt. The other gunmen watched his body flail to the ground and slide across the slippery floor.

The man in the middle reached behind him, his hands disappearing under the bottom of his jacket. In a blur, he pulled two guns, one in each hand, and rolled to his right, light flashing from the muzzles.

Kayla, Ashley, and Gavin all separated, taking cover behind several of the large stone pillars that supported the high ceiling in the police station's lobby. The two attackers dashed back and forth, firing countless rounds as dust and fragments of stone burst from the face of the pillars.

"Are you two alright?!" Gavin yelled over the gunfire.

"Yeah!" The girls shouted back.

"Then start shooting!" he screamed, spinning from behind a pillar, shooting at one of the men as he slid across the top of the receptionist's desk. Splinters from the counter flew through the air as Gavin's rounds slammed into it.

Kayla waited for a break in the other man's fire, then stepped from her cover. She let loose three quick rounds and slipped back behind to safety. Triton's soldier paused to reload, but as raised his gun, he felt his knees go weak and looked down at his chest: red splotches grew on his white shirt. Wide-eyed, he looked back at Kayla.

Ashley watched as he slumped to the ground. Everything felt like it was moving in slow motion. Every sound, every heartbeat echoed in her mind. She had thought about shooting, had thought she could, but it seemed that every time she peeked from behind the pillar that protected her, another bullet whizzed past. She couldn't do it. Scared, she slid to the floor, her gun resting next to her as she covered her ears, her eyes tightly closed.

Kayla spotted Ashley on the floor and used Gavin's fire as cover. She raced over to her sister and dropped down beside her.

"How are you holding up?" Kayla asked, ejecting her empty magazine and clicking another into place.

Ashley looked up, quivering.

"I can't do this, Kay, I can't!"

"It's okay," Kayla comforted, "it'll be over soon!"

While the two talked, they realized the room had fallen silent. The cracks of gunfire were still ringing in their ears.

Slowly, Kayla peered from behind the crumbling pillar. Gavin was standing in the middle of the lobby, spent casings scattered at his feet, his face glistening with sweat.

"I got him," he said, spotting Kayla. "Let's get moving before they send reinforcements."

Ashley grabbed Gavin's hand as they headed towards the rear exit.

"Three down," he said, his eyes fiery.

# XII

## MONDAY NIGHT

Smoke filled the alleyway as the rear tires on Gavin's old van spun loose, his big black boot holding the gas pedal to the floor. They had to get out of there, fast: more of Triton's men would surely be close behind. He shot recklessly into the busy street; car horns honking in disapproval as he cut through traffic, weaving back and forth between the lanes, his tires squealing with each sharp movement of the wheel.

"Well," Gavin shrugged, "that was a surprise."

"Were those the same men that attacked me and Kayla earlier today?" Ashley asked, leaning between the front seats.

"I'm sure they were. They're Triton's soldiers, he calls them his Tri-Six," Gavin explained. "Joseph trained me to take on Triton. That training also included his thugs. We just killed three of them. So that should leave us with fifteen."

"Wait!" Kayla exclaimed. "There are *fifteen* more of those guys?!"

"If everything Joseph told me is correct, and all my research is accurate, then yeah," he said, his grin fading as he considered the odds.

"I've never seen them all together and they all look alike, so I can never tell which ones are new and which ones I've seen before."

"So, what are we going to do?" Ashley questioned, sliding back into her seat.

"I don't think we've got enough guns to take on fifteen more assassins tonight!" Kayla exclaimed anxiously.

She was obviously beginning to doubt whether they would be able to save Jamie, if they weren't too late already. Even with Gavin's expertise, she was feeling helpless and it was coming across as anger.

"Why do they wear those suits anyway, and those masks?" Ashley squealed, her face contorted in disgust. "Freaky!"

"The Tri-Six are business men by day," Gavin answered, swerving around a bus, "killers by night. They all hold upper level positions at Tri-Corp. It's like Triton has bred his own army and uses his company as a front for everything he does. He even has thousands of followers that do his dirty work, all throughout the city. Triton calls them his *servants*, I call them 'sleepwalkers'."

"You said that before, *sleepwalkers*," Ashley wondered, "but why exactly?"

"Sleepwalkers look like us, but they are not. Their soul has been replaced by dark energy, demonic. There's no saving them. They've made their choice and sold their souls to the devil. They're faster than us, stronger than us."

"What happens when you kill one?"

"Do you mean, what happens to their soul?"

"Yeah," Ashley said.

"Like I said, they gave that up. They're already dead, they just don't know it."

"So last Thursday night, when Ashley had her first dream and those bodies were found in Harlem, people were shooting at the officers. They were holed up in there like it was their fortress or something. It had to have been some of his followers then," Kayla observed, thinking back to the report O'Donnell had given the detectives nearly a week ago.

"That explains a lot," Ashley said excitedly. "My dreams started and then all hell broke loose in the city. It was the sleepwalkers. Do you think Triton was controlling my dreams somehow, playing with my mind?"

Gavin smiled.

"You two are catching on. Everything Triton does is because of his arrogance. He thinks he's untouchable. Now that Joseph is dead, he'll think he can do anything he wants."

"But why me?" Ashley asked.

"Triton has his reasons. Maybe it's a coincidence, or maybe he knew that you would involve your sister and that would eventually lead you to me and Joseph? His goal could have been to use you to get him to Joseph and then have his men kill him, or me," Gavin reasoned, "or maybe, and this is scary, he thinks you have something he wants."

"Like what?" Kayla asked, running her fingers through her hair in frustration.

"That's something for us to try and figure out," Gavin answered.

"So why did he kill those thirteen people?" Kayla wondered.

"They were a sacrifice."

"A sacrifice?" Ashley chimed in from the back seat.

"Yeah," Gavin replied. "It's the only way Triton has lived as long as he has. Triton was once a man. But that was a long time ago. Who knows what he is anymore. He's more demon than human, I figure. Blood is what sustains him."

"Like a vampire?" Ashley smirked.

"Or maybe it was a cover-up!" Kayla interjected, her eyes glowing with thoughts of conspiracy and tangled webs.

"You're thinking like a cop," Gavin replied, wagging his finger.

"This is not like that."

"No, seriously!" Kayla continued. "Michael Hampton was one of the victims: he was also my brother's informant. He had serious dirt on Triton. Triton used Hampton to kill my brother, then used the sacrifice as a way to get rid of Hampton, not to mention discredit him and in so doing, discredit the findings of our investigation."

"And what about the other twelve people?" Gavin asked.

"Triton picked them at random. They were all good people, but he must have just viewed them as collateral damage," Kayla figured, piecing it all together in her mind.

"But the bodies were completely drained of blood. It was a sacrifice!" Gavin argued.

Kayla thought for a moment. Then it hit her.

"You're right, it was a sacrifice! It served two purposes! He got the blood he needed *and* he shut up a witness!"

"So he drinks blood?" Ashley imagined, still caught up in the earlier parts of the conversation.

"Well, not exactly *drinks*. Like I said, it's a sacrifice. In the Old Testament, the Israelites offered blood sacrifices as atonement to God."

"For their sins," Ashley added.

"Right. Triton reasons that if God valued blood sacrifice, how much more would Satan. He thinks he's taking their soul by killing them, or better yet, that he's capturing their soul for Satan, but he doesn't understand death. For all his power and all his knowledge, he doesn't see that he has no say in eternity, in the afterlife."

Gavin pressed a button on the garage door opener that hung on his sun visor and pulled the van to a stop inside the dark, old warehouse where Kayla and Ashley first met him.

"Home sweet home," he smiled, looking over his shoulder at Ashley, the garage door rattling shut behind them.

"What are we doing here?" Kayla demanded, angry and confused. "What about Jamie? We have to save him!"

"Take it easy!" Gavin said, as he climbed out of the van. "We'll save your boyfriend tomorrow when the sun is up. The trip to the police station really slowed us down, but I think we have a better idea of what we're up against. Besides, who knows what's creeping around Triton's place in the middle of the night."

"I don't like waiting and if you're so good at what you say you do," Kayla argued, her finger pointing Gavin in the face, "then why are you so afraid of whatever Triton has guarding his building? We handled those guys in the masks."

"It's not just the Tri-Six; it's what gives the Tri-Six their power. It's not mortal, not something we can face head on. You can't kill a spirit with a gun, only its host."

"What do you mean?" Ashley asked.

"It's demonic. And it's not a matter of fear. It's a matter of respect, respecting that this is a very dangerous, very real power that goes far beyond us. Without God's help, there's no chance of surviving," Gavin said, ending the conversation. "We don't want to play around with that kind of power."

Kayla huffed off to the living room area and plopped down on the old couch. Sitting there, she watched her sister and Gavin as he placed his tattooed arm around her, then led her over to the opposite couch were they sat down.

"We need to rethink our approach," Gavin began. "Sleepwalkers keep to the shadows, move at night. So striking during the day is our safest option, and I still think the front door is our best chance, but we need bigger guns."

Kayla stood up and walked into Gavin's makeshift kitchen. She opened his grimy fridge hoping to find more than moldy pizza.

"Whatever you say," she said, pulling out a can of pop and heading back to the old couch.

"We shouldn't argue," Ashley reasoned. "We should save our

strength for tomorrow. Gavin's right. We should rest."

Kayla ignored her. All she could think about was Jamie and whether or not he was still alive.

************

The heavy door slowly opened, light pouring in from the hallway. Jamie squinted as he watched the black outline of a figure step into the small room.

"What do you want from me?!" Jamie yelled angrily.

"Temper, temper, Detective," Thirteen mocked walking into the dim light cast by the hazy bulb that hung from the ceiling, the evil grin on his mask making Jamie shift uncomfortably, "Your girlfriend is giving us trouble. Do you have any idea what we do to people who give us trouble?"

"I don't believe you. You're just trying to scare me. It's not going to work."

"You don't sound so sure, Detective," Thirteen chuckled. "Tell me where she is."

"Tell *me* where the key is, the key from the wax covered table in that filthy basement," Jamie blurted.

"You want Triton's key?" Thirteen said with interest. "How do you know about that?"

"Someone I can trust told me," Jamie grunted, hoping he sounded tougher than he felt.

"Let me guess....*Sykes*?"

"Yeah, how..."

"Did I know?" Thirteen laughed. "I have eyes and ears everywhere. I saw the two of you sitting on that quant little bench, quite a rendezvous!"

Jamie felt a knot rising in his throat. He watched Thirteen as he paced slowly back and forth, in and out of the light.

"Sykes has been taken *care of*. He won't be mentioning the key to anyone else."

"You sick son of a..."

"Again, watch your temper," Thirteen interjected coolly. "Tell me where to find the woman and her sister."

"Leave her alone! She has nothing to do with this, with you. She's miles away, in hiding. You'll never find her."

"Actually, several of my men had a run in with her earlier today. I'm a little angry with your girlfriend right now."

"Why?" Jamie grunted, his curiosity overcoming his fear.

"Well, she managed to kill three of my men."

"What?" Jamie replied in disbelief.

"Yeah, that's exactly what I thought when I heard. She had her pathetic sister to help her, as well as the new man in her life...one with many, many tattoos. I'd watch out for him. He's pretty smooth with the ladies."

"I know what you're trying to do," Jamie grinned. "You're trying to make me jealous."

"Is it working?"

"No."

"Well then," Thirteen said, turning towards the door, "if you're lucky, you and your precious *partner* will be reunited. The two of you can patch up each other's wounds."

Jamie watched Thirteen head for the door when a thought hit him. He leaned forward in his chair.

"You have Triton's key don't you!"

Thirteen stopped. Slowly he turned to face Jamie once again.

"Mind your accusations, Detective. Triton is my master. I serve only him."

"Everything you've said is a lie isn't it?!" Jamie chided. "You're not as tough as you think...tough guy!"

Thirteen reached into his suit coat and pulled out a small blue pack of cigarettes.

"Smoke?" he offered Jamie, holding the pack out to him.

"No, I don't."

"Pity," Thirteen laughed, tossing the cigarettes onto the table and heading out the door, "these French ones are pretty good, very rare. You can only import them you know."

The door slammed behind Thirteen. Jamie sat staring at the cigarettes in front of him. The bulb hanging from the ceiling swayed lightly.

The pack was covered in dried blood. Jamie could just make out the name through the stains. *Gitanes*: the same kind O'Donnell smoked.

\*\*\*\*\*\*\*\*\*\*\*\*

Kayla was sleeping. Gavin looked over at the clock: 3:00am. Ashley was asleep too, her head resting on his lap. He set down the book he'd been reading and gently held Ashley's head as he stood, slipping a pillow under her. She stirred, but fell right back to sleep.

Gavin then pulled an old afghan from a crate under the stairs and covered Kayla with it. Her pop can had fallen on its side. What was left in it had spilled onto the concrete floor.

He headed up to the office turned bedroom and came back down with another blanket, a nicer blanket, and laid it across Ashley. He sat back down next to her on the couch as she cuddled up against him, pulling the warm blanket up to her chin.

Gavin picked the old leather-covered book back up from his coffee table and flipped it open to where he'd left off. It was his Bible, the page marked at the book of Hebrews, chapter eleven.

*Now faith is being sure of what we hope for and certain of what we do not see.*

*Hebrews 11:1*

As he read, his head began to tip forward, his eyes growing heavy. Finally, he dozed off, his Bible still sitting open. Ashley slept next to him: she felt safe. For the first time in days, she really slept.

Kayla flinched as she laid there: she was dreaming. Tossing and turning on the old couch, she nearly fell off, but in her sleepy struggle, she never woke.

************

Thirteen stood on the ledge of a building high above the street below, his jacket fluttering in the cool night air. As he looked down upon the city, he could feel his ever-growing power coursing through his body like electricity. He was now Triton's second in command. His replacement would soon be ready to join the Tri-Six. Joseph was dead, killed by the hand of Thirteen's apprentice. He felt as if he'd taken all of Joseph's strength and added it to his own. Now only Gavin and the girl stood in his way.

Without fear, Thirteen jumped from the ledge and landed on the rooftop just across the street. He began to sprint across the buildings, gliding over streets and alleyways. He felt invincible.

Leaping from one roof to another, he came upon the Empire State Building. In a flash of light, Thirteen stood at the top, the tall tower hundreds of feet above the surrounding buildings. From here, he could see for miles.

"So many people," he said, "walking in blindness, unaware of what is about to happen to them."

Kneeling down, he looked like a gargoyle hunched in the darkness, as black as his own shadow. He carried four handguns hidden under his jacket, two in rear holsters strapped upside down, within easy reach, then two more in shoulder holsters, the guns resting against his ribs. Across his back hung a leather sheath, a razor sharp katana inside, the intricately woven handle rising from the top, two blood-red ribbons tied to the hilt blowing whimsically in the wind.

Turning his attention far below, he watched the tiny dot-like cars making their way through the streets, their headlights glowing. He stood again, pulling his sword, the metal ringing as it slid free, the glint of perfectly forged steel glistening in the moonlight. He dropped from the top of the Empire State Building, diving headlong towards the traffic below, his arms outstretched like wings. Gracefully, he plummeted toward the pavement, the cars growing larger with every passing second. At the last possible moment, Thirteen swung his feet out below himself and guided his body into line with the street, poised to land.

With a crash, he smashed onto the hood of a passing taxi, the sheet metal twisting into a contorted mass of indistinguishable rubble, fluid spraying from hoses under the hood. He sprung off of it, back into the air, the impact sending the car flipping end over end. Traffic swerved out of control, collisions everywhere, as drivers slammed on the breaks, skidding into a mangled pileup. Large bursts of flame flickered in the night.

In the ensuing panic, Thirteen stood high above the chaotic street, admiring his handy work from the rooftops. Sirens wailed in the night. The wretched screams were music to his ears; the sound of innocent people dying in his symphony of madness. Feeling all the more powerful, the city had become his playground, and he loved the game.

\*\*\*\*\*\*\*\*\*\*\*\*

Jamie picked up the pack of cigarettes. He felt them shift to one side in the half empty box as he flipped open the lid. Only a few cigarettes were left. An expensive Zippo lighter was in the box as well. They were O'Donnell's alright, he recognized the smell.

*The Captain would never have left them lying around.*

Closing his eyes, fighting back tears, Jamie pushed the pack into his jacket pocket. He dropped his head onto his arms and began to sob. No one needed to tell him, he just knew, O'Donnell was gone.

\*\*\*\*\*\*\*\*\*\*\*

Luke Bradford woke with a start. His phone was ringing. Slowly, he clambered out of bed and answered it.

"Yeah," he said, half greeting, half yawn, as he looked at the clock that hung on his living room wall.

*4:15am.*

'You did as I asked?"

"Yeah."

"You cleared out the police station?"

"Yeah," Bradford replied impatiently, pacing from room to room in his apartment.

"How'd you do it?'

"I said a bomb threat had been called in and the Feds were handling it. Dimitri and Jones secured the building. O'Donnell was the only person left there, he wouldn't leave. Nobody asked any questions."

"Boy, you're lucky you're family..."

"What are you talking about?"

"Three of Triton's men were killed. If I wasn't the Mayor, Triton wouldn't have let it go. He was quite angry."

"Who killed them, O'Donnell?"

"That fat slob?!" Mayor Bradford laughed. "He's spent more time in front of the TV with a bottle of whiskey than he has at a firing range.

No, it was Detective Rose."

"Kayla?"

"Yes."

"You want me to take her out?"

"No, no," the Mayor replied. "Triton will take care of her. What I want to do is make sure you're ready for tomorrow."

Luke flopped down on his couch, his feet propped up on his coffee table. In one hand, he held his phone, with the other, he rubbed his sleepy eyes.

"What's happening tomorrow?'

"You are, my boy. You've been awarded a medal of recognition for exposing the murderous plot and revealing the threat: O'Donnell."

"What do you mean?"

"Dimitiri and Jones took your story a step further. Not only did they claim to find a bomb at the station and disarm it, but they said you tipped them off to whom the terrorist was, the Captain: angry, bitter, and drunk."

"What did they do to O'Donnell?" Luke questioned, a slight waiver in his voice.

"They neutralized the threat, that is, he's dead, which brings me back to your medal and your impending commendation. You've been promoted. You're the new Captain."

************

"Where have you been?" Triton demanded as he stood at his office window, Thirteen quietly approaching, their faces reflecting in the glass.

Thirteen shifted his weight from one foot to the other and smiled, looking out over the city, plumes of smoke rising in the distance from the chaos he created.

"...*playing*..." he laughed softly.

"And what of the detective, do you think he really knows as much as he claims?"

"I believe he knows enough, Master."

"Does he have my key?" Triton asked, turning to look Thirteen in his white glowing eyes. "That key is everything!"

"I don't believe so. Maybe his partner has it, or her sister?"

"The dreamer?"

"Possibly," Thirteen said seriously. "I think the detective and his girlfriend found the key at the sacrifice and gave it to the little girl for safe keeping."

"I knew it," Triton said dreamily, his gaze fixed on a large painting hanging on the wall, "from the first time I saw her, when I visited her art gallery. She is special, the one who will begin the end of all things."

"And the key?"

Triton leaned over the top of his desk, his strong, vein-covered hands clenched into tight fists, as he stared at the cluttered pile of folders, documents, and evidence photos taken from Jamie's desk at the police station.

"If she has it, then it is fitting. Go, search her apartment, and her sister's as well. Find what you can, hopefully the key. We need to make sure we destroy every piece of evidence they've collected that can connect us to any of this. And then..."

"Yes, my Master?"

"We destroy them."

\*\*\*\*\*\*\*\*\*\*\*

Gavin blinked. Something woke him. Ashley still lay next to him. He watched her for a moment. She was so beautiful.

The toilet flushed upstairs. He glanced at the couch were Kayla had been sleeping. Her blanket was there, but she wasn't.

"Can't sleep?' he asked her, as he watched her walk down the stairs.

"No. I had a bad dream. I can't stop thinking about Jamie."

"You love him don't you?" Gavin said, smiling.

"Yeah, I guess I do." Kayla answered thoughtfully. "I wanted to thank you for helping us. I know now we could never have survived the police station without you. We owe you our lives."

"It's no big deal, it's what Joseph trained me to do. Thank God I was ready."

"Oh, Joseph, I'm so sorry."

"Don't be," Gavin replied, "it's all part of the master plan, the grand design."

"But he's dead, doesn't that make you sad?"

"Yes, but...I can't change it. Joseph wouldn't want me to mourn him."

For a moment, they sat in silence, neither one looking at the other. Ashley rolled over, the blanket wrapped tightly around her.

"Can I get you something to drink?" Gavin asked, motioning towards his run-down kitchen. "Maybe some hot tea?"

"I'd like that," she said smiling.

Kayla followed Gavin around the counter and watched him fill a kettle with water. He placed it on the old stove and started a burner, the faint smell of gas lingering as his match ignited a blue flame.

"When we found your boss," Gavin started carefully, "you said he was like a father to Jamie. They were close?'

"Real close," Kayla frowned, picturing O'Donnell lying dead on the floor of the closet. "They hid their relationship well, almost as well as Jamie and I have kept our dating a secret at work, but it takes a long time for anyone to gain Jamie's trust."

"What happened?" Gavin asked, getting out two mugs from a cupboard and blowing dust out of them.

"Well I don't know if I'm the person to tell you this. It took Jamie a year before he shared his past with me. Like I said, he doesn't trust easily."

"I understand. You feel like you'd be betraying him by telling me."

"No. Ashley trusts you and I do too. I think Jamie would be okay with it."

Kayla thought for a moment as Gavin pulled the whistling kettle off the stove and poured the steaming water into the cups. He shuffled through a drawer for two teabags, then handed one to Kayla, dropping the other into his mug.

"I don't really know where to begin," she said, swishing the bag around in her cup, watching the tea mix with the water.

"How about the beginning?"

\*\*\*\*\*\*\*\*\*\*\*

Luke Bradford sat staring at the wall, his phone still in hand. Thoughts of commendation and praise danced through his head like a child anticipating Christmas morning, yet, oddly, he felt something unexpected: guilt.

*What have I done?*

\*\*\*\*\*\*\*\*\*\*\*

"Okay, here goes," Kayla began uncomfortably. "Jamie grew up

228

with his parents in a fancy penthouse near Central Park."

"Are we talking 1970's fancy," Gavin grinned, "like disco, macramé, and fondue?"

"Yeah," she sighed.

"Gotcha. I just wanted to get the setting right," he laughed, hoping to lighten the mood.

"Anyway," she continued, this time more relaxed, "his dad was a stockbroker, a real workaholic, he really raked in the dough, but Jamie was much closer to his mother. He didn't get along with the kids at school, so his mom was really one of his only friends."

"Hmmm," Gavin mumbled sipping at his steaming cup.

"Anyway, late one night, when he was twelve, three men broke into their apartment. They picked the lock, didn't leave any finger prints: professionals."

"What did they want?'

"Jamie's dad," Kayla said, adding some sugar into her tea. "As it turned out, his father wasn't really a stock broker. He was a very successful money launderer for the mob, one of their most trusted guys. But the bosses had taken notice of the high-life Jamie's dad was living, the expensive cars, the penthouse, the clothes: they figured he was skimming a little extra off the top of the money he cleaned for them."

"So they wanted revenge?" Gavin wondered.

"I think they just wanted to scare him, but they did a little more than that. That night, while they searched for Jamie's dad, his mom startled them; coming out of the hallway from around the corner, but she was just as surprised to see them. Without thinking, one of the men shot her, once in the stomach, and again in the chest. Jamie watched it all from his bedroom doorway."

Gavin stared at the floor. Kayla sipped her tea.

"So, Jamie raced to his mother and held her in his arms as she died. They stared into each other's eyes as she slipped away. Then he heard the sound of a gun hammer clicking back and he looked up. The gunman was standing over him, the barrel of his gun fixed at Jamie's forehead.

Jamie closed his eyes tight, still clinging to his mother, a tear running down his cheek. Then, silence; no shot. When he opened his eyes, they were gone. Jamie looked down at his mother, then at his blood stained hands and lost it, tears streaming down his face."

"I can't imagine what that would do to a kid," Gavin said, shaking his head.

"Well, when Jamie found out what happened, that his dad was actually working for the mob, he blamed his father for everything. The mob had put Jamie's dad in his place. The two of them moved into a really rundown apartment in Queens and scrimped by on food scraps and tattered clothing. The good life was over.

But there's a silver lining, *sort of.* When Jamie was fifteen, some kids from his high school were bullying him in an alley and it turned into a pretty heavy fight. A lot of punches were thrown, mostly by Jamie. He can be a bit of a hot-head. A passing cruiser stopped and an officer broke up the fight, scaring off the bullies. It was O'Donnell, just a beat cop back then, long before he made Lieutenant and eventually Captain.

O'Donnell took Jamie under his wing and taught him that regardless of his past, he could still make a difference in this world. By the time Jamie graduated high school, his father had disappeared. Jamie always figured that the mob got him, and in the end, Jamie was alone. O'Donnell was the only person there for him.

Jamie enlisted at the academy and was a standout. He spent his first two years on the force working narcotics. By this time, O'Donnell was just getting his feet wet as Captain. He moved Jamie to homicide so he could keep an eye on him. But Jamie started to pick up some of the Captain's habits."

"Like what?"

"Alcohol, for one," Kayla replied sadly. "Jamie was building a very successful career, earning real, honest money. O'Donnell saw to it that Jamie was making quite a bit."

"Enough to be comfortable, you mean?"

"More than enough, but even in his success, Jamie still felt the pain spawned from his memories. No matter how well he did, or how much he made, he couldn't forget what happened. He was haunted by the loss of his mother, still is really.

Jamie began drinking heavily, drowning his past. Then, a little over two years ago, not long before we were partners, Jamie was working with a detective named Luke Bradford. The guy wasn't the most ethical cop on the force, he looked the other way, *a lot*, even took some pretty hefty bribes. But he's protected. He's the Mayor's nephew.

While investigating a series of gangland murders in Hell's Kitchen, they questioned a couple of suspects at an apparently mob-owned restaurant. As always, Luke looked the other way. Jamie left the meeting with a bullet in his shoulder. That's when he started on painkillers: vicodin, percoset, oxycontin, anything he could get.

Now, it seems he's on them all the time. I feel so bad for him. He needs help, I just don't know who."

"I know someone who can help him," Gavin said, smiling with hope. "But Jamie will have to make the first move."

\*\*\*\*\*\*\*\*\*\*\*\*

"Hello again, Detective," Thirteen said, brushing dust from his sleeves as he pushed open the heavy door to the small, decrepit room.

"What do you want?" Jamie barked impatiently.

"I think you may have company soon."

"What are you talking about?"

"I'm talking about your little girlfriend," Thirteen grinned, crossing his arms, his mask hiding the pleased look on his face.

Jamie jumped up from the rickety, old chair. It creaked as he stood.

"I swear if you hurt her," he threatened, his face red, the veins in his neck bulging.

"Please, calm yourself, Detective," Thirteen said smugly, waiving his black gloved hand in a downward motion.

Jamie struggled, but found himself sitting. He tried to get back up, but it was as if an unseen force was holding him down, like invisible fingers were digging into his shoulders, locking him to the chair.

"What is this?!" Jamie yelled, straining with all his might.

"Something you wouldn't understand."

Jamie grunted. He couldn't get loose.

"Now to see to Ms. Rose," Thirteen said turning towards the door. "I wonder if she's at home?"

"I'll kill you if you even go near Kayla!"

"Now that I think about it, Detective," Thirteen shrugged, speaking in a sweet voice, "she is quite pretty and seeing how you're, *indisposed*, maybe I'll take little Ms. Rose out for a night on the town, you know, show her a good time, maybe a little...*more*? It starts to get cold at night this time of year. Good company is oh so...*warming*."

"You're dead, do you hear me? Dead!" Jamie screamed.

Thirteen gave him a little waive and stepped out into the dark hallway. As soon as the door closed, Jamie felt the grip release and he leapt from the chair, picking it up and sending it splintering into the cold metal door. He leaned against the wall and slumped to the dirty floor, his head in his hands, tears in his eyes, helpless, alone.

# XIII

## TUESDAY MORNING

Sunlight burst through the small windows that lined the ceiling of Gavin's warehouse. Ashley sat up, rubbing her eyes as they adjusted to the light. She blinked away her sleepiness, realizing Gavin was nowhere to be seen.

He'd been up most of the night, first; talking with Kayla; then, planning, praying, and preparing for morning, readying the van, checking it over, making sure it would keep running. The garage door stood wide open. Cool air blew in. Gavin had pulled his van right up to it, ready to leave. Now, he was in the back of the van making quite a bit of noise: so much so that it woke Kayla. Ashley caught Gavin's silhouette against the morning sun as he disappeared into the warehouse and headed for his tool bench. Looking over at Kayla, a broad yawn stretching across her face, Ashley stood and headed over to the old couch, sitting down at Kayla's feet.

"Sorry about last night," Kayla smiled. "I was just so worried about Jamie."

"I know," Ashley assured her as they stood and hugged, then made their way to the rusty black van, their blankets pulled over their shoulders to keep them warm.

"I was just loading up. Breakfast is on the table," Gavin said, nodding towards the kitchen as he stepped down over the bumper.

Not-so-fluffy pancakes were piled on a plate, a bottle of syrup just beside them.

In silence, they ate. The pancakes weren't very good. Kayla gave Ashley a funny look, the corner of her mouth perking into a slight smile.

"He really needs someone to help him with this kind of stuff," Kayla joked sarcastically. "He's great with guns, but not so good around the house."

"He got you a blanket, didn't he?" Ashley pointed out.

"Yeah," Kayla admitted with a grin, "I guess he's not that bad once you get to know him."

Just as she said that, something heavy clanked against the cement floor, the crash echoing through the warehouse, quickly followed by an unintelligible shout. The girls laughed as they finished their breakfast. Kayla washed the dishes while Ashley straightened up the kitchen counter and table top.

"You two sleep alright?" he asked, the smell of a night's worth of coffee on his breath as he came up behind Ashley and put his arms around her.

Ashley kissed him on his scruffy cheek. Kayla looked up, her expression growing sullen as her dream from the night before came back to her. She hadn't even thought about it, but now, her memory was flooding her mind. Kayla slumped onto a stool that stood along the counter as she felt her knees go weak beneath her.

"I saw Jamie in a dream again last night."

"What?!" Ashley exclaimed. "What kind of dream, the same dream?"

"He was suffering, worse than before, locked in a room. It was dark. All I could make out was his shadow, but I know it was him."

"We're going to find him," Ashley said confidently, sitting down on the stool next to Kayla and grabbing her hands. "He'll be alright."

\*\*\*\*\*\*\*\*\*\*\*\*

Gavin closed the hood of the van and headed for his secret armory. Pulling the cord attached to the overhead light, he began taking guns off the wall, the fluorescent bulb flickering above him, followed by a soft, electric hum.

"Come on," he called from the room, "let's load up."

Gavin turned to face them as they walked through the door, a bullet proof vest on, a tactical vest with pockets and pouches worn over that, and a pair of matching pistols strapped to his hips.

"I think you've been looking forward to this," Kayla chided, picking up a shotgun from the table and looking down the barrel.

Ashley picked up the same Heckler & Koch pistol she'd carried the day before and ejected the magazine, staring blankly at the 9mm rounds.

"I don't know if I can do this?" she admitted.

"You don't have to come along," Gavin said, loading the pockets on his tactical vest with extra magazines for his handguns and the AR15 rifle he planned on taking, "your sister and I will be just fine."

"Yeah," Kayla added, "I would never expect you to do this, to put yourself in such danger."

"I thought I could do it yesterday, but after the shootout at the police department, I don't think I'll be of much help."

Gavin pulled the assault rifle down of the wall and slung it over his shoulder, "I don't want you to do anything you're not ready for."

Ashley stared at the bullets again, then jammed the magazine into the gun and took a set of earmuffs off the shelf. Kayla watched her head for the door that led to the range.

"Give me a minute," Ashley said, the door closing behind her.

Gavin and Kayla stared at each other in silence, the repeated bangs of the gun reduced to subtle pops, muffled by the soundproofed walls. Then, silence.

The door to the range swung open. Ashley stepped through, her teeth gritted in determination.

"I can do this," she said, holding up a paper target for them to see. "I can help, you'll *need* my help!"

The target looked great, she'd fired tight groupings to the left and right of the bull's-eye, two shots clipped the red circle on the middle of the paper, a third hit nearly dead center.

"Only if you're up to it," Gavin conceded. "But if you get nervous, you take cover, hear me?"

Ashley nodded. Kayla patted Gavin on the shoulder reassuringly.

They finished gathering their supplies, then walked slowly to the van. The girls settled into the back. Gavin slid the door closed behind them and climbed into the driver's seat.

"What are we going to do when we get there?" Ashley asked.

"Just follow my lead," Gavin answered, "and shoot anything that moves."

"Anything?!" Kayla questioned.

"Anything wearing a black mask," he grinned, starting the van and flipping on the radio.

The growling engine sputtered a few times, then backfired as it rumbled to life. Sliding on his sunglasses, he glanced in his rear view mirror. Ashley and Kayla looked as if they were holding their breath, nervously awaiting what could be their death. Gavin smiled hopefully and pulled through the open garage door.

"Let's roll," he said, the gleam in his eyes hidden behind his dark lenses.

***********

The sky was beginning to cloud over: it looked like rain. A storm was on its way. Triton stood looking out his window on the one hundred and thirteenth floor, marveling at the city's beauty, his city, or so he thought. Thirteen leaned in the corner, looking down at the busy street below. His white eyes glowed with contempt.

A black van pulled up to the curb.

"They are here," Thirteen said, glaring down at them, his simple words reaching Triton's ears.

"Gather the troops," Triton commanded. "Today, goodness dies."

************

Gavin stepped from the van and opened the side door. Kayla and Ashley stared up at him from the rear seat, their eyes filled with hesitation.

"It'll be alright," he said as he led Ashley out by her hand.

Kayla froze as she stepped down onto the sidewalk. Jamie's white BMW was parked two spaces up. She approached the car, carefully looking in the windows.

"See anything?" Gavin wondered.

"No," Kayla frowned, trying the door handle, "it's locked."

She bent over; her hands raised on each side of her face as she pressed in on the glass, studying the dash, seats, searching for any clue that might give her hope.

*Hold on.*

Kayla walked to the front of the car and pulled a small, manila envelope from under the wiper blade.

"What's that?" Ashley asked.

"A parking ticket," Kayla muttered, throwing the pink slip of paper on the ground.

"Just make sure they don't write you up for littering," he joked, taking a short pause. "Now, let's go get your boyfriend."

They readied their guns, double checking the magazines and loading rounds into the chambers, then slowly approached the dual glass doors and peered into the lobby. It was empty. Kayla tugged on the handle.

*Locked.*

"Maybe we should knock?" Ashley wondered sarcastically.

"Yeah, knocking would be good. They'll let us right in," Gavin said, leaning back and kicking the doors open with his big black boots.

The doors flung inward, slamming against the stone walls, the glass clanking and rattling, then shattering into sparkling little glitters that scattered across the marble floor. The three reluctant heroes stood in the door way, Gavin taking the lead, his AR15 raised, ready for a fight. The girls stood one on each side, their hair blowing in the wind, a light drizzle falling outside behind their silhouettes, the sunlight glistening through the rain, surrounding them with glowing halos of pure light as they stood their ground.

It was dead silent. A stunned receptionist sat at the information desk, a phone held close to her head, but not to her ear, like she hadn't quite answered it. Her eyes were wide open, like a deer caught in headlights.

"Sorry about the door!" Gavin called to her, his rifle still aimed and ready.

The cold lobby echoed with the metallic sound of her phone receiver hitting the floor, quickly followed by the thud of her body right next to it. She'd fainted. Gavin looked at each of the girls, uneasiness in his eyes.

"I was expecting a bit more than her," he admitted.

Kayla kept her eyes peeled, the barrel of her shotgun following her gaze. Other than the receptionist, the room was empty.

High above them, shadowy creatures with leathery hides crawled across the walls and hung from the expansive ceiling, watching every move the intruders made. The smell of sulfur lingered.

Suddenly, a voice bellowed out in the room, a man's voice, dark and full of hate, "We don't open for another hour. Why don't you go get yourselves some coffee and check back during business hours?"

"Wow, you're pretty funny," Gavin mocked. "We came for our friend, that's it. This doesn't have to get ugly."

"Maybe they aren't keeping him here?" Ashley wondered, her voice dripping with disappointment. "Maybe he's in like a safe-house or something?"

"No, he's here," the voice echoed again.

They scanned the lobby, their feet seemingly fixed to the floor. Still, the room was empty.

"But I assure you," the voice spoke, "you will not set him free unless you have an answer for me, Ms. Rose."

"An answer to what?" Kayla asked.

A faint scratching sound, like nails on a chalkboard, pulled their attention to a dark, empty corner of the room, nothing but black shadows. They turned back; a figure now stood in the middle of the lobby: Thirteen.

"You know what we want, Ms. Rose," he said, an odd reverberating tone to his voice, almost unearthly.

"You want me to call off the investigation," she guessed.

"Do you really think we would go to such great lengths just to have you call off an investigation?" he mused. "Tell me, have you talked to your *boss* lately?"

Kayla ignored his attempt to unnerve her. She kept the barrel of her 12 gauge trained on him, "Then what do you want?"

"I want to know your decision. You have a choice to make. *What...will...it...be?*" he asked again, emphasizing each word.

"What choice!?" she asked, pumping a round into the chamber.

"Only one need die today, Ms. Rose: the one who has sight, the one my master has chosen. We already took your precious Joseph," Thirteen mocked, looking at Gavin. "But now, we will make a trade. We want the dreamer. She has an unusual bond with my master. She's the one we have searched for, that my master has searched for. He has invaded the minds of countless young girls looking for the one, and now he's found her! She's all that stands in the way of Armageddon. With her gone, the Dark Lord can wage his final battle for the souls of all mankind."

Ashley stared at his finger as it pointed at her.

"What's he talking about, Kayla?" she asked anxiously. "What Dark Lord?"

"I think he means the Devil, Ash," Gavin sighed.

"Like the Devil, Devil?"

"Pitchfork and everything."

"Laugh now, Hunter," Thirteen grunted, "but this is more serious than you think."

"Kayla," Ashley panicked, "what are we going to do?"

Kayla didn't answer. She continued staring down Thirteen, her eyes fixed on the white slits of his mask.

"You can't have her!" she yelled at him.

"Then Detective Branson will die."

"Why kill him if you want Ashley?" Gavin grunted.

Thirteen looked from Kayla to Gavin.

"Because," he shrugged, gesturing at the stitches on his mask, "it'll put a smile on my face."

He turned his gaze back to Kayla, "But only her blood will set Mr. Branson free. If she lives, then we will have to continue to kill for my master. And in the end, we'll still get her and begin this holy war. So it makes no difference to me. Now answer, *who...will...it...be?*"

Gavin whispered something in Kayla's ear. Ashley thought she heard him say the man was bluffing.

"We killed three of you last night," Kayla said, "there's only one of you now. Let Jamie go and we'll let you live."

The lobby echoed with Thirteen's laughter.

"You can't be serious, girl? I am not like the others. But you will not live to see the difference between me and my brothers."

As he finished, fifteen men, all in black suits and masks, stepped from the shadows. In silence, they raised their guns, surrounding them.

"I leave you to your fate," Thirteen said, leaping towards the ceiling and disappearing into thin air.

One of the Tri-Six spoke, "Kill the hunter and the woman, but leave the girl. Triton wants her alive."

"There's only one Man's blood that can save Triton," Gavin laughed, "it's the same blood that will free Jamie. I can tell you now, it's not Ashley's!"

The men cocked their guns, the hammers clicking back. Gavin smiled and stepped slowly ahead of Kayla and Ashley so that he faced the majority of the men. Ashley seemed confident. Kayla looked the same, but only on the surface.

"We don't stand a chance!" Kayla doubted as the men circled them, waiting to strike.

"Then let's even the odds," Gavin laughed.

\*\*\*\*\*\*\*\*\*\*\*\*

Flashes of gun fire flickered in the lobby. Black blurs lunged this way and that, dodging bullets and firing in retaliation.

Gavin rushed across the room, blasting at the men. Slowly, bodies began to hit the floor. Firing the last round from his gun, he swung his rifle to his side on its sling and pulled the pistols from his hips.

Ashley took cover behind a large marble pillar, bullets splintering its surface. Kayla ducked between plantings, firing to protect herself in the open.

Three of the men chased after Gavin as he jumped, turned onto his back, and slid across the floor, taking aim at the assailants.

*Bang... Bang...Bang...Bang!*

He pulled the triggers without hesitation and they collapsed to the ground, blood spurting into the air, their guns still firing in desperation. Two rounds hit Gavin in the chest: he didn't get up.

Ashley poked her head out of cover just enough to spot one of the Tri-Six flanking Kayla's position.

*It's now or never*, she told herself. *You can do it, just control your breathing...slow things down...*

She stepped from behind the pillar and took aim. Before she realized it, she felt the gun kick in her hands. The man paused but didn't fall. Had she hit him? She pulled the trigger again, her second shot hitting his shoulder. He turned, raising his gun to fight back, but she had him. Ashley let loose three more shots and he dropped to his knees, then the floor.

Ashley stepped back behind the safety of the pillar, relieved and shaking. She felt like minutes had passed, but it had all happened in mere seconds, but that was what she needed.

"You okay?" Kayla asked, taking cover next to her.

"I'm good," she managed, "a little crazy though. My adrenaline level must be off the chart and my heartbeat is like, WOO! But I'm okay."

"Thanks for getting my back," Kayla said, tossing her empty shotgun aside and pulling her Glock from its holster.

"I'm just glad I could!" Ashley grinned. "But where's Gavin?"

In all the commotion, they'd lost track of each other. Only now had the girls found each other. Kayla glanced around the pillar, a bullet smashing into the wall behind her. She barely glimpsed his boots on the floor as she pulled her head back. Dust from the crumbling walls and pillars filled the room. The thick cloud made it hard to breathe, let alone see. Kayla wanted to use this to their advantage.

"He's over there," she told Ashley, not wanting to tell her he was down. "He might be hurt. Let's split up and try to distract these guys. We need to get to Gavin."

She and Ashley dashed about the room, ducking from cover to cover, yelling at each other, firing whenever they had the chance. Round after round, Ashley grew thankful that Gavin had them carry extra magazines. The room was moving in slow motion. Every sound blurred into one.

It was difficult to tell how many of the men were left. Every time Kayla was sure she took one down, another seemed to fire at her. But, with a final crack, the last man fell. Fifteen black suited bodies laid strewn about the floor, blood-stained, resting in red pools.

Ashley ran to Gavin's body and dropped to his side, tears beginning to flow, fearing the worst. She felt his hand: still warm. As she held him, she suddenly felt him tense up and shake to life as he finally coughed, then tried to sit up. Ashley helped him slip out of his tactical vest. Silver splotches marked the Kevlar he wore beneath that. The bullets hadn't gone through, just knocked the wind out of him. Ashley grabbed his head with both hands and kissed him. She thought she'd lost him.

Gavin winced as he climbed to his feet, loosening the bulletproof vest and dropping it to the floor. Ashley gasped as she carefully lifted his tank-top. Large red welts had formed.

"You think that'll bruise?" he joked.

"I'm glad to see they didn't kill your sense of humor," Kayla responded with a relieved grin. "Come on, let's go find Jamie."

\*\*\*\*\*\*\*\*\*\*\*\*

"Master," Thirteen said kneeling at Triton's feet, "the apprentice is stronger than we thought. We should kill the man they seek and disappear."

"I'm not going anywhere," Triton said, his voice rumbling. "Not without my key: that key is everything. Did they bring it with them?"

"No, my Master; no key."

"Well we'll find it, soon enough. Branson couldn't have hid it that well. You will search his home. The young girl will be mine when this is over and the detectives as well as their helper will share her fate. We have nothing to fear from these humans. We are immortal, they are weak."

"I do not fear them, Master," Thirteen remarked. "I only worry for you, for your sake. I feel you are in danger if you stay here, key or no key."

"Are you saying I can't handle a couple of humans, as frail as they are? With my armies, I have killed thousands upon thousands. I have defeated hundreds of hunters. They play by the rules, but we, Thirteen, we break those rules. You have become more powerful than I ever imagined. And someday, when you are ready, you will move from my side and take my place. When the time has come, you will be invincible, as I am invincible."

Thirteen stood from his devoted pose and followed Triton to the windows overlooking the city. He looked out at the buildings, tall, shining in the sun. Triton smiled a guilty smile, full of arrogance and nodded towards Thirteen.

"Kill the man, do my will, and all this can be yours," he mused, gesturing at the skyline, "as far as the eye can see."

"I know it's not my place to question, Master, but why must you decide when I am ready?"

"For this reason: you are strong, but not patient. In your haste to conquer, you jeopardize your future. You must still follow me," Triton calmly answered. "You are strong, yes, but not *that* strong."

With those words, he put his apprentice in his place. Triton believed the world was his. He had never felt as strong as this.

"I am invincible," he grinned, relishing his words, his voice deep and gravely.

A quick movement reflected in the glass. His eyes widened, Triton watched a blur move behind him, but couldn't turn quick enough to see.

"Thirteen!" he exclaimed, a burst of blood spattering against the window.

Triton looked down at the burning in his stomach. Thirteen's blade was sticking through him, the razor-sharp tip screeching against the glass.

"I guess the time has come, Master," Thirteen whispered in Triton's ear.

Slowly, he raised his fist so that Triton could see it, then uncurled his fingers, an old rusty key resting in his gloved palm. Triton sputtered in disbelief, a trickle of blood in the corner of his mouth, his face straining in pain. Thirteen, as if performing a trick, flicked his fingers and it disappeared, then slipped his hand back into his jacket and removed a small golden-handled dagger.

Triton's eyes grew wide, he recognized it immediately. It was ancient, Babylonian, one of his relics.

"Superstitious old man..."

With another swift motion, he slit Triton's throat. Blood dripped from the ceremonial blade. As his master died, Thirteen held him, reveling in every jolt, every gurgle, as life fled from his body.

Removing his bloodied sword, Thirteen wiped the blade off on Triton's suit. His mask wrinkled in an odd way, as if a smile had erupted just below. The room was filled with a piercing howl, the sound coming from Triton's gaping, breathless mouth. Thirteen recited an ancient language and the howling stopped. Looking over Triton's dead form, Thirteen slid his sword back into its sheath.

************

Gavin, Ashley, and Kayla raced past the unconscious receptionist and stopped at the elevator, staring hopelessly at the directory that hung on the wall. Ashley's jaw dropped in disbelief.

"One hundred and thirteen floors, how will we ever know where to find him?!" she exclaimed.

Kayla stepped forward and reached for the buttons, but paused. Her own voice spoke to her inside her head, guided her.

*Strange*, she thought, *it sounds like me, but somehow different?!*

"Triton's up, Jamie's in the basement," she said.

"How do you know?" Ashley questioned.

"I just know," Kayla answered quickly.

Gavin pushed the button for the basement, "Going down."

\*\*\*\*\*\*\*\*\*\*\*\*

The elevator stopped, its doors slowly sliding open. They raised their guns, staring into the darkness of the hallway. It was difficult to see.

Cautiously, they began their search for Jamie. Every ten feet or so, they found a locked door, dim light shining out through a small window in its upper panel, the light glowing softly against the walls, illuminating their steps. Kayla led the way, her pistol hanging at her side. She didn't feel the need for it at the moment. There was an odd peace, everyone felt it.

The hallway seemed to go on forever. It turned here and there, leading them in different directions, like a labyrinth built to confuse anyone lost in its passage ways. Ashley peered through the small glass window in each door. Gavin followed close behind her. Kayla walked in silence, the hallways seeming so familiar, just as she'd seen in her dream.

They turned the last corner. Kayla stopped dead in her tracks. There it was, the door that led to Jamie, but standing just in front of it was a thin shadowy figure, a dark hood hiding its face, its back turned to them.

Kayla raised her gun, clicking off the safety, "Turn around slowly, or I'll shoot!"

The figure remained still.

"Fine, have it your way. Three...two..." she began to count.

Before she got to one, a familiar voice echoed in the dark hall.

"My dear Ms. Rose, if you shoot me, how can I help you?" he said, turning and removing his hood.

Kayla's jaw dropped. Ashley stared in shock. Gavin grinned.

"You're late," he said holstering his gun.

"Joseph!" Ashley squealed, "But you can't be, you're..."

"Dead?" Joseph smiled with a peaceful expression.

"Are you a, a, *ghost*?" Kayla asked, amazed to see him standing there.

"No, no, my dear, I'm quite alive, but not necessarily in the way you think," Joseph answered, still smiling. "God has allowed me to remain a little while longer. I'm no longer a fighter, but a guardian."

"But how?" Ashley asked.

"When the time comes, it will make perfect sense, I promise. But for now, Ms. Rose, I believe we could use one more ally," he said, nodding towards the door.

Kayla peered through the glass. Jamie sat slumped on the floor, the table overturned: he wasn't moving.

"I hope we're not too late!" Kayla exclaimed, trying the locked door knob.

"I've got this," Gavin said, stepping towards the door, ready to kick it in.

Joseph raised his hand and stopped him without a word. A burst of light illuminated the dark hall. Lowering his hand, the door clicked and gently opened.

Kayla opened the door wide and stepped through the frame. Fresh air from the hallway flooded in, masking the staleness of the small room. Jamie sat up slowly, expecting another beating, his bloodied bandage hanging to one side of his head.

"Kayla!" he yelled, jumping up from the cold, dirty floor, but stumbling back down, his legs weak. "The FBI agents are in on everything. They have masks, like the one I found on that body! And you were right, Triton is behind it all, the murders and O'Donnell; everything."

"I know," Kayla told him, helping him to his feet. "Are you strong enough to help us get Triton?"

"You bet," he said as they stepped into the hallway.

Kayla smiled, overwhelming relief and emotion dancing in her head. Jamie was back, safe and sound.

"I want to get that son of a..." he paused, "...Ashley! You're here too?"

Ashley's smile matched her sister's. She too was thankful.

"Who's the old man?" he asked, his gaze falling upon Joseph, then spotting Gavin, "and the guy with the tattoos?"

"I know you have many questions," Joseph smiled, "and they will be answered, but now is not the time. Can you fight?"

Jamie looked at the rag-tag crew and nodded yes. Gavin pulled the gun from his left holster and handed it to him with a smile.

"This girl has gone through more than you know to get you out of here!" Gavin said, tipping his head towards Kayla.

Jamie looked at her and smiled. She hadn't left his side now that they'd found him.

They made their way back to the elevator, Joseph hobbling just behind them. The doors slid open again and they all stepped inside its mirrored brass walls.

"What floor?" Ashley asked, ready to push a button.

Jamie loaded a bullet into the chamber of the gun as his voice rang with a vengeful note, "We're going all the way to the top."

************

The elevator climbed slowly, the floors passing by quietly, light jazz music playing softly in the background. The five looked at each other, wordless, each face intense with the expectations of what was coming.

Jamie eyed Gavin with uneasiness, but Gavin didn't notice. His eyes were closed, his brow furled. Kayla checked her gun, while Ashley nervously shifted from one foot to the other. Holding his chest, Joseph leaned in the corner, looking over his makeshift band of heroes, his worn robe stained in blood.

The elevator slowed. They'd reached the one hundred and thirteenth floor. With a ding, the metal doors smoothly slid open. They stepped out into the small entry hall, finding themselves in the dark once again, the lights off, the switch on the wall unresponsive. Gavin slowly opened the door into Triton's office as Jamie leaned through the frame, his gun raised, looking left then right.

"It's empty. He's not here," Jamie said, disappointed, dropping his gun to his side.

"This is his office?" Kayla asked, pushing past Jamie and into the room.

Ashley followed. Gavin and Jamie gave each other the same look, as if to ask why they were still there if Triton was gone. One wall housed a large, ornate bookshelf, reaching from ceiling to floor. Ashley browsed the collection while Kayla walked around the room. Although the lights were off, the windows glowed, the sun's warm rays illuminating the office. The museum-like oddities that filled the room cast strange shadows about the walls.

Kayla picked up a note from Triton's desk: it was sloppily written. The words scribbled on the page were hard to read, nearly flowing into each other. The note must have been written by Triton, but it talked of nothing more than a new civil project and a marketing campaign planned for Times Square. Placing the paper back where she'd found it, she glanced at the window just past the desk. A smear of blood glistened on the glass. Her eyes followed the streak downward and stopped at Triton's body lying in a puddle of sticky red mess.

"Jamie!" Kayla shouted. "It's Triton, he's dead!"

She stood up from where she'd knelt to check his pulse. Jamie raced over, followed closely by Gavin. Joseph lingered in the door way: he had yet to enter the room.

Triton's eyes were still open, their white glaze reflecting the faces of the two men as they looked down at his body. Ashley had seen enough death for one day. She continued to look at the books.

"How could this be? Triton can't be dead." Gavin said in frustration. "It would mean that I've done all this training, hunted sleepwalkers, all for nothing!"

Joseph looked ill. He didn't say a word. Gavin was the least of his concerns at the moment. Thought after thought echoed in his ears. He was trying to wrap his mind around Triton's death. He wondered who could be powerful enough to kill a sleepwalker like Triton. Joseph knew that he could handle the demon, especially with Gavin's help, but someone acting alone?

Ashley found a book called "Lucifer" and pulled it from the shelf. She hadn't opened it yet when she saw what looked like a set of flaming red eyes watching her through the space where the book had been.

The leather bound book thudded against the ground, drawing everyone's attention away from Triton's body. Ashley stared at the group with a horrified expression, then looked back to where the eyes had been. They were gone.

"What?" Gavin asked, heading towards the shelf, Jamie close behind him.

Her hands were shaking as she answered, "Something was watching me through the wall, through there!"

She pointed at the empty spot on the shelf. Jamie peered past the books and into the darkness. He couldn't see a thing, but a light draft filtered through. The air smelled foul.

"The wall is hollow behind here," Jamie said, feeling around the edges of the shelf for a lever or a gap, anything to open the bookcase.

"Do you think it's like a secret, trick door where you have to find the right one that opens it?" Ashley asked, tugging on the spines of several books.

"Give me a hand, Gavin," Jamie prompted and they grabbed the corners of the shelf and pulled as hard as they could.

Stubbornly, the bookcase finally began to move. They tried harder, pressing against the wall for leverage.

"Get back!" Joseph warned the girls.

With a slow creak, the shelf finally broke free from the wall and crashed to the ground, hundreds of books spilling onto the floor of Triton's office. Jamie climbed over the wreck and looked into the darkness, then remembered the lighter in the box of cigarettes. He reached into his pocket and pulled out O'Donnell's cigarettes, staring sadly at the blood-crusted blue box, then flipped it open and dumped the lighter into his palm. With a flick, he watched the orange flame dance to life.

"Where'd you get that?" Kayla asked, placing her hand on his shoulder.

"It was O'Donnell's."

Carefully, they climbed over the piles of books. Old wooden curios cabinets lined the small secret room, their shelves housing strange artifacts and tools. Yellow glass jars filled with odds and ends from different animals hung from coat hanger-like wires looped over rusty hooks twisted into the low rafters. Spiders crawled in every corner. The walls were covered in ancient, cryptic symbols. A small altar-like box sat on a table against the far wall, a photograph pinned to its lid by a small ornate dagger.

Kayla pulled the picture loose and took a better look. Jamie held the lighter close. It was Ashley, the photograph that had disappeared from its frame on Kayla's mantle. A lump grew in her throat.

"I think Triton wanted us to find this. He set this whole thing up," she said shakily.

251

"Set what up?" Gavin retorted. "Triton's dead. I don't think that was part of his plan."

Jamie lifted a jar off the floor, an old dried heart inside. The yellowing label that wrapped around it was faded, but the scrawling could still be made out, if just barely, "Triton."

"Maybe Triton never had any control," he said.

Joseph had yet to enter the secret room. The closer he got to the entryway, the worse he felt, but at this discovery, he quickly made his way over the broken shelf.

"Let me see that," he said curiously, reaching for the jar.

He pulled a pair of small wire-rimmed glasses from a pocket inside his robe and slid them on, nearly dropping the jar as the heart inside it jumped to life: it was beating. Joseph tried to slow his breathing as Gavin stood looking over the rickety wooden table, its legs covered in webs, every inch of its surface cluttered with various guns and weapons, unused bullets scattered about, the dagger on the shrine in the very middle. Something caught his eye. Carefully, he picked up the small black iron object.

"Check this out," he grinned, his hand outstretched, palm up, an old key resting in it.

"That's it," Jamie smiled, turning to Kayla excitedly as he took the key from Gavin, "that's the key, the one Sykes talked about!"

They stood staring at it, an odd disappointment washing over them. Now that they finally had it, did it really tell them anything they needed to know? It looked like any other old key.

"You've found my secret!" a loud voice called from Triton's office.

Joseph jumped, losing his grip, the jar tumbling to the ground, hitting the floor and rolling to a stop against Gavin's foot. The room filled with laughter as Gavin picked it up.

"Triton's dead," the voice taunted.

They headed back into the office, Joseph taking the lead, expecting to see Triton standing at his desk, but a man towered over the lifeless body, his dark silhouette outlined by the sun. Thirteen stood laughing at the sight of the heroes, his hands hanging empty at his sides.

"Hunter, you come to me with two little girls, an overzealous apprentice, and Triton's hostage? You were too old to kill my master, so I saved you the trouble. The problem is that you are now all that stands in my way from reaching my goal."

"What goal is that?" Gavin questioned, readying his gun.

"We have the key now. You're going to have to fight for it." Jamie challenged.

"Are you really that stupid?" Thirteen grunted. "The key was Triton's obsession, the dying dream of an old man. I could care less. Go ahead and keep it, a souvenir!"

"This man believes he is destined to be the right hand of the Devil, as it were, to be an extension of his evil on Earth," Joseph answered. "It was Triton's dream, the dream of the Order."

"The Order is dead, just like Triton," Thirteen chuckled, "nothing but myths and nonsense. And I'm not meant to be the right hand of the devil, Joseph is it? I'm nothing like Triton, I promise you that."

Gavin watched as Joseph placed his hands into the deep folds of his robe. Thirteen stood his ground.

"Where my master failed, I will not."

"You can't have Ashley," Kayla chimed in. "I told you that before."

"Silly girl, do you still think this was about you and your sister?"

"But what about her dreams, her vision of Triton," Kayla said confused.

"The girl was never of consequence, at least to me. Armageddon, blah, blah, blah...what could she possibly have to do with marking the beginning of the end? I played along with Triton's little game, adding fuel to his fire and giving him pieces to put together. I used her to make Triton feel as though I wasn't plotting his demise. I followed him like a dog and when the time was right, I bit, hard," Thirteen laughed, looking at Triton's bloody, dead body. "You were my distraction, you kept Triton's gaze off of me."

"If you're telling the truth, how did you manage to convince someone as powerful as Triton that we were a threat to him?" Ashley wondered.

"Please, the wheels were set in motion before you or I was even born. Each day has been played out already, an eternal battle between Heaven and Hell, and we've all been caught in the middle. It's not even our war. But we keep getting involved, on both sides, heroes and villains alike, just like your pathetic brother, pity," he scoffed. "You would think that God would use stronger people? But I have what I want. With Triton dead, there's no need for this to continue. Let's let bygones be bygones and go on with our lives."

"You really think we're just going to let you walk out of here?" Kayla argued in disbelief. "You're an accessory to murder, arson, kidnapping...and who knows what else."

"I gave you half the clues you needed to lead you right here to this office where you're standing now."

"The body in the park," Jamie muttered.

"What about Jamie?" Ashley added. "You kidnapped him, beat him!"

"No I didn't. It was Triton's other men, my lesser brothers; same with the fire at the site of the sacrifice," Thirteen explained.

"So then you deny killing the DA as well?" Jamie laughed.

"No. I did do that. But in killing Lister, I did this city a favor. He was dirty. And for the record, so are the Mayor and the Police Commissioner. That's why your boss is dead. They wanted you two shut up, your investigation ended, but he stood up to them. He died protecting you, Detective."

Jamie lowered his gun, confused. In a weird way, it did make sense. Could this be the truth?

"He's lying," Gavin shouted. "He's trying to worm his way out of this."

"I admit," Thirteen shrugged, "to get what I wanted, I did some things I'm not proud of, but Triton is the real monster here. In a way, I'm a victim in this just like you."

Gavin had enough. He raised his gun and opened fire.

"If you insist," Thirteen grinned beneath his mask, his gloved hands clenching into fists.

Bullets clacked into the windows, small shards scattering in the air. Kayla and Ashley followed Gavin, shooting wildly at Thirteen. Jamie waited, aiming steadily, trying for more precise shots. But Thirteen was too quick. He effortlessly dodged the bullets like they were traveling in slow motion. Gun smoke filled the air, a faint burning smell lingered. They stopped shooting and looked down at the dozens of spent bullet casings that lay scattered at their feet.

"We didn't even come close," Jamie grunted.

Thirteen straightened his suit coat, then applauded their feeble attempt, his hands slapping together mockingly.

"He can't be killed like this," Joseph spoke wisely. "We must use the strength God has given us. And even then, we will only prevail if it is His will."

"I thought that we could play a little longer," Thirteen said, kneeling over Triton's body, "but I'm getting bored with this. I gave you the chance to live, but now, I'm not feeling so generous."

They watched as he turned away from them, as if they were no longer even there.

"What do you think, Kay?" Ashley asked. "Is he for real, is he telling the truth?"

"I have no idea," she replied, "not taking her eyes off of Thirteen, the sights on her gun lined up with his head.

Thirteen began speaking once again in that same strange language. He held up Triton's lifeless head by his white hair and continued to speak softly.

Joseph closed his eyes. He'd hoped it wouldn't come to this, but he was ready. The truth would be shown.

Light shot from Triton's hollow eyes as a small shrill hiss grew inside his mouth. Thirteen stood back and watched as Triton's body lifted from the ground.

"I wanted this to end, I wanted to let you live. But you couldn't leave well enough alone, could you, *angel*?"

Everyone turned towards Joseph, the same confused looks across their faces. His eyes were still closed and his head bowed, his hands hidden within his robe.

"Oh," Thirteen laughed, seeing the looks on their faces, "he didn't tell you?! All this time I've been telling the truth and one of your own is the liar."

The screaming sound grew louder, drawing their attention back to Triton's now upright, floating body. In a blast of yellow light, Triton collapsed back to the ground, a massive leathery shadow with red glowing eyes standing in his place. It momentarily spread out its bat-like wings then wrapped them tightly around its midsection. Flexing its muscles, the creature tipped back its beastly, horned head and let out a deafening roar.

"Your will, not mine," Joseph said softly, his eyes flicking open.

He raised his head and dropped his robe, revealing a beautiful pair of white feathered wings. Joseph's appearance had changed. He was younger, stronger. The muscles in his arms rippled, his eyes glowed like the sun. A silver breastplate guarded his chest and a heavy leather belt hung around his waist, a beautifully detailed long sword sheathed at his side. His bracers matched his breastplate, as did his boots and Romanesque skirt, a blend of finally crafted leather and steel. Without a word, he lunged headlong towards the demon. The beast unfurled its wings and fanned out its skeletal fingers, ready to fight.

Joseph plowed into him, sending them flailing through the bullet riddled window. They fell, swinging wildly at each other in a frenzy of fists as small shards of glass glistened in the mid-day sun. Closer and closer, they raced to the ground, still beating on each other, then, SMASH! Chunks of asphalt flung into the air as they exploded through the pavement and into a utility access tunnel. Water sprayed from broken pipes, electrical lines sparked and flickered. On the street above, traffic skidded to a stop, vehicles ramming one into the next. Debris crashed down all around unsuspecting pedestrians, flooding the sidewalks with panic.

The fight continued as they staggered to their feet.

Joseph circled the monster, buying time to think.

"It's been a long time," the demon growled, snarling through his fangs.

"Yes," Joseph agreed, "it has, and you've remained one step ahead of me for centuries, but not today!"

"I should have killed you when I had the chance, in Jerusalem."

"I wish I'd done the same," Joseph smirked.

The demon roared and a glowing sword of flame materialized in his hand. He gripped its handle with both hands, raising it high over his head.

"Die, angel!"

Joseph pulled his sword and readied himself, anticipating the strike. The demon swung downward, Joseph's legs buckling under the force of the strike, his heels digging into the muddy clay. Sparks danced as their swords clanged. The demon raised his sword again, ready for another strike, and again, Joseph countered. The demon pushed harder, taking exhausting swings, his sword falling in huge fiery arcs.

Thirteen stood at the broken window, focusing on the fight far below. Gavin nodded. Jamie picked up on it and grinned, hoping to take advantage of the distraction. They opened fire on him once again. But Thirteen had grown impatient. As the bullets streaked towards him, he raised his hand. They slowed to a stop.

Gavin stared in disbelief, the bullets hanging in mid-air. He turned and looked at Ashley. She stood frozen in place, her gun razed, the slide on her gun half way though its cycle. Jamie and Kayla were the same.

"What is this?" Gavin asked.

Thirteen thought for a moment before speaking, the bullets hanging between him and Gavin, "I gave you the opportunity to live. I'm still giving you that chance. Tell the detectives to complete their investigation and implicate the Mayor and the Commissioner. They have all the evidence they need. There's one last thing I must do."

"And what's that?"

"I can't tell you. But if you want to live, don't follow me," Thirteen pleaded, lowering his hand, the bullets clattering to the ground.

In the crater below, the creature continued to swing his sword in huge, violent strikes, all the while slowing: Joseph was wearing him down. Again, the demon raised his sword high above his head. Feeling his energy dwindling, he readied for a powerful killing strike. But the angel was faster. Joseph tumbled to the side, evading the blow. The demon's blade smashed into the dirt. The angel spun around and thrust his sword into the belly of the beast. Shrieking, it stumbled backwards. A mixture of smoke and black, oily blood poured from the wound. His flaming sword evaporated into ash as he looked down at Joseph, the silver blade piercing deep in his stomach, and cursed Heaven in a grunting, unintelligible tongue. Joseph twisted his blade and the demon shuddered, bursting into a million tiny red particles that glowed like hot coals. He stepped back, watching as they slowly settled to the ground and crumbled into black char.

Joseph leapt into the air, sword in hand, his massive wings beating as he hurried upwards to Triton's office.

Thirteen saw him coming. Joseph glided back through the broken window and touched-down gracefully, his sword ready, the tip aimed at Thirteen.

"Your move," Joseph taunted.

Thirteen crossed his arms, unfazed by the angel's threat, "You killed a very powerful demon, old man. Good for you."

Joseph stood firm, his blade resolute.

"But I am not like Triton," Thirteen boasted. "I know your power and I respect it. God has willed all of this, and I have played my part."

Kayla and Ashley watched as Joseph lowered his sword. Gavin

chambered another round. Jamie followed suit.

"What do you mean?" Joseph asked, intrigued.

"Your quarrel was with Triton, not me. And I would think you'd be a bit more appreciative, maybe a 'thank you' is in order."

"Thank you for what?" Gavin laughed.

"For taking care of Triton. The angel could not hurt his human form and you *heroes* could never have killed the demon."

"What's he talking about, Joseph?" Kayla wondered.

"He speaks the truth," the angel admitted, "I cannot strike a human. It's why Triton survived so long. He trapped himself inside that fleshy disguise, outsmarted me, leaving me able to follow, but unable to do anything. Where I could only take on the appearance of a man, he actually possessed Triton: an abomination of both physical and spiritual."

"And our bullets, no matter how many, would never kill Triton in his true form," Gavin added. "The physical can't damage the spiritual."

Joseph smiled, understanding God's design, "Triton's physical body was protected by his demonic powers, powers shared by this young man. Just as he stopped your bullets, Triton would have done the same. Triton's trust in his apprentice was his demise. God knew that Triton would only be destroyed by someone he trusted. Amazing!"

"So is he really, you know, on our side?" Ashley asked.

Thirteen laughed, amused by their confusion, "I am not on any side but my own. I've gotten what I want. As far as I'm concerned, we're done."

"No!" Jamie growled. "You'll answer for what you've done, the people you've killed."

"We can't let you live, let the demon inside you live," Gavin agreed.

"I'm no sleepwalker," Thirteen laughed, "my *arrangement* with the Devil is far beyond your understanding."

"Are you saying you sold your soul to the devil?" Kayla mocked.

"No, no. That's so cliché. But you could say I owe him my life."

"Satan has no power to give life, only to destroy." Joseph said in disagreement.

"Like I said, you wouldn't understand, especially you, angel. You may have lived among humans, but don't be fooled, God made *man* in His image, not you. You're just a pet."

Gavin stepped in front of Joseph and pulled the trigger. Thirteen snatched the bullet out of the air and threw it back at him, sending it bouncing off Gavin's chest.

"So this is your choice then?" he asked.

"To fight!" Gavin confirmed.

"So be it. But not now; there are still more games to play and I'm having too much fun to end it like this, in Triton's tomb."

They raised their guns in opposition. This wasn't over.

"Catch me, if you can," he growled, vanishing.

\*\*\*\*\*\*\*\*\*\*\*\*

Joseph sheathed his sword. Gavin stood with his gun hanging limply at his side, confused, disappointed, and angry. He raised the old jar and looked inside. Triton's heart had stopped beating.

"I'm sorry I never told you, Gavin, but this is what I really am," Joseph said, pulling his robe back over his shoulders, his wings disappearing beneath it. "Thirteen was right, I'm not from your world."

Gavin turned and stared deep into Joseph's eyes, the angel gone, the old man Gavin remembered looking back sorrowfully.

"I understand," Gavin answered humbly. "Deep down, I always knew your story was too crazy; a man living for centuries, it's just not possible. And had you told me the truth, I would have asked too many questions, been more interested in what you are than what you could teach me. I would never have learned a thing, if I knew you were really an angel."

"It is a ridiculous story," Joseph smiled. "I thank God that you all had the faith to believe."

"But we believed a lie," Kayla frowned.

"No, not really," Joseph explained. "You believed in the ideals that I proposed, that you were called, at this moment in your life, to do something greater, something you'd never imagined. And I did chase after Triton for centuries."

They all stared at Joseph awkwardly.

Kayla spoke first, "So, Triton wasn't really a man? What was that...*thing*...inside of him?"

"That, my dear, is why I called Triton a sleepwalker. He lived with that demon inside him for centuries, like a host to a parasite, a spiritual disease. The demon's power kept the body alive. And actually, I confess, it was one of the most powerful demons I've ever seen," Joseph explained, stroking his thin gray beard. "But there is one thing that confuses me. Thirteen said this was over. He didn't want to harm any of us. With Triton gone, I assumed, maybe naively, that he used Triton, and you, to get to me, to allow him to kill me. But that was not his goal, all along. I'm afraid I didn't see it before. I should have, but I was focused on Triton and overlooked the real threat. I believe there's more to this, *Thirteen*, character that remains to be seen. I'm sorry I put you and your sister in danger, Ms. Rose. And I'm sorry I deceived you all."

Joseph stretched out his arms and embraced Gavin, then turned and smiled at Jamie, "So, my boy, still believe there's no God?"

"I, uh, really don't know," Jamie stammered. "I feel like I've been sleeping and now my eyes have been opened, but things are still fuzzy."

"The truth feels different for everyone," Joseph smiled, offering his hand in friendship.

Jamie grasped Joseph's hand, but said nothing. He was still processing everything he'd seen.

"And now, my sweet girls," Joseph said, turning to face them, "I thank you, for everything."

"Thank us?" Ashley smiled.

"Without the two of you, Gavin would not have struck when he did. God knew what role each of you would play, and you all played it to perfection. And you," he said, gently touching Ashley on the arm, "you're special to him. Though you've known each other for such a short time, he's let you see who he really is. For all his heroics, he's quite insecure, distrusting. I've never seen him take to anyone the way he's taken to you."

Ashley blushed as Joseph looked at Kayla, "Ms. Rose, you've faced great dangers, but it is not over. Jamie is now questioning everything he thought he knew. Show him the truth. He loves you, you know."

Joseph stepped towards the window, then turned, his face wrinkled and warm, goodbye glistening in his eyes, "My work here is finished. Gavin, continue to fight: Thirteen must be stopped. And I do not think you've seen the last of him. And remember, angels are always watching. They will help you see God's plan, even when it seems there is none."

Joseph looked to the heavens with satisfaction, knowing after so many years of service, his task was finally complete. He smiled one last time at Gavin and faded away, leaving the four of them standing in disbelief.

# XIV

## TUESDAY NIGHT

Jamie stood in the shower, hot water running down his face. It felt good to wash the blood away, to get clean. Resting his hands on the wall, his head hanging, he contemplated everything that had happened over the last few days, everything he'd seen, and what he was beginning to believe.

Faith was never one of his strong points. He'd rather talk about politics than religion, but something in him was changing: he could feel it. He felt it the first time he talked with Kayla. He felt it as he sat trapped in that room, alone, the darkness playing tricks with his mind. It made him *want* to change old habits, become a better person. But he didn't know why. Jamie had always seen such strength inside Kayla, a resolution he'd never experienced. Now, after all this, he understood where it came from and he wanted it too.

The small bathroom filled with steam. It was clouded, just like his head. Turning off the water and reaching for a towel, Jamie stepped out onto the cold tile floor and dried off, wrapping the towel around his waist; careful not to aggravate the many bruises covering his body: souvenirs from his visit to Tri-Corp. His face stung from the beating he'd taken in that elevator.

Wiping the condensation away from the mirror, Jamie inspected himself, bruised, broken, a large cut above his left eye. Stopping at his shoulder, he reached up and traced his finger around a small, raised scar just below his right collarbone: a bullet wound. It was still tender, even after two years. Slowly, he rubbed at it, trying to push the pain, or more so, the memory away.

Flipping open the medicine cabinet that hung on the wall in front of him, Jamie pulled out an orange prescription bottle of vicodin. He popped off the top, dumped two into his hand, and placed the bottle back on the shelf. As he closed the door, the mirror once again reflected his pain. He tilted his head back and swallowed the little white pills, then looked back in the mirror. A shiver ran down his spine. Standing just over his shoulder was a large winged creature, black as night, its eyes a phosphorous yellow. Dark, wispy fog seemed to emanate from its body.

Jamie spun around, nearly dropping his towel. His razor fell from the edge of the white porcelain sink, skittering across the floor. Turning circles in his bathroom, he found himself alone.

A soft knock at the door pulled Jamie back to reality.

"Everything okay?" Kayla asked, leaning against the wall.

Jamie thought for a moment, still frantically scanning the steam-filled room, his eyes darting back and forth.

"Yeah," he finally answered, as he opened the door and smiled as calmly as he could, "just drying off."

"Those don't look too bad," she said, eyeing the small bruises on his face as she gently touched his cheek.

"These are the ones that hurt," he replied, motioning downward.

Large brown and purple bruises were scattered about his chest and stomach, onto his sides, and around his back. Scratches and cuts covered his arms.

Kayla winced as he walked past her and into the bedroom. She turned towards the living room: Ashley and Gavin were sitting quietly on the couch. The warm glow of the television flickered as they flipped through the channels. Kayla knew Jamie needed her now. Quietly, she followed him into his bedroom, the door closing behind them.

"That cut looks pretty bad," Kayla asked as she eyed the gash on his brow, "did you put anything on it?"

Jamie stepped out of his walk-in closet zipping up a pair of faded-wash blue jeans and headed for his dresser. Kayla sat down on the end of his bed.

"I had some antibacterial stuff," he said as he pulled a neatly folded white undershirt out from the top drawer and slid his arms into it. "I used it on my face and on a couple of the deeper cuts on my arms."

Kayla watched as he slowly pulled it down over his bruised shoulders, obviously hurting. But it wasn't his wounds, it was his eyes. He seemed distant.

"I feel like you're not telling me something?" she prodded.

Jamie sat down next to her, a pair of white socks he'd grabbed from his dresser in his hand, the cuffs folded over to hold them in a perfect little ball.

"It's, *him*," Jamie said pulling the socks on, "the guy in the mask. He wouldn't leave me alone while they were holding me at Tri-Corp. He kept messing with my head, even talking about you."

"What did he say?"

"He told me about O'Donnell," Jamie cringed, his sore ribs aching as he bent down to tie a pair of sneakers, "he told me he was going to, *see* you."

"*See?*" Kayla asked uncomfortably.

"Well I'm sure he meant something...else."

"I'm sorry, but, you know he was lying about me, about *seeing* me, right?"

"I know," Jamie said with a half smile, the fire Kayla knew and loved returning to his eyes. "He'll pay for what he's done."

"I'm sure he will. I know you'll make sure he does," she laughed softly. "But are *you* okay?"

"Not being okay won't bring O'Donnell back, Kayla."

They sat silently, looking into each other's eyes. Kayla leaned in closely and kissed him softly on the cheek, trying to find a spot that wasn't black and blue. Slowly, Jamie ran his hands along her neck and up through her hair. They kissed. A flash of lightning illuminated the room. Kayla turned and looked out the window. Large drops of rain pelted the glass.

"When is it ever going to stop?"

"You have to admit," he smiled mischievously, "it is kind of romantic, in a cheesy, classic movie sort of way."

Kayla laid back on the bed. Jamie eased down on top of her and kissed her again. She caressed his arms, her fingers gently pressing into his biceps. He propped himself up on one elbow and reached down with his other hand, unbuttoning her jeans and tugging on the zipper. She smiled as his hand slipped inside her pants.

"Kayla," Ashley's voice called from the hall, "How's Jamie doing. Is he alright?"

"Um...yeah," Kayla answered between kisses.

"The pizza guy is here."

Jamie sighed, rolling onto his back.

"Okay, we're really hungry," Kayla laughed, "be right out."

Kayla stood up and fastened her jeans then bent over Jamie and gave him another kiss, "When this is all over..."

"And we're alone," he interjected.

"And we're alone," Kayla smiled, "I'll make it up to you, I promise."

Jamie sat up, then took her by the hand as they headed out into the sitting area of his loft.

"This is a really nice TV," Gavin grinned, still flipping through channels on Jamie's forty-seven inch LCD display, stopping on a sci-fi movie: two men locked in combat, their laser swords glowing. "Incredible, I love this movie!"

Kayla sat down next to Ashley on the couch and looked around Jamie's cluttered loft. It could use some cleaning. Magazines and old newspapers were piled up in one corner; empty Chinese take-out cartons littered his coffee table.

"We need to figure out what we're doing next," Kayla said, turning her attention back to Gavin, Ashley, and Jamie.

"I agree," Ashley said, grabbing the remote from Gavin and clicking off the television with a smile.

"It's an old movie anyway," Gavin gave in, "besides, I have it on DVD."

Jamie forced a painful smile as he settled into his leather armchair, "So how do we find the guy with the mask?"

"Well, he's definitely not going back to Tri-Corp," Ashley reasoned.

"Yeah, He'll never set foot in there again. And, there's still something bothering me. You know what I can't believe after all this, the whole investigation into Triton, is that he wasn't even the big fish behind everything," Kayla said thoughtfully. "That guy, what did he call himself?"

"He called himself *Thirteen*," Gavin shrugged.

"Right, Thirteen," she continued. "He had us looking the other way the entire time."

"Oh my gosh!" Jamie said, jumping up, his hands raised in frustration. "I can't believe I didn't see it earlier! Think about it, the roman numerals etched in the wall in the basement where the bodies were found, the number *thirteen* was circled in blood..."

"Oh, and at Lister's house," Kayla added enthusiastically. "A *thirteen* was carved into the top of his desk!"

"He's like an artist signing his work," Ashley laughed in disbelief.

"He's sick is what he is," Kayla replied disgusted at the thought of Thirteen taking pride in killing innocent people.

"But he gave himself away, from the very beginning, leaving clues for us to catch," Jamie mused. "Like he wanted us to know, just like he said."

"They weren't very subtle either," Ashley added

"What do you think?" Jamie asked, turning to Gavin.

"I haven't figured this guy out yet," he said scratching his beard. "He's so...*evil*, is the only word I can think of. But he said he only played his part, that he was finished. I can't figure out what he meant. I mean, he let us live. Why?"

\*\*\*\*\*\*\*\*\*\*\*

Thirteen looked out over the city. With Triton gone, he no longer needed to hold back, to hide any of his intentions. Quickly, he turned and walked across the roof of the Tri-Corp building.

The last glimpses of sunlight slipped away into the western most sky. Darkness had come. Black rain clouds shrouded the horizon. Thunder rumbled in the distance.

Glaring down over the ledge, Thirteen stared at the giant Tri-Corp moniker glowing bright blue in the shadows below. Slowly, he knelt down.

"The last of Triton's empire," he said as he closed his eyes, relishing every moment, focusing his will.

Thirteen's mind strained against the weight of the sign. As he concentrated, he felt the world around him fade into a haze. Then, with a horrifying screech, the marquee twisted and jerked as it worked its way loose from the side of the building. Metal ground on stone, as pieces of mortar dropped into the darkness. The letters flickered, then went black. With one final thought, Thirteen dislodged the sign, sending it plummeting to the street below.

\*\*\*\*\*\*\*\*\*\*\*\*

"What about the tapes?" Ashley pointed out as she paced the room. "Maybe there's something we missed?"

"I wouldn't mind hearing them," Gavin thought aloud. "They could lead us to Thirteen."

"Do you have them with you, Kayla?" Jamie asked, rubbing the stiffness from his shoulder.

"No. I hid them in my apartment."

"Then that's where we need to go next," Jamie decided. "Let's get moving."

\*\*\*\*\*\*\*\*\*\*\*\*

Gavin pulled to a stop. Jamie parked his BMW next to him. The parking garage was dark: all the lights were off.

"Strange..." Kayla mumbled, her thought trailing off.

Gavin and Ashley stepped from the van as the sound of Kayla and Jamie closing their car doors echoed off the cold cement walls and pillars. The four walked quickly towards the elevator, their footsteps clicking down the aisles of cars.

"Gavin," Jamie said, stumbling over his words, "back at my apartment...I saw something...a reflection in the mirror."

"What kind of reflection?" he wondered as he watched Kayla push the *up* button.

"It looked similar to what came out of Triton."

The girls eyed each other and stepped into the elevator. Gavin stared at the ground.

"What do you think?" Jamie asked, following the girls through the doors.

"I'll get back to you on it," Gavin finally answered. "Every man has his demons. Maybe you saw yours?"

The elevator stopped on Kayla's floor. Silently, they headed towards her apartment, the lights flickering in the hall. Ashley shivered. Kayla fit her key into the lock and turned.

"That's funny; the door's already...unlocked?"

Gavin pushed past her and led the way into the apartment. All he could do was shake his head.

"What happened?" Ashley cried out as she panned the room.

Kayla felt like she couldn't breathe. Jamie grabbed her around the waist and picked up a toppled chair for her to sit in. The couch was overturned. Papers and magazines lay scattered all over the place. The kitchen cupboards all stood open, the contents dumped onto the floor. Every room was the same.

"Where did you put the tapes, Kayla?" Gavin asked as he cracked his knuckles.

"I, uh, I put them in a cereal box on top of the fridge," she answered, gathering herself.

Gavin grabbed the box of frosted cereal and reached deep inside, then flipped the box upside down and shook it with an exasperated look. It was empty.

"I guess they found what they were looking for," Jamie frowned as he rubbed Kayla's shoulders.

Ashley walked out from the bedroom holding a teddy bear, its belly torn open, stuffing pulled through the ragged hole.

"We need to get somewhere safe," she said. "This had to have been Thirteen."

"How about my place?" Gavin offered.

Kayla nodded with a dazed expression. The rest agreed as well. They had to find a place to rest. Thirteen was still out there.

"Ashley," Jamie said, his instincts taking over, "you and Kayla gather up some clothes to take to Gavin's. We don't know how long we could have to hide out, but we need to be prepared."

Kayla stood, still in a daze, as Ashley grabbed her by the hand and led her through the mess and into the bedroom. Flipping on the light, Kayla gasped as she surveyed her room. Drawers were pulled open, clothes piled everywhere. Her closet stood empty. A few hangers rocked back and forth on a clothes rack running inside it. Every pair of shoes she owned was thrown about the room and, oddly, all of her underwear was spread out on the bed.

"This is nuts!" Ashley said, her hands on her hips.

"Yeah," Kayla laughed; waking from her daze as she picked up a pair of underwear, then tossed them back down.

She stepped around the piles of clothing and pulled a large, rather expensive looking overnight bag out from the mess on the floor of the closet, little tan L-V's patterned on its brown leather cover. The two girls filled it with Kayla's favorite sweater, several t-shirts, and extra jeans, as well as a few pairs of socks Kayla picked up from the floor. Ashley sat on the bed examining all of her sister's underwear.

"Grab a couple pairs for each of us and put them in the bag," Kayla said before heading into the bathroom for her toothbrush and a few other necessities.

"You still have the best taste, Kay. I like these," Ashley laughed, stretching out a particularly lacey pair. "Can I wear these?"

"I don't care," Kayla grinned, dropping a small bag of items from the bathroom into a side pocket. "Just hurry up. I don't feel safe here."

Ashley tossed them in with several other pair, then zipped the bag shut and slung it over her shoulder as they stepped back into the living room.

"All set," Kayla said, nodding at Jamie.

"Good," he grinned, heading for the door, checking to make sure the hallway outside was clear. "Let's get going."

\*\*\*\*\*\*\*\*\*\*\*\*

"Do you see those flashers ahead?" Ashley asked, pointing out the front window of Gavin's van as they slowed to a stop, Jamie's car right behind them.

Gavin rolled down his window and leaned his head out. Emergency vehicles were blocking all the lanes of traffic. A handful of police officers were talking with paramedics a few car lengths away.

Kayla jumped out of the BMW and headed for the cops. Flashing her badge at the officers, she had a quick conversation, then turned to see Jamie standing next to Gavin's window.

"So?" Jamie asked as she stepped alongside him.

"There was an accident outside of the Tri-Corp building," she explained. "Somehow, the big sign that was suspended on the side of the building fell down. Lots of people are hurt. It's a huge mess. They don't know how it happened."

Jamie sighed. Ashley let out a frustrated grunt.

"Alright," Gavin conceded, "we'll take the long way around."

He turned the van down an alleyway, knocking over some trash cans as he cut through to the next street. Jamie and Kayla jumped back in the BMW and followed.

In silence, they wound their way back to Gavin's warehouse: the feelings were overwhelming. Thirteen was getting out of control. No one wanted to admit it, but each person was sure they all thought the same thing: they were no match for him.

Gavin flipped off his headlights and pressed the button on his garage-door opener. With a jolt, it rattled to life. He pulled the van into the warehouse. Jamie squeezed through and pulled off to the right.

Tired and despairing, they headed towards Gavin's dirty old couches.

"You live here?" Jamie laughed as he flopped down next to Kayla.

"You bet. I'll give you the tour later," Gavin grinned.

"So where's the bathroom again?" Ashley asked Gavin, squeezing his arm.

"Follow me."

Gavin took her hand and headed up the stairs. He closed the bedroom door as they passed: the bathroom was in the adjoining room.

"Can I see your room?" Ashley asked as they walked by.

"Oh, um..." Gavin thought a moment, suddenly shy, "yeah, when you're done in the bathroom."

Ashley smiled as she stepped into the bathroom and flipped on the light. Gavin pulled the door shut behind her. The walls were unfinished fiber board. Exposed pipes led to a shower on the wall, a rusty drain in the floor. A work sink stood on the opposite wall with a dirty mirror hanging above it. She laughed to herself as she washed her hands. At least the toilet was clean. Closing the bathroom door behind her, she found Gavin leaning against the railing, looking down over the warehouse. She stepped over to him and wrapped her arms around him.

"See that over there?" he asked, pointing at a half-built motorcycle leaning against a workbench in the far corner of the room.

She nodded.

"I've been working on that bike for three years now. I don't know if I'll ever finish it. You know, in a way, that bike is kind of like me."

"What do you mean?" she asked.

"It's incomplete. It has most of the parts it needs to run, but there's still something, *missing*. Something I haven't found yet..."

He trailed off. Ashley wasn't sure, but she thought she might have seen a tear in his eye as he turned his head away.

"Anyway, did you still want to see my bedroom?" he wondered, rubbing his eyes."

"Are you okay?"

"Yeah," he said sadly, faking a yawn, "just getting tired. That's all. "

He put his hand on her lower back and led her to his room. She opened the door and smiled. It wasn't quite what she pictured, but it was definitely him.

His mattress rested on top of a set of box springs that sat right on the floor. The bed wasn't made: his flannel gray sheets lay tangled about. Simple wood paneling hung on the walls, a well cut square of beige remnant carpet stretched to all four corners. Several skateboard decks and famous movie posters decorated the walls. A small chest of drawers sat on the left, to one side of the bed, and a nightstand balanced it out on the other side; an odd, antique lamp resting on it, several books lay scattered beneath it on the floor. An acoustic guitar rested on the bed.

Ashley looked past the door and stepped into the room. On the wall to the right was a modest flat-screen television. However, on each side of the TV were large shelves running from floor to ceiling, each filled with countless DVD's. Another set of smaller shelves, overflowing with action figures, collectibles, and movie memorabilia, framed the movies on each side. She turned and grinned at Gavin.

"It's my collection," he said blushing. "I'm kind of a movie buff."

"How many do you have?" Ashley asked as she read the names on the spines of the cases.

"I'm not exactly sure," he laughed. "It's almost a compulsion. But, I'd say somewhere around, twelve hundred, maybe more, not including the video games, of course."

"*Oh, of course*," she said heading over to him and kissing him first on the cheek, then on the lips. "I think you definitely have a problem."

He held her close and kissed her again. Then, he walked her out of his bedroom and back down to the others in the living area. Jamie was already asleep on the couch, Kayla resting in his arms, her eyes growing heavy. Gavin glanced at the clock on the kitchen wall: 12:54 am.

"We should get some sleep too," he said as he unfolded a blanket and handed it to Ashley. "Get comfortable. I'll be back in a second."

Gavin headed for the chain-link room and quickly returned with a box of .45 auto ammunition, then pulled his holster, gun and all, from his hip. Ashley was waiting for him, all wrapped up in the blanket. He placed the gun within arms reach, then wedged himself onto the couch between Ashley and the armrest. Kayla stirred and mumbled something, but she never woke. Silently, they smiled at each other.

Ashley quickly drifted off. Gavin reloaded the magazine for his HK USP and then set it beside the gun. He wasn't sure when he finally fell asleep. For a while, he prayed; but soon, he was dreaming. Darkness clouded his mind as doubt filled his thoughts. Thirteen stood laughing inside his head.

\*\*\*\*\*\*\*\*\*\*\*\*

"Master, an ambulance just pulled up at the emergency room. What should we do?"

Thirteen stared out the sliding doors, then fixed his gaze back at the man, Sergeant Keller, a sleepwalker, who stood in front of him.

"Let them in," he smiled beneath his mask. "Invite them to join us. Do the same with any others who stumble upon us."

Slowly, Keller unlocked the door and slid it open. Two paramedics raced past him, a stretcher between them, a man lying deathly still beneath a white sheet, an oxygen mask covering his pale face. As they approached the desk, they froze, the stretchers squeaky wheels coming to a stop. A dozen sleepwalkers stood staring them down hungrily, their shiny black eyes full of anticipation. Slowly, the paramedics stepped back towards the door, but as they turned, they faced another handful of expressionless, hollow faces. They were surrounded. Frantically, the sleepwalkers swarmed down on them. The medics fought back, swinging violently, screaming with every bite, but they couldn't stop the attack.

"Come with me," Thirteen commanded, watching the sleepwalkers with a satisfied grin. "I want to give you something."

Thirteen and Keller turned and left the paramedics to their fate. They wound their way through the corridors and down a flight of stairs into the dark hallways of the basement level.

"This is the psych ward," Thirteen smiled happily as they walked beneath dim, flickering lights, their shoes clicking against the cold floor with each step.

Keller leaned closely to the wall and looked through the glass in one of the doors. A man slumped huddled in the corner of a padded room, covered in sweat, staring blankly at the ceiling. The man's lips were moving, quickly mouthing horrified, unintelligible words as several pairs of red, glowing eyes blinked at him from the darkness. Muffled shouts and screams reverberated from behind other doors as the men approached the end of the hall. Keller stopped and stood next to Thirteen as he opened a heavy, reinforced steel door. Thirteen led the way as they entered into a large room, the walls lined with steel paneling, chains and restraints bolted to the metal. Scratches dug deep into the walls and floor where each set of shackles hung loosely. He stooped down in the middle of the room and picked up a pair of bloody restraints, a heavy chain securing them firmly to the cement. A rusted drain was cut into the floor, centered beneath his feet.

"I have *special* plans for you," he said, nodding at Keller, beckoning him to come closer.

He approached nervously. Thirteen clamped the shackles around each of Keller's wrists and stepped back, patting Keller on the shoulder reassuringly.

"I also have a new name for you," Thirteen laughed softly as he knelt down in front of the man and began a deep, dark chant.

A faint hissing grew from the corners of the room, then turned into an unearthly roar as the sound of beating wings filled the air. Keller fought against the restraints, his eyes opened wide. As he struggled, the rusty metal cut deep into his arms, black blood streaming from the wounds. The roar engulfed him as the stench of sulfur filled his nostrils, forcing him to inhale an evil, shadowy mist. With every second that passed, Keller grew larger and larger, a vast number of demons coursing through him, the dark veins in his arms bursting through his flesh as he felt his muscles tear and stretch. Then, as suddenly as it began, the howling stopped. Keller collapsed wearily to the floor, the blood from his wrists running down the old circular drain.

Thirteen stood proudly, staring at the monster he created. He circled Keller's motionless body, a very satisfied expression wrinkling his mask.

"Can you hear me?" he asked softly.

Keller's eyes flinched, but didn't open. His massive hands rested limp against the floor.

"As I said, I have a new name for you," Thirteen whispered in Keller's ear as he knelt down beside the man. "I will call you Legion, for you are many."

# XV

## WEDNESDAY MORNING

Gray September skies shrouded the rising sun. The city woke in anticipation of another day. A light sprinkle spotted windshields as clouds circled the tallest buildings.

Ashley stretched and headed towards Gavin's kitchen. He was already busy making coffee. The toilet flushed upstairs. Kayla turned and watched Jamie walk down the stairs. He looked much stronger today. A feeling of hope seemed to fill the room this morning: last night's despair was gone. Kayla took the mug Gavin handed her and pulled out a stool at the kitchen counter.

"Good morning," Jamie yawned, pouring himself a cup of coffee as he took the stool next to Kayla.

"Aren't you chipper?" Ashley teased with a shiver, a blanket wrapped tightly around her.

Gavin silently finished his coffee and headed up to his room. Quickly, he returned with two zip-up hooded sweatshirts. Handing one to Ashley, he put the other on, then disappeared around the corner.

"What's up with him?" Kayla wondered.

"I don't know," Ashley said as she zipped up the brown sweatshirt he gave her. "I'll go see what's going on."

Jamie stopped her, his hand on her shoulder, "Would you mind if I talked to him?"

"Oh, sure, alright. I just hope he's okay. He seems, sort of, not himself. You know what I mean?"

Jamie followed the ratcheting sound of a socket wrench and found Gavin hunched over next to his motorcycle. A mess of tools laid spread out on a grease stained grey quilt, the stitching frayed, some of the filling working its way out through holes.

"So..." Jamie paused, feeling out the words, "Harley Davidson, huh?"

"Yeah," Gavin answered without looking up, "it needs new paint though."

"This isn't that bad," Jamie said, examining the badly scratched and worn black tank. "What are you working on?"

"I'm having some trouble with the carburetor," he grunted as he removed the last bolt, dirt flaking off the motor as he pulled it away from its mount.

"Mind if I take a look?"

"Knock yourself out," Gavin said, handing the part to Jamie, then leaning against the tool bench.

Jamie flipped the butterfly open and closed on the manifold then grabbed a rag off the bench and cleaned a decade's worth of gunk from the carburetor.

"So, why so quiet this morning?" Jamie finally asked as he checked the manifold again, carefully easing into the conversation.

"It's nothing really," Gavin shrugged as he watched Jamie work, "I just didn't sleep well."

"Come on, we need to trust each other," Jamie said, standing up, setting the part on the bench and rubbing his dirty hands together, "After all, I trust you."

Gavin stared at him a moment, weighing his thoughts. Jamie was right: they were all in this together now.

"Last night, as I slept," Gavin said thoughtfully, almost sadly, "I saw Thirteen in a dream, laughing at me. I think he's starting to get to me."

"It doesn't matter," Jamie replied, shaking his head, "you're the strongest of us. He can't do a thing to you. Don't let him manipulate you like this."

"You can be strong too," Gavin shrugged, "but you're going to have to face your demons first."

"How, with guns?"

"No. You can't fight demons that way. They aren't from *this* world, so they can't be fought with anything from *this* world."

"Where do they come from then?"

Gavin leaned next to Jamie against the work bench and crossed his arms.

"They come out of the darkness," he answered, "from Hell."

Jamie stared at him with an odd, confused look.

"What do you mean *darkness*? I thought Hell was supposed to be all fire and brimstone?"

"The Bible talks about a lake of fire, but only refers to Hell as a place of darkness," Gavin explained.

"So the flames of Hell are just a scare tactic that preachers use to frighten people into believing, huh?" Jamie grinned.

"You could say so. I just know we're definitely not sinners in the hands of an angry God."

"Anyway, back to my first question. As a hunter, a *demon* hunter, how do you hunt something you can't kill?"

"Guns are used only when necessary, in circumstances of physical manifestations."

"Possessions?"

"No, possessions are a spiritual conflict, like oppression. Physical manifestations are not common. They're what Joseph referred to as *sleepwalkers*. In possession, the demon can be cast out, fought through prayer. In the same way, with oppression, the demon is tied to bonds of sin or temptation, also countered by prayer, but a sleepwalker has shared its soul with the demon. They are no longer human. Their body has become a host for the demon. They died the moment they asked the demon to enter them. For that reason, I hunt them."

"So what about *my* demon?"

"I've seen him," Gavin said very matter-of-factly. "He's here now."

"What?"

"Over there," Gavin explained, pointing toward a dark corner of the room, "he's been watching us and he doesn't like what I'm telling you."

Jamie stared into the shadows, but couldn't see a thing.

"Is he going to attack us?" he asked nervously.

"No," Gavin grinned.

"Why not?"

"Because, a couple of angels are standing by the girls."

Jamie looked over at the kitchen. Ashley and Kayla were sitting on the stools, chatting away, sipping from their mugs. He still didn't see anything.

"The demon won't move as long as the angels are here."

"So you see them too?" Jamie sighed.

"All the time."

\*\*\*\*\*\*\*\*\*\*\*\*

"Lock those doors, barricade them. I want no access from the outside," Thirteen ordered. "If they want a war, they'll have a war."

At once, his sleepwalkers hurried about, doing his bidding, barring the doors to the hospital with anything they could find: chairs, benches, tables, desks. All of them worked thoughtlessly, like he controlled their will. The young nurse approached Thirteen, staring at him with her black, glazed eyes, blood stains on her bright white scrubs.

"Master," she whispered, "how do you know they will come?"

"Because," he laughed cruelly, "I've sent them an invitation."

\*\*\*\*\*\*\*\*\*\*\*\*

Ashley stood. Kayla turned quickly, an alarmed look on her face.

"Did you hear that?" Ashley asked.

Kayla cocked her head to one side, listening intently.

"It sounded like a knock," she finally answered, "at the garage door."

They turned as the sound faintly echoed again, this time from the small door that led out onto the dock at the front of the building.

"Jamie?!" Kayla called, "I think someone's outside."

Gavin glared at the demon in the dark corner then turned to Jamie.

"You cover me, I'll answer the door."

"What do you mean *cover you*," Jamie asked, "maybe it's just somebody you know, a friend?"

282

"I don't have any friends. No one knows about this place," Gavin said sternly. "Come on!"

Jamie followed Gavin across the warehouse and picked up the HK pistol from the coffee table as they headed towards the door. Sliding all the locks free and pulling on the large, rusted handle, Gavin peeked outside, Jamie peering over his shoulder.

A large man stood facing them, slightly hunched, but very well-built. His head was down; a hospital green gown, torn and blood-stained, hung loosely from his huge shoulders.

"Sorry, I only buy cookies from girl scouts," Gavin mocked, ready to close the door.

"Wait," Jamie said as he stepped around Gavin to get a better look.

The man slowly raised his head and stared at them with dark, hollow eyes.

"Keller?!" Jamie cried out.

"Get back!" Gavin said, pushing Jamie through the door and slamming it in the man's face. "He's a sleepwalker, a big one!"

The door pushed open as Keller slammed his heavy body against it. Gavin leaned into the door, but his feet slid on the floor.

"Help!"

Jamie dove against the door, putting all his weight into it. They pushed, the door teetering back and forth, opening, then closing, till finally, with one strong shove, the door clanked shut. Gavin slid the bar locks in place and stepped back. Keller was still beating on the other side.

The girls ran over to them. Ashley handed Gavin her gun.

"What's going on?" Kayla asked staring at the door. "Did I hear you call that man Keller?"

"Yeah," Jamie said thoughtfully, "isn't he supposed to be dead?"

"Comatose," Kayla replied, "that's what O'Donnell said after he visited him at New York General."

The banging stopped. They stood in silence, looking at each other uneasily, not sure what to expect. Suddenly, the sound of grating metal filled the warehouse. It echoed across the ceiling and between the heavy steel pillars.

"Is he on the roof?" Ashley whispered.

Their heads spun around in circles, all searching in different directions. The sound was too indistinct. He could be anywhere.

Before they could react, a loud creak filled the air, followed by the shrill cry of twisting metal as Keller ripped the door from the wall, right off its hinges. He held it high over his head as sunlight filtered in behind him, dust particles floating in the air illuminated by the early morning glow. The broken sliding locks clanked to the floor. Gavin raised his gun.

"Is this the kind you pray for or is this a, a physical manifest...thingy?" Jamie trailed off, his gun raised as well.

"Manifestation," Gavin answered. "He's already dead. There's nothing to cast out. He is the demon. We have to kill the host."

"Kill the host? He's huge!" Ashley said as she stared at Keller.

Keller grinned, a steely grin, his eyes black as night, his colossal, vein covered muscles hardly straining under the weight of the door.

"We shoot on *three*," Jamie said taking charge, pulling back the hammer on the HK, "you girls get out of here, find some cover!"

Gavin readied himself, the sound of his gun cocking echoed in the silence. Kayla and Ashley ran for the stairs, taking refuge in the bedroom.

"*One...two...*"

"*Three!*" Keller growled, hurling the door towards them.

It smashed into the corrugated steel wall and buckled in the middle. Gavin and Jamie looked first at the door sitting crumpled behind them, then at each other. Keller's hellish laugh broke their stare. With a determined nod, they rushed at the monster, guns blazing. Round after round plunged into his chest, but still he stood, laughing at them, their efforts wasted. Keller batted Jamie aside with his left arm as he lifted Gavin off the ground, choking him with his humongous right hand. Keller turned and slammed Gavin into the wall, denting the metal where he hit. Jamie gathered himself from the floor and elbowed Keller in the back, but it did nothing. Raising his gun and aiming it point blank at Keller's forearm, Jamie pulled the trigger.

Keller growled, letting Gavin drop to the floor, gasping for air. He turned and stomped towards Jamie, oily blood running from the hole in his arm.

Jamie headed off in full sprint and dove across the living room as Keller took chase, then lifted the couch up and flung it at him, sending it smashing into the other sofa, splinters of wood and springs flying everywhere. Jamie looked up from behind the coffee table, his eyes wide. Racing past Keller, Gavin grabbed Jamie by the shirt and pulled him up.

"I'm out!" Jamie yelled over Keller's shouts and the crashes of things he threw at them hitting the walls.

Gavin turned and fired wildly over his shoulder as they ran around the corner of the kitchen.

*Bang...Bang...Bang...Bang!*

"Me too," he said as they entered the armory.

Gavin pulled a string hanging from a bulb on the ceiling. The light flickered and illuminated the room.

"Pick one," Gavin shouted, heading for the wall of semi-auto rifles, "something big!"

Jamie pulled a suppressed Smith & Wesson MP15 5.56 off the wall and checked the magazine, then clicked on the Eotech sight, "let's make some noise!"

Gavin headed out of the room, an HK UMP 45 raised and ready. Keller stood in the middle of the warehouse, debris scattered everywhere. Gavin's hideout, his home, was destroyed. The faint smell of sulfur pulled his attention to a dark corner in the room.

"You're next!" he threatened Jamie's demon still laughing and pointing from the corner.

Jamie stared down Keller through the sight and squeezed off bursts of fire. Gavin turned and did the same, the rattle of spent shells bouncing off the cement floor muted by the barking of the guns. Black blood covered Keller's arms and chest as he pushed towards the men. The green of his robe now stained, almost indistinguishable.

"What are we going to do!?" Jamie yelled over the noise of the guns.

"We have to slow him down. Go for his legs!"

They focused their fire at Keller's knees. After several rounds, he finally stumbled, but didn't fall.

"It's not working!" Jamie cried out.

"It will!" Gavin yelled, reloading. "Keep shooting!"

The bullets continued to fly. Keller began to slow, then, finally, he dropped to his knees, clawing at the ground, dragging himself forward.

"He doesn't give up does he?" Jamie shouted.

Gavin surged forward, leaping over the struggling sleepwalker, then turned, digging his knee into his back, pinning Keller to the ground. He put his gun to the back of his head and emptied his magazine. Keller slumped to the ground. Gavin stood, wiping black muck from his arms.

"What a mess."

"That was crazy!" Jamie sighed, relieved, but still cautious of the monster's body, its fingers twitching, half a dozen empty magazines cast about on the floor.

Jamie rolled the beast over as the smell of sulfur filled the room. Yellow smoke poured from what was left of Keller's face.

"Did we kill him?" Jamie asked. "I mean the demon?"

"No, you never kill the demon, just the host. The demon is a spirit.

All we did was send him back to hell, and I think it was more like *demons*. He was way too powerful to be filled by a single entity."

"How do you think he found us?" Jamie wondered, tearing off a shredded piece of Keller's clothing, a patch embroidered on it.

"He didn't," Gavin frowned, casting a glance at the corner where Jamie's demon sat, "Thirteen sent him, I'm sure of it."

"New York General Hospital: that's where O'Donnell went to visit him."

"Then I bet that's where we'll find Thirteen," Gavin said heading up to the bedroom.

Ashley opened the door before he got to the top of the stairs. She stared at him, spattered in Keller's blood.

"Oh...my...gosh!"

"I'm okay. It's over," he smiled. "We got him."

Kayla came to the door and gasped, her hand over her mouth as she surveyed the wreckage of Gavin's warehouse. It was like a bomb went off.

Jamie looked up at her from the bottom of the stairs. "Talk about intense!"

She raced down the stairs and leapt towards him, her arms wrapped firmly around him, her legs locked around his waist. "I thought that thing was going to kill you!"

"Stop," he urged, holding her, not wanting to let go, "you'll get blood all over you."

Jamie lowered her to the floor and she stepped back, frowning as she inspected the stains on her shirt.

"You really think Thirteen sent him?" Kayla said, turning to Gavin.

"There's only one way to find out."

"But why a hospital?" Ashley wondered.

"After Christ's resurrection, Mary Magdalene went to His tomb searching for Him. An angel appeared and asked why she looked for the living among the dead? I figure it's the same sort of thing now; only the dead among the living. Thirteen would have had to have access to that man to call those demons into him, to transform him into that monster, and the way I see it, Thirteen has learned a lot from Triton."

"Meaning what?" Jamie asked, examining a scrape on his forearm.

"I think he's going to assemble an army as well, but not an army of servants, an army of sleepwalkers."

"It makes sense," Jamie agreed. "O'Donnell visited Keller at that hospital. Keller was wearing a shirt from that hospital..."

"And a hospital would ensure that Thirteen would have plenty of people at his disposal," Kayla added, "the perfect place to *recruit*."

"So what are we going to do?" Ashley sighed.

"There's only one thing we can do," Jamie nodded firmly, knowing what Gavin was thinking. "We've got to get to the hospital. Thirteen's waiting."

\*\*\*\*\*\*\*\*\*\*\*\*

Pale sunlight filtered through the bullet-riddled walls of the warehouse as Jamie knelt over the bloodied corpse of Officer Keller. Cool air flowed through the open door. Gavin laid a blanket across the dead body.

"You okay?" he asked, covering Keller's disfigured face.

"Uh huh," Jamie answered thoughtfully. "I knew him. We were in the academy together. I went detective, he went S.W.A.T."

"You say 'knew him' like it goes a little deeper,"

"Yeah," Jamie said, standing and walking over to the only chair

Keller hadn't smashed, "we were like brothers back then."

"Something happen between you two?" Gavin asked as he pulled a crate over and sat down facing Jamie.

"You could say that," he grinned, staring at the floor. "We went after the same girl a few years back and he ended up taking a swing at me. Things were never the same after that."

Gavin laughed as he rested his elbows on his knees, "Who'd she pick then?"

"Neither of us," Jamie said, his smirk breaking into laughter. "She's a coroner. She says any man with a pulse is too complicated for her."

"So she *sees* dead people?" Gavin added, their laughter growing louder.

"Not quite."

"Look, it's nice to see you boys getting along so well," Kayla said as she tugged on Jamie's sleeve, "but we need to get a plan together here."

"First, we need to see what we're up against," Gavin said.

"Are you thinking front door?" Ashley smiled.

"No. I was thinking reconnaissance this time," he said, "I'm going to take a drive past the hospital and take a look at what he's up to before we make our move."

"If Keller is any clue as to what Thirteen's plan is, we're in trouble," Kayla replied.

"There's only one way to find out," Gavin said as he stood and headed for his van.

"I'm going with you," Ashley said, hurrying past him and jumping in the passenger side.

\*\*\*\*\*\*\*\*\*\*\*\*

Gavin eased his van around the corner and parked in an alleyway across the street from the hospital. He pulled a pair of binoculars from a cubbyhole on the dash and a digital SLR camera with a 55-300 zoom lens from the glove box, then they clambered out of the van. Ducking behind a dumpster, he handed Ashley the camera.

"Is it big enough?" Ashley teased, looking at the lens protruding from the frame of the camera.

"I don't want to get too close," Gavin replied cautiously with a wink before peeking out at the hospital. "If Thirteen is there, he'll be watching the street. We need to get higher."

Gavin spotted a fire escape on the side of the building and climbed up onto a dumpster, then jumped to reach the bottom rung of the ladder. He grasped the cold metal bar as the ladder slammed down with a screeching clank.

"Here, Ash," he said, dropping back onto the heavy plastic lid of the dumpster, his arms outstretched towards her.

Ashley took hold of Gavin's hands, a sudden rush of weightlessness hitting her as he lifted her up, then boosted her towards the ladder. Quickly, they made their way to the rooftop.

"There's a lot of steps," Ashley huffed as they hurried up level by level, the metal steps clunking beneath them.

"Almost there," Gavin assured.

They stepped onto the crumbling asphalt roof and began looking for the best vantage point. They ducked around HVAC units and vents till they reached the edge of the building and peered down at the street below, then across at the hospital. Ambulances blocked the entrance and exit to the emergency room. Cars jammed up the auxiliary parking lots and deck.

"Does that look normal to you?" Ashley asked as she surveyed the scene.

Gavin spied through the binoculars, scanning the doors and windows, searching for movement. He went back and forth from one window to another, till finally, he nearly dropped the binoculars, his heart skipping a beat. A security guard was staring out at them, a hand pressed against the glass, his eyes black and hollow. Then, one by one, each window began to fill with people; guards, doctors, nurses, patients, all with haunting black eyes.

"Quick," Gavin said, "take some pictures."

Ashley started snapping away at the twisted faces gazing out at them till she let out a squeal.

"What is it?" Gavin asked, still searching the windows.

"Here," she said, pulling the binoculars away from his face and holding the camera up in front of him.

The display showed a picture of a window, the screen filled with hollow faces, in a room directly across from where they stood. Thirteen lurked in the very middle, his white eyes staring right at them.

"We've got to go," he said, pulling her away from the ledge and heading for the fire escape.

*************

Thirteen turned away from the window as he watched them disappear over the side of the building.

"They'll be coming soon," he laughed.

*************

"So how many of them are there?" Kayla asked as they passed around the digital camera, taking turns flipping through the pictures.

"Dozens," Ashley said throwing her hands up in frustration.

"There has to be something we can do?" Kayla frowned.

Gavin stood, thinking as he watched Jamie sort through the pictures.

"Hey," Jamie thought aloud, "a lot of these people in the windows are cops! Do you recognize that guy there? He worked the desk in narcotics."

Kayla leaned in for a better look. Ashley sunk into the lone chair.

"That would explain why the police station was empty when we went down there the other day looking for the Captain," Kayla said.

"He's been getting ready," Gavin sighed, the photos confirming what they feared. "He's holed himself up with an army of sleepwalkers and then told us it's our move."

"There's no way we can handle this," Jamie said as he turned the camera off. "What about your angel friends, can't they get involved?"

"This isn't their fight."

Gavin headed towards his arsenal as the rest followed, arguing their points. They stopped as he pulled a case of smoke grenades from their spot on the shelf and set them down on the table.

"Here's the deal," Gavin explained, "you're right. We can't handle this, at least not in a straight fight. What we need is a diversion. Then, we take advantage of Thirteen's weakness."

"Oh yeah, his weakness; what's that?" Kayla asked sarcastically.

"His arrogance," Gavin answered. "He wants this to be his Rome, and I say we burn it to the ground."

"So what do we do for weapons?" Jamie asked, looking over the walls of guns.

"That part we keep simple. Small, tactical, we carry nothing that will limit our mobility; I'm thinking pistols and suppressors. If we're lucky, we'll be able to keep the shooting to a minimum. As far as a plan, I'll be the distraction, the bait. I'll keep Thirteen busy. You guys just need to promise you can do your part. We won't have much time if everything unfolds the way I see it."

"What's our part?" Ashley asked sitting next to him on a stool.

"Here, look at this," Gavin said, grabbing a notebook that sat in a pile of papers and books on the table and drawing a quick diagram on a blank page. "I've been in this hospital, I know the layout: there are six main structural supports. So if you guys can plant six of these charges throughout the building, while I keep Thirteen occupied, then we can end this and have our best chance of stopping him. Bullets won't do a thing, but I think fire will. I'm sure he can't dodge heat or explosions."

"And what about his followers?" Jamie asked.

"The sleepwalkers," Kayla added, "won't they try to stop us?"

"Just think of them as a speed bump," Gavin grinned. "Besides, you saw the pictures. Most of them won't be armed at all. None of them will be like Keller. He was special, something Thirteen cooked up just for us. But they're still dangerous, don't take any unnecessary risks."

"So we just shoot them?" Ashley frowned unconvinced.

"Well, yeah," Gavin answered matter-of-factly. "They are dead, remember?"

"Then that's that," Jamie finally said after looking over the roughly sketched plans. "We do it, and we do it quick."

Ashley took her now familiar gun down from its place on the wall as Kayla gathered rounds of ammo, loading magazine after magazine with bullets. Gavin pulled an aluminum case out from under the table and cleared a spot for it amongst the mess of papers. Lining up the combinations on the locks and flipping open the thumb sliders, Gavin pulled out his homemade bombs. Jamie watched over his shoulder.

"I have to admit," Jamie laughed, "I'm impressed, all these guns, this case: you're one big surprise, kind of scary though."

Gavin smiled as he pulled a remote detonator out from alongside the charges and set it down next to the case, "What can I say, I'm a collector."

"No seriously," Jamie replied, turning and scanning the wall again, "you really use all these too! It's amazing."

"Well, actually," Gavin said leaning in close to Jamie so the girls couldn't hear, "like I said, I'm a collector. I have guns on this wall I've never fired. I have my favorites that I always use, but most of these have never even seen a round."

"That's a shame," Jamie joked as he placed his hand on Gavin's shoulder. "If we make it through this, I'll personally help you explore the many facets of your gun collection, as a favor. Don't thank me now."

"You'd do that for me?" Gavin laughed.

"Of course," Jamie smiled. "Hey, is that a real AK-47?"

"You bet, a restored 1947 original. You've got to love the Kalashnikov."

"Da," Jamie replied in an exaggerated attempt at a Russian accent.

Gavin and Jamie broke out in laughter. The girls hardly took notice as they continued to ready themselves for what lay ahead.

"Can you hand me that bag?" Gavin asked Ashley, pointing at a brown leather satchel hanging on the wall.

Ashley gave it to him and went back to loading rounds. Gavin placed the charges in the bag.

"Jamie," he said, holding the last one out to him, "I want to show you how to arm these. Placing them won't be enough."

"Oh yeah," Jamie said, hanging the AK-47 back on the wall."

"The bottom of the charge peels away, leaving a very strong adhesive. Once it's in place, you won't get it off. After you've secured it, twist the top and push down, locking it in. This green LED will light up. After that, it's the point of no return."

"Got it," Jamie nodded.

"Are they on a timer?" Kayla asked, putting her last magazine down.

"Nope, that's what the remote is for," Gavin said solemnly. "I'll take care of detonating the bombs. I push this button and they all go off simultaneously."

"How will you know we have them all in place?" Ashley wondered.

"I won't. You guys will have ten minutes to get through the hospital, set the charges, and get out."

"Ten minutes!?" Jamie laughed.

"Fifteen at the most," Gavin said as he rubbed his hands across his buzzed head.

"How about I call you on a cell phone when we have the last charge in place?" Kayla reasoned.

"Here's the deal. I'm trying to stall Thirteen here, not fight him. The longer I have to try to hold his attention, the more he's going to want to kill me. That's not really a win-win situation."

"I thought Joseph trained you to fight him?" Ashley asked.

"He did train me to fight, but maybe this isn't that kind of fight. In the end, that's what I really learned from Joseph."

"Is that what you believe?" Kayla wondered, leaning against the table.

"I know what I believe," Gavin said, taking a darker tone," and before we go after Thirteen, before we go into that hospital, we have to realize that this is serious, something that could end it for all of us. Death is a real possibility. I've tiptoed around it with each of you, but the time to take inventory on where you stand is now."

"You mean like believing in God and all that stuff?" Jamie smiled.

"If by stuff you mean salvation, then yeah," Gavin grinned, "stuff."

"I guess I've never bought into the whole religion thing," Jamie said, "in my line of work, you see too many things that make a just, loving God seem like a lie."

"Maybe you've just looked in the wrong place," Gavin explained. "After all you've witnessed now, hasn't everything changed?"

"Seeing *is* believing," Jamie sighed.

"No, faith is believing," Kayla spoke up. "It's taken me nearly this entire time to figure it out. I haven't been myself recently, and this is why. I've felt it in my heart. I've heard a voice in my head, calling me back to what I used to know. You know it too, Ashley, I can tell. You can feel it."

"I feel, *something*," Ashley answered, looking at the floor.

"It's conviction," Gavin said, "God has called you to be His. Christ died for you. Believing He can save you doesn't mean life will be perfect. That's what this whole thing with Thirteen is about. But I'm telling you now, going into that building without God on our side is the last thing we want to do. Let's take some time to focus, get our heads straight, then we'll roll out."

Jamie and Kayla headed out to the kitchen, softly discussing what Gavin had said. Ashley stood close to Gavin, taking his hands in hers.

"I want to let you know that I've been thinking a lot about things, and you've shown me what needs changed in my life," Ashley smiled. "Thank you. I don't know where my life would be headed if I hadn't met you. Even if we don't survive this..."

"It's okay," Gavin said, "you don't have to say any more. I'm really glad I've had the chance to get to know you."

Ashley squeezed his hands and blushed, "Will you help me pray, get back to where I need to be?"

Gavin sat down with Ashley at the table and dug an old age-worn Bible out from the pile of books. Flipping it open to the gospel of John, he turned it around to face her.

"I can help you go this far," he said, "but only you can ask for forgiveness. That's between you and God."

He stood and rubbed her shoulder then turned and left her alone in the room, just Ashley and the Bible. It was time for her to make things right.

Jamie leaned over the kitchen counter, his head in his hands, his bruised body aching. Kayla bent over next to him.

"Kayla," he said, "is this all for real? I mean, God and everything?"

She stared at him, not sure what to say. She'd grown up hearing all the stories, Christian parents, grandparents, but it was hard to put her feelings into words. Kayla closed her eyes and mouthed a silent prayer. As a shiver ran down her arms, she heard the words she wanted to say speak inside her, soft at first, then louder as the Holy Spirit guided her.

"Sometimes life leaves you feeling empty," she began, "work...friends...money, none of it adds up to the happiness you strive for. It's like you could have the whole world in your hands, but what good would it do you if you lost your soul in the process? There's a peace that comes through knowing Jesus. Even as a cop, I find it calming. I guess I'd just forgotten what my faith meant to me till all this started. But now, I can't imagine life without it."

"See, that's what I want," Jamie said looking at the excitement in her eyes.

"You can have it," she said, lowering her voice to a whisper, "you just need to put yourself aside and accept that you can't control everything that goes on around you."

They sat in the kitchen in silence. Jamie thought about all she'd said, all he had experienced in these last several days. He was afraid his pride would stand between himself and an all-powerful, all-knowing God, but he also knew that Kayla was right. If he could just believe, he could find the hope he was searching for.

"I'm ready to make that choice," he said turning to her. "I want to believe."

Kayla led Jamie in prayer as Ashley sat in the other room rededicating her life to Christ. Gavin knelt at his broken coffee table. As he prayed, angels surrounded him; their wings spread high above him in a canopy of shining brilliant feathers. Suddenly, he opened his eyes. The time had come.

\*\*\*\*\*\*\*\*\*\*\*\*

Jamie and Kayla held each other in the kitchen as Gavin stood and surveyed the room. Ashley ran up to him, tears covering her face. A howl erupted from the corner of the room. Jamie's demon was hysterical with laughter.

"What a tender moment!" he gasped. "Hold on, I think I have a greeting card here somewhere."

Gavin nodded at the angels and they unsheathed their swords. The demon froze, panic across his face as his chest heaved with each sulfurous breath. In an explosion of light, the angels swept down upon the demon. He darted up and down, back and forth, the angels in close pursuit, till finally, he slipped out the open door and disappeared into the gray sky.

"What's going on?" Ashley wondered as she watched Gavin's eyes following the action. She strained to see, but could only imagine.

"Angels," he smiled, wrapping his arms around her as she wiped her tears away, "they just took care of a demon that's been hanging around."

With a confused half-smile, she hugged him back. As she held him, she was certain she heard the sound of beating wings above them, but looking up, she saw nothing but air.

"I can't believe how much better I feel," Jamie smiled, his face red with excitement. "It's like I was carrying this weight and it's just been lifted off my shoulders."

"This is only the beginning," Kayla said as she stepped away from him and headed out of the kitchen.

Jamie looked like a new man. His countenance had changed, even the way he walked.

"You know," Gavin said with a very intense expression, "for the first time since we've come together, I feel like we can really work as a team. Maybe we should get costumes, like the *X-Men*?"

Ashley grinned as Kayla shot the idea down right there with her eyes.

"I'm just kidding," he smiled, "besides, I don't know if you could pull off the spandex look anyway?"

"Hey!" Kayla laughed, a warm blush filling her cheeks.

"Seriously," Gavin said turning to Jamie and extending his hand to him, "I'm proud of you. It's not easy to let go, to let someone else have control. But soon, you'll see how much better life is when choices are made through the perspective of the cross. It will change every aspect of your life."

# XVI

## WEDNESDAY AFTERNOON

Jamie stood next to Gavin's van, his hand in his pocket as he watched the setting sun slowly sinking away in the distance, inadvertently playing with the key they'd found in the secret room of Triton's office. Staring out the open garage door, Kayla gently rubbed his shoulders as she tried to fill in the blanks from all the events that had taken place that week.

"I wonder what this key is for," Jamie thought aloud, pulling it from his pocket.

"Looks pretty old..." Kayla replied.

He held it up in the fading light. Small, intricate writing was engraved on its rusty surface.

"What do you think that says?" he asked, holding it so Kayla could read it.

"It looks like something European, maybe Latin?" she wondered.

"I think you're right," Gavin agreed, "but I haven't a clue what it says."

Jamie rubbed his finger tip across the engraving, feeling the etching, "So what do you think Triton wanted with it? Thirteen said it wasn't important."

"Yeah," Kayla frowned, "why waste so much energy on it if it's worthless?"

"Maybe we'll never know. Either way, keep it," Gavin smiled, "think of it as a memento of something that changed your life."

Jamie squeezed his fingers around the key tightly and held it to his chest for a moment, thinking how true Gavin's words were. Kayla continued to rub his shoulders.

"What if it opens a really old chest," Ashley imagined, "and it's filled with like, millions of dollars? Or, oh, ancient treasure!"

"I really don't think so," Gavin reasoned. "From any relics I've ever seen, this is too simple to be something kingly, though the engraving makes me question its purpose."

"Well regardless, Thirteen didn't seem to care about it, so it must be nothing more than an ordinary, old key." Kayla concluded.

"But what if it has some magical power," Ashley pressed, not wanting to drop the possibility that it could be more, "it was at the sacrifice wasn't it, Jamie? Maybe it's got some hidden power?"

"That doesn't really matter," Gavin said seriously. "It wouldn't have to be magical to have power. If someone believes that it has power; that can make it quite real, especially if it opens the door to something demonic."

"And you think this is what Thirteen was really after?" Kayla smiled curiously.

"I think it's what Triton was after. Thirteen took it simply to distract him, make him look for it after the sacrifice was complete, have him drop his guard rather than watch his back.

"So then what's all this really about?" Kayla sighed.

"All Thirteen wanted was power. By killing Triton, he took his place. This guy is big time scary. So Ashley, the sacrifice, the *key*, they were all of no consequence. He probably didn't even care about Joseph."

*************

Thirteen slouched against a sink in one of the hospital's many restrooms, his hands lying flat on the counter, his arms propping him up. Alone, he stood in silence, contemplating everything that had unfolded and each move he'd made, his head hanging as he thought.

"I've done all I could. Everything is falling into place, am I right?"

"Yes, Master," a voice hissed from somewhere in the dark.

"I just want to know that I've been right all along," Thirteen questioned as he raised one hand and rapped his gloved knuckles on the tile surface in frustration and self-doubt, "that all of this was not for nothing."

"You are right," another voice squealed, "the cleansing of Triton was necessary."

"Besides, you're only watching out for your best interests," yet another voice growled.

Thirteen raised his head, looking into the mirror. His masked reflection stared back, five demonic, twisted faces moved about just behind him. He turned towards the empty room, crossing his arms as he faced another tiled wall.

"Show yourselves!"

The blackness of the shadows began to move in wisps of gray smoke as cruel forms began to take shape, winged and evil.

"The Dark Lord knows I haven't done what he asked, right?" Thirteen asked solemnly, reaching up and pulling off his mask, revealing his handsome face, his dark hair messy. "And when this is over..."

"The Dark One is not fond of forgiveness," one of the demons laughed with a sickly cackle, "but he knows selfishness, he'll understand."

"This isn't out of selfishness," Thirteen barked back angrily, his eyes a steely blue, "it's security, for the future."

Quietly, his cell phone chirped from an inner pocket in his suit. Thirteen pulled the phone from his jacket.

"Leave me."

The demons faded away into the shadows as Thirteen answered his phone. The restroom fell silent again.

"Sweetheart," he smiled, his temper calming, "I've missed you."

"I've missed you too!" a young woman's soft voice replied. "How's work?"

"Murder," he grinned, "as always. So how did it go?"

"Fantastic. The buyers were thrilled with the opportunity; they made an enormous offer."

"Enormous?"

"More than you could ever have imagined, for everything: all the research, the labs, proprietary technologies, all that Tri-Corp owns."

"So you accepted it then?"

"Of course," she laughed innocently. "So when are you coming home?"

"Soon, soon, I promise. I just have one more loose end to tie up and we'll never have to worry about anything again."

"I know. It's just that this house is so empty without you."

"I'll be home this weekend," Thirteen smiled. "How's the baby?"

"Sleeping like an angel," she mused.

"That's my boy."

Thirteen turned back to the mirror, pulling his mask down over his face, his eyes glowing bright white, proudly shining in the reflection.

"Did you get a chance to look at Triton's will yet?" he asked sweetly.

"Yeah, honey," she answered excitedly, "the house, the cars, the yachts, the plane: Daddy left them all to us, everything!"

Thirteen tilted his head back, closing his eyes thankfully as he faced the ceiling. All his hopes were coming true. His plan had worked.

"I love you, Elizabeth."

"I love you too, Michael."

\*\*\*\*\*\*\*\*\*\*\*\*

A soft thud against the side of the corrugated metal wall startled Ashley as she sat talking with Gavin, her sweet smile turning to a look of sudden fear. Jamie raced to the front door of the warehouse, his gun drawn, leaning against the wall, cautiously peering around the mangled doorframe. He panned the dock.

*Nothing.*

Jamie dropped his gaze, a newspaper, tightly wrapped and secured with a thick rubber band, rested at the base of the wall outside. Kneeling, he picked it up and slipped his gun into the holster on his belt.

"It's alright, someone just dropped off a copy of the New York Times," he smiled in disbelief as he headed towards the lone undamaged chair. "I didn't know they delivered to the docks?"

"Oh good, the evening edition is here," Gavin said facetiously as he wrapped his arm around Ashley's shoulders.

"You get it delivered here?" Kayla laughed.

"Sure. I know a guy that works over at the paper. We give each other leads, share work. He always makes sure I get a copy."

Dropping the rubber band on the makeshift coffee table, Jamie opened the paper and stared at the front page, his jaw dropping with shock.

"What!?" Kayla asked, seeing his expression.

"There's a big picture of the Captain," Jamie exclaimed, his voice cracking.

"What's it say?"

Jamie looked like he was going to cry as he read the headline aloud: "Bomb Scare Shakes Police Dept."

"After twenty-seven years of commendable service," Jamie continued, "disgruntled Police Capt., Patrick O'Donnell, took control of the 3rd precinct downtown, threatening to detonate a bomb planted somewhere in the building if city officials did not meet his demands. In a statement, Mayor Bradford reconfirmed his stance on terrorism saying 'We have not and will not negotiate with those who threaten us with violence'. An FBI task force was sent in and reports have confirmed that the threat was neutralized and the bomb disarmed. Patrick O'Donnell was killed as he defended the explosives. It is believed he worked alone. An investigation is underway and the station will be temporarily closed..."

Jamie tossed the newspaper onto the coffee table and covered his red face with his hands. Kayla hugged him, softly kissing the side of his head.

"I'm sorry," Gavin frowned as he picked the paper back up and skimmed through the rest of the article.

"I can't believe they're doing this to O'Donnell!" Jamie said, his voice muffled behind his hands.

"There's more," Gavin replied, shaking his head as he read a smaller section at the bottom of the page. "In a decision that rocked Wall Street today, Elizabeth Triton, daughter of Dr. Maurice Triton and sole heir to the Tri-Corp Empire, within hours of her father's alleged suicide, negotiated the board approved sale of the company the famed Dr. Triton successfully built from nothing to an undisclosed European firm. Though no figures have been released, it is assumed that Tri-Corp, as well as its many subsidiaries, one of Forbes highest rated companies, would be valued in the trillions. Tri-Corp spokesman, Blaire Vaughn had this to say: 'Though saddened by the tragic loss of Maurice, we are excited at the announcement of this new endeavor. Merging with this global partner will expand the possibilities and enhance the potential outreach of our company.' Many investors stand to reap huge profits as these two companies come together; however, many analysts speculate that, as we've seen so many times before, an acquisition of this magnitude could lead to the possible loss of thousands of jobs here in America as the future of this great company, at least for the time being, is unknown..."

"So O'Donnell and Triton, how are they connected? Why would Thirteen bring the Captain into this?" Jamie whispered.

"I hate to say it, but I think Thirteen was telling the truth," Kayla said solemnly. "Maybe the question is how were Triton and the Mayor involved. Thirteen said that Triton was partnered with city officials. If they really are dirty, then it follows that they could have set this up to protect themselves and the truth about their relationship with Triton."

"And the sale of Tri-Corp, that seems awful quick, wouldn't you say?" Gavin said, slamming the paper down. "But what could Thirteen possibly gain from the sale?"

"If Triton paid him in stock options, then I would assume a lot," Jamie thought aloud.

"Like hundreds of thousands?" Ashley asked.

"More like a couple million," Kayla replied. "The paper said Tri-Corp was valued in the trillions! Just think of what that would pay an investor."

"Not to mention an heir," Ashley sighed.

"But I can't believe this was all about money," Jamie reasoned. "Don't forget what we uncovered in our investigation: your brother, Hampton, even Dennis Lister. They're all linked."

"To Triton, not Thirteen," Kayla answered. "There's no evidence that would conclude that Thirteen knew Jack or Michael Hampton."

"But he admitted to the murder of Dennis Lister," Jamie argued.

"Only because he was part of Triton's conspiracy," Gavin reminded.

"So that's it then? Our investigation was for nothing?" Jamie asked angrily, looking at Kayla.

"I guess so."

************

They gathered their gear and began loading the van. Kayla and Ashley sat down to say another prayer together as Gavin pulled Jamie aside.

"Can I talk to you for just a second?" he asked.

Jamie nodded and followed Gavin over to the dark corner where the demon had been lingering that day.

"I know this has been a rough week for you, especially concerning your boss and all, but I just wondered if you were feeling anything, *strange*?"

"Like what?" Jamie asked furrowing his brow.

"A presence, or anything...dark?"

"No," Jamie smiled, "I feel, peaceful."

"Okay," Gavin said, smiling back, "I just wanted to be sure. Earlier, the angels chased your demon out of here."

"So it's gone?" Jamie asked excitedly.

"Gone, but not necessarily gone for good. I want to help you as much as I can, but you have to decide what parts of your life you've been living can be given up so that you can continue to know this peace."

"What kind of demon is it?" Jamie said in a hushed tone, not wanting to disturb the girls.

"It was a demon of addiction," Gavin said carefully. "I know because I used to have one following me around."

"I don't know what you're talking about?" Jamie replied, trying not to sound defensive.

"Look, I'm on your side," Gavin explained, "and I'm telling you this because I really care about you. Even in such a short time, you've become a good friend, truthfully, one of my only friends, and I wouldn't be returning the favor if I didn't say anything. I used to drink, a lot. When I stopped, I felt the kind of peace you're talking about now."

"Other than the tattoos and, well, pretty much everything about your appearance, I'd never have thought you were much of a drinker," Jamie said sarcastically, letting his guard down.

Gavin smiled, he was used to those types of judgments. For years, those stereotypes had made him avoid church, now it helped him embrace it.

"Yeah, I drank. Not to party, but to escape; escape from the pressure of being alone."

"You didn't have to be alone," Jamie said sadly. "We all think you're great. You'd have been the life of any party."

"But that's not the life I chose, it's not the path that was laid before me. A demon hunter's life is a lonely life," Gavin said as he turned and looked at Ashley.

"Well I drink a little," Jamie admitted.

"I'd say more than a little," Gavin smirked. "Have you seen your fridge?"

"Okay, more than a little," Jamie laughed. "But my problem isn't completely alcohol, it's pills too. I can't let go of the painkillers."

"I know. I saw a bottle of them on the kitchen counter at your loft."

"They just help me *feel* better. You know? They take away my pain, ease my thoughts."

"But you have to have faith that God can take away your pain, the same as He did mine," Gavin smiled, motioning towards the scar running down his neck and beneath his collar, then holding up his wrists for Jamie to see the marks of a failed suicide attempt, now camouflaged by tattoos.

"You tried to kill yourself?"

"Yeah," Gavin said slowly, thoughtfully, the memories pouring through his head, "but God decided to save me, keep me alive. It's how I know I have purpose. You have that same opportunity now."

Jamie smiled. For the first time since his mother's murder, he began to see that life can still be fully lived.

"I didn't want to talk about this with you to make you feel bad or guilty, but I wanted to let you know that I'm here for you, to help you stay accountable."

"I appreciate it," Jamie said. "It's something for me to work on."

"Yeah," Gavin smiled sincerely as he heard Kayla and Ashley say *amen*. "Oh, and one more thing, I didn't get to tell you earlier, but I wanted to make sure I explained it now, before we got down to New York General. The charges you're setting up won't detonate unless all six are armed. It has to do with the frequencies I programmed into the receivers, they chain together in a sequence. So make sure you have them all set."

"No problem," Jamie grinned, full of new found hope.

************

"Okay, do we have everything?" Gavin asked, looking in the back of the van at the bag of charges and their supplies.

"Yeah," Ashley said hugging him nervously.

"Good, then everybody ready?"

The girls nodded their heads. Jamie was once again looking at the key. He slipped it away into his pocket, but as he did, his hand brushed against the little silver pill box.

"I just have to go to the bathroom real quick."

"Alright, Jamie," Kayla said as she sat down on the floor in the opening of the van's sliding door, her feet hanging out the side. "Hurry, I want to get this over with."

Gavin watched him head up the stairs and into the bathroom, his hand still curiously deep in his pocket. Silently, he mouthed a quick prayer for Jamie.

The bathroom door clicked shut. Jamie stood in front of the dirty mirror and pulled the pill box from his jeans. He stared at its shiny surface, traced his finger along the initials engraved delicately on its lid, *I.L.B.*: Ileana Lane Branson, his mother.

Slowly, he popped open the lid and stared at the small white pills scattered across the bottom of the box. Each one called out to him, as if he could hear them whispering his name. He looked at himself in the mirror, then looked back at the box. Jamie imagined what his mother would have looked like if she were standing there, her brown hair and green eyes still vividly real in his mind. Again, he dropped his gaze to the pills. Shuffling the box so they rolled back and forth, he tried to fight off the absolute hunger to take one, just one. It made him feel like an animal. Killing the pain, the hurt, the memories, had become instinct.

Jamie set the little silver box down on the edge of the sink and headed over to the urinal. He whispered a prayer as he stood there. He really wanted to let go of the pills. He didn't want to rely on them any more, yet with each passing moment, his desire to take one, to swallow it, to go numb, drove him absolutely mad. His mouth was watering. Again, he prayed.

As he flushed the toilet, he heard a metallic clink inside the basin of the porcelain sink, quickly followed by the soft sound of little pills spilling across the faded white surface and tinking down the open drain.

*No!*

Jamie raced to the sink and grabbed the pill box. It was empty. A single white pill rested on the edge of the drain, teetering, ready to fall down and be lost forever. He felt like the world was in slow motion as he reached for the pill, feeling it between his finger and thumb just as it was about to disappear.

Now, he stood staring at the pill, his last pill. All he had to do was take it, he'd feel better. He'd be able to forget about the Captain and focus on the mission. He would be able to set the charges and save the day. All he had to do was take the pill, his last pill. Longingly, he raised it to his lips. He could feel the smooth coating as he readied to slip it into his mouth. But, as he hesitated, he felt a sudden calm wash over him.

*No*, a small voice echoed in his head. *You don't need it.*

For a moment, he felt betrayed, his own thoughts fighting against him. He pushed the guilt away and prepared to swallow it. And again he heard the voice.

"Why not?" he asked aloud.

*Trust Me.*

Jamie lowered his hand, the pill still firmly grasped in his fingers. Without another thought, he tossed it into the sink, watched it circle the basin, then slip away into the darkness of the drain.

The door opened slowly. All eyes were on him as he stepped out of the bathroom and headed down to meet them at the van.

"You were in there a long time," Kayla commented with a worried expression, "everything alright?"

Jamie thought for a moment, his eyes connecting with Gavin's, "I just had one more thing to take care of before we headed out."

"And?"

"It's over."

Confused, Kayla looked at Jamie, then at Gavin. She and Ashley were both surprised as the two men suddenly hugged, Gavin patting Jamie congratulatory on the back.

"Just always be ready," Gavin encouraged, "the urge can hit you when you least expect it. Remember where your strength comes from."

Kayla tipped her head to the side, her lips curling into a question, but the words never came.

"I'll explain later," Jamie grinned happily at her, like a burden was lifted from his shoulders.

Ashley and Kayla shrugged at each other and climbed into the back of the van. Jamie jumped in the passenger side as Gavin hurriedly slid the door shut with a bang.

"You know, when this is over, I can never come back here. It'll never be secure again," Gavin confided, Jamie listening through the open window. "We'll pick up your car, pack up as much of my stuff as we can carry in the two vehicles, and that's it."

He looked like a lost puppy as he scanned his home for what could be the last time. "After this, I'll have nowhere to go."

Gavin gathered himself. He had to focus. Silently, he asked God for courage.

"All set?" he asked climbing into the driver's seat and adjusting his rear-view mirror.

They all shared a look of reluctant agreement as Gavin pulled out of the garage. They had no idea what to expect.

# XVII

## WEDNESDAY NIGHT

Kayla stared out the window of Gavin's rusty, black van, raindrops streaking across the dirty glass. Gray clouds covered the city. Lightning flashed.

*This is it, really it; the end.*

So many unbelievable things had happened, were happening, she found it hard to reason through them, rationalize the truth, even though she'd been involved since the beginning, been witness to every strange occurrence. She ran her fingers nervously through her hair, her head hanging down, her elbows resting on her knees. Reluctantly, she looked out the window again. Kayla could see an old sign, its fluorescent bulbs dimly flickering in the quickly darkening sky: New York General Hospital. They'd arrived.

Gavin parked across the street from the aging building; its once bright white façade now fading away. The side door slid open as Kayla and Ashley stepped out into the cool air, joining Gavin and Jamie where they stood. The light shower was growing heavier with each passing moment.

"Why is it always raining?" Ashley wondered as she lifted the brown satchel onto her shoulder.

"Consider it baptism," Gavin said, casting a glance in Jamie's direction.

Gavin pulled a toolbox to the edge of the back of the van and flipped open the lid. He quickly removed the thread protector from the end of his pistol's barrel and picked up a suppressor stamped *.45 cal.* He twisted it carefully onto the gun, making sure it was aligned properly.

"Here," he said handing Jamie and Kayla each a Glock 17 and pointing at the 9mm suppressors, "put these cans on and take these extra magazines. They're loaded with subsonic 9mm hollow-points. You have to be as quiet as possible."

Kayla set her pistol down in the toolbox and clipped two magazine holders on her belt, "How many rounds in each mag?"

"Seventeen," Jamie said, ejecting the one in his Glock, inspecting it quickly, then clicking it back into the grip.

"You ready?" Gavin asked, staring up at the hospital.

"All set," Kayla answered, loading a round into the chamber.

Jamie smiled confidently, the gun Gavin gave him in his hand, his duty gun holstered on the back of his belt; four magazine holders clipped alongside his backup firearm.

Ashley tucked her gun into the waist of her jeans: hopefully she wouldn't need to use it. She was planning on helping Jamie with the charges while Kayla provided cover.

They trudged through puddles as they approached the E.R. A crack of thunder rumbled above. The rain came down harder.

"Ash?" Gavin asked solemnly, "You still alright with this?"

"Yeah," she said, gently patting the side of the bag, the bombs securely inside.

They stopped at the entrance. A couch was pushed up against it, as well as a small table. Shadows crept inside. Jamie grabbed the sliding doors by their frames and tried to push them apart, but they were locked.

"Maybe we should knock?" Ashley suggested.

"That's what you said at Tri-Corp," Kayla quipped, "Why would we knock?"

"Cause, you know, it's polite. The last time, we busted down the door and look where that got us: a huge gunfight! Maybe we should try a calmer approach? What would it hurt?"

Jamie shrugged, "Other than the element of surprise, nothing."

"No, they already know we're here. Thirteen is expecting us." Gavin grunted, trying to see into the dark building.

"Well then, give it a shot," Kayla prompted, tugging again at the doors." I don't think any of us will be kicking these down."

Gavin reached out and rapped on the thick glass, water spattering from beneath his knuckles. One of the bodies came closer, till finally, they could see its hollow, black eyes.

"What do you want, hunter!?" it growled from inside the barricaded hospital, its shrill voice piercing and cold.

Gavin grinned, raising his finger to the glass. Slowly, he traced a backwards number thirteen on the rain-soaked window, large water droplets streaking from his markings.

The sleepwalker nodded and more creatures joined him as they began to move away the furniture that blocked the entrance. Finally, a path was cleared and they unlocked the door, sliding it open.

"Only one may enter. You, the hunter, he'll see you," one of the sleepwalkers hissed, his gnarled finger pointing at Gavin.

Gavin turned and faced his friends. Tears welled up in Ashley's eyes.

"We're playing by his rules, for now."

\*\*\*\*\*\*\*\*\*\*\*\*

Gavin stepped through the door, the sleepwalkers securing it behind him. Silently, they led him down the hall and up three flights of stairs, the shuffling of their feet against the age-worn cement steps the only sound. As they walked, he pulled the hood of his sweatshirt up over his head, his face disappearing into shadow.

"I feel just like Daniel..." Gavin laughed aloud with no response from his escorts, "...into the lion's den."

They turned the last corner. Gavin saw him standing at the end of the long, dark corridor. Thirteen had his sword drawn, the blade reflecting what little light shone through the windows.

\*\*\*\*\*\*\*\*\*\*\*\*

Jamie paced in front of the emergency room doors. Kayla wrung her hands as Ashley watched the sleepwalkers slowly stalking about inside.

"How long has it been?" Jamie asked.

"About five minutes," she estimated, pulling her rain-soaked hair away from her face.

"Do you think he's met up with Thirteen yet?" Ashley wondered, her arms crossed as she shivered.

They looked at each other for a moment, hoping everything was going to plan. But they knew there was no room for error. They had to do everything right.

"We have to get in there," Jamie said as he stopped pacing and slammed his fist on the glass.

It didn't budge. The sleepwalkers stopped, their empty gazes fixed at the door.

Jamie stepped back and raised his gun. Taking aim, he fired two shots. The muffled *thwap, thwap*, of the silencer was followed by the *tink* of the bullets hitting the window. Two small holes, thin cracks emanating from the centers, stared at Jamie as he leaned back and kicked in the glass, sending it shattering to the ground.

"Aim for their heads," he said as he stepped through the empty frame, broken glass crunching beneath his feet.

Kayla followed behind him, her gun raised. They cleared the area of sleepwalkers; a dozen bodies strewn about the lobby. Ashley entered after they'd neutralized the threat.

"Alright," Jamie said, wiping the rain from his face, then pulling out the makeshift map Gavin had drawn them, "there are six rooms that make the most effective targets, three on each side of the building, each one with a large, main support beam. We set the charges and we get out."

"We'll have to move fast," Kayla said as she looked down the main hall, "should we do one side, then the other?"

Jamie looked at the map again and nodded.

"I think that will be the quickest. Each room is off of a main hall. See here?" he said, pointing at the map, tracing his finger along the path, "there's a large middle section, ignore that. We take the corridor to the left. It jogs around in a big square, then brings us back here: our exit in the emergency room. Just keep your eyes open."

\*\*\*\*\*\*\*\*\*\*\*\*

"So tell me, hunter," Thirteen taunted, the tip of his blade pointed at Gavin, "would you like to die quickly or slowly? I don't care. Either way, I get to have all the fun."

Gavin stopped, the sleepwalkers still stood alongside him.

"You don't need their help do you?" he laughed.

"Leave us!" Thirteen ordered.

The sleepwalkers turned and headed back to the stairwell. Gavin waited till they were gone to speak.

"I'm unarmed," he said, raising his hands above his head.

"You shoot your mouth off like it was a weapon," Thirteen mocked.

"To each his own, my friend."

Thirteen grinned. Gavin watched his mask wrinkle. Slowly, he lowered his sword and pulled a handgun out from under his suit coat.

"Would you prefer a bullet or my blade?"

"I just came to talk," Gavin smiled, his hands still raised. "I mean, don't you ever get lonely with all these stupid sleepwalkers around saying, *yes, Master* this; *yes, Master* that..."

Thirteen clicked the hammer back with his thumb.

"Guess not," Gavin said as he slowly dropped his arms to his sides.

\*\*\*\*\*\*\*\*\*\*\*\*

Three more sleepwalkers thudded to the floor. Kayla lowered her gun as she slipped around the first corner and into a large waiting room. A receptionist's window marked the entrance to the doctors' offices, comfortable looking seats lined the walls. And there, in the middle of the room was a thick, circular, plaster wrapped beam running from the floor to the ceiling.

*Bingo!*

Jamie motioned to Ashley. She followed, as Kayla checked the rest of the office and the door that led to the examination rooms. Another two bodies hit the floor while Ashley opened the satchel and handed Jamie the first charge. Peeling the plastic cover off the bottom, Jamie firmly attached the explosive to the support pillar and twisted the top. The green light blinked to life.

"One down," Jamie said, turning and heading back out to the main hall.

\*\*\*\*\*\*\*\*\*\*\*\*

As cold rain drops swept across the rooftops, a battle line was drawn. On one side, angels stood high above the street, lining the edge of the roof, their swords ready, the hilts held in front of them, the blades pointing downward. Yelps and howls echoed from the hospital's rooftop across the street. Demons bantered back and forth, beating their leathery wings and taunting the angels. But, the angels stood by patiently. This wasn't their fight.

\*\*\*\*\*\*\*\*\*\*\*\*

Ashley handed Jamie the second charge. Kayla panned the empty room, gun raised, just in case. Jamie set the charge, a faint beep signaling as it armed.

"Keep moving."

\*\*\*\*\*\*\*\*\*\*\*\*

"So tell me about the key?"

Thirteen stared at Gavin, cocking his head to the side, "What's with the key? Triton obsessed over it, and now, frankly, I'm sick of hearing about it."

"All I want to know is where it came from, why Triton valued it so much?"

"The key is old, as old as time for all I know." Thirteen explained, already bored with the conversation. "Triton was entrusted with the key centuries ago, or so his story went. He said it's supposed to be the key to the Abyss, the one that would be used to seal away the dragon for a thousand years."

"Right," Gavin nodded, "Revelation 20."

"As long as the key was in Triton's possession, then the Devil could do whatever he wanted on Earth, with no fear of retribution."

"I thought Christ took the key from Hades when He overcame Death, at the resurrection?"

"Yes, and then He gave the key to Michael the Archangel till the day that it would be used to lock Satan away and there would be hallelujahs and rejoicing in the land. An angelic choir would sing and lo and behold, TV evangelists everywhere would proclaim that the end has come, so send us money...blah, blah, blah..."

"So how did Triton get the key if an archangel held it?"

"Oh come on, it's just a story. If you're so worried about it, ask God after I kill you."

\*\*\*\*\*\*\*\*\*\*\*\*

"Hurry," Ashley yelled as they ran down the corridor and into the next room, "this is it: number three!"

Jamie fired off another two shots as they entered. Kayla stepped over the sleepwalker's bodies and checked the corners of the room.

"All clear," she smiled, Jamie preparing another charge, "just three more to go!"

\*\*\*\*\*\*\*\*\*\*\*\*

"Enough about the key, tell me, hunter, did you come here to kill me?"

Gavin shifted his weight from one foot to the other as he eyed the shiny metal blade in Thirteen's hand.

"That's not for me to decide."

\*\*\*\*\*\*\*\*\*\*\*\*

Jamie, Kayla, and Ashley managed to set the fourth and fifth charges with no trouble. Things were going just as Gavin had said.

"This is the last one," Ashley whispered, looking at the map and pointing ahead, "down there, the last room on the left."

Jamie stepped from the room with the fifth support pillar, sweat trickling down his brow. Kayla followed closely behind, her gun aimed and ready.

They eased past the doors lining the dark hall, checking the rooms. Sleepwalkers lurked inside, creeping in the shadows, hiding from the last rays of sunlight that shone through the breaks in the clouds outside. Quietly, they made their way to the end of the hall.

"This has been surprisingly easy!" Ashley said with a perplexed frown.

A sleepwalker groaned, scratching at its scabbed arms, as it hobbled into the hall ahead of them. Kayla fired. The creature slumped against the wall, then slid to the floor.

"What do you mean?" Jamie asked, spotting the room just ahead.

"These sleepwalkers have all been slow. They haven't given much of a fight."

"There's still a little daylight left outside. I don't want to see what they're like in the dark." Jamie grunted.

They cautiously stepped through the door frame. The room was dark, no windows. Kayla grabbed Ashley by the shoulder as a fire extinguisher whizzed past, nearly hitting her in the face. Jamie turned and pulled the trigger. A body collapsed from the corner, dropping out of the shadows. A yellow wisp of smoke swirled into the air from a small hole in its forehead.

"You were saying?"

Kayla reached into the satchel and carefully removed the last bomb. Ashley shrugged off her fear as Jamie took the charge and headed toward the support. Drawing closer, an odd sensation rushed through him. His pace slowed, till finally, he stopped, just short of the pillar. With a scratching of claws and a sickening, asthmatic laugh, Jamie's demon twisted his way out from behind the pillar, its leathery wings wrapped tightly around its small body.

"Didn't think you'd see me again, did you?" he cackled. "But you just can't seem to get rid of me."

"You aren't going to get to me," Jamie said, shaking his head in disbelief as he took a step backwards, "not this time!"

"Are your hands shaking, boy? I bet a drink would do the trick, or maybe a little something from this bottle to ease your nerves?" the demon taunted as he held up a little orange prescription bottle and shook it, his bony clawed fingers wrapped tightly around it, the rattle of pills tapping against the plastic ringing in Jamie's ears. "Just one wouldn't hurt."

Jamie stared hard, hoping he was imagining, until he felt Kayla grab his hand. He couldn't break his gaze. The demon had him locked down, frozen.

"He can't control you anymore," Kayla encouraged, giving his elbow a squeeze. "You're stronger than him because of what you believe."

Jamie tried to take a step forward, but his legs wouldn't move. It was like he was paralyzed.

"Look at the big, bad cop!" the demon howled. "Aren't you going to rig that little bomb of yours up here, or am I in your way?"

Jamie winced at each word. It was as if they pierced his soul. He looked down at the charge in his hand, then at Kayla, and finally, back at the demon, its mouth wide in an evil toothy grin, its short tail flicking back and forth. Slowly, he shook off Kayla's hand and raised his gun. Aiming at the demon, he fired off his entire magazine, the sound of the suppressor masked by the shrill demonic laughter.

"You can't kill me, mortal."

\*\*\*\*\*\*\*\*\*\*\*\*

"I didn't come to make threats," Gavin said solemnly, "but you had to realize that this couldn't go on forever."

"What are you talking about?" Thirteen chuckled, lowering his sword.

"I'm talking about your little world here, this fantasy you've created. Triton died. In the end, you will too. We all answer for our actions in this life. I'd hate to be in your shoes."

"My, my, ever the cocky one," Thirteen mocked. "Don't you ever shut up? As I told you before, my fight was not with you. You chose this fate. It was never Triton's power I desired. I gave you the chance to walk away once. I will not allow it a second time."

Gavin grinned. Thirteen raised his sword again.

"Look," Gavin smiled, "I'm not going to pretend I came in here thinking you would let me live. I'm ready to die. My life has been paid for. If you kill me, you're just doing me a favor and sending me to God sooner than I thought I'd see Him. How does that make you feel?"

"First off, Triton died because I killed him, or did you forget that, hunter. Second," Thirteen answered, relishing each word, "I'll make sure that when I kill you, it will be slow and painful, so in the end, when you meet Him, it will be well worth it."

"The way I see it," Gavin said as he glanced down at his watch, checking his time, "death isn't the end, it's only the beginning."

\*\*\*\*\*\*\*\*\*\*\*\*

"You have to set the charge!" Ashley yelled as Jamie stood locked in a stare down with the demon.

Kayla checked the clock on her cell phone. It had been just over fifteen minutes. They were out of time.

"Please Jamie," Kayla urged him, "you have to do it!"

Jamie prayed silently. At first the words escaped him, but slowly, he found what he needed to say. With new found strength, he pushed forward, but the demon pushed back. Jamie stepped closer and closer to the support and with each step, the demon grew bigger and bigger, till he stood between Jamie and the pillar like a giant leathery golem.

At that moment, Jamie felt his resolve, and his faith slip away. Instead of reaching for the pillar, he ran away from the demon. Frantically, he tore off the protective cover exposing the adhesive and slammed the charge against the wall as the monster roared behind him.

Jamie twisted the top. The green light blinked.

"We need to go," he yelled over the demon's ruckus, "NOW!"

"But that's not the right place!" Kayla said racing over and pulling at the charge, trying to free it from the wall so she could attach it to the pillar.

"It's too late!" Ashley cried out as sleepwalkers raced into the room. "Gavin said once it's in place it's stuck there!"

"It'll still work!" Jamie yelled as he reloaded his gun and fired rounds into the oncoming sleepwalkers.

Kayla was still trying to get the charge off the wall when Ashley grabbed her by the arm.

"Come on!" she yelled. "We're going to have to shoot our way out of here!"

Jamie pulled his second handgun from its holster and continued to take aim, a gun in each hand. Kayla followed closely behind him with Ashley next to her, shooting at anything that moved.

Through a haze of gun smoke and sulfurous laughter, they shot their way down to the main hall and through the lobby, a mess of bloodied, broken bodies in their wake, their hollow black eyes staring blankly up to heaven.

\*\*\*\*\*\*\*\*\*\*\*\*

"I've had enough of your tongue," Thirteen said spitefully.

"Uh huh," Gavin said as he reached into his back pocket and pulled out the small remote detonator, "I think I've said enough."

"Are you ready to die then?" Thirteen grinned raising his razor sharp blade high above his head.

"Yes," Gavin smiled, closing his eyes.

Thirteen leapt high into the air, his blade swinging in a whistling arc. Gavin pushed the button.

************

Jamie grabbed Ashley around the waist as she fought against him, kicking and screaming, tears flooding her face as he held her back. Kayla prayed the same words over and over.

Flames burst through the windows, shattering the glass. The ground shook beneath their feet as the charges exploded, simultaneously, just as Gavin had planned: perfect synchronization. Quickly, the entire hospital was engulfed in bright fire as black plumes of smoke billowed into the night sky. Sleepwalkers wailed from within the crumbling building as the flames consumed them.

Kayla and Ashley collapsed to the ground embracing, wiping away tears. Jamie ran his fingers through his hair in frustration, reason telling him that no one could have survived that explosion, that there was no hope.

A low rumble echoed in the night. They watched in horror as the roof caved in, each level collapsing onto the one below it, till the bottom floor stood beneath a burning pile of rubble and ash.

# XVIII

## FOUR MONTHS LATER

"How's your arm?" Ashley asked, sipping at her coffee, watching snow fall outside the café window.

"Better now the cast is off," Gavin smiled as he flexed his fingers, feeling the muscles tighten beneath his sleeve.

"I still can't believe you survived!" she grinned.

"Like I said, I blacked out. When I woke up, an angel was standing over me in the lobby of the hospital, shrouding me from the flames with his wings. He told me I was meant for greater things."

"That's amazing," she laughed as she bit her lip and picked up a pencil, sketching an outline of his face in her sketchbook.

Gavin leaned back in his chair and enjoyed a long drink from his mug. Snow covered the window ledge as frost filled the corners of the glass. He turned and looked around the room. A man sat on a small couch reading a newspaper, another sat at a bar-like counter typing away on his laptop, a group of girls giggled at a corner table: this was something he'd never done, just sit and enjoy a cup of coffee.

"So, what do you want to do tonight?" Ashley asked, smiling up at him with her big blue eyes.

"I don't know; do you want to watch a movie?" he grinned, looking down at the simple silver band on her left ring finger.

"Stay in?" she thought aloud as she looked outside at the white snowflakes falling to the ground.

"Sounds like a plan, Mrs. Dering," he smiled.

\*\*\*\*\*\*\*\*\*\*\*\*

"I can't believe they're shutting down the precinct!" Jamie exclaimed as he threw his cup into a trash can and flopped down behind his desk.

"It could be worse," Dennis McKenzie, his new partner, said from across the desk. "At least we can transfer across town."

"Still," Jamie frowned, reaching in his pocket for his iPhone, "the Mayor's nephew takes over as Captain and this place goes to Hell."

"I know what you mean," McKenzie chuckled. "Everybody fights, no one works together. We never did solve that nonsense down at New York General."

"Yeah," Jamie said thoughtfully, resting his phone against his lips.

"Anyway, I'm going to go get some fresh coffee," McKenzie said. "You want some?"

"Hmmm?" Jamie mumbled, waking from his trance. "No, I'm good, just going to make a quick call."

\*\*\*\*\*\*\*\*\*\*\*\*

The shriek of packing tape peeling off the roll echoed through Kayla's apartment as she closed another box. Dressed in sweats and a t-shirt, she sat down on her couch and surveyed the living room. Moving boxes stood high, stacked against the wall where her television used to sit.

She'd been at it for days, packing, cleaning, and preparing to move: she'd already signed the lease for her new apartment in Chicago and FedEx'ed it to the landlord. So much had changed: leaving active duty behind, she took a desk job at the lab where her brother worked forensics.

Her cell phone rang to life. She flipped it open and smiled as she heard Jamie on the other end.

"Hey," she grinned.

"Are you all packed up?"

"Almost..."

"I have something really important I need to talk to you about."

"Sure," she said, ready to listen.

"Not now, tonight, 6 o'clock," he replied, "the Chinese restaurant we always go to."

"Okay," Kayla answered, closing her phone and placing it on the box she'd just sealed.

\*\*\*\*\*\*\*\*\*\*\*\*

"I don't think I can do this anymore, Dennis," Jamie said, as his partner sat down stirring cream into his coffee.

"Do what?"

"Police work; or at least police work here."

McKenzie leaned onto his desk, his elbows rustling on a messy pile of papers as he listened.

"They've cut our pay, demoted detectives, never accounted for any of the good men and women who went missing on the job last September, and now they want us to just forget about the hospital bombing? Come on!

Kayla quit because of all the politics, I'm thinking about doing the same."

"You've got to do what you've got to do."

"Yeah," Jamie said, a sparkle of hope in his eye, "I know what I've got to do."

\*\*\*\*\*\*\*\*\*\*\*

Ashley smiled as she looked at the name for the incoming call on her cell phone.

"Hi, Kayla," she answered, smiling at Gavin as he finished his coffee.

"Hey there, sis, how's married life?" Kayla teased.

"I hate it when people ask that!"

"I know," Kayla grinned, "you told me, about ten times. Anyway, I'm all set to move this weekend."

"I can't believe you're leaving in three days," Ashley moaned. "I'm going to miss you *so* much!"

"You've got Gavin now."

"I know," Ashley said sadly, "but you're still my sister. You'll be like half a country away!"

"It's only a fourteen hour drive," Kayla answered as she tucked her legs up under herself on the couch, "and you guys can visit whenever you want."

"We will," Ashley smiled, wiping a happy tear from the corner of her eye, "anytime we can."

\*\*\*\*\*\*\*\*\*\*\*

"Keep going! Move that pile over there!" the foremen yelled over the roar of generators and construction machinery. "We need to get this site clear by the end of the month; we break ground on the new hospital in March!"

Bulldozers moved earth and debris as diggers clawed their way through the fallen, charred walls of New York General Hospital. Diligently, they worked, clearing the land, yellow caution tape and fencing cordoning off the site.

"Sir," one of the workers cried out as he ran from the remains of the building, his fist wrapped tightly around something small, black, "you've got to take a look at this!"

The foreman hurried over to the worker, his boots sloshing in the thick mud.

"What is it?" he asked, impatiently placing his hands on his waist. "You find another body in there?"

"No," the worker said, removing his hard hat, wiping away a mix of sweat and soot from his brow, "I don't know what it is."

The worker held out his hand, the small piece of black cloth wadded up in his palm. Slowly, the foreman took it and unfolded it, spreading it out and holding it up in the sunlight. The cloth was dirtied with ash, but otherwise undamaged. They stared at it in confusion, an evil chill running down their spines as a cold January snow swept across the work site. It was a mask, the mouth stitched shut, the eyes two empty black slits. As they stood in silence, they could have sworn they heard a laugh hidden in the howling wind.

************

Jamie packed up his laptop and pulled on his suit coat. Walking into Capt. Bradford's office, he dropped an envelope on the desk, then turned and stopped back at his workspace. Picking up a cardboard box filled with his desk's contents, a framed photograph of Kayla on top, Jamie looked over the office for the last time. McKenzie nodded at him, his lips pursed as if to say *good luck*. Jamie smiled and walked out the door.

He dropped the box in his trunk. Heading for the driver's door,

Jamie paused, catching a faint movement out of the corner of his eye. He scanned the garage, but no one was there.

*Probably just a bird, or…something.*

Jamie slid into the seat of his BMW and fastened his seatbelt, then turned the ignition key, the exhaust note echoing through the parking garage as the engine revved to life. He flicked the shifter into reverse, backed out of his space, and flicked the knob into first gear, then sped towards the exit, never looking back.

Heading for Chinatown, he groaned, looking at the clock on the dash: 5:45pm. He dialed Kayla's cell phone, his head clouded. Jamie had so many thoughts jumbled together in his mind. The phone was ringing, but she wasn't picking up. Driving through the busy streets, he dialed her again, still no answer. Jamie tried one more time, holding the phone to his ear, hoping she'd pick up.

Suddenly, he hit the brakes, realizing he'd passed the Chinese restaurant. Glancing back in his rear view mirror, he saw her blue Honda parked on the side of the street. Flipping on his blinker, he pulled over.

*You idiot, think straight.*

Stepping from the car, he glanced up at the neon sign on the building next to him, his hands shaking, his thoughts racing.

*Cold Beer.*

He dialed her number one more time. Finally, she answered.

"Hey," he said looking at the clock, then back at the sign, "I've been trying to call."

"Sorry, I was in the bathroom. I left my phone at the table."

"Anyway," he continued nervously, "I'm running a little late and there's still something I have to take care of before I meet you. Is that okay?"

"Yeah," she answered, "take your time. I can't wait to see you. I've missed you all day."

"Okay," he said, staring at the bar as he hung up.

\*\*\*\*\*\*\*\*\*\*\*\*

"Sorry I'm late," Jamie said, brushing snowflakes from his hair as he sat down across from Kayla. "You look great!"

She leaned across the table and kissed him.

"You're shaking!" she exclaimed. "What's wrong?"

"Well I kind of had a rough day. I made some big decisions," he confessed.

"Like?"

"I gave Luke Bradford my resignation."

"Are you serious?!" Kayla asked in surprise.

"Yeah, I've just felt out of place there recently, since you've left. I belong somewhere else."

"Where?" Kayla wondered with a slight smile.

"I was thinking maybe, Chicago?" he said, hesitation in his voice.

Kayla wasn't sure what to say. She felt so many different emotions, but none of them brought words to mind.

"Jamie, I don't want you to quit your job to be close to me," she finally responded. "I love you, but you have a good thing here."

"No," he said, shaking his head emphatically, "you're my good thing. If you go, there's nothing left for me in New York."

They sat in silence as the waitress brought their food: Kayla's pad Thai chicken and Jamie's sweet and sour shrimp. Picking up their chopsticks, they ate without a word, each with too much to say.

\*\*\*\*\*\*\*\*\*\*\*\*

Jamie smiled at their waitress as he left money for the bill. The old Asian women bowed quaintly as she brought his change, then left three fortune cookies on the edge of the table. Kayla tore the plastic wrapper open and cracked her cookie down the middle, pulling the fortune out from between the two halves.

"Spring has sprung: life is blooming," she read aloud.

"Not quite," Jamie smirked, watching the snow fall outside the window.

"What's yours say?" Kayla grinned.

Jamie opened his and laughed, then handed it to her, "You will be crowned king at a Memphis rock concert."

They stood, sharing big smiles.

"There's still a fortune left," Jamie said, looking down at the extra cookie the waitress had inexplicably left. "You want it?"

"No. I don't need wise old proverbs wrapped in plastic," she smiled.

"I'll save it for later," he grinned slipping it into his coat pocket.

Kayla took Jamie's hand and they headed towards the door.

"I definitely won't miss the snow" he joked as they walked into the cold night air.

"It snows in Chicago too, you know?"

Kayla gave Jamie a kiss, then dug through her purse for her keys, "I had a good time tonight."

Jamie nervously rocked back and forth from one foot to the other.

"Do you think we could go for a little walk?" he asked, his hands deep in his pants pockets. "They still have Christmas lights up on some of the trees in Central Park. I drove past them on my way. It would be nice to do something like that one last time before you leave."

Dropping her keys back into her purse, she smiled. With a slight shiver, she followed him down the side walk as Jamie hailed a cab. He wrapped his arm tightly around her as they headed towards the car, snowflakes sparkling in the moonlight.

The cabbie dropped them off across the street from the park. Cars sped about the busy streets as people hurried on their way. Jamie and Kayla ignored them, lost in their own little world. Even with all the traffic, it was like they were the only two people in the entire city.

When they reached the park, Kayla paused, in awe as she saw the snow covered grass and trees glowing white and yellow under the reflection of the lights. She'd never noticed how beautiful it was, or maybe it was just because Jamie was there sharing the moment. Hand in hand, they walked beneath sparkling branches coated in glistening icicles as snow fell lightly around them. Ice skaters swirled and spun on the pond, their scarves dancing in the breeze, thick stocking caps pulled down over their ears. Another couple passed them, nodding and whispering hello.

Moonlight shone down on them like a spotlight, illuminating their path, a trail of footprints marking where they'd been.

Snow crunched beneath their feet as they turned down another path. They laughed at a squatty round snowman, an odd-shaped carrot for a nose. This was one of the most beautiful moments Kayla could have ever asked for.

Stopping under the shadow of a tree, the white lights strung from the branches reflecting in Kayla's eyes, Jamie pulled a small black velvet box from his pocket and smiled in a way that Kayla had never seen him smile before. She turned to him, happiness and confusion spreading across her pretty face, her cheeks red from the crisp night air.

"Jamie?" she whispered, looking down at the small box, her heart racing.

"Shhh," he said, putting his finger up to his lips, then wiping a tear from her soft cheek.

"Kayla Rose," he smiled, dropping to one knee on the snow covered path, "Will you marry me?"

# EPILOGUE

Sunshine beamed over the hood of Jamie's car as he sped through the countryside. Kayla watched in the passenger side mirror as the New York City skyline finally disappeared behind the last bend. A smile filled her face every time she looked down at the diamond sparkling on her finger. Jamie happily tapped away a rhythm on his steering wheel, playing along with the CD they were listening to.

It felt good to get away from the city, away from the traffic, the noise. There wasn't another car in site on the tree-lined road. Light gusts of wind sent wisps of drifting snow across the highway as they passed mile markers and speed limit signs. Kayla recognized an old rusty water tower covered in ivy, now white with a fresh dusting.

"We're nearly there," she said softly, staring out the window.

Jamie continued on, still drumming away on his leather-wrapped wheel.

"So last night," she asked quietly, "when you said you had something to take care of, what were you doing?"

Jamie glanced over at her, a smile taking shape as he thought about the night before.

"When I talked to you on the phone, I was sitting in front of a bar..."

"I thought you said you weren't going to drink anymore?" she said, cutting him off before he could say anymore.

"That's just it," Jamie explained, "last night, I was sitting in front of a bar when I had what I guess you would call an epiphany or whatever, and I knew at that moment, I didn't need beer or pills, only you, for the rest of my life."

"So what did you take care of then?"

"Right after I hung up the phone, I hurried to the jewelers, the same one my dad bought my mom her wedding ring at. I was so lucky he was still open. Anyway, I knew exactly which ring to get you as soon as I saw it. It was perfect."

"It's even my size," Kayla grinned, holding her hand up in the bright morning sunlight.

"Like I said, perfect," Jamie laughed.

They smiled at each other. She held his hand tightly as it rested in her lap.

"Oh, okay, okay, up there!" she said excitedly, pointing off to the left, the icy reservoir on their right. "There should be a gravel drive leading into the trees."

Jamie searched and finally pulled the car to a stop.

"You sure?"

"Yeah?" she said disappointed, looking around for a break in the scrub.

"There's something over there, looks like an old mailbox," Jamie said, easing the car forward.

"That's it! But I don't remember all this overgrown brush. It couldn't have grown up this quickly, could it?"

Jamie looked at the brown leafless shrubs lining the old gravel drive and the large rotting limbs blocking the turn off.

"They look old to me. Are you sure this is the place?"

"I'm positive!" she said, jumping out of the car and tossing the old, fallen branches off to the side of the drive.

"All clear!" she said, climbing back into the car and fastening her seat belt.

With a sigh, Jamie turned down the snowy gravel drive and wound his way deep into the trees.

"It should be just ahead," Kayla promised as she tried to see through the maze of brush. "I'm telling you, the monastery is here."

"Alright," Jamie conceded, avoiding ditch after ditch in the rough, rocky path.

Finally, they reached an opening in the trees. The path led around a small circle. Jamie followed as far as he could, till a fallen tree trunk blocked their way.

"On foot?" he asked, pulling to a stop.

"On foot," she said, opening her door and stepping from the car.

They continued around the tree. Kayla knew they had to be close. As soon as they cleared the large vein like roots, they saw it. The monastery stood in ruins, an empty shell. Its walls caved in: its beautiful tall tower broken and toppled.

"There's no way!" Kayla cried out, running up to the broken wooden doors hanging off their hinges. "I don't believe it!"

Jamie took her hand and led her over a small pile of rubble standing in the door way. Slowly, they walked down the cold halls and empty corridors. Several times, Kayla called out for Joseph, but he never answered. He wasn't there.

Turning a corner, they came upon his study. Kayla leaned against the heavy door as it slowly fought against her, creaking with age.

"I sat here," she explained, pointing at a dust covered chair, "and Joseph was there, at his desk. This is where he told me his whole story."

Together, they looked around the room, each curious artifact covered in decades of grime. Every now and again, a strong gust of wind would howl down a corridor, sending a shiver up their arms. But, this was the same place Kayla had visited, where she first remembered what she was missing in her life.

"Look at this," she said, pulling an intricately carved wooden cross down off the wall and wiping the dust away.

"It's beautiful," Jamie smiled as she handed it to him.

"Do you think we could take it for our new home in Chicago?" Kayla wondered, looking around, a slight look of guilt on her face.

"I don't think anyone's coming back here," Jamie grinned. "Besides, I think Joseph would want you to have it."

Kayla smiled and grabbed Jamie's hand. Heading out of the study, she led him down the hall and up to the large double doors that opened into the chapel.

They pushed as hard as they could, but the doors wouldn't budge. Disappointed, they turned and made their way back towards the front of the monastery.

Just as they turned the corner that led down the main corridor, a loud crash echoed through the dark halls. They quickly raced back to the chapel doors, now lying on the stone floor, a cloud of dust settling around them. Cautiously, they entered the room. Cold, fresh air hit them in the face. Part of the ceiling was gone. Several of the tall stone pillars had collapsed, wooden pews lying broken and splintered beneath them. But there, at the front of the chapel, hung the crucifix. Snow had gathered on the cross and dust covered Christ's arms, but His face was still as loving, as compassionate, and as strong as Kayla remembered.

Kayla wiped the tears from her eyes as Jamie fought with the lump in his throat. Kneeling down in the dirty, debris-covered chapel, they prayed. They prayed for Gavin and Ashley, Kayla's brother and his family, for the lives affected by Thirteen, and for the new life they were starting together.

*************

Jamie pulled his BMW out onto the highway and headed back towards the city. Kayla turned, staring out the rear window as the rusty mailbox disappeared in the distance.

"You going to be okay?" Jamie asked, looking down at the old wooden cross resting across her legs.

"Yeah," Kayla smiled, her eyes meeting his, "everything's going to be fine."

*"Thirteen"* - original concept art by Timothy James Reese

www.ingramcontent.com/pod-product-compliance
Lightning Source LLC
Chambersburg PA
CBHW071847220626
47052CB00002B/11